J. G. Turner

The Pioneer Missionary

life of the Rev. Nathaniel Turner, missionary in New Zealand, Tonga, and Australia

J. G. Turner

The Pioneer Missionary
life of the Rev. Nathaniel Turner, missionary in New Zealand, Tonga, and Australia

ISBN/EAN: 9783337313111

Printed in Europe, USA, Canada, Australia, Japan

Cover: Foto ©Andreas Hilbeck / pixelio.de

More available books at **www.hansebooks.com**

THE PIONEER MISSIONARY:

LIFE OF THE

REV. NATHANIEL TURNER,

MISSIONARY IN NEW ZEALAND, TONGA, AND
AUSTRALIA.

BY HIS SON,

THE REV. J. G. TURNER,

OF THE AUSTRALASIAN CONFERENCE.

WITH A PORTRAIT.

LONDON:
PUBLISHED FOR THE AUTHOR AT
THE WESLEYAN CONFERENCE OFFICE,
CASTLE STREET, CITY ROAD;
SOLD AT 66, PATERNOSTER ROW.
1872.

LONDON :
PRINTED BY WILLIAM NICHOLS,
HOXTON SQUARE.

PREFACE.

THIS book is not a history. If its scope and connecting links appear to give it somewhat of that character, it is but very partially, and only incidentally. The book purports simply to be the Life of a godly and useful man. The writer's inducements to publish it were, First, That a large circle of relatives and friends might have preserved to them in permanent form authentic reminiscences of one they honoured and loved; Secondly, That the story of his labours might serve in some degree to encourage and stimulate the succeeding race of toilers in the same service; and, Thirdly, That as the biography would afford glimpses of the formative age of the Christian Church in the Southern World,—its peculiar trials and signal triumphs,—it might awaken or revive the missionary spirit, both in England and Australia, where Christian sympathies and benevolence are unduly restricted by local claims.

Special acknowledgments are thankfully made to the Rev. James Buller, to whose correspondence the biographer is indebted for portions of the material from which the chapters on New Zealand have been prepared. Also to the Rev. W. Butters, and Mr. Thomas Hayes, of the Wesleyan Mission House, London, whose friendly offices have secured the revision of printers' proofs in England.

Methodist Preachers have not the leisure for authorship, and this memoir has been prepared amid many disadvantages, during a year of Circuit work. The author is conscious of its manifold imperfections; but in the hope that it will do good, he submits it, not to reviewers and critics, as such, but to all who take an interest in the world's salvation.

WESLEYAN CONFERENCE, HOBART TOWN,
   February 1st, 1871.

CONTENTS.

THE PIONEER MISSIONARY:

LIFE OF THE REV. NATHANIEL TURNER.

CHAPTER I.

1793—1822.

THE birthday of Nathaniel Turner is not known. He was baptized in the parish church of his native town, Wybunbury, in Cheshire, on March 10th, 1793. His parents, Thomas and Elizabeth Turner, had for many years resided on a small farm on the estate of Sir Robert Hill, of The Hough. They were members of the Church of England. The careful training of their eight children was suddenly interrupted by death. Within the space of twelve months both parents and one daughter died, thus leaving an orphan family of five brothers and two sisters. In them, however, was fulfilled the assurance, " In Thee the fatherless findeth mercy."

Nathaniel was but nine years old, and keenly felt his privation. Sorrowing for the loved ones gone, he sought relief in tears and much prayer; but he had now no Christian counsellor. At his mother's knee he had learnt to pray, and now the daily cry of his orphan heart was, " My Father, be Thou the Guide of my youth." That prayer was heard: his path was directed. Yet though he feared the Lord, read His holy Word, prayed much, and regularly attended the services of the church, he did not know the way of peace.

The home of childhood was broken up, and the guardianship of friends supplied in some degree the care of parents. At fifteen years of age he resided with his uncle, who when advanced in life had found the Saviour, under Wesleyan instrumentality. Under his roof boyish prejudices against the Methodists were entirely dispelled. The power of God accompanied the first sermon he heard amongst that people. It was on Easter Sunday, when Mr. Joseph Mellor preached from the words, "Did not our heart burn within us, while He talked with us by the way, and while He opened to us the Scriptures?"

In June, 1811, he was awakened by the Spirit of God under an impressive sermon by Mr. Joseph Lowe.* The text was, "And in hell he lift up his eyes, being in torments," &c. During his walk home, conviction and fear so

---

* At twenty-one years of age Mr. Joseph Lowe was awakened to a sense of his sins, joined the Wesleyan-Methodist Society, and within its communion found peace through believing in Christ. For sixty years from that time he was ardently attached to the church of his choice, and served his generation by the will of God. His loving spirit and deep piety, together with a remarkable persuasiveness of manner, and ingenuity of address, gave him great influence over others. As a local preacher he was eminently successful in winning souls. He held that office to the close of a long and honoured life, and during most of the time was also a valuable class-leader. The Head of the Church, however, seems to have allotted him a special sphere of permanent influence. From the beginning of his spiritual life, he took a deep interest in young men converted to God, and evincing ability for the service of His church. Several successful labourers in his own church, and one in that of the Church of England, trace, under God, their entry upon the Christian ministry to his encouraging and stimulating intercourse with them. When the infirmities of age were upon him, he still exhibited the beauties of holiness; and till within two months of his death was able occasionally to conduct religious services. He died in Geelong, Victoria, on November 23rd, 1863.

affected him, that his cousins on seeing him thought him very unwell. He now earnestly sought religion, but with insufficient light. He wept, prayed, and strove in Christian ordinances, but to no saving result. His outward deportment was noticed in the village. Some called him "the good young man;" others, "the Pharisee." This led him to self-content, in which he too soon cried, "Peace, peace."

Dark clouds settled for a season on his spiritual path. A pious Calvinist minister, under whose guidance one of his cousins was preaching, and for whose services another cousin had opened his house, disturbed his mind on the subject of election. The effect was distressing, and was only relieved by the truth. A young Wesleyan friend lent him Mr. Fletcher's "Scripture Scales," and the honest examination of this book left him no doubt that God was willing to save all mankind. He was at once affectionately advised and urged to decide for God.

Then followed a struggle for life, which was maintained as well in the prayer-meeting and class-meeting, as in the closet and the church. On the 5th of February, 1812, while at class-meeting for the second or third time, he found peace with God. Fifty years afterwards, on referring to the memorable occasion, he wrote, "So clear to me was the removal of my guilt, and so satisfactory the evidence of my acceptance in the Beloved, that I have never doubted to this day, that I then passed from death unto life."

Satan harassed him, but by faithfulness in private prayer he held fast the beginning of his confidence. He diligently strove to grow in grace, using all the means. The deceiver sought to ensnare him. At one time he struggled for many hours with the temptation that he had fallen from grace. When the conflict was at its height, the hour of the weekly class-meeting came round; and while in the fellowship of saints, after telling of his con-

flict, the snare was broken, and confidence and peace were
regained.

Almost coeval with his conversion, was an intense desire
for the salvation of others. The earliest objects of his
solicitude were his brothers and sisters : and, by his efforts
and God's blessing upon them, the three youngest were
soon led to the Saviour. Thereupon followed a conviction
that God intended him for usefulness in the public
services of His church. His successful exercises in the
prayer-meeting became the subject of general notice, and
more public labours were soon put upon him. From
frequent conversation with pious persons on the subject,
and from the expressed views of the Circuit ministers, the
Revs. Joseph Brookhouse and James Allen, (the latter of
whom especially evinced an interest in his career,) his mind
became drawn towards preaching the Gospel. In earnest
prayer he entreated the Lord to show him His will, and to
shine upon his path. The answer came. One Sunday
evening, at Coppenhall, he was " constrained " to preach by
Mr. Joseph Lowe. The subject of his first address, at which
several local preachers were present, was, " These shall go
away into everlasting punishment."

From that time he took many services as a substitute for
others ; and when the next Circuit plan appeared, which was
for a term of six months, he found that the superintendent
had given him forty-two appointments. He had but scanty
material for such service ; but with simplicity of purpose,
and a heart warm to the work, he obeyed God's call.
The Lord gave him favour in the eyes of the people, and
the word he preached was owned in the salvation of many.
His situation being somewhat unfriendly to the work nearest
his heart, he removed to Blakenhall, where he resided
for several years with Mr. Thomas Salmon, finding full
scope for the powers and zeal which God gave him. Besides
preaching two or three times on the Sabbath, and not un-

frequently on the week nights for the ministers, he was almost constantly engaged in holding prayer-meetings, or meeting classes. To meet the mental demands for this course of toil, and the better to qualify himself, it was his custom to spend till midnight in study. In these exercises his soul delighted, and his knowledge and piety grew.

Frequent intercourse with the ministers and the reading of missionary intelligence were much blessed to him. He soon found his sympathies drawn towards the heathen. The feeling warmed into a holy passion. The requisite qualifications for the life service of the Gospel were not to be had without much effort; and he prayerfully set himself to prepare for the work, should God clearly call him to it. At the March Quarterly Meeting, 1820, he was nominated for the missionary service. Having been examined and recommended by the District Meeting at Congleton, he was received by the Conference, and placed on the President's list of candidates for the foreign work, to be sent out under the direction of the Missionary Committee; but was given to understand that, from the low state of the funds and other causes, it would be some time before he could be sent to a Mission station. His Divine Master meanwhile found him other work to do. What it was, and how he did it, shall be told in his own words.

"There were a number of populous villages and hamlets, which were sadly benighted and demoralized. They lay chiefly between the Nantwich, Newcastle, Staffordshire, and Whitchurch Circuits, but beyond the reach of the ministers generally. My Circuit Quarterly Meeting, at the instance of Mr. Richard Vernon, of Buerton, unanimously resolved to originate a mission among them. They subscribed among themselves some five or six pounds for the purpose, and appointed a Sub-Committee to carry out their views. The Committee, after consideration, wrote to me, and I at once entered into their plans. It was not known that there was one pious person in the whole region into which I was sent; and I was interdicted from going into any place where the Gospel was preached.

" I began my mission on the last Sabbath of April, 1820, preaching on the green at *Audlem*. The few who attended listened attentively as I bade them 'behold the Lamb of God.' Though former preachers here had been persecuted, I met with but little molestation. A house was opened for preaching, and a tolerably good congregation collected. Several persons turned to God, and a class was formed, which I left doing well at the close of my mission.

" In the village of *Norton*, we were successfully hindered by the vigorous and persevering opposition of the clergy-man, and the leading gentleman of the place, a Captain ——. These worthies regularly attended at the time and place notified for Divine service, and, each bearing a stick, warned off the villagers from forming a congregation. One Tuesday evening, just as the service was beginning in the square, they personally headed a band with drums and fifes, and came with a mob of fellows of the baser sort right into the congregation. Already the village bells were ringing in derision; and when the voice and yells of these intruders were added, the service was effectually stopped.

" In *Neigton* we were similarly opposed, but not with such flagrant impiety. The outward leader of the opposition was a publican. But he was instigated by the clergyman of the parish, known to be living in gross sin. Some good was effected here, and not long after a Wesleyan chapel was built.

" Though *Ashby* was a notoriously wicked place, our introduction into it was peaceable, and for some time we preached in a private house unmolested. The house being small, and but few attending, we ventured to hold service in the open air. After singing through the village, the preacher took his stand on the seat of the stocks. A goodly number assembled, and though there was some disturbance, many listened seriously. This daring on the part of the Methodists so aroused the leading Churchmen of the place, that in the course of the week a public meeting was held on the subject. It resulted in a great manifestation of popular loyalty to the Church. A crowd assembled at the Methodist preacher's stand, and, preceded by the clergyman and a band of musicians, marched from it to the church ground. They then clasped hands around the building, and exclaimed, ' The Methodists shall never take the church.' Money was given them, which they freely spent at the neighbouring public-house, kept by the clerk of the parish. Here they drank the health of the clergyman, success to Church and State, and damnation to the Methodists. This statement I received from one who had taken part in the movement, but who soon afterwards became converted to God under my ministry. Some lasting good was done in this village.

" A hamlet named *Podmore* witnessed some special triumphs of the Gospel. The villagers of *Bowers* had baffled many previous efforts. But here my way was providentially open, and the Lord gave me great success. At the close of my mission, some twenty members, who had been gathered from the paths of sin, were walking together in love, and adorning a Christian profession.

" My centre was *Black Brook.* This was the scene of my hardest labours and greatest success. By day I went from house to house, holding religious conversation ; and this, as intended, led many to come to the evening services. After some months of varying encouragement, the Lord poured out His Spirit, and many were saved. On one occasion, under a sermon on ' the blood of sprinkling,' an old woman who had passed eighty winters was convinced of sin, and the next week she found peace. At a lovefeast fifteen souls were set at liberty.

"At *Woore*, where the clergyman was a ' blind leader of the blind,' the parish clerk personally assaulted me : here some few were brought to God. Several minor places were included in my mission.

"In this delightful employment I had been laboriously engaged for eighteen months, when I was summoned to the foreign work. Upwards of seventy souls had been gathered into classes, and were being watched over by duly appointed leaders, chiefly chosen from among the new converts during the mission. For these I ascribe, now as then, all honour to God. From the first the villages paid the expenses of my maintenance, except the five or six pounds originally subscribed."

The scene of the labours above narrated is now the abode of a flourishing commercial community. The population has received its increase during the half century from all parts of the British empire. Religion flourishes. Methodism has won many triumphs over Satan, and now wields a wide-spread influence among the masses. Its growth is represented by several Circuits and many large churches.

During Mr. Turner's home missionary career he formed the friendship of many excellent young men, who afterwards did good service in the cause of Christ, and with several of whom he carried on an affectionate correspondence. Among them were Thomas Jones, Missionary to the West Indies, and who was lost in " the Maria " mail boat ; Thomas Turner, Missionary to Canada, Alfred Bourne, who died at Oxford, Andrew Doncaster, William Hare, and Thomas Ford, who died in the English work.

In November, 1820, he was examined before the Committee in London, in company with Mr. John Morgan, who, at a later date, was appointed to begin a Mission at St. Mary's, River Gambia. At the Mission House he came in contact with several excellent brethren who were going out as Missionaries, among whom were Messrs. Duncan and Young, about to embark for the West Indies.

Another year's delay occurred, and Mr. Turner continued in his loved work as an evangelist. Towards the end of 1821 he was instructed to prepare for New Zealand. On the 10th of January, 1822, he was married to Anne Sargent, daughter of Mr. John Sargent of Ipstones, Etruria, Staffordshire. The marriage was solemnized in the parish church of Stoke-upon-Trent. It is an interesting fact that the social religious services connected with the event, and with the family leave-taking, were made, under God, the occasion of the conversion of Mrs. Turner's relatives.

To say "good bye" to his numerous children in the Gospel, and other friends, was no common trial to the young Missionary, or to his wife. It was night when they took coach at Newcastle-under-Lyne for London. Though at a late hour, in the depth of winter, and bitterly cold, more than a thousand friends, numbers of whom had travelled many miles, assembled around the coach to bid them "farewell." The townsfolk near the stage tavern had not been unused to street gatherings; but they looked on with wonder to see so large a company standing for some ten or fifteen minutes. Amid the falling of the snow there was but one sound to break the stillness. It was the preacher's voice giving a farewell address, from the box of the coach. As the coachman hailed his team, kind impulses seemed to move some good sisters, who bethought them of the pitiless weather, and Mrs. Turner's adieus were given from within, amid a shower of shawls. The latest words they heard, as the coach was driven through the crowd, were those of Mr. Turner's brother: "We shall now be as sheep without a shepherd." They were entertained in London by Mr. and Mrs. Taylor.

In company with Mr. William White, Mr. Turner was

ordained on January 23rd, 1822. Among those who took
part in the service were the Revs. Richard Watson, Jabez
Bunting, and Joseph Taylor. The vows of that evening
were most prayerfully and solemnly undertaken, and for
more than forty years faithfully observed, by the grace of
God.

On the 15th of February he left England in the brig
"Deveron," bound for Van Diemen's Land and New
South Wales. Among his fellow voyagers was the
Rev. William White, also appointed to New Zealand, and
who had been received by the Conference before Mr.
Turner. He went out unmarried. There were more than
twenty passengers, some of whom were very profane, and
occasioned the Mission party much annoyance and grief.
When in the Bay of Biscay, the brig being kept out of her
course for several days, the Missionaries went to special
prayer. They had but just risen from their knees when the
captain cheerily called out, " Ladies and gentlemen, I am
happy to inform you that the wind has suddenly veered
round, and that the brig is laying her course." The passengers landed at Madeira, where they found "the houses
low and wretched, and the inhabitants poor and miserable-
looking." Fruit was cheap, but everything else dear
enough. During the latter part of the voyage several
storms were encountered, in one of which they were well
nigh lost. The rudder tackling and stern boats were carried away, and the deadlights stove in. The alarm and
confusion were not lessened by the terrified mate calling
out, " She is sinking ! She is sinking ! "

Van Diemen's Land was sighted on the one hundred and
twenty-fourth day out, a passage at that time considered
very good for a vessel of but two hundred and fifty tons.
Some of the passengers, whose profanity had caused much
annoyance to Mr. Turner, begged his pardon, and thanked
him for his Christian counsel and example while with them.

As the brig stood up Storm Bay, the voyagers were delighted with the picturesque coast fringing the base of a hundred hills, clothed with verdure to their very summits; and when, a few hours later, they had rounded Crawfish Point, and opened upon Sandy Bay, with Mount Nelson on their left, and before them the majestic Mount Wellington, four thousand feet high, with its grand white cliffs and snowy crown glittering in the sunshine, and Hobart Town sleeping at its feet, their admiration was unbounded.

CHAPTER II.

In March, 1787, eleven vessels, under command of Captain Arthur Phillip, R.N., left Old England for New South Wales, with five hundred and sixty-five male and one hundred and ninety-two female prisoners, and a proportionate military guard. After a tedious voyage of eight months, relieved by calls at Madeira and the Cape, they anchored in Botany Bay. Anticipations formed from Captain Cook's report of the place were not realized, and the ships' boats were employed in coasting northward, in search of a better harbour and more promising country. Quite unexpectedly they found Port Jackson, which had been descried from Cook's vessel, and described as a " boat harbour," to be a spacious and inviting one; and on January 26th, 1788, the expedition by "the First Fleet" landed from Sydney Cove. The wood resounded with the echoes of the axe, and in a few hours a camp of tents and huts replaced the trees which had skirted the lovely crescent bay. Governor Phillip's colony numbered one thousand and thirty persons. The circumstances were new and eventful to all.

The next Sydney-bound vessel from England was " The Guardian : " she was wrecked at the Cape. Complicated difficulties at Port Jackson, and fears of starvation, from want of supplies, induced the Governor to relieve the community by sending some of the prisoners to Norfolk Island. The " Sirius," which conveyed them, was wrecked on its rough coast. A second fleet arrived with stores from the Cape in 1790. After Phillip's day, the government was administered successively by Hunter, Bligh, and Macquarie. The rule of the last-named Governor, from 1809 to 1821, was marked by the improvement of the community, considerable exploration, and much progress in public works.

Fifteen years after the occupation of New South Wales the penal population numbered some six or seven thousands; but the harvests were so redundant, and no market for the surplus available, that the convicts became a burden on the hands of the Government, and relief was a second time sought by expatriation. It was with this intent that Van Diemen's Land was selected; and in August, 1803, it became the exile home of the worst of the Botany Bay community. Its founders debarked at Risdon, on the eastern bank of the Derwent, from the ship "Lady Nelson," Lieutenant Boner Commander, and Dr. Mountserrat surgeon. They were in all but a few prisoners and soldiers, and were soon unexpectedly joined by a large number from England, under Colonel Collins. It occurred on this wise.

The result of the British policy had led to the contemplated founding of a new penal colony in the south of the continent, and Colonel Collins sailed in charge of the expedition. He was not more fortunate than his pioneer predecessor, Phillip, in the place chosen for his debarkation,—Port Phillip,—and became so disgusted with his first difficulties as to recommend the abandonment of the place. The expeditions were removed to Van Diemen's Land, where, in due time, they established themselves at Hobart Town and Launceston. They were conveyed from Port Phillip in "The Lady Nelson" and "The Ocean," and arrived in two parties, on January 30th, and February 16th, 1804. The ships' companies comprised Lieutenant-

Governor Collins, Rev. Robert Knopwood, chaplain, several other gentlemen holding commissions in the enterprise, a competent marine guard, and three hundred and sixty-seven male prisoners. In October, 1804, the "Lady Nelson" having meanwhile surveyed the entrance to the Tamar, a small number of prisoners were sent round under Colonel Paterson to found a settlement in the north. For some time they held little intercourse with their neighbours on the south of the island.

Soon after this, on the recommendation of Governor King, the penal station at Norfolk Island was abandoned, and many of its families were removed to Van Diemen's Land, where as grantees they originated the settlement of New Norfolk in the south, and Norfolk Plains in the north. The second Governor of Van Diemen's Land, Colonel Davey, arrived in February, 1813. He was succeeded in April, 1817, by William Sorrell, Esq., Governor Macquarie, of New South Wales, being then in the ninth year of his administration.

It would serve no good purpose to dwell upon the moral darkness and social disorder of the early days of British settlement in these parts. Through a long, distressful night of iniquity, a watchman here and there waited for the morning, and when at length a few faint grey streaks struggled into the mournful gloom, they came but to reveal its density. Several administrations had passed away, and governmental systems changed, before the bonds of iniquity, whether self-imposed or ordered by home authority, relaxed. Society of all classes was knee-deep in oppression, dishonesty, and shameless vice. The habits of the military officers discouraged moral reform. The first Colonial Chaplain, the Rev. Mr. Johnson, of Sydney, had much opposition. In 1803 the priest of a Spanish vessel, visiting Port Jackson, was surprised on finding that no church had been provided, and that the clergyman sought some shady spot in the open air, for his public ministrations. For four years Mr. Johnson vainly waited for official help, and then, at his own cost, built a church of "wattle and dab," and roofed with thatch. The Governor now sought to enforce attendance upon public worship. The sentiments of the prisoners, as to this improvement, were read in the flames which reduced the church to ashes. His Excellency, it is said, threatened to punish them by employing them on Sundays in erecting a stone church. That threat, however, if made, was not carried out, and a store which became available was fitted up for public worship. Before Mr. Johnson's removal to England, the Rev. Samuel Marsden* arrived, and settled at Parramatta. His earliest religious efforts do not appear to have been very successful. In 1808 he returned to

---

* The Rev. Samuel Marsden was the son of a tradesman in the village of Horsforth, near Leeds, where he was born on the 28th of July, 1764. Both his parents were of repute as upright and pious. They are known to have been favourable towards the Wesleyan Methodists of their day. In his boyhood he was placed at the grammar school at Hull, of which Dr. Joseph Milner was the head master. Thence he went into his father's business, but his mind was not in it. He was a member of the Methodist Church, and zealous in the service of Christ. The Elland Society opened his way to Cambridge, where he studied in St. John's College. Before he had completed his studies he was offered, it is supposed through the influence of Mr. Wilberforce, the appointment of "Chaplain in His Majesty's territory of New South Wales." At first he declined the offer,—it would seem, from motives of diffidence. His objections, however, were overruled, and he received his commission under date January 1st, 1793. He married Miss Elizabeth Ristan, and voyaged to Sydney. His course in New South Wales was one of high public spirit, guided by piety and benevolence. His varied difficulties and labours in the interest of the aborigines and of prisoners are matters of history, as also his deep and practical interest in the welfare of the New Zealand race. He voyaged to England once, and to New Zealand seven times. He died on the 12th of May, 1838, at Parramatta.

England for a season, during which time the colony was
without a clergyman.   His representations, however,
secured further appointments, and he was afterwards aided
by the Revs. Messrs. Cartwright and Cowper.

In Van Diemen's Land religion was nominally represented by a gentleman, who, though he combined the
magisterial with the clerical functions, was quite unable to
cope with the abounding iniquity.

The time will come, within this century, when the Christian world will accord to Methodism no small honour, as
the pioneer of advanced civilization in both hemispheres.
The tone of Samuel Marsden's character and life purpose
was doubtless received and matured under Methodist teaching; for in early days he was a member of the Methodist
Society.   Through life he practically honoured his parents'
views of Methodism. It was at his request that Mr. Bowden,
a teacher of the Great Queen Street charity schools, and
highly respected for his personal qualities as well as for his
piety in the London West Circuit, of which he was a member, went to New South Wales as a schoolmaster.   He
was joined by another Wesleyan, Mr. John Hosking, who
was introduced to the chaplain by Joseph Butterworth,
Esq., M.P.   The value of their presence and piety is
apparent from the following communication to the Wesleyan Mission House, forwarded by a zealous member of
the society which they founded in Sydney, soon after their
arrival. It was published in the January Missionary Notices
for 1814, and is the earliest authentic account of Methodism
in the southern world of which I have any knowledge :—

" SYDNEY, NEW SOUTH WALES, *July* 20*th*, 1812.

" On the 28th we got safely into this port, which is a most
astonishingly beautiful, romantic, capacious, and commo-
dious harbour, (*sic,*) of which I need say but little, several
authors having done this better than I can do .....Of

Methodists we have here in Society the following persons :
in Sydney, Mr. John H., who leads a class in his own house,
consisting of Mrs. H., Mrs. B., and Mrs. I., and three of the
senior girls in the school. Mr. B. has also a class in his
house, consisting of Mr. H., I. F., T. J., husband of the
above, and a soldier or two of the 75th Regiment. Our
meetings generally are very comfortable and profitable.
At Windsor, we have a class under the care of Mr. E.,
consisting of six. Mr. E. is a pious, sensible young man,
sent here from Ireland, where he was converted while
under sentence of death for forgery. He was bred to the
bar ; and being of a humble, affectionate disposition,
and zealous in the cause of God, I doubt not (especially
could his reproach be wiped away) would make an useful
man among us. He has been employed for some months
past in teaching school, and he goes some miles into the
country on Sunday, where he reads the Church Liturgy,
and expounds or preaches to the settlers, several of whom
are thankful for his labours. This is a very recent undertaking, only of a few weeks, so that we can speak but very
little of its success.

" March 6th, 1812.—We held our first class meeting, and
it has continued ever since.

" April 3rd.—Our friends at Windsor came down, and we
held a lovefeast, which was a most blessed season. God
was eminently present, and gave us such a meek, humble,
simple, loving spirit, that the place was a little heaven ; and
each thought himself the most unworthy of so great a
blessing. We had been consulting on the most effectual
means of procuring the Gospel among us by means of
itinerant preaching. We had justly concluded that,
although we have a few worthy clergymen here, yet till
we see more labourers going forth in the spirit of their
work, with pure, disinterested principles, labouring only to
win souls to Christ, we cannot reasonably hope that

God will make bare His arm, and display His saving power.

"We therefore determined to address our Missionary Committee, and to solicit their aid in sending us some Ministers whom God has anointed for so great a work. Of such men we doubt not our native country has several, whose desire is only to spend and to be spent in the work of saving souls......One of the most powerful arguments we can urge is,—here are thousands of souls perishing for lack of knowledge, both in high and low life. Iniquity exceedingly abounds; and in many cases the only difference between the one and the other is that which avarice or oppression has made......The statement made will show that abundance of work might be found for one or two Missionaries; and could two be obtained it would be of very great advantage, as they could act in concert, strengthen each other's hands in God, and their work would be far pleasanter. As for their support I am allowed to state that could they be sent out to us with a good allowance of books, wearing apparel, furniture for a house apiece, we would be answerable for the rest. I am sure Mr. Marsden would be glad to see the different settlements provided, and especially if we proceed in the primitive way of Methodism, not in hostility against the Church, but rather in unison with it; not so much to make a party distinct from the Church, as to save souls in the Church. Of course, the preacher should not be radically a Dissenter; if possible, one attached to the Establishment, as Mr. Wesley, Dr. Clarke, and most of our primitive preachers were.

"I am," &c.

The official action of the society appears to have been delayed for a short season, from some unexplained cause, as their communication, which is in harmony with that above given, did not reach the Mission House till March of 1814. From it ample extracts are made.

"*To the Preachers and Members of the Committee of the Methodist Missionary Society.*

" REVEREND FATHERS,—

"THERE are probably twenty thousand souls in this colony, natives of the British Isles, and their descendants. From the description of people sent hither, much good cannot be expected. The higher ranks of those who were formerly convicts, are, in general, either solely occupied in amassing wealth, or rioting in sensuality. The lower orders are indeed the filth and offscouring of the earth, in point of wickedness. Long accustomed to idleness and iniquity of every kind, here they indulge their vicious inclinations without a blush : drunkenness, adultery, Sabbath-breaking, and blasphemy, are no longer considered even as indecencies. All those ties of social order and feelings of decency which bind society together are not only relaxed, but almost *extinct*. This is the *general* character of the convicts, high and low ; and, excepting the civil and military departments of the government, there is no other difference than that which wealth naturally creates, in the means it affords for the greater indulgence in vice.......

" The present Governor of the colony is a respectable man, mild, moral, and attentive to the forms of religion. He encourages every attempt to reclaim or improve the people. ......We have here four chaplains, sent out from England, with handsome salaries.......With respect to them all, from their characters, we have full reason to conclude that they would approve of further exertions being made among us, provided these exertions did not imply an opposition to the Established Church. There are some Calvinist Dissenters, Missionaries that were some years since sent by the London

Missionary Society to Otaheite and the South Sea Islands.
Having been forced to leave the islands, they came to this
colony, and many of them have settled here in trade and
business.

" Blessed be God, notwithstanding the general depravity,
there are a few endeavouring to escape the overflowing of
iniquity, and to serve the Lord in simplicity and godly
fear.   We have formed two classes at Sydney, and
one at Windsor.   Our numbers now are nineteen
in class, besides occasional attendants, and by God's
blessing we look for an increase.   At first there was only
one family.   There are numbers who, from some remains of
former impressions, and many other causes, would join us
heartily, if we were a settled people, and had a pious, upright
man, to preach to and watch over us.   Most of us have
been but a short time in the country.   We are, however,
endeavouring to do as much as we can in the way of
prayer-meetings, &c.

" Thus circumstanced, and in such a country, your children
begotten by you in Christ call upon you, reverend fathers,
for help.   Send us your aid.   We doubt not that you will
think of the offspring of your labours, your tears, and your
prayers.   Send a faithful servant of the Lord to us.   Surely
there are many willing, yea, desirous to succour the disciples
of our common Lord, to proclaim His salvation to perishing sinners, even in this distant land.   Find out one such,
and send him among us.   Deny us not : our hearts, our
expectations, are turned to you.   Our hope is from you :
disappoint us not.   We call upon you in our *own* behalf,
leave us not in this benighted land.   We call upon you in
behalf of *our children* : let them not be left to perish for
lack of instruction.   We call upon you in behalf of those
who have neither opportunity nor inclination to speak for
themselves,—perishing, dying sinners : leave them not in
their blood.   We call upon you in the name of *the outcasts*

of society, sent and daily sending hither: administer to them that word of life which may make their exile a blessing. Send us that Gospel which you have received from the Lord *to preach to every creature. Send among us one of yourselves,* and we and a seed to the Lord shall rise to bless you.

" You have now our state and circumstances laid before you, and are best judges of the qualifications necessary in the person you might be disposed to send out to us. Yet we would beg leave to suggest these necessary considerations: (1.) That he be a single man.......(2.) That he be legally qualified. A certificate obtained in the usual way in England will be in force here. (3.) That he be rendered perfectly independent, in all points, of us and everybody else, and a regular credit established for him to draw on as he may deem fit. *This suggestion arises not from our unwillingness or inability to support a preacher ; for, thanks to God, we are all able, and fully determined, and hereby pledge ourselves so to do.* But, for other reasons, which we need not here specify, he should (4.) have a good supply of wearing apparel, house furniture, and particularly books.

" With a filial confidence on your pastoral love, we subscribe ourselves,

" Reverend and honoured fathers,

"Your children and servants in the Gospel of the Lord Jesus Christ,—

" Signed in the name and $\left\{\begin{array}{l}\text{Thomas Bowden,} \\ \text{J. Hosking,}\end{array}\right\}$ *Leaders.*"
on behalf of the Society,

Who that is acquainted with the results of that communication, can fail to mark in Methodism the gift of God's mind and heart to the Southern World ?

That letter received prompt consideration by the Missionary Committee, and the Conference Station list, adopted three months later, included New South Wales in its Asia division. The record is,—

" *N. S. Wales—Two to be sent by the Committee.*"

In the same Station list, there is in the Nova Scotia and New Brunswick District this appointment :—

" 27. *Montreal—Samuel Leigh, if wanted.*"

In due time Mr. Leigh left his Staffordshire home for London, and for America. He was on the eve of sailing when the Secretaries received a letter from Montreal, requesting that at present no Missionary might be sent, as the country was in a very disturbed state. Whereupon half his passage money was recovered, and he was appointed to New South Wales. He sailed from Portsmouth in the " Hebe," on February the 28th, 1815, and reached Port Jackson on the 10th of August. His biographer tells of his having been much depressed the first day and night after his arrival, but of encouragement quickly following.

" It was regarded as a primary duty on the part of Mr. Leigh to pay his respects to His Excellency the Governor, present his credentials, and, if possible, obtain his official sanction. Accordingly, the next day, at eleven o'clock, he called at Government House. After waiting some time, he was ushered into the presence of His Excellency by his aide-de-camp, and received with much formality."

His Excellency.—" Who sent you here, in the capacity of a Wesleyan Missionary ? "

Mr. Leigh.—" The Committee of the Society, at the request of several British emigrants, and, as I understood, with the concurrence of His Majesty's Government."

His Excellency.—" I regret you have come here as a Missionary, and feel sorry that I cannot give you any encouragement in that capacity."

Mr. Leigh.—" The documents which I now present to your Excellency will show you that I am legally and duly authorized to preach the Gospel in any part of His Majesty's dominions."

His Excellency.—" You have come to a strange country.

Those documents are of no value here. It is necessary we should be jealous and cautious; for a few years since we had a religious rebellion, aggravated by the bitter hostility of both Papists and Protestants. If you will take office under Government, I will find you a situation in which you may become rich, and one in which you will be much more comfortable than in going about preaching in such a colony as this."

Mr. Leigh.—" I thank your Excellency for your generous offer ; but having come to New South Wales as a Wesleyan Missionary, I cannot act in any other capacity while I remain in the country." He then briefly stated the object of his Mission, and the means he intended to employ.

The Governor, who had listened with marked attention to his statement, observed: " If those be your objects, they are certainly of the first importance ; and if you will endeavour to compass them by the means you have now specified, I cannot but wish you all the success you can reasonably wish or desire. Call at the Surveyor General's office; present my compliments, and say that I wish him to afford you every facility in his power in travelling from one township to another." At the close of the interview, his Excellency advanced towards Mr. Leigh, and shook hands with him in the most cordial manner.

The Wesleyans then resident in Sydney rented a house on The Rocks, one of the most densely peopled and Sodomlike neighbourhoods of the place. They removed the partition walls, and fitted up the building for worship. The Sabbath services, held at six in the morning and at six in the evening, were attended by a promiscuous crowd of soldiers, sailors, immigrants, and prisoners. A Sabbath school which had lately languished was revived, and regularly attended to by a few pious soldiers and some reformed convicts. This arrangement was not only useful in itself, but it secured Mr. Leigh's access to many houses of the scholars. A worthy soldier, Sergeant James Scott, who had been converted in the West Indies, opened his house for week-evening services. He afterwards purchased some property in Prince's Street, part of which he sold to the Missionary Society. It is the site of the oldest church property in the Southern World now held by the Wesleyan Connexion, and its Trust Deed is the model deed of the Australasian Conference property.

The notice of Mr. Leigh's early visits to the country,— "the interior," as it was then called,—gives many interesting details of the first services among the settlers on the Nepean and Hawkesbury, where Methodism has since witnessed many a blessed revival. His course of Mission labour is shown in the following extract from a letter to the Rev. Joseph Benson, eighteen months after his arrival in Sydney.

"In this distant and barren land, I have had the satisfaction of seeing six classes formed ; the fourth class at a place fourteen miles from Sydney ; the fifth, thirty-five miles ; and the sixth, upwards of forty miles. And in some of them the people seldom meet without experiencing the power of God among them. Thanks be to God, there are some who are earnestly seeking the salvation of their souls ; and others are willing to receive instruction. Several have set their hands to the Gospel plough, and have been added to the Society this week: may they never look back, but soon enjoy and live in the full assurance of faith."

The same communication notices the founding in Sydney of an Auxiliary Bible Society, under the auspices of His Excellency the Governor. From another source it appears that Mr. Leigh, in connexion with the aide-de-camp, was the first Australian collector for that noble institution.

For the sake of its historic interest I append the first notice of Van Diemen's Land submitted to our Committee as a suitable Mission field. It is from the last paragraph of the same letter.

" I now beg leave to recommend to the notice of the Committee the present state of a settlement distant from this, though within the jurisdiction of this territory, a place called *Van Diemen's Land*, where there are two or three places of trade, one called *Hobart Town*, (which is the seat of Government there,) and the other *Port Dalrymple* (Launceston). I would earnestly request that some of our Missionaries should be authorized to visit each place, previous to any regular appointment being made."

About this time Mr. Leigh conducted service occasionally at fourteen different places, the chief in importance of which appear to have been Parramatta, Windsor, and Castlereagh. At the last named settlement, resided a worthy Methodist whose good deed ought not to be omitted by any chronicler of Church events in those times. John Lees, of Castlereagh, built at his own cost the first Wesleyan church in the Southern World. It was a substantial building of weather boards. It still stands, surrounded by numerous Methodist homes. It was filled with attentive hearers when dedicated to God on October 7th, 1817. Mr. Leigh's text was, " The Lord hath done great things for us, whereof we are glad." (Psalm cxxvi. 3.) It was a day of spiritual joy. The people were not willing to leave ; so, in the evening Mr. Leigh conducted a prayer-meeting, at which they pleaded for the prosperity of God's cause especially in that place.

On the door of this church in the wilderness were painted the words " Methodist Chapel ; " and below them, " Prepare to meet thy God." Mr. James Burns, for many years a successful class leader, was convinced of sin by reading that text.

During his first two years' residence in the colony, Mr Leigh appears to have taken as many as eight preaching tours through the settlements of the interior, his course comprising, in addition to the places named, Portland Head,

Wilberforce, Richmond, Liverpool, and Camden. He also occasionally visited Newcastle, and preached to the prisoners.

His labours aroused persecution on the part of some godless friends of the Established Church. While on a visit to Windsor, the Governor invited a number of official personages to dine with him;—magistrates, military officers, and the Windsor Chaplain. The resident Magistrate inquired whether His Excellency knew that a Missionary was " going up and down in the several townships, collecting large bodies of people together, and persuading them to become Methodists." He stated that "unless some restraint were laid upon him, they would soon, in his opinion, become a colony of Methodists." The worthy Magistrate concluded by recommending, "that Missionary Leigh be sent to work in the chain-gang in the coal mines of Newcastle." " You had better," said another officer, " let Missionary Leigh remain where he is; and keep a vigilant eye upon him." Governor Macquarie's reply was worthy of his office : " Gentlemen," he said, " I am neither unacquainted with the person to whom you refer, nor with his proceedings. As I did not in the first instance approve of his mission, I have, I assure you, kept a vigilant eye upon him. I have now sufficient evidence that he is doing good everywhere." Then, turning to the Magistrate who preferred the complaint, His Excellency added, " Sir, when Mr. Leigh comes here again, I desire that you will call the servants of the Government into the store-room, that he may preach to them. Remember, I wish this to be regularly done in future."

As the Governor was returning from the country, Mr. Leigh met him. His Excellency stopped his carriage, and asked how he was getting on, and why he had not applied for land, that, like the clergy and others, he might improve his circumstances by breeding cattle and sheep. The

Missionary thanked him, but respectfully intimated that he "had been sent to the land for purely spiritual objects." He then informed the Governor that though he could not accept of any gifts for his own use, he felt at liberty to avail himself of any offer that might be made of land, on which to build chapels or school-houses for the Society.

Once in three years there was a general muster of the colonists, when each one had to present a schedule of his landed property, houses, cattle, and grain. On looking over the Missionary's schedule the Governor remarked, " Mr. Leigh, have you nothing to return but your old horse ? You seem to have neither cattle nor grain yet. Why, you will always be poor at this rate." About five hundred persons were present, including Magistrates, Clergymen, military officers, and wealthy settlers, who had assembled to pay their respects to His Excellency; and Mr. Leigh embraced the singular opportunity afforded him of explaining the regulations of the Missionary Committee, and the design of the Mission.*

Success and the many open doors for usefulness induced Mr. Leigh to write to the Committee for more Missionaries ; and on the 1st of May, 1818, the Rev. Walter Lawry arrived in Sydney. Upon his first Sabbath he preached with great power and acceptance. Of his pioneer he wrote :—" He is everything I could wish in a colleague. In commencing this Mission he has not only been alone, like a sparrow upon the house top, but has endured calumny and opposition from those from whom he expected assistance. I need not dwell upon his wanderings in these forests without food, having no shelter by day nor bed by night. His patient soul endured all in quietness, and the effects of his labours will be seen after many days. By his exemplary conduct he has established himself in the good opinion of almost every one, from His Excellency the Governor to the

* Strachan's Life of the Rev. S. Leigh.

fisherman at the stall.   We are agreed to live upon two meals a day if we may have another Missionary and a printing press."

For nearly two years, reckoning the short interval of Mr. Leigh's visit to New Zealand, these brethren laboured zealously and successfully together, without further ministerial help.   In September, 1818, the foundation stone of the Windsor chapel was laid, on a site generously given by the Rev. Samuel Marsden.   On the 1st of January, 1819, Mr. Leigh laid the foundation stone of the Macquarie Street chapel in Sydney, the site having been the joint gift of His Excellency Governor Macquarie and Thomas Wylde, Esq., from adjoining parts of their separate properties.   Meanwhile Sergeant Scott was erecting, at his own expense, a chapel in Princes Street.   It cost him more than £500.   It was opened one Sunday evening in March, 1819, by the Rev. Walter Lawry.

Early the next year Mr. Leigh, whose health had given way, went to England, with the approval of the New South Wales Church ; and for some weeks Mr. Lawry was alone.

With 1820 begins the history of Methodism in Van Diemen's Land.   The third Wesleyan Missionary sent to the South Seas was the Rev. Benjamin Carvosso, appointed to New South Wales.   In May, 1820, his vessel touched at Hobart Town.   The Rev. Mr. Knopwood introduced him to Governor Sorrell, who authorized his teaching. The man of God from Cornwall stood upon the street steps by a house doorway, his congregation being part within and part without.   His text was appropriate to the times, and characteristic of the man, "Awake, thou that sleepest."   During his two or three weeks' sojourn he preached to numerous congregations, visiting both Pittwater and New Norfolk, where, up to that time, no religious service had been held.   Mr. Carvosso described the Van Diemen's Land people as being "kind, but dissolute."   He heard of a religious settler in the country, and went fifteen miles to see him, but found him swearing.

Soon after this a detachment of the 58th Regiment were quartered in Hobart Town. Some of these soldiers had been converted in Sydney. They obtained a room for worship in Collins Street, where eight persons met on October 29th, 1820. Their leader was Corporal Waddy. They shortly removed their meetings to the house of Mr. Wallis. Here they met with some rude disturbances, which, however, were put down by the interference of the Governor. Their landlord soon tired of his lively tenants, and they had again to turn out. There was a workshop belonging to one Charles Donne, a carpenter, who had been a prisoner, but who had lived to acquire the confidence and respect of his neighbours. His proper name was *Cranmer*, and he was a descendant of the illustrious archbishop. After much entreaty he promised to arrange the place for worship. His wife, who was a vigorous Romanist, violently refused her consent. But that night, in the midst of a dreadful storm, which rocked the house, she started up in terror, and exclaimed, "The Methodists shall have the room!" Those who flocked to the services of the soldiers and their pious civilian friends, could not find room within the building: they therefore had it enlarged.

Some few months later the Rev. Ralph Mansfield, the fourth Wesleyan Missionary appointed to the South Seas, called at Van Diemen's Land, on his way to his station, New South Wales. Like Mr. Carvosso, he heartily embraced the opportunities offered during his two or three weeks' stay, and engaged in the delightful work on which his heart was set. On May 13th, 1821, the first Sunday-school was established by the Methodist Church, as yet without a Minister.

In 1820, about fifty years ago, the Wesleyan-Methodist Church was represented in this hemisphere by three Missionaries, the Revs. Walter Lawry, Benjamin Carvosso, and Ralph Mansfield, all of New South Wales.

Early in 1821 a reinforcement arrived, in company with the Rev. Samuel Leigh, who had been appointed by the British Conference General Superintendent of the Mission to New Zealand and the Friendly Islands. They were the Revs. William Walker and William Horton, both for New South Wales,—the former to found a Mission among the aborigines. They touched at Hobart Town, where the claims of the Society and the openings for usefulness so impressed them, that although they were not able to seek official sanction, it was agreed that Mr. Horton* should remain in Van Diemen's Land.

* The Rev. William Horton was born in Louth, and at twenty-one years of age was received into the ministry of the Wesleyan Church. For eight years he laboured in Van Diemen's Land and New South Wales, and for twenty-two years afterwards in England. In 1852 his health failed, and he became a Supernumerary. On the 18th of June, 1867, he was seized with apoplexy, and suddenly called to his reward.

CHAPTER III.

1822—1823.

MR. TURNER'S first night in Van Diemen's Land was spent without sleep, but in grateful Christian fellowship with Mr. Horton, and in conversation upon the work of God in these ends of the earth.

As most of the cargo and passengers were for Hobart Town, it was expected that the vessel would be detained there about a month, and Mr. Turner was to have proceeded by her to Sydney. Intelligence, however, arrived, which forbade the establishing, at that time, a Mission in New Zealand. The ferocious cannibal warrior, "Hongi," (or, as then generally called, "Shonsghei,") had lately returned from England, where, having seen something of the glory of George the Fourth, he had resolved on becoming King in his own country. He had brought with him muskets and ammunition,—weapons scarcely before known among the New Zealanders, and had begun a destructive war upon the tribes south of the Bay of Islands. Many had been taken captive, of whom large numbers had been killed and eaten. The natives in every part were so disturbed and given up to war, that missionary operations for the time had ceased, and Mr. Leigh and his wife were residing with the Church Missionary, awaiting brighter days.

Besides the Rev. Mr. Horton, there was at this time but one Clergyman in all Van Diemen's Land,—the Rev. Robert Knopwood. It was judged expedient that Mr. White should go on to Sydney, either to join Mr. Lawry in the Tongan

Mission, or to await, in Sydney, more favourable tidings
from the New Zealand Mission, and that meanwhile Mr.
Turner should assist Mr. Horton in extending his labours
in Van Diemen's Land.

It was the depth of winter, and the appearance of the
young town was anything but cheering. The streets were
unmade and very dirty, and the houses were chiefly small
weather-board erections of a rude character. The moral
surroundings were more wintry still. Most of the inhabitants were prisoners, and in a deeply degraded condition.
Until long after their eyes had become familiarized with
the scene, the Missionaries were made sad by witnessing
large gangs of the unhappy men marched to and from the
public works in chains, in charge of overseers.

The Lieutenant-Governor, Sorrell, who had expressed a
desire that Mr. Turner would remain in Van Diemen's
Land, gave instructions that the men should be mustered
for Divine worship whenever the Missionaries desired it.
They immediately began visiting the prison gangs around,
and itinerating among the sparsely scattered settlers.
Many of the latter were leading grossly immoral lives,
family sanctity being shamefully disregarded. Mr. Turner
often found it hard, after travelling all day from house to
house, conversing with the families, and inviting them
to the services in the evening, " to preach to from five to
ten persons." Yet he did not labour in vain. Good was
effected among them, and in several instances among the
prisoners also. In Hobart Town itself " the word grew."
Many flocked to hear, until Charles Donne's room, which
had been rented, required enlargement. Souls were converted, and added to the newly-formed classes. God gave
the preachers favour in the eyes of the people. An eligible
site of land for Mission premises in Melville Street was
secured, and the erection of a chapel commenced.

Towards the close of the year they were greatly cheered.

by the arrival, as settlers, of several valuable families of Wesleyans and Independents. Among these were Messrs. Mather, Dunn, Hopkins, Chapman, Hiddlestone, John Walker, Turnbull, and others, with their excellent families. This has been regarded by many as the most important addition of Christian families Van Diemen's Land society ever received. Most of them had been members of our Churches at home, and some of them honoured office-bearers. They gladly and heartily joined the infant Church, and the widespread results of their piety and labours remain to this day. With some of them Mr. and Mrs. Turner formed an intimate and lasting Christian friendship. Mr. Henry Hopkins, a pious Independent, but who joined the Wesleyan Church until a Minister of his own denomination should arrive, rendered valuable service in the systematic distribution of tracts, and in gathering children for the Sabbath school. Early in 1823 the number and working power of the Church were further increased by the arrival of Messrs. Pullen and Hobbs, two valuable Local Preachers. Mr. Hobbs afterwards became a successful Missionary in New Zealand. Messrs. Sherwin and Barrett arrived in the same vessel.

The fierceness of the Maori wars was soon over, and general tranquillity reported ; and though Van Diemen's Land friends would have detained him, Mr. Turner sought to reach New Zealand, his appointed Mission. With his wife and infant daughter, about the close of April he sailed for Sydney, where, after a fifteen days' passage, he was welcomed by the Rev. Benjamin Carvosso.

CHAPTER IV.

1823.

MR. WHITE had sailed for New Zealand, and his colleagues waited an opportunity to follow. A day or two after landing Mr. Turner went to Parramatta, to see the Rev. W. Walker, whom he had previously met at the Mission House in London. There he was welcomed by the Rev. Ralph Mansfield, of whose public ability he had heard much. They were from neighbouring Circuits in "the old country." The friendship which followed proved lasting as life. He then accompanied Mr. Carvosso to the opening of a little chapel on the banks of the Nepean, where, as being a stranger, he was "almost compelled" to preach. It was "an interesting and profitable occasion." From Castlereagh they proceeded to Windsor, where they spent a short time with the Rev. George Erskine and his wife. A few months before this Mr. Turner had met Mr. Erskine in Hobart Town, an invalid Missionary from India, on his way to Sydney under Conference appointment, as the General Superintendent of the New South Wales Mission. He had then appeared exceedingly delicate, and by many was believed to be dying. But during the few months of his residence in New South Wales he had become quite vigorous.

In Sydney Mr. Turner entered heartily into the work of God as occasion arose. Mr. Carvosso * and he daily

---

* The Life of this devoted servant of God is a stirring manual. He was a man of eminent faith, energy, and zeal. For five years he preached twice each Sabbath in the Melville Street church, and in the

renewed the consecration of their lives to God and to the objects of their Mission, and were honoured with success. Entering open doors where they found them, and opening doors which they found closed, they bestirred themselves in exhorting the Church to holiness, and in warning sinners. Their numerous prayer-meetings in the neighbourhood of " The Rocks " were seasons of much power, and witnessed many triumphs of grace.

The few memoranda of Mr. Turner's course during his brief sojourn in Sydney are those of various labours " in season and out of season." One afternoon, while he was meeting the female class for tickets, there occurred a fearful storm of thunder and lightning. Returning from the meeting a Mr. Challinor fell down in the street, and suddenly expired. On the following Sabbath, preparatory to the funeral, he stood beside the bier, in the verandah, and preached to a multitude in the street below, from, " The night cometh, when no man can work."

After eight or ten weeks in Sydney Mr. Turner proceeded to New Zealand, accompanied by Mr. Hobbs. Among his fellow voyagers were the Rev. Samuel Marsden, the Rev. Henry Williams, and Mr. Fairbourne, of the Church Mission. They endured eleven days at sea with one of the most profane captains they ever knew. The voyage terminated on Sabbath evening, August 3rd, 1823, when the ship " Brompton " cast anchor in the Bay of Islands.

It is time now to say a few words about the people to whose welfare Mr. Turner was about to devote himself.

afternoon spent an hour with the chain gang. Twice each week he visited the inmates of the gaol, and as frequently those of the hospital. A favourite theme of his ministry was the doctrine of sanctification. He had unusual tact and power in leading meetings for prayer. He valued the moments of life, rose early, and observed personal discipline for his work's sake. He left Australia on the 30th of March, 1830, for England, where he laboured successfully for many years.

The name *Maoris* was given to themselves by the
inhabitants of New Zealand. It signifies *native* or *indigenous*. The race evidently belong to the Malay family.
Though calling themselves indigenous, they are, by their
own tradition, immigrants from Hawaiki, by some supposed to mean *Hawaii*, of the Sandwich Islands, and by
others, *Savaii*, of the Navigator's Group. Their story is,
that they came to New Zealand in seven canoes, about five
hundred years ago. It is thought by some that they are a
mixed race, the immigrants of the tradition having inter-
mingled with the people to whose land they had come.
The Maoris have a powerful muscular development, and an
intellectual cast of head. Their hair, which is either
black or sandy colour, is not frizzled, but wavy. They
have large eyes, thick lips, and irregularly set teeth, very
suggestive of their native savageism. The women are less
than the men, and in all respects their inferiors. Prior to
Christianity both sexes practised *tattooing*. It was a painful operation. The flesh was punctured over the face, hips,
thighs, &c., in scrolls and figures, denoting various ranks.
The punctures were then stained with vegetable dyes.
Among their religious institutions there was one having
political as well as religious respect, called *Taboo*. Whatever thing or person the priest had made *sacred* was left
unharmed even in war. Their social condition was very
degraded, and, except to men of faith and prayer, appeared
hopeless of redemption. Polygamy, infanticide, slavery,
and cannibalism prevailed among all the tribes. Their
graces were indolence, treachery, and revenge. Their god
was war, and their sacrament blood. The Maori language
comprises our five vowels, and but nine consonants. In
conversation they are animated, and deal largely in figure.
Their public addresses in tribal conference or controversy
are said to show great oratorical power. They have numerous proverbs and legends in metrical form. In their

native games they evince the highest athletic skill. Acquaintanceship with them, under their changing condition during the last fifty years, has impressed all observers with their great superiority over most, if not over all other coloured races.

CHAPTER V.

THE history of the New Zealand Mission, up to that time, is briefly as follows. In 1814, the Rev. Samuel Marsden, then senior Chaplain at New South Wales, had established at the Bay of Islands some Clergymen and lay settlers, whose object was to civilize the Maoris, and teach them Christianity. Many Maori chiefs and others had visited New South Wales, and Mr. Marsden's intercourse with them in the colony, which had been considerable, had deepened his interest in their religious welfare; and the New Zealand Church Mission was the outcome of this feeling. The principle adopted was the then popular idea, that in attempting to Christianize a heathen race, it is essential to success first of all to civilize them. Accordingly, the pioneer agents of that Mission, who were excellent men, sought by example and instruction to introduce among the natives the trades and habits of European colonists.

The anxiety and arduous labours of Mr. Leigh in New South Wales, during its dark days of immorality, had told seriously upon his health; and in 1818, at the instance of Mr. Marsden, the way being open by the arrival of the Rev. Walter Lawry to reinforce the Australian Mission, he took a voyage to New Zealand, in the hope of recovery. He found that the well meant effort of the Church Mission had been, up to that time, a failure. Amid the disadvantages of their false position, the lay settlers had found but little encouragement in attempting the religious instruction of the natives. Mr. Leigh gave them such sympathy and counsel as became him. From the first he loved the New Zealanders. His short visit afforded him many opportunities of estimating their character. He judged that the time had come for direct evangelistic effort to save them, and there arose within him an intense desire for New Zealand Missionaries. Early in 1820, he proceeded to England, and there devoted himself with great zeal to the advocacy of New Zealand as an important field for missionary enterprise. His first representations to the Missionary Secretaries were met by the matter-of-fact difficulty, that the Treasurers already showed *a deficit of ten thousand pounds.* Mr. Leigh was disconsolate. One sleepless morning, however, while ruminating upon the question, the thought seized him, that the Mission might be successfully undertaken without any immediate demand upon the General Treasury. "Could not the Methodists of England contribute a good supply of articles suitable for barter among the natives?" The Secretaries neither endorsed nor discarded his project, but referred him to the Conference. To that body Mr. Leigh made his statements, proposal, and appeal. After mature consideration, the Conference passed the following

Resolution.—"That Mr. Samuel Leigh having been appointed as a Wesleyan Missionary to New Zealand, the Conference authorizes the Missionary Committee to direct him to visit, before his departure, any places in this kingdom, where it is probable that he may obtain the present of various articles of manufacture, in aid of the South Sea Mission."

Armed with this authority, and encouraged by the general co-operation of the Ministers, he made a tour through the manufacturing provinces. The result of his morning vision was a confused accumulation of prints and pots, calicoes and axes, razors, fish-hooks, &c. These goods, which passed through the office of the Mission House in London, were shipped to Sydney, and afterwards forwarded to order as occasion required, for the establishment and service of the New Zealand Mission. They furnished the means for purchasing the first Mission property there, and for erecting the Missionaries' dwelling and schools ; indeed, they almost met the expenses of the first five years.

The financial hindrance having been thus removed, Mr. Leigh landed, as the first Wesleyan Missionary to New Zealand, on February 22nd, 1822. His biographer says : "The natives of the Bay of Islands hastened to bid him welcome, which they did by rubbing noses. While a succession of individuals saluted him until the skin was entirely rubbed off the point of his nose, they shouted, ' Glad, very glad to see the white teacher.'"

Several exploring trips, by boat and otherwise, were taken, in search of an appropriate site for the Mission. On the 11th of June of that year, after having been flooded out of a booth which they had the day before erected upon their intended site, the Mission party laid the foundation of their dwelling upon a hill side near Wangaroa Bay. From that time Mr. Leigh continued amid many hardships, until August, 1823, when Mr. Turner found him seriously invalided, and quite unequal to Missionary toil. It is right to say, that though Mr. Leigh had not been able to preach or offer a public address in Maori, he had so far acquired the language as to have held religious conversations with the tribe.

CHAPTER VI.

1823–1825.

On arrival in New Zealand Mr. Turner was received with much cordiality by the friends of the Church Mission and the other residents at the Bay of Islands. Mr. White had joined Mr. Leigh at Wangaroa, forty miles north. The first trial in the Mission field came early. An agreement with the captain of "The Brompton," under which £70 had been paid, provided that if the Wesleyan Mission station should prove to be within fifty miles of the Bay of Islands, the Mission family were to be landed at it, either by the ship or ship's boats, free of extra expense. But having landed his passengers at the Bay, the worthy captain would neither take his ship nor send his boats to Wangaroa, and Mr. Turner might get there as best he could. Leaving his family in care of Mr. Hall of Rangakoo, he and Mr. Hobbs proceeded overland to the station, under conduct of a native guide.

It was on their third day in New Zealand when they found their brethren, tools in hand, working at their dwelling. They returned to the Bay, and chartered a small schooner, "The Schnapper," to convey them and their luggage round. Mr. Marsden went with them, to see his friend Mr. Leigh. They reached the station the second evening. The weather had been unusually wet, and when they had clambered up the clay bank to their first home in the Southern World, they found it cheerless in the extreme.

It was wintry August, and the site chosen for the log and

roupo tenement proved very unsuitable. Nor had the construction of the building improved matters. The severe and continued rains had made no account of the roof; and, in order to save his failing health, Mr. Leigh had for some time been obliged to sleep in a cask, which formerly had contained Mission stores. Mrs. Leigh's welcome to her European sister was very hearty, and the gratitude of all was great. It was well that it was so; for the aspect of things would have chilled a cooler love, and quenched a weaker faith.

Mr. Leigh's state of health necessitated his leaving New Zealand for a time. Preparation was made accordingly; and on the third day after Mr. Turner's arrival, he left Wangaroa by " The Schnapper," for the Bay of Islands, *en route* for Sydney.

The Mission party felt their dependent position ; but knew where to look for wisdom and strength. They comprised Mr. White, who had then been eight weeks at Wangaroa, Mr. and Mrs. Turner, Mr. Hobbs, Mr. Stack,* late Missionary associate of Mr. Leigh, and Luke Wade,† formerly a sailor, but latterly engaged as general servant on the station. Wade was not at that time pious. Besides these there was a young nurse girl, whom Mrs. Turner had taken with her from Sydney.

The station was about twelve miles inland from the heads of the Wangaroa harbour. The Mission dwelling stood on a jutting point of land on the south-east side of a beautiful vale, through which ran the Kaio, a fine serpentine river, which emptied itself into the harbour six miles below. The entrance to Wangaroa is singularly beautiful

* Mr. Stack was in later years associated with the Church Missionary Society. The Rev. J. Stack, who has the religious oversight of the Maoris in the Canterbury province, is his son.

† After leaving Wangaroa with Mr. Turner, in 1827, Luke Wade removed to Sydney, where for many years he has led a consistent life.

and romantic. Near the northern head is a large perforated rock, resembling, in one aspect, a deep Gothic archway. The sea rolls through it, and in moderate weather canoes find it a safe passage. The entrance is not more than half a mile wide, and, as an island is abreast of it, cannot be discerned from any distance at sea. The water is deep close to the land, which is bold and steep on both sides. When entered, the harbour is found one of the finest in the world. The largest fleet might ride securely sheltered from any wind. Close to the western shore is a series of huge volcanic rocks of immense height and most fantastic shapes. An insulated rock, three hundred feet high, and excessively steep, is the site of the principal native *pa*. The interior of the country is very hilly and thickly wooded. The Mission valley was sequestered among hills and mountains of almost every size and shape ; most of them covered with excellent pine trees; many running from sixty to a hundred feet high without a branch, and their trunks from three to six feet in diameter. The soil around, as will be imagined, was very fertile.

In selecting the tribes of Wangaroa as the subjects of the first Missionary experiment of our Church in New Zealand, Mr. Leigh certainly adopted the maxim of our venerable founder, " We are to go to those who need us most." Those who knew the Maoris regarded the Wangaroa tribes as the vilest in the land : and among them all the most distinguished for villany were the Ngatehure tribe, in whose midst the enterprise had been planted. A dreadful notoriety had attached to them, from the tragedy of the ship " Boyd " in 1809, when the captain, crew, and all the passengers, save two,—seventy persons,—had been betrayed and murdered, and most of them eaten.

The subjoined notice, which differs in some details from other accounts of this atrocious carnage, is from Mr. Turner's pen. From his daily intercourse with several of the perpetrators, and the circumstantial character of the narrative, it may be taken as correct.

" The awful tragedy had taken place in sight of where we afterwards erected our dwelling. Our tribe had been the chief actors, our chiefs the principals. These chiefs were three brothers,—Te Puhi, Ahera or *George*, and Ahududu. The occurrence, as narrated to me by one of the party, was as follows. George and Teroehide, another young chief, had visited New South Wales, and after residing there for nearly two years were returning in the ship ' Boyd,' five-hundred tons' burthen, Captain Thompson." [This vessel was the first loaded for England with Australian produce, and many of her full complement of passengers were reputed wealthy.] " The ' Boyd' was to call at some port of New Zealand for spars. During the voyage, the cook complained to the captain, that he had lost some silver spoons and other small articles, and charged George with having stolen them. The captain, very injudiciously, had the Maori chieftain tied and flogged. In the proud and vengeful spirit of his race, George at once vowed to have satisfaction ; but he concealed his purpose. Knowing that Captain Thompson purposed to obtain spars, George desired him to put in at Wangaroa, and in the kindest manner promised to procure him as many as he wanted without delay. From the authority he had as a chief, he could easily have fulfilled his promise.

" George's counsel was taken, and the vessel safely anchored in Wangaroa. Accompanied by his Maori associate, the chief soon made his way up the Kaio to his own tribe, at the head of which was his father. The insult and degradation received, and the great value of the cargo, were no sooner told, than Maori villany and keenness devised an atrocious scheme of murder and pillage, as *utu* or *satisfaction*. The tribe selected a convenient spot on the bank of the river, near their principal *pa* or residence, and at once felled a few spars. A number of armed natives having been placed in ambush, George went down to the ship, told the captain that the spars were fallen, and invited him to look at them, and see if they would answer. Two boats were manned, and as many of the passengers as wished to go and see the country, were invited to do so. When all were on shore, and while the captain was in the act of measuring a tree, an appointed signal was given, and the natives instantly sprang from their ambush, and murdered every one. They afterwards stripped the slaughtered sailors, and attired themselves in their garments. Then sending before them many of their friends to the vicinity of ' The Boyd,' they manned the boats, and by evening light pulled to the ship. Before those on board suspected danger, the tribe fell upon them, and murdered every one. It was the Sabbath, and a few passengers had gone ashore to another part of the bay. These too were sought for, and all killed, except a Mrs. Broughton and her little girl, for whose lives a friendly chief interceded. They alone were spared to tell the tale of horror. .

" On the following day, the natives feasted upon the bodies, until nearly all were devoured. The ship had anchored near the mouth of the harbour ; but for greater convenience in taking the plunder up their own river, the cable was slipped under direction of George, and the vessel towed up the bay, until she grounded on the flats. The work of plunder was then begun with avidity. George knew that there were muskets and ammunition on board, and these were the first things he sought. The hold was broken into, and several casks of powder brought on deck, and their heads knocked out. While some of the excited natives were in the act of trying the muskets, the powder caught fire. Most of those on board were blown into the air, and among the killed was George's father. The vessel was burnt to the water's edge. [The bodies of the captain and officers of the ship were hanged from limbs of trees, and the natives, as they pointed out the tree to the Mission families, stated that it had been the intention of the tribe to eat them a slice at a time, but that they 'tasted salt,' and were not even such good eating as Maori flesh.]"

The guns and some other relics which had been got on shore by the natives, were for years to be seen here and there in the neighbourhood. The tribe acknowledged that a great mortality had set in among them soon afterwards ; and Mr. Turner told them it was to be regarded as a judgment from Almighty God for their wickedness.

It was resolved that for the present the Mission party should live together as one family, and observe family prayer morning and evening; prayer-meeting each Wednesday evening, class-meeting each Saturday evening, and at least one English service on the Sabbath.

A more eligible site was now selected for the Mission dwelling, affording, with other advantages, rich garden soil and abundant good water. The levelling for a foundation proved hard work ; but in due time it was effected by the willing hands of the Missionaries. They then proceeded to erect the wooden frame of a cottage which Mr. Leigh had taken with him from Sydney.

On the death of his father, George had become the head chief of his tribe; and, notwithstanding frequent disputes with his elder brothers, had maintained that position. From his character and that of the tribe, as illustrated in "The Boyd" massacre, and from the isolation of the Mission party, Mr. Turner from the first felt that the Mission enterprise would be attended by peculiar peril,— that he had indeed before him "a great fight of afflictions."

For the severest trials of his career he was gradually educated, beginning early. Though the chief, George, professed friendship, he caused much trouble. One day he drove off all the natives employed on the premises, claimed the house which was being built, said he would knock it down, and that the Missionaries should not remain. Three natives forcibly seized the spades with which the Missionaries were levelling the ground for their house. For several days and nights consecutively the family were " almost stunned " by the turbulent broil and vociferations around them. One day George took Mr. Turner a pig for which he had prepaid him, and demanded a second payment. After long refusal, Mr. Turner gave him an iron pot, the article he desired. The man immediately seized an axe and a frying-pan, and then dashed the pot to pieces against an anvil. Mr. Turner walked towards Messrs. Hobbs and Stack, who were at work not far off. George at once followed in fiendish rage, and twice levelled his loaded musket at him, and threatened to take his life. But the Lord mercifully withheld him. He then raged dreadfully, and pushed him about the bank, saying, " You want to make the New Zealanders slaves : we want muskets, and powder, and tomahawks ; but you give us nothing but *karakia*," " prayers ;" on which he poured the greatest contempt, saying, " We don't want to hear about Jesus Christ : if you love us, as you say you do, give us blankets, axes," &c. In a short time he went to the house, and threatened Mrs. Turner and the servant, saying he would serve them as he had done the crew of " The Boyd." The girl became alarmed, and ran screaming to the Missionaries. Mr. Turner feared his wife had been murdered, but on reaching the house found her courageously braving the chief. After a while George's fury abated. In excusing himself he said, putting his hand to his heart, " When my heart rests here, then I love Mr. Turner very much ; but when my heart rises to my throat, then I could kill him in a minute."

When Mr. Turner arose the next morning, it was to a yet more offensive trial. A small tribe close by had killed a slave, and were preparing to eat the body. Unattended, he went over the hills, and found the chiefs sitting near a large fire. They feigned gladness to see the Missionary. Mr. Turner saluted them, and asked what they were roasting? Guilt and confusion were written on their faces. He says, "I went towards the fire; and God only knows my feelings, when I beheld a human being laid at length, and roasting between two logs drawn together for the purpose." After very much ado, he succeeded, with the assistance of his brethren, in securing the unburnt remains for burial. The tribe explained that "the man was old and troublesome."

Three canoes with friendly visitors from the Bay of Islands reached the settlement. Whereupon there was a great stir; old and young running, leaping, shouting, and firing muskets, in token of their good will. After a lively dance, the visitors went to see the white people. They were more free than welcome: but the watch-dog understood them.

Mr. Turner noted Maori customs and character. Te Puhi's son having behaved ill, he warned the father that the lad might be corrected. The chief answered that he durst not punish him; for if a Maori beat his child, the child would go and hang himself through vexation, and that then his friend would either kill the father, or strip him of all that he possessed. One evening a girl was cruelly mangled with a hatchet, for divulging some dark deed of her master.

Maori filth, covetousness, and impudence constantly disturbed hearts and home. Among some youths received into the premises, to be fed, clothed, and instructed, was Hongi, son of Te Puhi, the chief. The boy was scrofulous. His unbearably filthy garments called into use the only large iron boiler, and on that account valued. Attended by two or three of his men, Te Puhi went to the house in great excitement, and demanded the boiler, declaring that it had been made *taboo*, inasmuch as, he being a chief and a priest, his son and all belonging to him were sacred. "The thing in which Hongi's clothing has been boiled is sacred." Saying this, he seized the pot, and was in the act of lifting it over a high fence to his men, when he found his ownership more than disputed. By great effort Mrs. Turner, who had followed him, managed to ungrasp his hold, and defeat the chief. He tried all means short of violence, but in vain, and then retired, vowing that he would yet have the pot. To terminate this annoyance, the Missionaries resolved to make the pot "common" again. So they boiled some rice in it for the native youths under their care. The lads, however, refused to eat; not that they feared their god, but from dread of their chief's anger. "That or nothing," was the Missionaries' reply. Firmness conquered. The old chief softened: he took a biscuit to the pot of rice, and after mumbling over it said, "The *taboo* is taken away, and the lads may eat."

Such incidents as the following were frequent:—During English worship one evening in the outer room the chief managed, unperceived, to secrete the teapot within his native garment, and carry it away. One day the dinner was cooked in the yard, and while the cloth was being laid a hawk-eyed and quick-footed fellow got over the fence, and carried off oven, dinner, and all. Washing days were watchful days. Basket and clothes-line were a weekly temptation.

Meum et tuum was somewhat more seriously disregarded in Maori intercourse with traders. A Sydney captain purchased some pigs, and engaged the natives to help his crew in salting and packing them on board. He soon found the natives too many for him. Some crafty fellows on deck, good judges of pork, handed over the best pieces to their friends in the canoes at the ship's side. Alterca-

tions arising, they were in their very element. They cut
away the ship's boat, on purpose to increase confusion, and
then pulled her round the vessel, demanding from her
exasperated captain a large salvage. They had "found
her adrift." In a note to Mr. Turner the captain declared
that but for the Missionaries he would have "taught them
a lesson with powder and ball." Captain Berridge, of
the "St. Michael," asked Mr. Turner to conduct Divine
service on board. The weather being rough, all the ship's
hands attended in the cabin. After service, the "lord of
the galley" went to serve up dinner. It was "done to a
nicety." Some natives were enjoying it with great gusto,
up the river. Preferring it hot, they had taken the cooking
apparatus too.

When they had been six months at the station, the
Missionaries found themselves able to teach the children
in the open air. From this step they proceeded to erect
two temporary rough buildings at the chief villages, to serve
as schools and chapels. These structures they put up
themselves, before their own dwelling was completed.
They were the first Wesleyan churches built in New
Zealand, and on Sabbath, June 13th, 1824, were formally
consecrated to God.

They had requested Mr. Shepherd, of the Church
Mission at Kere Kere, to assist them on the occasion. The
Rev. Mr. Kendall,* of the Bay of Islands, being also with
them on an unexpected visit, the services were as follows :—
At half-past ten they assembled at Te Puhi's chapel, '
and began by singing a hymn in Maori. The Rev. Mr.
Kendall then offered prayer in the same language. After

---

* The Rev. Mr. Kendall was one of the first of the Church of England
Missionaries in New Zealand. He was the author of a Grammar and
Vocabulary of the Maori Language, which was printed in Sydney in
1818. The Messrs. Kendall, of Sydney, Kiama, and Ulladulla, are
his sons.

Mr. White had prayed in English, he addressed the congregation, some fifty in number, Mr. Shepherd interpreting with great fluency. The natives paid the utmost attention. His address was followed by some of the chiefs asking several important questions, which evidenced that their minds were to be reached by Gospel light. Then followed the singing in English of the grand missionary prayer,—

> " From all that dwell below the skies,
>   Let the Creator's praise arise."

At the dedication of the second chapel, the same afternoon, there were more natives present, but their attention was not so good.

In May they prepared to move into their own house. Family flitting usually vexes the husband, and worries the wife, and that at Wesley Vale proved no exception. Arrangements were made to reduce as much as possible the risk of plunder. The property was to be removed during the early part of the night, an hour when most of the Maoris would be asleep. Under private permission a few " trusty " natives assisted in lifting some of the heavy packages. A valuable case of chisels, plane-irons, &c., was missing. Search being made, the party of thieves, with Te Puhi the chief at their head, were pounced upon in the act of dividing their spoil. Te Puhi repudiated any share of the blame, because he was *taboo*,—" sacred !" Next morning family prayer at the old house was disturbed by dreadful yelling outside. Te Puhi and a large armed party had surrounded the house, and were forcing their way for plunder. In trying to prevent their carrying off some linen, Mr. Turner received a blow on his left arm from a marè,—a native weapon. Fortunately it was by the flat side of the weapon, otherwise it would have broken his arm. The chief then entered the house, and a general plunder would have ensued, only that his brother George interfered, and threatened his life if he did not desist. The disappointed savages then made off to the new house. Mrs. Turner and the servant had the courage to bar them out. The diary entry of that date is as follows :—" After a day of extreme difficulty and trial we all assembled in the evening in the new house, together to worship God. Surely goodness and mercy have followed us all the days of our life. We will trust in our God, and praise His name for ever and ever."

In the opinion of the Secretaries in London, the Mission began at this time to wear a brighter aspect. They wrote, " There is now promise of success." This impression they received from a communication by Messrs. Tyerman and Bennett, who had just completed a visiting tour of the London Society's Missions in the South Seas. Their vessel, " The Endeavour," when bound for the Bay of Islands, had taken refuge from adverse weather in Wangaroa Bay. They had thus providentially an opportunity to see and encourage Mr. Turner and his associates.

The subjoined allusion to this casual visit which appeared in the " Sydney Gazette" of August 26th, 1824, will assist the imagination to realize " perils among the heathen : "—

" The ' Endeavour ' was nearly cut off while at anchor at Wangaroa. The following are briefly the circumstances :—Mr. Dacre, with some others, had gone in the boat up to Wesley Dale, the Mission station, leaving the gentlemen of the deputation, Mr. Threlkeld and his son, and some of the crew on board. The natives at the mouth of the harbour, who are as savage and barbarous as ever, thickly crowded the deck of the little vessel, and committed several thefts. An attempt was then made to clear the deck, in effecting which one of the natives fell overboard from the bows. Supposing that their countryman had been thrown overboard, they made the shores resound with the hideous alarm of war. The deck was presently thronged. The natives armed themselves with axes, billets of wood, and whatever else their hands could grasp. Not one of the passengers or crew on deck could stir. An attempt at resistance would have been followed by death. The cries of, 'We are dead;' 'It is all over,' burst from every tongue. Some of the monsters felt the bodies of our affrighted countrymen, and seemed intensely delighted, while others held the uplifted axe, anxious for the signal to give the blow. Mr. Threlkeld prepared himself to receive the impending club, that he might the more easily be despatched. His little boy inquired of him whether it would 'hurt them to be eaten.' Mr. Bennett awaited in silence, but with unshaken confidence, in the hopes of a better world, the stroke that would lay his body low. Mr. Tyerman, though confidently looking forward to the glorious realities of eternity, still felt it his duty to speak in a friendly manner to the savages. All on board, though certain of death, prepared to meet the shock with heroic fortitude, excepting the poor cook, who, rather than be devoured, thought of appending shot to his feet, and leaping overboard. While in this state of suspense, the Mission boat hove in sight, and with it a ray of hope inspired every breast. The natives, too, relaxed their ferocious appearance. In the boat were the chieftain George and the Rev. Mr. White. The latter, with amazement and gratitude, saw the destruction from which all had escaped so narrowly. He addressed the savages on their conduct, while George exerted all his power and influence. The natives soon dispersed."

It seems that George had previously expressed a wish to afford every proof possible of his sorrow for the " Boyd " massacre, though done in revenge for un-Briton-like cruelty; and the opportunity offered in the case of " The Endeavour." He was the cause of that vessel's deliverance, and of the saving of the lives of all on board. Is it too much to ascribe that deliverance to the influence of Missions ?

On August 3rd, 1824, Mr. Turner wrote :—

" This day completes my first year's residence amongst this barbarous people ;—a year of hard labour and great trials, but of abounding mercy from my God. The angel of His presence has saved us. In our great work we have had many discouragements ; but we do not despair of planting the tree of life in this barren soil, and, if spared a few years, of seeing it bend with fruit to the glory of God."

The remainder of the year saw many changes of hope

and fear; and, though fully occupied in Mission toil, was unmarked either by failure or triumph. The sappers and miners at the foundations of heathenism had not much to cheer, but they were not disheartened. I select a few extracts from the correspondence of the day :—

"Sunday, August 15th.—To-day we were fully assured by a respectable chief that female infanticide obtains. He had, but a few days since, saved his own child, a second time, from this fate at the hands of its inhuman mother. The natives freely spoke of the custom, and with pleasure rather than otherwise. They referred to several of the most respectable native women around us who had thus destroyed their children. The mode is called, '*romca*,'—that is, ' squeezing the nose.' It is done soon after the child is born; and then the hypocritical mother cuts herself with shells, and makes a great outcry about her dead child. Two reasons were assigned :—women are of no use in war; and when the offspring are numerous, the girls make the mother too much work. We pointed out both the impolicy and the wickedness of this custom, saying that it was ' murder in the sight of God.' They persisted that it was only '*romca*,'—' squeezing the nose.'

"Monday, 16th.—Gladdened by letters, papers, and magazines from England.

"Saturday, 28th.—I have spent much of this week in the schools. Most of the children have been froward and disobedient. Sometimes I have had as many as eighteen or twenty. They do not progress.

"Sunday, September 5th.—Mr. Hobbs and I held service with Te Pere and upwards of a hundred of his people. They listened attentively. We were favoured with a gracious influence. The people said they understood what was said, and I believe many of them felt it too. As soon as we left, the native boys we had with us advised us never to go there again, as the tribe had been speaking evil of us, and had said they would ' kill, roast, and eat us, as a sweet bit to their turnips;' but this we believed had only been said in a jest to vex the lads. We also preached to the people of another village. I have seldom seen greater attention. We were pleased to find that they had well remembered the particulars of a former address, on the Deluge.

"Sunday, 19th.—One of our best days in New Zealand. After a sermon on the Sabbath, to more than two hundred attentive listeners, we had a long discussion before all with the chief, on the Two Eternal States. The gainsayer was put to silence.

"Monday, 20th.—Visited the schools. Some children show a little improvement, but most get their lessons like parrots. The girls' school is doing well, particularly in needlework.

"Saturday, October 2nd.—Wet weather lately. Correspondence. Yesterday James heard one of our chiefs tell a visiting chief that when he first came, the Wangaroans had tried all they could to make us afraid, but had failed. Said he : '*They are a courageous tribe.*'

" Tuesday, 12th.—The doctrine of the Resurrection is new and strange to this people. Some contended strongly against it, while others (some women in particular) seemed much pleased at the thought of seeing their friends and children again."

Mission experiences were reviewed on December 31st; and it is not simply as a tribute of filial affection to a noble Christian mother, but in the hope of encouraging Missionaries, that I copy my father's entry :—

" This has been the most trying period of my life. Being the only married man, I had trials and anxieties to which my associates were necessarily strangers. Yet I had great support in the piety, zeal, and courage of my devoted wife. She bore her trials with more than common Christian heroism, and not unfrequently held up my hands, when ready to hang down. Her exalted piety and praying faith were a great help to the whole Mission party. We could only keep our own souls alive by regular and sincere attention to the English services among ourselves....... Generally, our most soul-stirring services were our class-meetings on Saturday nights. O, what seasons of humiliation, gratitude, love, and prayer were these!...... I fully believe that had we not adopted such means we should not have borne our trials and sustained our Mission. Not unto us, not unto us, but unto Thy name be praise."

I am not able to offer an account of the early labours of 1825. No serious interruption to the work occurred during January or February, but from that time the natives became hostile.

The Missionary Committee thus prefaced their publication of interesting Journal extracts of that date, some of which are appended.

"The extracts will show the exercises, dangers, and capricious changes to which the messengers of peace are exposed amongst these warlike, ferocious, and untamed savages. The difficulties of such undertakings, it is obvious, are greatest at the commencement, and nothing has occurred as yet in the history of New Zealand Missions, either as to our brethren of the Church Missionary Society or our own, which it was not reasonable to expect as exceedingly probable, though often sufficiently discouraging, and sometimes distressing. The great struggle is, indeed, *to begin* the work ;—to make an effectual impression upon the rude and boisterous barbarism, caprice, and ignorance of such a people, by the conversion of a few. Nothing less than this gives to a Mission, properly speaking, an *entrance* among them ; and when that, by the gracious influence of God, shall be effected,—when a small society of faithful native Christians shall be raised up,—the work will be so rooted as to defy opposition, and the influence of Christian knowledge and Christian example will acquire a force constantly accumulating, and in a very short time be triumphant over the most inveterate practices of these islanders. We have no doubt of the result, whilst men and women can be found to make the sacrifices, and to face the dangers of such Missions. Their faith and love will triumph, and the result will add new trophies to the power of the Gospel, even when unaided by human strength and influence."

Under date of March 25th, 1825, Mr. Turner wrote to the Committee :—

"Of late things have been far from quiet and encouraging amongst us. On the 5th instant the natives gave us a proof that our lives are in some danger. Many of them gathered around our settlement, and became troublesome. Several got into the yard. Ahudu, a principal chief, in a menacing mood, came direct to the house. On my remonstrating, he became enraged, and stormed at me, shaking his weapon over my head, as though he would have instantly cut it off. On Brother White coming up, he reproved the chief; and as this had not been the first insult of the kind, ordered him out of the yard. He refused to go, and began storming and threatening in an alarming manner. Presently he left, followed by his party. We soon missed a favourite young dog, which during the affray one of them had taken away under his mat. Learning the whereabouts of the dog, Mr. White went and recovered it. Young Te Puhi, for whom it had been stolen, attempted a rescue, and in doing so broke its leg. He then set upon Mr. White with his spear, but was prevented from injuring him much. Seeing the occurrence from my room window, Mr. Hobbs and I ran to render assistance. Before I had half crossed the field, Te Puhi left Mr. White, and ran towards me, with vengeance in his looks, and, I believe, with destruction in his design. Without saying a word, he aimed a blow at my head with his spear. I received the blow on my left arm. The spear broke in two, and with the longest part he attempted to spear me, and gave me a severe thrust, or blow, in my left side. Fortunately for me, it happened to be the blunt end of the spear. On receiving this blow, I believe I fell senseless, not knowing the injury I had received. On seeing him upon me, another chief, who is very friendly to us, ran and prevented him from doing me further injury. At this time Ahudu, the father of my assailant, had got Mr. White down, by the side of the fence, and it is likely would have injured him seriously, if not murdered him, had he not been rescued by other natives. He escaped with a few cuts and bruises."

Mr. Turner was taken up for dead and carried into his house by his supposed murderers. While this was being done, another party of excited natives were hurriedly stealing all they could lay their hands on in another part of the house. They purposed to completely strip the premises, and were only prevented by the general alarm which arose on account of the supposed murder of the Missionary. The injuries and shock Mr. Turner received laid him on his bed for several days.

Published at the same time with the foregoing extract is

a long and interesting detailed narrative by Mr. White of the seizure by the Wangaroans of the whaling brig " Mercury." For brevity's sake we give an outline of it from Mr. Turner's pen. It may be regarded as one among a hundred instances afforded by our South Sea Missions of the great services which the Missionaries have rendered in opening up the way for European commerce, and at the same time of the hindrances to their success caused by godless captains and sailors.

" On the same day the whaling brig ' Mercury ' entered our harbour for supplies. Early next morning we heard of her arrival, and, simultaneously, of an intended attack upon her by the Ngatepo tribe at The Heads. From the injuries received the previous day, I was unable to leave my bed, but advised my brethren, White and Stack, to go down in the boat at once, that they might, if possible, prevent the plunder of the ship and loss of life. Taking with them our principal chief, Te Puhi, they pulled down immediately, and found the vessel surrounded by canoes, and crowded with natives. Although it was the Sabbath day, the captain and officers were busy bartering. After surveying the ship, Te Puhi accosted the brethren thus:—'*E mata ana korua tene ivi?*' Know you this tribe?' pointing to the ship's company. They answered, ' No.' He asked further, ' Is this their sacred day? I know it is yours.' ' They acknowledge this to be their Sabbath,' was the reply. He then exclaimed, ' See how they trade;—an evil people is this tribe.' Perceiving that the Maoris contemplated a disturbance, the Missionaries advised the captain to go out at night, with the ebb tide, when the people would have gone on shore. Messrs. White and Stack then got into their boat, to return home. They had, however, not long left the ship when the anchors were uplifted, the sails unfurled, and orders given to clear the decks. In the execution of these commands, several natives were thrown overboard, and among them young Te Puhi, who had wounded me with his spear the day before. Upon this there was a general rising. During the confusion the wind veered round, and the vessel went on shore. According to New Zealand custom, she was now the lawful prize of the chief on whose coast she had grounded. A general plunder was ordered. With astonishing alacrity the dead lights were torn out, and the sails cut down, while chests, boxes, and other moveable articles were passed over the ship in every direction. The captain and crew, being driven from the decks, took to their boats, and fled for their lives. My brethren, observing from a distance what had transpired, turned their boat's head, and made for the ship. Te Puhi, armed with a musket, beckoned them on board.. The scene was both ludicrous and distressing: the rigging cut away, the hatches off, and the decks swimming with oil, and manned by naked natives. They had washed, or rather bathed, themselves with oil so copiously that they were nearly blinded. The chiefs listened to the earnest entreaties of my brethren, and delivered the vessel up to them. Leaving the brig in the hands of some friendly chief in whom they had a degree of confidence, Messrs. White and Stack first went after the fugitive captain and crew. But to no purpose. In great terror they pulled right off for the Bay of Islands. My poor brethren brought their unusual Sabbath exertions to a close by pulling to our station. Here they rested for the night, resolving to attempt, next morning, with such assistance as they might get, to take the brig out themselves, and sail her to the Bay. On reaching the ship, next morning, they found that she had been stripped of nearly everything moveable. By the assistance of three seamen whom, from the captain's directions the previous day, they had found on shore, they succeeded, though with much hazard from native resistance, in getting her well to sea. Their hope of making the head of the Bay by evening was disappointed by a perverse change of wind. In this critical state,—short-handed and crippled,— many sails gone, most of their rigging cut away, and without sextant or compass, they were obliged, for personal safety, to abandon her altogether, and pull to shore, fully twenty miles. Here further troubles met them. They landed in the neighbourhood of a villanous set of natives, who plundered them of all they had in the boat. The brethren and their sailor companions arrived in safety at the Mission station late the same evening. The sailors, who had literally lost their all, were thankful enough that their lives had been spared."*

Wangaroa went mad. The plunderers paddled up the river, shouting their triumph, and forthwith began a hideous dance in front of the Mission premises. Some had drawn the arms of pea coats over their legs ; others were jacketed in trousers, and in every inconceivably grotesque style.

* The almost invariable custom had previously been for captains, when seeking wood, water, or other supplies, to send armed men on shore, and not upon any account to allow a native to board the vessel.

Each man disported himself in European dress. They were all dripping with oil, and as they brandished their marling-spikes or harpoons, the hills resounded with their furious yells. The Chief George, who was approaching his end, entered into the excitement with amazing zest. The Missionaries were depressed by the general result on the native mind. However, they heard a voice saying, "Cease ye from man, and trust in the Lord for ever."

CHAPTER VII.

1825—1826.

TRUE Christian Missionaries, of whatever name, have always and everywhere sympathized with one another; and the pioneers in New Zealand were notable examples. It is to the honour of the Church Mission families, whose lines had fallen to them in comparatively pleasant places, that with hearts and homes they cherished the Wesleyan Mission, and relieved its agents when occasion arose. When a retired veteran, Mr. Turner often related to his children incidents of his first campaign against heathenism ; and he always spoke with affectionate remembrance of his excellent friends of the Church Mission.

The troubles of Wangaroa gave much concern at the Bay, and Messrs. Williams and Kemp kindly went over to offer aid. They desired to remove Mrs. Turner and the children, which was consented to only on the ground of apparent necessity. Indeed, the Missionaries themselves considered seriously whether it would not be their duty also to remove. They sought counsel. On the 18th and 19th of March they conferred with several of their brethren from the Church Mission. Of the result of their deliberations Mr. Turner sent to the Home Committee the following notice :—

" It was the unanimous opinion of our friends present that our lives were in danger, and that we ought to leave as speedily as we could, and in the best way possible. Their decision was influenced by the following considerations :—1st. The conduct of the natives towards ourselves in the affair above mentioned ; *i. e.*, spearing me and assaulting Mr. White. 2nd. The taking of the brig ' Mercury.' 3rd. The speculation that the different tribes around the Bay of Islands would come against our people, and punish them. 4th. The probability that Europeans might call them to account, and, if so, it being very likely that we should fall victims to their rage and malice. 5th. That, after such base conduct, should we continue amongst them, it might be injurious to our brethren at the Bay of Islands, as their natives might take occasion, from the conduct of ours, to behave ill towards them. 6th. That George, one of our principal chiefs, was dangerously ill, and had requested, in case of his death, that the natives of Shukeanga would come, and strip us of all we possess, if not kill us, as *utu*, or payment for the death of his father, who had been killed through the taking of the ' Boyd,' and for whom he says he has never yet had '*satisfaction.*' This report is believed by our friends ; and I have been repeatedly told by his brothers that when he dies we shall be '*ka wali,*' ' broken,' or stripped of all ; and that this request must be looked upon as the last *will* of one who was about to enter the world of spirits; and made to those to whom revenge is sweet.

" Viewing the case in this serious light, we could not disapprove of the conclusion come to by our brethren, who, I believe, as brethren, feel for us and our cause. But, though our judgment approved of the measures recommended, our feelings have not suffered us to take any step towards carrying it into execution. And we now think it will be best to continue at our post for the present, and ' quietly wait for the salvation of God.' "

The temporary residence of Mrs. Turner and the children at the refuge kindly supplied them at the Kere Kere occasioned Mr. Turner much labour and fatigue, as it was necessary for him to divide his time between the duties of the Mission station and the claims of his family, to reach whom involved eight hours' walking. In some of the British settlements of New Zealand at the present day, (1870,) when the war spirit prevails, family ties are held, and arrangements made, under the constant dread of native butchery. The chills and thrill of horror by the tragedies of Gascoigne, and of the martyrs Whiteley and Volkner, will not soon be forgotten. But if we throw the mind back forty-six years, and imagine the unmodified savageism of natural heathen Maoris, the loneliness of the Missionaries, separated from all friends by hills, streams, thickets, and treacherous enemies, for twenty or thirty miles, it will be seen, as the narrative is followed, that the Wangaroa Mission was indeed " God's peculiar care."

When making his way homeward on March 21st, Mr. Turner was overtaken by messengers to The Heads. Their errand was to apprise some people there to prepare to receive two large parties of natives, who were under instruction to take away the Missionary to the Bay of Islands. This step had unceremoniously been taken by the warrior chief " Shunghee," preparatory to his making war upon the Wangaroans. It seems that Shunghee's proximity to the vessels trading to the Bay gave his tribe much advantage in the way of procuring muskets and ammunition ; and, from a policy of self-interest, he was angered with the Wangaroans for their recent depredations. He knowingly argued that, if Maori intercourse with the ships should be stopped, his own tribe would not be able to get ammunition ; and in this way his power to tyrannize would end. The Bay of Island chiefs had long desired to destroy the people of Wangaroa, but, heretofore, Shunghee had restrained them.

The Chief George was sitting in the Mission house, very ill, when Mr. Turner arrived. Observing the Missionaries pretty closely, he was anxious to know what they were talking about. When told, he became terribly agitated, and left the house, believing his end had come. And no wonder, if the following incident, supplied by Mr. Leigh to the Committee in London, the year before the date of which we write, was a true illustration of the warrior's character as an enemy.

" Soon after Shunghee had returned from England, he learned that, during his absence, one of his relatives had been slain by one of his friends at Mercury Bay. Shunghee immediately declared war against the people, although they were relatives. The chief who belonged to

Mercury Bay, and with whom Shunghee had sailed from New South Wales, earnestly desired reconciliation, but in vain. Nothing but war could satisfy him. He soon collected three thousand fighting men, and commenced his march. The battle was dreadful, and many fell on both sides; but Shunghee proved victorious, and returned to the Bay of Islands in great triumph..... After my arrival in New Zealand I learned that he and his party slew one thousand men, three hundred of whom they roasted and ate before they left the field of battle. Shunghee killed the chief above mentioned; after which he cut off his head, poured the blood into his hands, and drank it. This account I had from Shunghee himself, and Whycaboa, who related it with the greatest satisfaction."

This warrior could be magnanimous when it suited him. In kindness to the Mission party, whom he wished to remove, he caused a canoe, seventy feet long and seven feet wide, to be prepared for their special accommodation.

As Te Puhi reported the progress of events the next Sunday, the Missionaries were thankful for some evidence of regard for themselves. They had often seen him like an incarnate fiend, but now that they were to be taken away, he wept tears of real friendship.

During that week there was a public heathen ceremony. A large number of the bodies of the natives were taken from their sepulchre, and the skulls arranged in line, anointed with oil, and decked with turkeys' feathers. At this *morgue* there was a monster meeting of natives. Mr. Hobbs preached to them on the Resurrection. But they listened as to a dream. The same evening, Wednesday, they learned that Shunghee's expedition had been recalled.

The Missionaries felt perplexed as to their duty. Monday revealed a complication of threatened intertribal wars, which foreboded bloodshed; and only a conviction that their continuing at the station would save many Maori lives elsewhere, induced them to remain. Mr. White left on Tuesday, with a second boat-load of moveables, in anticipation of the worst. Mr. Turner returned from visiting his family on Wednesday, and spent next day in anxious conversation with his brother Missionaries, and with George. Though apparently on the brink of eternity, the chief could be persuaded to talk of nothing but the coming of ships and of war. The result of a council on Friday I give in Mr. Turner's words :—

" Though the whole of our friends at the Church station had given it as their decided opinion that we ought to leave, and though our judgment could not disapprove, still some of us, myself in particular, could not bring our feelings to consent. The thought of leaving the place which a few months before had seemed so promising, was almost more than I could bear. Though our lives appeared in danger, it was one of the greatest crosses I ever had to take up, to give my voice that we should depart."

It was then resolved that Messrs. White and Hobbs should take the boat, with as many things as they could carry, to the Kidda Kidda, and Mr. Turner and Mr. Stack should remain at the station till Monday, when, if all remained quiet, the brethren could be recalled by letter.

On the following Thursday, when Messrs. White and Hobbs had returned, Mr. Turner went on to the Church station. The Missionaries and friendly natives at Wesleydale passed the next Sunday night in great apprehension : for that evening the head chief George died, and the event had been anticipated as the signal for a murderous onslaught on the Mission party. It transpired afterwards, that an attack had been designed and debated by some of the tribe, but that Te Puhi had prevented it. By daylight it was known that George had expressed his will that his people should be kind to the Missionaries.

In a fortnight, there being the prospect of tranquillity, the family returned to Wesley Vale, Mrs. Turner travelling palanquin fashion. "We got along very well, so long as the road was open. When we reached the woods, heavy rains set in, which made travelling difficult. Mrs. Turner was obliged to walk over country which at best is never fit for any woman to travel. But the Lord gave her strength and courage. We reached our settlement at nine P.M., wet and weary enough. After changing clothing we got supper, and then read our letters received in the morning, *per* favour of the Rev. Mr. Pitman, of the London Missionary Society: they were treasures indeed. The Committee's Circular of 1824 we read with great interest. I was thankful to have got back to my station and work. Not less grateful was Mrs. Turner. She had left with extreme reluctance, but had gladly returned to share the trials of the Mission."

Sunday, the 17th, was a day of fear. During the morning service a cry was raised that two children had been speared, and at the same moment a number of savages, armed with spears, were seen running towards the house with all speed. On reaching the outer gate, they were stopped by Ahududu. Two chiefs from a distance had just come to the settlement. One of them, in bloodthirsty rage, had wounded two children in the head, as *utu* for George's death. Several natives and the distressed mother abused him in return. In a fit of exasperation, he and his men had resolved on destroying the Mission premises.

On Wednesday they learned by letter from their Church Mission friends, that native tribes were proceeding to take satisfaction out of the Wangaroas for the affair of the "Mercury:" next day Te Puhi besought their mediation. The invasion quickly followed, but happily without any sanguinary result. On the Saturday the Missionary associates visited the Pa, but found the preparations harmless, if indeed war was meant. Large numbers had assembled, but no fortifications had been built ; and the energy of the tribe seemed to find vent chiefly in accumulating and dispersing quantities of food. The Wangaroas, having judged "discretion to be the better part of valour," had collected all the food they could, with the double object, first, of gorging their enemies, and, secondly, of saving for themselves what might remain. About a mile distant, Shunghee's party, several hundreds strong, were engaged in an exciting war dance, and in destroying fences and building a temporary town with the material.

The adoption of the Scripture rule, (in this instance from policy,) " If thine enemy hunger, feed him," won a victory. Indeed, the Missionaries suffered more than the natives. For some days, they had to keep open house for the visiting chiefs and principal people, in order to conciliate their good will. The invaders departed, having done nothing more serious than feast for four days at the expense of the Wangaroas and their Missionaries.

About this time Mr. White left for England, and Mr. Turner was now the only recognised Missionary of the Wesleyan Church in New Zealand. Depressed by difficulties and cares, he sought and found comfort in God. The Missionary trio, Turner, Hobbs, and Stack, proceeded to complete several buildings then in progress, and to reorganize the schools. They strove hard to lead the young people to the knowledge of Christ, assured that when converted they would efficiently teach, and by the blessing of the Holy Spirit instrumentally save, those around them. In this work they were not without encouragement.

On the 30th of December of that year, 1825, Mr. Turner had great joy in receiving a letter from Mr. Williams, informing him of a native of whose conversion he had hope. The person referred to gave evidence of a thorough change of heart, and for many years adorned the profession of Christianity. He was the first fruits of a harvest of souls.

At the watchnight hour the Missionary friends at Wesley Vale partook together of the emblems of their Saviour's love, and 1826 was entered upon in the strength of renewed consecration.

Besides labouring zealously in the schools, among the sick, and in preaching in the villages, they had much to do in the way of gardening and of wheat-growing. In addition to a considerable area on the station they sowed many patches of the natives' fields with wheat. They afterwards purchased from them the produce......Both parents and children showing much indifference about the schools, a new plan was tried, and at first with success. A large, inexpensive native building was erected adjoining the Mission house. After two or three hours' morning instruction, the scholars were rewarded with a little boiled rice, or other prepared food.

A deep shadow now fell upon the Mission home. Mr. Turner's infant child, eleven months old, Nathaniel Bailey, was claimed by death. But,

> " Not in cruelty, not in wrath
> The Reaper came that day."

The parents laid " the beautiful clay " in the lone sepulchre of the Mission garden, and knew that he slept in Jesus.

Difficulties increased. Though at no period did the zeal of the Missionaries flag, the general and continued unrest and excitement around them not only neutralized their work, but rendered their further stay perilous.

One Sunday, when Mr. Turner went to Te Puhi's village to preach, he had no congregation, for the people had gone gathering fern root, which was in general use as food. The chief had just mutilated one of his slaves with a hatchet, and, when spoken to on the matter, became very excited, and afterwards proceeded to kill the poor creature, and then to bake and eat her. Next morning he shot a near relative dead, and for hours made the valley ring with his mad vociferations, excitedly exclaiming, "Let us have a general massacre." On the Sabbath after, Mr. Turner met him, wild with passion, with two muskets in his hands.

The severity of winter had scarcely passed, when they were threatened with another invasion by Maoris. Hongi, with characteristic magnanimity, sent the Wesley Vale tribes word to leave their "food, and fly for their lives; for, if he saw the face of any of them, they would be killed." The valley was filled with consternation. The Maoris entered the harbour on Sunday the 19th, and at once seized three of Te Puhi's slaves, while gathering shellfish. They murdered one, a fine young woman, and made prisoners of the other two. On the Monday morning, about three hundred strong, they reached Wesley Vale, and at once destroyed all the crops. They broke into the boat-house, and were carrying off the rudder, when Mr. Hobbs interfered. They then made for the garden: the Missionaries exposed themselves much in trying to save it from destruction; but to no purpose, for the savages looked as if they would like to eat them as well as their vegetables. They threatened to spear Mr. Hobbs, but were mercifully withheld.

During the afternoon, another party broke into the premises, and demanded the surrender of a slave girl, whom Mr. Turner had redeemed some eighteen months before. Resistance was considered useless, as the chief was very fierce, and his men were armed. Te Puhi spent much of the day lying secreted in the bush, lest he should be shot. It was reported to be the invaders' purpose to strip the Mission dwelling that night. The story seemed very likely, and the Missionaries prepared for the worst. The children were put to bed with their day clothing on, that they might not be turned out naked: the adults equipped and nerved themselves for escape. Next morning peace was made, and the invaders left at the turn of the tide.   Overnight, Mr. Turner had written in his diary, " How little do our English friends know of our insecurity here ! Before daylight we may be plundered of all, and our persons cruelly treated."

CHAPTER VIII.

1827.

THE loyalty of Missionaries was illustriously exemplified at Wesley Vale. Until all hope of remaining was cut off, Messrs. Turner and Hobbs, and their associates, stood for Christ, true as steel.

On the watchnight, after a hard day's religious toil, Mr. Turner preached on the wise and foolish virgins, and the Mission band commemorated their dying Saviour's love. The diary closed with acknowledgments of God's mercy, and with forebodings concerning another expected invasion by Hongi, now on his way to take and occupy the settlement. What ground there was for fear the sequel will tell.

Mr. Turner wrote to his friends at the Bay of Islands :—

"WESLEY VALE, *January 9th*, 1827.

" DEAR FRIENDS,

" WE are now left without a single inhabitant,—man, woman, or child,—save our boy Taweira, (David,) who has returned, to remain with us. On Friday evening last our chiefs, with some of their slaves, fled for fear of the *Uqa Puhi*, (Bay of Islanders,) who have entered the harbour, and commenced their work of plunder and bloodshed. On Sunday morning a deputation of note came from Hongi, requesting our people to go down and join him against the *Uqa Tipo*. Nearly all the men complied, and went, but returned yesterday morning for their wives and children. This they have done from a fear lest, during the absence of the men, other parties, hearing of their defenceless state, should come and destroy them, or make them prisoners. Our people left us in perfect good will, and appeared concerned on parting. The school children were compelled, by their parents and guardians, to go with them, much against their will. Many have gone with heavy hearts respecting their own fate. Several, on leaving, expressed apprehension for our safety, saying the *Karawa* tribe would probably come and plunder, if not kill, us ; and stragglers might come and do so. You now see our state as nearly as I can give it you."

" Tuesday evening, after eight o'clock.

" I wrote the above in haste, about noon to-day, intending to send it immediately by Mr. Stack.   But at that juncture the boy Pui arrived with your letters ; and, about the same time, a party of some twelve of the *Uqa Puhi* came to the house.   We inquired what they had come for ; to which they replied, ' To take away your things, and burn down your house ; for your place is deserted, and you are broken.'   We felt a little troubled, regarding their intentions as of a serious nature.   After annoying us for a while, and taking away a few articles, they left to load their canoes with potatoes, &c.   On their return they broke into one of the outhouses, and carried away several things.   The principal persons being known to Miss Davies prevented their going to greater lengths. On leaving, they said we should certainly have a general plunder to-mor- row.   We hope it may not be so ; yet we think it very likely.   Dear friends, you now see our situation, and will, I know, feel for us, and be ready to give us all the counsel and help you can.   I have a particular wish that Mr. H. Williams should come over as soon as possible.   We may be obliged to leave the place, and we wish for his mature judgment in the matter.   Our females begin to wish themselves under your protection ; but we have no power to move them, for we have no natives to assist, and we cannot leave the station ourselves.   Mrs. Turner and Miss Davies bear up well ; but poor Mrs. Wade is very low.

" Yours affectionately,

" NATHANIEL TURNER."

What followed shall be told in Mr. Turner's own words, slightly abridged, to save space.

" At ten P.M. Brother Stack, accompanied by Taurina, left with the letter for the Kere Kere.   I was sorry for my dear brother to have to undertake such a journey in the night ; but the boy was afraid to go alone, and the errand was urgent.   Just as we had commended our- selves to the care of our Heavenly Father, and were preparing to take a little rest, two of our native girls came up from the harbour.   They gave us much information concerning Hongi's proceedings, but nothing cheering as to our own situation.   They said they had heard the people talking about robbing us.   For several nights we had kept watch by turns. That night the duty devolved upon Luke Wade. About midnight we retired, though not free from anxiety ; yet for myself, bless the Lord, free from all distressing fear !

" About daybreak Luke knocked me up in haste, for the natives were coming up to the house. Mr. Hobbs, Luke, and I met them outside. They said, ' We have come to take away your property, and you must be gone.' One party broke into Luke's dwelling, and another into the toolhouse. They then burst into the outer kitchen, the store over it, and the carpenter's shop, and carried away with all speed their contents to the canoes. Being now satisfied that nothing short of an entire clearance of all we possessed was intended, we made all possible haste, and equipped ourselves for flight. I urged the two girls aforementioned to get a little tea ready, as, if their lives should be spared, the women and children could not travel a distance of nearly twenty miles, over a rough country, without some refreshment. Locked inside, we got the children and ourselves ready, while the food was being prepared. Then we ate our passover. At this instant four of our school boys came up to the door, and were let in. They saw our situation, and offered to go with us. We thankfully accepted their aid, which, indeed, we regarded as essential to our safe escape. The plunderers now smashed all the windows to pieces, broke open the back door, and began in earnest to spoil the house. Still we lingered, until we saw them carrying away the beds from which we had just arisen.

" During our many dangers and trials I had often prayed that I might not quit my post until absolutely compelled. My prayer was answered. Our boys and girls urged us to be gone. ' Go ye, go ; for, unless ye be gone speedily, you will go with your skins only ; ' meaning, ' When they have stripped the house, they will strip you too.' Being now fully satisfied that all we possessed would be taken from us, we were glad to escape with our lives. While most of the natives were at the back of the house, we passed through the front door."

At this moment the special providence of God saved Mrs. Turner from a violent death. Over the outer doorway were some loose boards, which formed at once a ceiling to the room, and a floor, upon which had been placed some stores, which were not known of, except by the Mission family. When stripping the premises, the natives began to poke and disturb these boards, upon which there seemed to lie some weighty substance, the nature of which they did not at the instant comprehend. This discovery of concealed property was made at the very instant of the escape. During the excitement of the last few minutes the wildness of the furious savages had become uncontrollable. Life or death was in every moment. Mrs. Turner was escaping through the doorway. A chief had raised his weapon to cleave her to the ground, when a shower of nails fell upon his head, which so surprised and confounded him and those near, as to arrest the bloody stroke, and save a valuable life.

"Hastening down the garden, we made our way through the fences, and across the wheat field. On passing out of the house Tungahei, one of my boys, remembered that my fowling piece (with which the Committee had supplied me) was hanging up in my bedroom. He asked and obtained permission to bring it. God only knows what my feelings were at this moment, when thus obliged to quit the place on which we had bestowed nearly four years' labour and anxiety. Never, never, had I been called to such a trial. But the Lord proportioned our strength to our day. Amid all this distress I could not but praise the Lord at almost every step I took. I many times looked back, fearing lest some of those whom we had left plundering the house should pursue us." [It afterwards transpired that one man did get over the fence for that purpose.]

"Our company comprised myself, Mrs. Turner, and three children, the youngest an infant of five weeks and two days old; Luke Wade and his wife, who had not long arrived from England; Mr. Hobbs and Miss Davies from Paihia. The property we secured consisted of the clothes we had on, our small trunks of changes for the children, which Mrs. Turner had thoughtfully packed overnight, and a few bundles we carried in our hands. We made the best of our way over the *kumera* grounds, now no longer sacred. As the morning was foggy, and a heavy dew lay upon the ground, Mrs. Turner and her fugitive sisters got very wet in passing through the growing corn. Just as we had waded through the river the second time, we met three of our natives who had fled to Hokianga on the evening of Friday last. One of these was Te Puhi Nehi, the young chief who had nearly murdered me eighteen months before. They informed us that a powerful party from Hokianga were just at hand, going to defend the place against the *Uqa Puhi*. They strongly advised us to turn out of the way, and hide in the bush, until the *tana* (war-party) had passed, for they would strip and murder us.

" This was a trying moment. Danger and death stared us in the face. I felt a strong impression that we ought to go forward, but this was not the feeling of all our company ; and through the urgent entreaties of our natives, we turned out of the way, ascended a hill, and hid ourselves among the bushes. Such, however, were my feelings that I could not sit for two minutes, being strongly persuaded that if we remained where we were, the very men we had met would themselves fall upon and murder us, for what little we had about us. Others shared my fears ; but the native boys objected to go forward, saying they dared not. We resolved to proceed without them. Seeing us move, they moved too. Having descended the hill and regained the road, we met our chief Agahuduhudu, and Warenui, a friendly chief of the Bay of Islands, of whom we had some knowledge. They also advised us to hide until the war-party should have passed ; but we pleaded hard to go forward, and asked Warenui to protect us. He noticed the fowling-piece in the hands of my native lad. I said to Tungahe, ' Give it to him.' The old chief shouldered the piece, and in the most friendly manner said, ' Come along.' Thus led and defended, we followed our guide.

"We crossed the serpentine river twice more. Just as we were turning a sharp bend, and while on its bend, we suddenly met the war party. They were all armed, and presented the most formidable appearance, as they marched in a compact body, ready for action. They were headed by several chiefs, the principal of whom was Patuone, of Hokianga, a friend to Europeans. On seeing us in the bend of the river, he instantly turned round upon his army, and commanded them to halt. Never before had I seen in New Zealand such an exhibition of authority and obedience. Some few attempted to press forward, but he instantly repressed them with his spear. Others ran into the water, to get past him, but he was with them in a moment. Having secured a halt, he with other chiefs came towards us, and pointing to the edge of the water, said, ' *Noho koutou ki reria*,' ' Kneel there.' This was, I think, the most trying time of my life. With the tender babe in my arms, and my wife, children, and friends kneeling close beside me, I felt that the fatal hour had come. But thank God it was not so. Patuone and the other chiefs came and rubbed noses with us, in token of sympathy. One poor old chief in broken English said, ' No more *patu patu*,'— ' No more white man.' This he said to remove our fears. Our situation was told them by the chiefs he had met. Having deliberated for a few minutes, they asked me to go back with them and remain ; but we declined, as all we had was gone. After we had conversed a little, they told us to stand nearer the water. The chiefs now placed themselves in front of us, and ordered the *tana* to march on the other side. When they had passed us, and the chief had said in a friendly way, '*Haere ata koutou,*' 'Go ye onward,' a burden was taken from my heart, and we rejoiced together for this great deliverance.

"Warenui, bearing my fowling-piece as his own, was our guard, and we then proceeded. We passed through the wood, about six miles, better than I had expected. A little further we met Brother Stack and Mr. Clarke, accompanied by eight or ten of Mr. Clarke's schoolboys. It was a gladdening sight. One of the lads was despatched to the Kere Kere, to procure the means of carrying Mrs. Turner and Miss Davies the latter part of the journey. We were now able to render a little assistance to the weaker of our travellers. At the waterfalls, six miles from our first asylum, we were delighted to meet the Rev. H. Williams, Mr. R. Davies, Mr. Puckey, and about a dozen natives, who had hastened to our relief on receipt of my letter. Mr. Hamlin also met us, with refreshments and chairs, to form palanquins. We reached the Kere Kere by sundown, weary enough; and were received with every possible mark of Christian kindness and sympathy.

"While we were at tea, the old chief Wairemu, and Isitori, another chief, came in, and wished to know where we were going. They said, 'If you remain at this settlement, different parties will come and strip our friends and kill us.' All judged that we should go to the Pahia settlement, at the Bay, and there remain until our course of duty should be more plain. We retired to rest very weary, but very thankful to the God of our lives.

"Early on the 11th, my friends took us in their boats to the Church station at Marsden's Vale, where, with great kindness, many articles were supplied us, of which we were in absolute need. The rest of our party were distributed among Christian friends, whilst Mrs. Turner, myself, and children, were very lovingly entertained by the Rev. H. Williams and his excellent wife. Sunday, the 14th, was a blessed day. By special request I preached to the Mission families. My subject was, 'These are they which came out of great tribulation.' We afterwards partook, with our dear friends, of the Lord's Supper. At the evening service I baptized my infant son, calling him John Sargent, after his maternal grandfather. The Lord gave him to us in perilous times, and we have now solemnly dedicated him to His service and glory.

"On Wednesday, 17th, we heard from two chiefs what became of our station. On the arrival of the Hokianga party on the 10th, they drove away the first plunderers, who belonged to Hongi's tribe, and who were able to carry only the more portable of the booty. They seized the remainder for themselves, and returned the following morning to Hoki-anga with their spoil. The Mission premises, together with about one hundred bushels of wheat which we had left in the straw, had been burnt to ashes, and the eight head of cattle, goats, fowls, &c., had all been killed. Of the dwelling itself, not a vestige remained standing, except the brick chimney. Not content with what they had found above ground, the ruthless barbarians had dug up the coffin of my dear child, merely for the sake of the blanket in which they supposed it had been wrapped, and had left the remains to moulder on the surface of the earth."

The Church brethren were afraid their Mission would share a similar fate. They secreted some portion of their property, and forwarded some to Sydney, for safety. Upon this their alarm communicated itself to their venerable founder Mr. Marsden. He was greatly moved with sympathy. Imagining that his presence in New Zealand would tend to quell the native disturbances and re-assure the Missionaries, he proceeded thither with that intent. Though he went in a sloop of war, he met with little reward. Upon the scene of Mr. Turner's hardships he sought to recover some of the plunder. All he obtained was two books. He learned that with those exceptions the whole of a considerable library had been torn up, for making cartridges.

The heroes of an authenticated missionary story like that above given need no commendation. If they did, filial duty and admiration would justify it here. The late Rev. Alexander Strachan, whose Life of the Rev. Samuel Leigh was laboriously prepared in great part from the Mission House records in London, had access to much of Mr. Turner's original correspondence. Alluding to the disaster related in this chapter, he says, " Thus terminated for the present one of the most noble, best sustained, and protracted struggles to graft Christianity upon a nation savage and ferocious, which the history of the Church of Christ supplies."

CHAPTER IX.

1827.

THE whole Mission party, having with them two native lads and a girl, proceeded to Sydney by the whaling ship "Sisters," Captain Duke. The voyage was but a change of peril, anything but pleasant. While in the Bay of Islands, the "Sisters" had captured the brig "Wellington," which had been piratically seized by a number of doubly convicted prisoners, on their passage from Sydney to the penal settlement at Norfolk Island. The villains, while making for South America, had called at Korarika Bay for water. Here they had been retaken, made prisoners, and transferred to the "Sisters," about to sail for Sydney. While yet in the Bay, they almost executed a second diabolical conspiracy. The manacles of some of them had been filed almost through; and they were within a few hours of a murderous outbreak, when one of their number informed, and a bloody outrage was prevented. These desperadoes, now ready for any practicable form of vengeance, were fellow passengers with Mr. Turner and family.

One of the ringleaders was chained on one side of the quarterdeck, and his informant on the other; and to each was allotted a tun-butt, as a sleeping room. The nearness of their apartments to the cabin must have made the promenade of the passengers anything but agreeable. Some twenty or thirty crime companions were in ignominious hold below; the remainder were on board the "Wellington," which sailed in company. Though extreme measures had been taken for the security of the gang, their presence occasioned much alarm on board. Yet Mr. Turner's heart yearned over them; and after much entreaty, he got the captain's permission to go down into the hold, to talk and pray with them. The consent had been reluctantly given, and the mate stood over the hatchway with a loaded musket, fearing that the Missionary would be murdered; for the prisoners knew that their piracy had been discovered and reported by one of his brethren at the Bay. The men received his visits apparently with thankfulness.

The Christian colonists of New South Wales were much affected by the sad tidings from the Mission field; and Mr. Turner's arrival caused some sensation. Yet he had, almost immediately, to bear a trial in some respect severer than any he had hitherto passed through. "A wounded spirit who can bear?" He and his missionary associates were calumniated, in a most unexpected quarter, as having deserted their station and work. An official investigation was held; his brethren amply justified and honoured the deserters (so called).

Since that day, other zealous servants of God have been subjected to injury by unfounded rumours. As a caution to sinners against the law of charity, as well as in filial gratitude for the bright example of a model Missionary father, I here anticipate my narrative by many years, to append a sentence or two calmly and humbly uttered by Mr. Turner forty years afterwards, when on his death couch, waiting for his reward. He said, "For more than fifty years I have loved and served God. I have made many mistakes, but I do not know that I have once willingly departed from Him." To a man of high spirit and Paul-like love for souls, as was he, such a calumny could not but give great pain. He thus alluded to it in a manuscript autobiography written for his children.

"This unfounded report, and the proceeding based upon

it, wounded me to the very soul; for I had never for an hour, amidst all our trials and dangers at Wangaroa, entertained the thought of leaving the place unless absolutely compelled. And had I ever contemplated an act so dishonourable to my Missionary character, she who shared in all my trials would have done her utmost to hold me back from such a deed; for, even when literally stripped of everything, she wished to remain, and commence anew in the best way we could. While contemplating taking her and the children to Sydney, she often imploringly asked, ' Cannot we remain and prosecute our Mission somewhere in the land ? ' "

After having been kindly entertained for a few days by the Rev. Mr. Mansfield in Sydney, Mr. Turner resided in Parramatta. His zeal for God found many occasions when he heartily entered into his Master's work, sometimes in Sydney, but chiefly in Parramatta.

The Conference of 1826 had formed New Zealand and Tonga into a separate district, and had appointed the Rev. William White chairman; but upon Mr. White's arrival in England Mr. Turner was appointed to that position. Who courts office in the Methodist ministry? let him reckon on trouble. Mr. Turner was apprised of his new responsibilities by his Sydney brethren. They at the same time introduced to him Mr. I. V. M. Weiss, a highly esteemed Local Preacher, whom the New South Wales District Meeting had recently appointed assistant in the Tongan Mission, and who was then with his family living at Mission expense, awaiting a passage. Mr. Turner demurred to the action taken by the District Meeting, as being invalid, but was at length overruled. When several months had passed without any opportunity arising, he chartered a small schooner to convey Mr. Weiss and family, and also to take supplies to the brethren Thomas and Hutchinson, then supposed to be in real want. The charter (for a specified sum per month) was expected to run out in four or five weeks. The arrangement resulted unsatisfactorily. The Tonga brethren were found in painful circumstances, prepared and anxious to leave the station, which they regarded as being in a hopeless state. Such were their apprehensions, that they feared to let Mr. Weiss set foot upon land, and sent him back in the schooner immediately. They also sent away part of their own luggage, and would themselves have left, had there been accommodation on board.

On the 3rd of August, the brethren in Sydney, while hoping the best as to Tonga, welcomed from England a reinforcement for the New Zealand work, consisting of the Rev. William Cross and Mrs. Cross, Miss Brogriff, (the affianced of Mr. Hobbs,) and Miss Bedford, whose zeal for the Saviour had led her to engage herself as assistant to Mrs. Turner in the New Zealand schools. Miss Bedford afterwards became Mrs. Launcelot Iredale, of Sydney, where, for many years, her heart and home afforded true welcome and comfort to our Missionaries and their families, when passing through the city, to or from their Mission stations ; or when tarrying for a few days or weeks under instructions. They were of course surprised to find that the New Zealand Mission had been suspended, and that, for the present, their own prospects were completely altered.

Six months had passed since the Wangaroan disaster, and now, in the hope of resuming the Maori Mission, Mr. Stack was sent to New Zealand to report and prepare the way. His communications to Sydney arrived unexpectedly early, and were found highly favourable. Patuone, the friendly chief of Hokianga, was anxious that Mr. Turner and the Mission party should reside here, and teach his people. The locality being known as suitable, and the chief confided in, it was determined to re-occupy the cannibal land in the name of the Lord.

They were about to embark, when, to Mr. Turner's surprise and disappointment, who should arrive in Sydney but Mr. Weiss! He had been to the Friendly Islands, and had returned by the same schooner, the bearer of mournful intelligence from the brethren there. Their letters entreated that a vessel might be sent to rescue them from their perilous situation. This conjuncture of difficulties caused much anxiety. The Committee had already been subjected to great expense, and now there was the likelihood of the immediate abandonment, a second time, of the Tongan Mission.

The counsel of the New South Wales Ministers was sought. After anxious conversation and much prayer, they advised that Mr. Turner should proceed to Tonga without delay, to help to sustain the work there; and that Mr. Cross should accompany him, as it was quite possible Messrs. Thomas and Hutchinson would have left by some whaler or trader. This course was acceded to: meanwhile Mr. Hobbs and party prepared for New Zealand.

The heavy expense, and the falling through of London arrangements, at this crisis, involved Mr. Turner with the Mission House, through the Committee's misapprehension. Conscious that his proceedings were both right and discreet, he found it galling to bear their censure. Afterwards, however, when better informed, they did him the justice to acknowledge that he had acted wisely and well, and to make such reparation as was in their power. At the same time they expressed devout thankfulness that Providence had led him to the course he had adopted.

The Missionary voyagers to Tonga were Mr. and Mrs. Cross, Mr. and Mrs. Weiss and family of three, Mr. and Mrs. Turner and three children, two New Zealand boys and one girl, and two European servants. They sailed through the lovely Sydney harbour on the 8th of October, 1827, in a schooner of but seventy or eighty tons. The sailing master did his best to make them comfortable; but he had his own troubles, having to combine the duties of cook and captain, the cook having rather unhandsomely fallen sick the second day out. After weathering the North Cape of New Zealand, where the craft had to lie to for twenty-four hours, they got fine weather and pleasant sailing. The passengers went ashore at Sunday Island; and were fortunate in getting off again. On landing they were nearly buried in lava. The sides of the hill were distinctly marked by the recent streaming of molten masses from the volcano.

The scenery of the pine-covered islets was lovely and peaceful: but as the "Endeavour" bore him towards another sphere of labour, Mr. Turner found it hard to keep his mind in harmony with tranquil nature. He was anxious. Slow sailing on a calm sea favoured reflection; and memory recalled his "deaths oft" in the land behind him. This gave vividness to his imagination, awakened and excited by the tidings received in Sydney of the state of things before him. Pacing the deck, he connected the future with the past, and honoured God in all. Reflection was not embittered by murmuring, nor hope by unbelief. He sought the God of Missionaries, and heard His promise, "My presence shall go with thee, and I will give thee rest."

They learned from some natives in a canoe off Ahaki, that their brethren were still at Hihifo, and "all well." Seeing a vessel working into the Bay, Messrs. Thomas and Hutchinson concluded she had come in answer to their pressing appeals to Sydney. They were soon on board, and much surprised to see three Missionaries. Their astonishment, however, was greater, on learning that their object was not to remove them, but to sustain them in their trying position. The unexpected reinforcement gave great pleasure to Mr. Thomas, who, despite severe trial, was strong to labour. His colleague was in an enfeebled state.

On reaching the Mission house, it was found the scene of busy preparations for removal,—the good wives having somewhat anticipated their destiny. When informed that three Missionary sisters and several children were on board, they exclaimed, "Madness to bring them here, and subject them to such trials as we have had to endure!" However, the wives and children, with their mad husbands and fathers, were soon welcomed to their home, to remain there until observation and counsel should decide their future.

It was verdant spring: the clothing of nature was so beautiful and luxuriant that Mr. Turner could scarcely believe the scene real. The agreeable contrast with the scenery of his former station almost enchanted him. But scenery was not the chief charm; the cleanliness and dignified friendly bearing of the natives, as contrasted with the filth, degradation, and ferocity he had lately left, were very marked. In a few hours he felt himself at home, and the subject of a cheering conviction, that God would make his way and his Mission prosperous.

CHAPTER X.*

EARLY HISTORY OF THE TONGA MISSION.

THE honour of having discovered Tongataboo belongs to the renowned Dutchman, Jan Tasman, who in 1643 was in the southern group of the archipelago,—afterwards ascertained to embrace the Tongan, Vavau, and Haabai clusters, and now usually known as the Friendly Islands. We are indebted to the celebrated Captain Cook for the discovery in 1773 of the middle group, Haabai, and of that to the north, Vavau; also for the earliest knowledge of the native character.

The three clusters comprise about one hundred and fifty islands, of which Tongataboo, Lafuka, and Vavau are of considerable size. Except about fifteen, all of them are low: an elevation of fifty or sixty feet above the sea is high land.

They are situate between 18° and 20° south latitude, and 174° and 176° west longitude. The soil is of the richest quality, and, from the humid heat prevailing, produces a wealth of tropical vegetation which has astonished visitors from every part of the world. Besides the ordinary soil-products which in great variety and abundance serve for domestic use, Providence has planted the cocoa-nut and bread-fruit trees, the food, oil, and manufactures from which contribute in a hundred ways to the happiness of the islanders.

As to climate, the thermometer sometimes shows nearly

---

* For the substance of these pages on Tonga and the Tonguese, I am indebted to the Rev. Dr. Hoole. It is taken from his Appendix to the Rev. Walter Lawry's Journal.

100° in the shade. From the abundance of rain which periodically falls, and the heavy night dews, there are often transitions from heat to cold, unfriendly to the health of persons from colder climates. The inconstancy of the winds renders navigation somewhat critical. Hurricanes are as capricious in their seasons as they are destructive in their course. There are several active volcanoes, and occasionally an earthquake is felt, but not severely.

The population, according to the estimate of resident Missionaries, is about fifty thousand, of whom ten thousand are of the Tonga cluster.

The natives are a remarkably fine and well formed race, and of pleasing appearance, especially in the case of the higher class families. The complexion is of a rich, clear brown, sometimes approaching a light copper colour. Many of the young children are nearly white. The youth of the better families, who from their childhood have been well cared for, are much admired by European visitors.

Their political constitution is an hereditary but elective monarchy. From time immemorial there has been a royal family in Tonga : yet sovereignty has been by the franchise of the chiefs, who choose a son, brother, or nephew of the late monarch. The qualities which they seek in their sovereign elect are judgment, gravity, and kindness; that the nation may have some guarantee of a wise and happy government. The investiture of royalty is by a very formal ceremony of kava drinking.

The social rank comprises king, chief, *matabooles*, *tuas*, and *tamaiocikis*. In the heathen days there was another class, called *bobulas*, or slaves. The Gospel, however, has removed this distinction. Next to the chiefs, who are the heads of tribes, districts, or towns, are the *matabooles*, who are the chiefs' counsellors, and are responsible for good order.

The habits of the Tonguese exhibit much that is

pleasing. Their cleanliness is remarkable. In this respect they will not unfavourably compare with the civilized nations of Europe. Interesting notes abound of their habits of bathing, washing, anointing with scented oil, delight in flowers, hospitality to strangers, &c. Old persons of both sexes are highly respected on account of their age and experience. This is regarded as a religious duty. It is said there is scarcely an instance of old age having been wantonly insulted. Women are honoured with consideration and respect, according to their rank. They are not made to do any hard or very menial work, and it is considered unmanly not to show them regard and attention.

It is scarcely justice to retain the popular idea that the Tonguese are an idle people,—nature having so bountifully provided for their wants, which are but few and simple. Years ago they used to ask, with as much philosophy as self-content, " What need is there for us to exert ourselves in manufacturing things of which we do not feel the want, or know the use ? " Yet even then they delighted in carpentering and in ornamental and useful fabrics. But the recent intermingling with Europeans, and King George's visit to Sydney, have resulted favourably in this particular. The toils of our native Missionaries, and the laborious studies of our native ministerial students, should be noticed to the honour of the people, misrepresented in some respects.

Their *language* is a dialect of the great Polynesian language spoken, but with perplexing variations, by the New Zealanders of the South Pacific, and the Sandwich Islanders of the North, as well as by the dwellers on all the known groups between. Their dialect, which is very methodical in construction, is very soft and euphonious, but copious and expressive withal. The beginning of every word, and indeed of every syllable, with a vowel, makes it

mellifluous. Double consonants never occur. To adopt
English words requires their being so much altered as to
run the risk of non-recognition. It is said that the natives
can number distinctly to thousands of millions.

As to their *origin*, the Tonguese have the well known
comforting tradition that they are directly descended from
the gods. It is to the following effect :—Centuries back,
before the Tonga islands, which had been recently fished
up, had been peopled, some of the gods put to sea in a large
canoe, and arrived at Tonga. Delighted with the land,
they resolved to remain. Soon, to the surprise of the
survivors, two or three of them died. Afterwards one of
the number became inspired, and told the rest that for
coming to Tonga, they were to remain there, and people
it, but as mortal beings. Having vainly attempted to
escape, they remained on the island, and there multiplied.

In their heathen mythology there are four principal gods,
—brothers,—and one goddess. 1. *Maui* is said to have
fished up the islands from the depths of the sea, with hook
and line. The mountainous islands are those he did not
tread down. 2. *Hikulco*, "the god of spirits." He is a
being without love or goodness, has absolute power over
all, and all are forced to go to him. 3. *Tangaloa*, who
resides in the sky, and sends the thunder and lightning.
Being their god of carpenters, he is supposed to be the god
of foreigners, and to have instructed them in the art of
ship-building. 4. *Hcamoauha-uli-uli*, who governs the sea,
and controls all fish. On him fishermen depend for success. 5. The goddess *Maleckoola*, and the god *Maui*, were
the parents of the inferior gods and goddesses.

It is not difficult to trace or to imagine a connexion
between some of their popular traditions, and several of the
monumental verities of Bible revelation. They believe in
Bulotu, "a place of departed spirits." They speak of " the
water of life " in *Bulotu*, the properties of which heal the

dumb, lame, or blind, or revive the dead. It renews the youth of the aged, and makes them immortal.

At Tungua, Haabai, there is a rock, which tradition says was formerly a woman. While yet a virgin, she was found with child. The surprise of her friends was increased, when she told them she had committed no sin, but was with child by the sun. As the boy-child grew up, he was naughty; they therefore sent him in a canoe, to be in the sky with his father, the sun.

The faith of the Tonguese, as to the future existence of the soul, is that the souls of chiefs, *mataboolcs*, and, at furthest, *tuas*, are immortal ; none else.

The Friendly Islanders have been so called from their peacefulness of disposition and habits. At the date of their acquaintanceship with Christian Missionaries, from some quarrels arising out of intertribal trading with the Fijians, they had adopted a more warlike character than of old ; and from the neighbouring savage they had adopted some implements and customs of war.

The early history of the Friendly Islands Mission, which in later years has witnessed apostolic successes, has been already given to the Christian world ; but, as is hoped not inappropriately, it is here summarized. For ampler information, readers are referred to the well-known manuals by South Sea Island Missionaries, and to the charming history by the late Miss Farmer.

The first efforts to evangelize the Friendly Islanders were made by the London Missionary Society in 1797. On the 12th of April of that year, Captain Wilson, of the Missionary ship "Duff," landed ten agents at Hihifo. They were Messrs. Shelley, Kelso, Wilkinson, Bowell, Harper, Buchanan, Cooper, Nobbs, Veeson, and Gaulton. They were not ordained Ministers, but were nevertheless accredited as right-minded servants of Christ. From a variety of causes, chiefly the ungodliness of runaway sailors resident on the islands, their labours were all but fruitless. In the midst of a native war, three of them were murdered. Sadder still to tell, one apostatized to Paganism. For the honour of the others his name is given,—*Veeson.* The remaining brethren saw little prospect of success, and became discouraged; and, in the year 1800, embraced an opportunity which offered for their removal to Sydney.

Many years after, apart from the counsels of any Missionary Society, the Providence of God again favoured the Tonguese with Christian truth. It was on this wise. The Rev. Mr. Davies, of the London Missionary Society, was at Tahiti. His church appointed two Tahitian teachers, to labour as pioneers on one of the Fiji Islands. Their vessel sprang a leak. The captain, for some reason fearing to proceed to Fiji, left the teachers at Tonga. This casual and apparently trivial circumstance led to important results, as will be seen by and by.

On August 16th, 1822, the Rev. Walter Lawry, pursuant to appointment by the British Wesleyan Conference of 1821, arrived at Tongataboo. Besides Mrs. Lawry and their infant child, he was accompanied by three Europeans, regarded as living in the fear of God. They were Thomas Wright, general servant; George Lilley, carpenter; and Charles Tindall, blacksmith. The Mission opened favourably. Mr. Lawry was welcomed by the notably great and obese chief, Fatu. The chiefs in general not only promised to send thousands of children to be instructed, but also to attend themselves upon the teaching of the *papalangi,* "white teacher."

Mr. Lawry was at first pleased and encouraged to believe his Mission would prosper; but, in fourteen months, he left for England by way of Sydney. The Rev. Dr. Hoole says, he was obliged to leave on account of domestic circumstances. Lilley returned to the colony in about a year,* and Tindall went to reside with a chief in another part of the island.

Although the expenditure of much time, anxiety, and money by our Committee had resulted so unsatisfactorily as to show neither school, nor church, nor acquirement of the language, they still cherished the belief that a successful Mission might be established. In 1825, they appointed the Revs. John Thomas and John Hutchinson to labour in Tongataboo. These Missionaries landed in June, 1826, and chose Hihifo as their station.

Here they were at first favourably treated by the chief Ata. They erected a substantial dwelling, which they had taken with them in frame from Sydney. Both Mr. and Mrs. Thomas were full of ardour and purpose. Their vigorous constitutions and health contributed not a little to their zeal and hope. The enfeebling climate, however, was too much for Mr. Hutchinson's frame, and in a few months he desired to return to the colonies, whence he had been taken into the work. Confidence in the chief proved to have been misplaced. He soon began to throw difficulties in the Missionaries' way, suffering boys and youths to rob them with impunity, and threatening to burn their premises. He summoned together those who attended Divine worship, and commanded them to leave the district.

It was in the midst of these trials, and while they were fearing for their personal safety, that the brethren's appeal to Sydney, as we have seen, led to the withdrawal of Mr. Turner from his contemplated re-occupation of New Zealand, and to his going, in company with Mr. Cross, to Tongataboo.

* Mr. Lilley died in Ballarat in 1868.

CHAPTER XI

HAVING considered well the existing state of things, Mr. Turner concluded that a new station should be formed elsewhere in the group, and with some other chief and tribe. Feeling intensely his responsibility, he sought Divine guidance. Nor in vain. He had heard of the Tahitian teachers at Nukualofa, and wished to know more of the state of the work there; for he attached importance to the fact that Tubou, the principal chief of Nukualofa, was king, by right, of the whole group, and that upon Mr. Weiss's recent visit he had expressed a strong desire for an European Missionary. So he arranged with Messrs. Cross and Weiss to go over with him and be present at their Sabbath service, that they might see, hear, and judge for themselves.

It was their first Sabbath, and they started at daybreak. The morning service had begun when they arrived. It was conducted by Haepe, one of the Tahitian teachers. He appeared an earnest, good man, and the people listened attentively. The chief was among the hearers. The Missionaries afterwards learned that about two hundred and forty had begun to *lotu*, though there were not so many present on that occasion.

When service was over, Tubou ordered refreshments for the visitors. Fortunately, an English sailor was available as interpreter on common subjects. When the chief had learned who the white worshippers were, and what was their object, he arranged that the people's views and wishes should be ascertained the next morning at a public meeting, and that then his decision should be given. Monday came, and the meeting. The procedure was conducted with the solemnity of the kava ring. The objects of the Missionaries and their expectation from the chief were stated; when Tubou, through his chief speaker, intimated his approval. He had made up his mind to *lotu*, and wished to be instructed in the knowledge of Jehovah, the true God. He added, "These Tahitian teachers cannot speak the Tonguese language, and we cannot understand them."

Haepe was distinctly given to understand that the Society with which Mr. Turner and his associates were connected, was not the same as that by whose representatives he and his companions had been sent forth. Possessing this knowledge, he united his entreaties with those of the chief that the Missionaries would go and reside at Nukualofa. He entered fully into the particulars of his having come to Tonga, and stated his longing desire to go to Fiji, to which place he and his colleagues had been appointed.

The chief promised two of his best houses, and another building for stores, for the use of the Missionaries, until suitable erections could be completed. The cloudy pillar rested at Nukualofa, and thither, in the name of the Lord, the Missionary trio resolved to go. The community was filled with joy. Men, women, and children set to work to clear the public paths, and provide a comfortable reception. Captain Ebriel took the vessel round, and in an incredibly short time the property of the Mission was safely stored in the native houses.

Haepe was a small man, with a hump-back, and singularly unprepossessing. Yet in spirit he was amiable, and Mr. Turner loved him for his Master's sake, and for his work's sake. At Mission expense he supplied him with food and raiment,.

the latter of which he much needed. Referring to the above circumstances, and to his subsequent relations with Haepe, Mr. Turner wrote, "But it never entered into my head to liberally reward him for giving up the station to me, as implied in the language of Williams's 'Missionary Enterprise,' page 304. I was justly concerned to do that which was right and honourable by this good man, and the noble Society to which he belonged; and therefore, when an opportunity offered in the person of Captain Ebriel, who was about to sail for Tahiti, I wrote to the Rev. Mr. Davies, the pastor of the church who had sent Haepe forth, detailing the circumstances under which we had occupied the station, and desiring him to write me explicitly whether he would approve of Haepe continuing to assist us at Nukualofa, or whether we should forward him to his original destination, Fiji. In reply, Mr. Davies expressed in warm terms his gratitude to Heaven for directing my way to Tongataboo, and his most cordial approval of the steps we had taken in commencing our Mission with Tubou at Nukualofa; stating at the same time most distinctly, that it had never been his wish that the place should be occupied by their teachers. He expressed his thanks also for my kindness to Haepe, and desired me to send him back to Tahiti, which I accordingly did by the first opportunity." Mr. Turner made little account of Tafita, the other Tahitian teacher, whom he judged a worthless man.

Tubou's people had erected a homely building to accommodate two hundred and fifty persons, and Haepe had held religious services in it for some months, in the Tahitian language. Though several had been taught to read Tahitian, the people did not and could not rightly comprehend their teacher. On his part Haepe was not able to make himself understood in Tonguese; so that but little instruction had been imparted. Nevertheless, the people had been favourably impressed, and were very desirous to know the truth. This the Missionaries felt, and for it gave honour to Haepe, and ascribed glory to God.

Mr. Turner saw that the work before him would require much patient continuance. There to his hand were a people anxious to be instructed, but he and all with whom he could converse were ignorant of their language. Not a scrap had been written from which he could teach, nor had an orthography of their dialect been formed. His four years' experience in New Zealand proved a great advantage, inasmuch as his knowledge of Maori assisted him in acquiring the Tongan, and in reducing it for the advantage of others.

So soon as he had fairly domiciled his family, he applied himself to learn the language as of great importance. During his voyage, by the aid of Mariner's Vocabulary, he had learned a few sentences that would serve as common subjects; and so furnished, he at once went forth among the people, slate and pencil in hand, sat down in their houses, and made inquiries, as best he could. When his questions seemed to be understood, he wrote down the answers. He thus proceeded from day to day with much encouragement. The idiom resembling that of New Zealand, and the dialect embracing many words and phrases exactly similar, (though differently applied,) he was soon able to write and speak so as to be partially understood. The natives became interested, and set themselves to help him.

After a few unsuccessful attempts through a sailor interpreter, he felt constrained to begin public teaching with even the very slight knowledge of the language which he had. Within a few weeks after his arrival, he composed a hymn, wrote a short prayer and a short sermon, and after due preparation used all three in public worship. It was but a feeble effort, but it was in the right direction. It interested the people, showed that the Missionaries were in earnest, and kept the religious inquirers together.

Residents of Tonga must expect Tongan law and usage. Prior to their arrival, a great feast had been arranged for, and the Missionaries judged it a good opportunity to observe native customs. From two to three thousand persons assembled, from all parts of the island. A large proportion were athletes, the flower of the young men, eager to display their agility and strength in wrestling and boxing. Many tons of baked yams were distributed upon the lawn; and conspicuous in the midst of the spread were several fat hogs, baked whole, beside fowl, fish, turtle, and baked puddings innumerable, with fruit in tempting variety and abundance. The multitude assembled in front of the great town house, where they formed an immense ring, enclosing space enough for the competitors. To get a better view of the sports, Mr. Turner and his associates stepped upon a little mound close by. They were instantly warned off, as, being a burial place, the spot was sacred. They submissively moved away, and to get a good view got on to the lower branch of a toa tree. The limb broke with their weight, and let them fall. Before Mr. Turner could well regain his feet, a native was over him with an uplifted club to kill him : but his arm was arrested by a mightier Hand unseen. It was his superstition that the gods were in the toa tree, and were offended at the Missionaries having violated the *tabu* upon the burial ground. Though the incident caused a momentary sensation, it did not interrupt the festival.

After the feast, Tubou dealt with the matter as serious. The native's conduct was an affront to himself; for the Missionaries were known to be under his protection. He ordered that the chief, whose subject had thus behaved, should humble himself before him by way of atonement: this under penalty of war upon his tribe. Commissioners bearing this judgment were despatched to his town, Maofanga, two miles distant. The Missionaries were alarmed, and became intercessors : but to no purpose. For two hours they were very anxious. Happily, the Maofanga chief knew his interest, and in a short time, attended by many of his principal people, came into Tubou's presence, wearing the Tongan badges of penitence. Each man had on the most tattered mat he could procure, and a wreath of green leaves around his neck. The penitents sat with their faces bent to the ground, and, in a moaning tone, sued for mercy. Presently Tubou pronounced their pardon, and bade them rise. One lesson was learned by the Missionaries, and another by the natives.

Satan resisted the attack being made on his kingdom. No doubt he was the chief actor in a singular tragedy which occurred at that time. The cook of " The Endeavour " was so dangerously ill with dropsy that the captain would not take him further on his voyage, but left him in Mr. Turner's care. He was utterly ignorant of God, and the Missionaries were concerned for his conversion ; but their efforts were in vain. One day, when his end seemed near, he persuaded some of the natives to carry him into the chapel, and lay him beside the pulpit, under pretence of getting more air. When left alone, he took a razor which he had concealed about him, and cut his throat.

" The heathen raged." The chiefs were wild with Tubou, for having at the head of his people bowed the knee before Jehovah. They tried to dissuade him by argument, and then seriously threatened him. Late one evening, after Mr. Turner had returned from Hihifo, Tubou sent him a message, desiring to see him immediately. He went, and found the king in solemn conference with all his principal men. Uhila, by the king's direction, then informed him that the heathen chiefs were determined that the gods of Tonga should not be superseded by the *lotu.*

H

or be neglected on account of it, and that they had banded together to compel Tubou either to renounce the *lotu*, or to submit to war, and that a deputation had that evening brought this intimation as their *ultimatum.* Uhila further stated, " The Tui desires your counsel in the matter." He then remarked, " War is a bad thing, and the Tui does not want to fight; on the other hand, the *lotu* is a good thing, and he does not want to abandon it. Tubou puts to you this question : ' Shall I continue the *lotu* and prepare for war, or shall I give up the *lotu* and preserve peace ? ' " Mr. Turner's situation was serious, and so was Tubou's. To advise giving up the *lotu* was out of the question : to advise war was equally so, as opposed to God's teaching, and as likely to break up the Mission. He offered no definite answer; but ventured to suggest that it was important to devise some means by which, if possible, war might be prevented. Instantly Tubou conceived a plan which appeared to offer him an honourable escape from his dilemma, and announced it under powerful excitement :—" Let all the *lotu* people and the Missionaries go to one of the uninhabited islands of the group, where we may worship Jehovah unmolested, and live in peace." Uhila replied, but Mr. Turner did not understand what he said. Tubou was evidently offended at his chief speaker, and said in an unmistakeable manner, " I shall go at once to launch my canoes, and prepare for sailing from Tonga in the morning." He then added with dignity, " So many of you as are for Jehovah, rise and follow me ; those who are for the devil, sit still :" and suiting his action to the word, he marched out towards his canoes, followed by every member of the assembly. Not one for Satan was left. Mr. Turner had walked twelve miles that day under the burning sun, and returned home from the strange midnight scene wearied and anxious.

Some of the Mission party who had never seen heathen

war were terror-struck, and hastily prepared for flight, though it was not very apparent whither; but those who had passed through many a fight of affliction in New Zealand were tranquil: they again took hold of God's strength. Mr. Turner tried hard to calm his agitated friends, but in vain; so he comforted himself by sleep: but not for long. Another deputation from Tubou knocked him up,—the king wanted to see him on the beach. He went with his brethren. There in the deep water was the large double canoe, which the men had just succeeded in conveying over the reef, and launching. Women and children were hastily carrying to the water's edge food, clothing, and other necessaries. The king was seated in his canoe house with his weary men around him. He stated that he had determined to leave at once for one of the Haabai Islands, and begged that the Missionaries would go with him. It was his intention in the morning to launch the other large canoe, and they could manage to take with them all the Mission property, excepting some bricks and one or two other articles he named.

The Missionaries deferred their answer till morning. Returning home they found greater excitement still. An English sailor had said in the hearing of their families that they would be all despatched before the noon of to-morrow. Mrs. Turner felt, "It *is* hard to be driven away again, after having so lately suffered the wreck of all in New Zealand." The morning, however, presented an altered condition of things. When the Missionaries had left the beach, Tubou and his chiefs had resumed their delibera-tions, and had resolved to wait a few days, and watch the effect upon their persecutors of the chiefs' intended action.

It has been stated that Tubou was king of Tonga by right. Owing to various circumstances, he had not been yet installed. Satan knew Tubou and his people, as surely as he had known Messiah and Israel. So soon as his strange purpose had become generally known, the heathen chiefs assembled, and resolved forthwith to instal him *Tui Kanukobulu*, or king. This was a crafty move, inasmuch as the obligations of royalty implied the support of the gods of Tonga, and the maintenance of idol worship. Tubou stepped into the snare. Mr. Turner wrote, however, " But I never heard what has been stated by others, that he verbally promised to give up the *lotu*."

Treachery was feared, for the heathen chiefs had openly said that unless the Missionaries were sent away they should be killed ; so Tubou placed armed guards at the Mission house gates, to prevent the entrance of strangers who might prove assassins,—an uncomfortable position truly for the messengers of peace and their families.

After some days' preparation, the king was installed at Hihifo. Mr. Turner was present at the ceremony, which " was most imposing." This movement reconciled the tribes, but boded disaster to the Mission. Though no interdict was placed upon the Missionaries or their native friends within the Mission enclosure, the chapel was closed. Tubou dared not show himself among the *lotu* people. Under the circumstances, the worship of God was carried on in Mr. Turner's house, it being the largest ; or at times under a shady tree in front of it. Tubou was manifestly unhappy : he was carefully watched, and did not for a while join in any of the public services. By and by, however, when spies got careless, he would steal into Mr. Turner's bedroom, and join him in the worship of God.

The first District Meeting in Tonga was held late that year. The lessons of experience were noted, and the future arranged for. The brethren Thomas and Cross had made much progress with the language. The alphabet and plan of the orthography which Mr. Turner had prepared were approved, and it was decided to prepare a First School Book, to be printed in Sydney. Meanwhile a written book was to be used at the schools of the several stations. The characters then fixed have continued without a single exception in use till this day. Mr. Hutchinson obtained permission to return to the colony on account of ill health. The unhealthfulness of the season, and his exertion and anxiety in acquiring the language, had seriously told on Mr. Turner's health; and it became a question for the Meeting whether he should not, on the return of Captain Ebriel, leave Tonga, and resume his Mission in New Zealand. To meet this, it was resolved that he should remove to Mr. Hutchinson's residence.

Early in 1828 this temporary exchange between the two sickly brethren took place, Tubou engaging to build for Mr. Turner's use at Nukualofa a suitable residence. While in daily fellowship, Mr. Thomas and Mr. Turner were mutually helpful in composing hymns and the school book. The chief Ata and the people generally seemed more favourable toward the Missionaries, and Mr. Turner felt freedom in talking to them in their dwellings. Ata, however, perversely opposed the instruction of his people. For their own strengthening and comfort in God, the Mission families regularly held English worship. Mr. Hutchinson at Nukualofa was not without his trials, and Mr. Turner occasionally visited him.

A native school for children and adults was begun in March. There were fifty present the first day. The number rapidly increased, and proved more than the Missionaries could instruct. At this, they carefully selected the most promising pupils, taught them the alphabet, and appointed them monitors over the rest, whom they divided into classes. By this training system, which was not inspected by critics, they prepared for the instruction of the entire people; and, by exercising a careful personal supervision, they succeeded in a high degree. Simultaneously they began a school at Hihifo, and were encouraged by an average attendance of about twenty, including the children of some of the first families.

A few weeks before this, a large party of friendly visitors had gone to Vavau, and the Tui had secretly sent among them a chief of high rank, named Tubou-Totai, to confer with Finau, the king of Vavau, on the subject of the *lotu.* On his return, the chief reported that at first Finau had been very angry; but that he had succeeded in obtaining from him a patient hearing for fourteen days on all subjects connected with the *lotu*, and that it had led to his becoming so concerned as that he could not sleep. He had sent two letters, written for him by an Englishman who resided near him. One was for Tubou, the other for Mr. Turner. The letter to the king acknowledged that Finau had been a very bad man, and stated that he was tired of his evil spirits' and wanted to turn to Jehovah. The other letter is here copied :—

" Mr. Turner.

" Sir,—I am so glad to hear that you are at Tonga-taboo, teaching my friend Tubou to know the Great God. I hope you will be so kind as to send to Port Jackson for some Missionaries to come to my land, to teach me and my people. I am tired of my spirits. They tell me so many lies that I am sick of them. Since Tubou-Totai came to see me, I have had no sleep for fear Missionaries will be so long before they get here. But if a ship should come to your island, be so good as to send one of your Missionaries to me, so that my people may see I have turned my evil spirits away. My island, Sir, will turn to the great God, because I am the only chief on the island. I have no one to control me : when I turn they all turn. To be sure I did try to take a ship," [a vessel they had tried to take some months previously,] " but there will be no more of that. Tubou-Totai tells them all that their spirits are lies.

Be so kind, Sir, as to go quick about Missionaries as time will allow. So no more from me a wicked sinner.

"(Signed,) FINAU, (his mark,) × × ×."

The result delighted all the friends of the *lotu*. The chiefs requested Mr. Turner to pay a visit to Vavau, which he cheerfully consented to do, when again settled at Nukualofa. At this time Taafahau, the king of the Haabai group, visited the Missionaries : he was accompanied by his principal wife. Mr. Turner was struck with his fine form, and uncommonly expressive and intelligent countenance. He was with him a long time, during which he seriously and carefully presented to him in his own language the truths of revelation. Taafahau sat and listened with marked attention. Of that interview Mr. Turner wrote : " From this conversation alone, I have reason to believe, sprang the first sincere desire to *lotu* on the part of Taafahau, who has since become celebrated as the great and good King George of the Friendly Islands." He tarried some time at Nukualofa, carefully marking the proceedings there ; and, before his departure, earnestly requested that a Missionary might be sent to Haabai to instruct him and his people.

The joy of Gospel triumph was tempered by domestic trial. Mr. Turner's infant son, given in time of extreme peril in New Zealand, and endeared by more than ordinary natural ties, was seriously afflicted, and for some days lay at the gate of death. His father had occasion to visit Nukualofa, and while there sorrowfully selected some boards, with which on his return to make the little coffin he feared would be needed.

When Mr. Turner again took up his abode at Nukualofa, having improved health, he entered with zest upon the work before him. The scholars had so increased, that a new arrangement was needed ; so he took charge of the boys

and men in the mornings, while Mr. and Mrs. Cross and
Mrs. Turner instructed the women and girls each afternoon. They found it difficult to keep the monitors sufficiently a-head of the classes. Their special trouble was to
write out sufficient lesson-papers; so they selected the
smartest youths, taught them to write a legible hand, and
then set them to work to prepare copies. As all who had
learned to read thirsted for knowledge, the young scribes
were kept busy in preparing a manuscript Loan Library.
The contents were simply some selections of instructive
Scripture, with words of exhortation and application
added. One copy of each book of this class from the Missionaries' pens sufficed; they were quickly multiplied.
For the credit of the Wangaroa Mission, I must add that
Tunqahoo, the Maori lad who had accompanied Mr. Turner
to Tonga, and had learned to write in the school at Wesley
Vale, proved a most valuable scribe. It is noteworthy
that, by means of this Loan Library, many natives who had
long sat in darkness had much of God's truth graven on
their minds long before the printing press arrived.

Their paper was soon all used up, and the Missionaries
were at their wits' end for more. How to supply them was
a question of great interest to the schools. The captain of
a Sandwich island trader called in at the station, seeking
some articles for barter, and offering in exchange anything
he had on board. He had a quantity of paper, and Mr.
Turner let him have for it a few dozen worthless axes, by
the supply of which the Mission agents had been deceived
by some Sydney sharpers. The Tongan natives would not
look at the hatchets, they were so worthless. Thus the
Library was increased.

Tubou, the king, had now been undecided for six
months. Between Jehovah and Baal he had halted, much
to the anxiety of the friends of the *lotu*, and of the Missionaries. But on the 1st of June, 1828, he again worshipped

Jehovah in the presence of his people. That he would do so had become known, and many from a distance attended the service. Mr. Thomas, from Hihifo, came over and assisted. The event caused great joy: indeed, a large number left their heathen homes to reside at Nukua-lofa, where they might the better enjoy the means of grace.

Now came lively times for the Missionaries. It was not easy to secure rest: recreation was out of the question. Head, heart, and hands were fully consecrated to the work. Beside studying the language, composing hymns, translating Scripture for Sabbath services, and preparing lessons for the pulpits, there was the superintending of the daily schools, and the care of the sick.

In the course of Missions everywhere, medical attention to the sick has proved an important auxiliary to the special object, by winning general confidence and goodwill. In Tonga, skill was not acquired without anxiety. Men generally are not born physicians: nor was Nathaniel Turner. The islanders were subject to what they termed *bala*; a scrofulous gangrenous disease, affecting any part of the body, in the form of boils or ulcers. No outward application they knew of could heal the suppurating wounds, which spread and ate into the flesh till they brought on death. Solohea and Tubou-Totai, two nephews of the king, were among its victims. The latter, who had some smattering of English, had found out that a similar affection had been cured by the Missionaries at Tahiti. He asked Mr. Turner if he had any mercury, and begged him to try to cure him by the use of it. From want of experience, and with becoming caution, the risk was declined, though with reluctance. The king then interceded: so, upon a distinct understanding that the responsibility would not be with the Missionary, who yet would do his best, Tubou-Totai was salivated. It was Mr.

Turner's first attempt, and he administered too much mercury in the earlier doses. One morning he was summoned to his patient, and found him in a frightful state. There he lay, with his head swollen, his jaws extended, his tongue fourfold its natural size, standing out. He said to himself, "This is a gone case;" and then carefully consulted his medical books. His subsequent treatment had the best effect. The alarming symptoms subsided; and it was some satisfaction to him to find that though he had nearly killed the man, he had healed his "*bala.*" The wound which had covered half the calf of his leg, and had eaten into the bone, was now reduced to the size of a crown piece. By the further use of mercury in more approved doses, the cure was perfected.

From Dan to Beersheba the cure was published, and now the Mission enclosure became a Bethesda. Of a large number of cases treated, in two only, which had been late taken in hand, was there failure: this was satisfactory; but there was another result far more so: not a few earnest persons found their way to the feet of Jesus, crying, "Lord, if Thou wilt, Thou canst make me whole."

Mr. Turner had a friendly critic. A young convert, named Vi, by request came to the Mission house every Monday morning, that the Missionary might have the advantage of his strictures upon the public deliverances of the previous day. He had previously assisted him much in acquiring the language. Vi's frequent visits made him almost as one of the household, and led to his daily attendance at family prayer. At these services he was greatly blessed; for, the servants being natives, Mr. Turner offered prayer as well in their language as in his own. Vi was a married man, though but young; and naturally enough considered that such prayer would be appropriate and right in his own family. So he introduced it. Within his enclosure were several other families, and some of them were early privileged to attend his domestic worship. Then he was invited to pray in the homes of others, and in a very short time regular and appropriate family worship became general. Thus originated an institution which has become one of the brightest glories of the land.

Vi was afterwards baptized by the name of Peter, and became an apostle to his countrymen. As a native Assistant Missionary he has for many years been honourably employed, seeing much success.

About three miles from Nukualofa, in different directions, were three villages, Hofoa, Havelu, and Manfauqa : to each of these the Gospel was carried. Nearly all their inhabitants renounced idolatry, and schools were established.

So mightily grew the word of God and prevailed, that the neighbouring groups clamoured for it. On the 4th of October, Mr. Turner thus wrote to the London Committee:—

" My mind is at this time affected by the absolute necessity there is of more help being sent to this infant Mission. Captain Samuel Henry, son of the Rev. Mr. Henry of Tahiti, has just arrived here on a trading voyage. He has come from the Navigators', Vavau, and the Haabai Islands. At nearly every place he has touched at, the first inquiries have been, ' Have you any Missionaries on board for us?' At some places the natives have been really troublesome on this account. On one island, where no Missionary has set his foot, a chapel has been erected by the poor natives in full expectation of one. On one of the Haabai Islands they have persuaded an ungodly sailor to become their instructor. Do, my dear fathers and brethren, pity and help these thousands of perishing souls. Tell their wants, publish their cries throughout England, and I doubt not the increased liberality of those who love Jesus. will enable you to send a press and a printer, and men who will gladly rush into these open doors, and cry, ' Behold the Lamb of God.' "

The first Methodist class-meeting in Tonga was conducted by Mr. Turner on October 14th, 1828. The number was about ten. To these other members were added, and a second class was formed. Before the close of the year the Missionaries rejoiced over about twenty souls gathered from wild heathenism into the fellowship of the church of God. In a letter to Mr. Leigh about this date, Mr. Turner says :—

"The work is unquestionably begun. Many have entirely laid aside their heathen customs and superstitions, and, according to the light they possess, sincerely worship the true God. I can hear them pray to Jehovah in their little communities with such solemnity of spirit and propriety of expression as quite affect me. Observe, I do not say that any are evangelically converted, but we expect this soon. We have above one hundred natives under daily instruction. Our congregations on the Lord's day average from three to four hundred, and they listen with eager attention. My diligent and laborious colleagues make great progress with the language. Thousands in the neighbouring islands are crying, 'Come over and help us.' Our trials are severe, but they are swallowed up in our mighty concern to instruct and save the race."

Meanwhile, Mr. Thomas was persecuted at Hihifo by the chief Ata, and his work much hindered. But the Lord not only supported His faithful servant, but made "the wrath of man to praise Him."

The pleasing hopes of the new year were justified. The first convert to Christ from among the Tonguese was baptized by Mr. Thomas at Hihifo in January, 1829. Solohea was a young chief of the highest rank, being son of the late king, and nephew of the reigning monarch. During a long affliction he received instruction from the Missionaries. His baptism was witnessed by his heathen mother and friends. He soon after fell asleep in Jesus. Miss Farmer has supplied an interesting account of his illness, death, and funeral, as he is regarded as the first-fruits of Mission toil in the Friendly Islands.

In a short time six of the most promising of the catechumens were publicly received into the church by baptism. The names assigned them were Noah, Moses, Peter, Barnabas, Joseph, and John. The whole of these first six converts became preachers of the Gospel to their countrymen. John, who was of frail constitution, died young. Noah and Moses were reliable and useful in the church at Nukualofa ; while Peter, Joseph, and Barnabas were early sent forth as evangelists to other islands. Mr. Turner wrote : " I regarded the leading of these converts to Christ and to His church as the highest honour which up to that time God had conferred upon me."

The second public baptism was on the 29th of March, when the Rev. Mr. Cross administered the sacrament to the wife of the king, and to four other women, two of whom were wives of members of the native church. On the 4th of April the Missionaries of Nukualofa and Mr. Thomas had "a laborious meeting" in reference to the language and the enlargement of their school book. This little volume, which they were hastening to complete for printing in Sydney, comprised Scripture lessons, catechisms, and hymns.......During this month the sloop of war, "Satellite," was in the harbour for a few days. Her commander, Captain Lawes, and his officers showed much courtesy to the Mission families, and evinced an interest in their work. The commander had visited the Society Islands and New Zealand, but said he had seen nothing to equal the progress of the Gospel in Tonga, for the time the Mission had been established.

The first Christian marriage in Tonga took place on the 3rd of May, Sunday. Mr. Cross preached a preparatory sermon on David and Goliath. What special adaptation he found in the subject my readers may guess. The husbands' names were Noah, Peter, Joseph. They had been married before in Tonga fashion, but now desired a Christian union under the sanction and ceremony of a Christian marriage. A translation of the Book of Common Prayer was used on the occasion.

There was a large concourse at the first Christian funeral of a Tongan native. It was that of a chief who had renounced heathenism and had found the Saviour during his affliction. He had been baptized " Job " because of his patience. English order was pretty closely adopted. The Missionaries preceded, and the mourners followed the bier to the ground. When the corpse had been placed at the door of its long home, the followers and spectators seated themselves around. To the sympathizing and confiding natives, newly blessed with the light and hope of heaven, the service was peculiarly affecting.

When the novelty of going to school had somewhat worn off, the attendance decreased. So the king's influence was sought. Next day two hundred and fifty were present. The building was inconveniently small for the scholars or worshippers; and Tubou promised to have it enlarged.

Sunday, the 7th of June, was a Pentecostal day. At the nine o'clock service a very gracious influence rested upon five hundred persons during the whole meeting. Ten men, two of them being chiefs of rank, solemnly renounced heathenism. At the afternoon service eight adult females and three children were baptized. Better still, many were pricked in the heart by the word. In the evening, twenty-six native converts, who had been previously instructed in the nature and design of the ordinance, united with their Missionaries in partaking of the emblems of the Body and Blood given for the life of the world.

The candidates for baptism were chary as to the names proposed to be given them; especially as to the moral character of their Scripture namesakes. A chief, whose native name was Lightning, and who had been a celebrity as a heathen priest, was baptized with his wife and son. The trio were named "Zechariah," "Elizabeth," and "John." Each native was allowed to retain his Tonga name, when not an improper one.

All Nukualofa felt the influence of God's truth and Spirit. The people would talk of nothing else than learning to read, attending the class, being baptized, and going to heaven. Twenty-two anxious inquirers were met for the first time at class the same evening. All ranks and conditions were represented in the general movement for Christ and His salvation.

On the 10th of June, Mr. Turner's diary recorded a memorable event:—"To-day Tubou, the *Tui*, or king, met in class for the first time. Another chief, Mafeleo Toutai, has met with him. Agreeably with their request, I met them alone in my study. With the *Tui* I have much cause to be encouraged. He engaged in prayer after I had spoken to them, and, seriously, he prayed as one who had been accustomed to prayer for years. The Lord keep him humble, and assist me to guide him in the good and right way."

In painful contrast with this was the funeral ceremony of Mafeleo's mother, two days afterwards. The mourning women had no sooner poured their bags of fine sand over the corpse, and the slab door been placed upon the tomb, than there arose a piteous orgy of heathenish fury; some of the men turned maniacs, and gashed their heads with axes, or other sharp instruments, until their bodies were drenched in blood; others thrust sharp-pointed spears through the fleshy parts of their arms and thighs; some burned themselves in different parts with firebrands; meanwhile the women persisted in uttering the most piercing wails. It was "the sorrow that worketh death."

The chief Ata was a tough piece of heathenism. He had now for about three years frustrated to a great extent the labours of the Missionaries at Hihifo, and on the 16th of July the brethren held a consultation as to giving up the station. It was known that a favourable opening offered at Haabai; indeed, as many as from five to seven hundred could be gathered for Christian worship, if only a Missionary could go to them. It was judged that they might with advantage occupy Haabai instead of Hihifo; but there was a difficulty. Unless Ata should consent, of which there was some uncertainty, there would be trouble. Divine guidance was sought, and then the chief was conferred with. Ata was found civil and candid. He "loved Mr. Thomas, but would not turn for him or any one else who might come. He had always told Mr. Thomas so, and in that mind he would remain. Mr. Thomas might go to Haabai if he liked." Thereupon it was decided to form a new station at Lifuka, the king's town at Haabai. They resolved on this course, anticipating the mind of the Committee in London; but did so with little reluctance, as but little expense would be incurred. A fortnight later the Hihifo station was given up, and Mr. Thomas removed to Nukualofa. The king of Haabai visited him there, and desired him to tarry awhile until he should have prepared to accommodate him.

The diary notes following are of incidents of school progress, of triumphs of grace in sickness, and of happy death beds......The case of Fau, whose only son "the Lord took," brought out Christian faith and submission...... On the 19th of September there was an earthquake. Tongan superstition regarded earthquakes as caused by the god Mui shifting the island from one shoulder to another.

From the experience of Ata's insincerity and other causes, some doubt arose as to the trustworthiness of the king of Haabai in his profession of desire for the *lotu*. To satisfy themselves, the Missionaries had a long talk with him on the evening of the 8th of October. It established their confidence.

The first native lovefeast was held on the afternoon of October 11th. About one hundred and fifty members were present, of whom only forty-six spoke. "O, how our hearts were melted while we heard them with simplicity and earnestness state their conversion from heathenism to Christ! Glory to God for what our eyes behold!"

The origin of Tonga Sabbath schools is noticed in an entry of the same date. "Commenced a Sabbath school to-day, which, we believe, will be productive of good to the rising generation."

Mr. Thomas's removal to Haabai was deferred, pending expected communications from the Committee. It was resolved, however, that Peter Vi should go as a temporary supply.

The Missionaries had now to endure serious personal and family loss. The brig "Minerva," with supplies, was wrecked upon a reef, and went to pieces; not a single article of food or apparel, or even a document, was saved. The sailing master, Peter Bags, reached Nukualofa.

Not hearing from the Committee on the subject, the Missionaries for some time hesitated as to occupying the Haabai group. Their suspense was removed by a mysterious providence, a notice of which I copy from Miss Farmer's "Tonga." Mr. Turner judged that Miss Farmer had taken it from his written journal forwarded to the Committee after the occurrence. "While waiting anxiously, not daring to add to the difficulties of the Society by further outlay, a small box, or packet, was washed on shore, and brought to Mr. Turner. It was found to convey a letter that set their minds at rest. Things at home were not so bad, after all. A Missionary might go to Haabai. The vessel that bore that letter (a schooner from Sydney)

had foundered, and all on board had perished. Neither
the vessel, nor any of her crew, nor any of the goods with
which she had been freighted, was heard of again. That
letter alone, the messenger of mercy to a people waiting
for the law of the Lord, guided by Him whom winds and
seas obey, escaped the general ruin, and was cast on the
right shore at the right time."

Cheering tidings from Haabai soon reached Tonga. The
king was in earnest. On the very day after his return
home he had publicly demonstrated his resolve to *lotu*.
He had taken to pieces a large sacred canoe which had
been deified, had set himself to learn to read, and had
counselled his people to turn to Jehovah. Meanwhile the
work grew in Tonga. The classes increased. On the
20th of December no less than eighty-four persons received
Christian baptism. Many of the old folk rejoiced in the
names of the patriarchs. One simple sister, having a taste
for antiquity, chose to be called " Eve." Next week she
wanted to be unbaptized, complaining to the Missionaries,
" All the children of the place make sport of me, calling
me ' the mother of all evil.' "

As the flock had greatly multiplied, it became necessary
to provide under-shepherds ; and the most experienced and
eligible of the church members were chosen, and appointed
leaders. These the Missionaries met weekly by themselves, in the hope of keeping them in advance of the
members in knowledge and experience. Most of them
quite fulfilled these expectations. The wisdom of this
arrangement was in its necessity. Some of the new
leaders must have had but a dull moral perception. At
one of their meetings, after Mr. Turner had been speaking
plainly on the duty of restitution, he was voluntarily
informed by several that they had kept back as their own
sundry articles they had found, but to which they had no
other than a finder's right. One characteristic of first love

is tenderness of conscience ; and next morning numerous lads and lasses were seen at the Mission house, each laying something down. They had been told over-night by their leaders of this doctrine of restitution. The ready recovery of knives, scissors, spoons, and other articles mysteriously missed, was not so pleasing to the family as this new evidence of the power of truth.

On the 9th of January, 1830, Peter Vi arrived from Haabai, to accompany Mr. Thomas thither. He brought glad news ; the king and several hundreds of his people had cast away their idols. The next day,—the Sabbath,— was one of great interest. Mr. Turner had the high honour of receiving into the church Tubou, the king of Tonga. He stood beside the pulpit, with his wife and children standing at his left hand. His manly form was neatly attired in native cloth, and his countenance indicated that he was calm and full of purpose. The large assembly and their teachers looked on with joyous admiration. Having asked their attention, he seriously and openly renounced the gods of Tonga, calling them " vanity and lies." He assured the people that he had " cast away everything that he knew to be sinful; that Jehovah was his God, and Jesus Christ his only Saviour ; that he made an offering that day of himself, his wife, and children, unto the Lord, that He might dispose of them as He would see good." He exhorted his people to follow his example, and attend to the things of God. He then knelt down, and in that position was baptized in the Name of the Triune God. He was named Josiah. Rising from his knees, he presented his three sons and his daughter to the Missionary ; and they also were dedicated to God. In the afternoon another notable person was baptized. He had been one of the greatest priests of the land ; indeed, Tubou himself had often prayed to him as his god. Both the king and his god were received into the church the same day.

Early in March, the whaling ship " L'Aigle " was wrecked on a Tonga reef, on to which, strangely enough, her master had sailed her direct. The loss to the owners was three hundred tuns of sperm oil. The captain and crew made for Nukualofa in four whaleboats. They were afraid of their lives, and sought the protection of the Missionaries. Tubou and his men acted the part of Christians, showing much hospitality, and doing their best to save the property from the wreck.

One result of the success of the Tonga Mission was, that its chief port soon became a convenient station for the shipping in the South Eastern Seas. On the 11th of April, there were present at the English service three captains, three doctors, and many from the crews from their three vessels. We hope the prayer in Mr. Turner's diary was heard : " O, may the word of God take hold upon their hearts, and do them everlasting good ! "

The church and school building at Nukualofa was found too small, and a new one was erected. The first post was put in the ground on the 5th of May, amid the prayers and praises of a grateful people. The site was the centre and summit of an old fortification. It is the highest point of land,—eighty feet above the sea level,—and, as it commands the opening of the Nukualofa harbour, the church has become a guide to captains sailing in.

As Captain Ebriels was going over to Haabai, Mr. Turner had a trip for his health. The schooner's course would admit of his spending but one day there. It was the Sabbath. At nine A.M. he preached to four hundred attentive hearers. The return was perilous. He writes :—" We had not proceeded far before it began to blow and rain tremendously. The narrow, sinuous channel being fringed with coral reefs on every hand, and the schooner running with gunwale under water, our danger was great. Tubou Totai, our pilot, was lashed to the mast, that he might preserve his position, and guide the vessel. The captain said he had never been in greater peril."

Early in June the war frigate " Seringapatam " called in. The commander, the Honourable William Waldegrave, and his officers exhibited with much courtesy a kindly interest in the Mission. The attentions of the medical officer to Mr. Turner were timely, as he had been very unwell. On the commander offering whatever assistance he could render to the Mission, he was told of some runaway sailors at Vavau, whose rascality was a hindrance to the influence of the Gospel among the natives. He promptly replied, " Although it was not my intention to visit Vavau, I will sail direct for that port, and take them away." To the honour of the British navy, he fulfilled his promise. In a few days he wrote to Mr. Turner from " off Lifuka, " stating that he· had succeeded in taking on board five of the men referred to.

About the same time he received another letter which he valued much. It was in the handwriting of the king of Haabai. It accompanied a significant token of his sincerity in turning Christian. The present was a rude wooden image of one of the goddesses. It was about twenty inches long, and represented a decrepit, ugly old woman. The dishonoured deity had a cord around her neck, by which she had lately been hanging from the rafters of a now abandoned god-house.

On June 25th, the Rev. Messrs. Williams and Barff, of the London Missionary Society, arrived from the Society Islands. They had with them a number of teachers, designed for the Navigator's and other islands. The Nukualofa Missionaries received them as brethren and fellow labourers in the kingdom of Christ. Mr. Williams sojourned at Mr. Turner's, and Mr. Barff with Mr. Cross. All the native teachers took up their abode with the king by invitation. At daylight a Tahitian service was held in the chapel, attended by the Tahitian teachers, and the crew of their little vessel, "The Olive Branch." Mr. Turner was present, although he did not understand the language.

At nine A.M. he addressed a great congregation with freedom and power, the Missionary visitors attending. At that service Mr. Cross and he baptized thirty male adults, and Samuel the infant son of Tubou the king. Mr. Williams afterwards conducted an English service, in which he preached "a good sermon" for the benefit of the Mission families, and the Europeans from the vessels. In the afternoon Mr. Cross preached, in Tongan, and baptized about thirty women, most of them the wives of those baptized in the morning. Later in the day forty couples were publicly married. On the Wednesday evening at the prayer-meeting, Mr. Williams delivered an address, narrating Missionary adventures and triumphs in Rarotonga and elsewhere. The following is from Mr. Turner's diary :—

"July 4th.—Another very blessed Sabbath in the sanctuary, among our people, and at our English services morning and evening, conducted by our dear brethren Barff and Williams. The latter gave us a very profitable sermon in the evening from, ' And there they crucified Him ;' at the close of which we partook together of the sacred emblems of our Saviour's body and blood. This was indeed a soul-hallowing season, in which we held communion with our Lord, and silent fellowship one with another.

"Tuesday 6th.—This morning our dear brethren Barff and Williams, with their band of native teachers, sailed for the Haabais, accompanied by Mr. and Mrs. Cross, who have gone to spend a few weeks with brother and sister Thomas at Lifuka. The Lord bless and prosper the enterprise of these devoted men ! "

In heathen times the burial of a young prince was attended by the frantic shrieks and bleeding wounds of mock mourners; but all this ceased under the softening influence of the Gospel. Both parents and some hundreds of the people were present at the funeral of Samuel, the king's infant son, but there was not the sign of a heathen rite; and as Mr. Turner addressed them upon the "home above," it was evident that many of those who wept believed the words he spoke, and were able to comfort one another.

On August 5th, Thomas Olley was soundly converted to God under a sermon on "the Many Mansions." He was an old man-of-war's man, and had been " sinning hard in many lands." Lately, while much afflicted, he had fallen under Mr. Turner's care. He testified in the clearest manner to two shipmates and to two others, strangers, that God had pardoned all his sins. The diary entry reads : " I have not met with a clearer conversion since I left England. Glory to God for putting honour upon His truth in saving this poor aged sinner!"

The new chapel was opened on Sabbath, September 3rd. The day had been anticipated with the liveliest interest. Not all of it perhaps of the most spiritual kind. The occasion had been fixed upon for the first appearance by many in European costume. The Missionaries' wives turned dressmakers, and instructed scores of anxious learners, who rivalled each other's skill. However becoming their dresses, the women would not like to appear without bonnets. So they made their plait, and plied their skill. Their millinery was a native art, adopted from Tahiti on the recent visit of the Tahitian teachers, who had been accompanied by their wives. At an early hour numbers assembled around the sanctuary, and in Christian thought and conversation waited the opening service. The king had suggested, with true Tongan delicacy, that many of his own people should remain outside, so that, as far as possible, strangers should be accommodated. At nine o'clock the building, seventy by thirty feet, was packed from side to side, principally with strangers: the throng within and without numbered two thousand. Those inside sat upon matting, native fashion. For once in Methodism the people sat to sing, for they had not room to rise. At the sides of the pulpit, made by the carpenter of " L'Aigle," were two pews, one for the Mission families, and the other for the king and chiefs.

Next Sunday Mr. Turner fell in with the brother of the chief walking to and fro, with his eyes steadily lifted upwards.

Mr. Turner.—" What are you doing, Abraham ? "

Abraham.—" O ! I am thinking of what you preached about,—the mercy of the Lord toward us being higher than the heavens are above the earth ! "

Mr. Turner.—" Have you not been home for dinner ? "

Abraham.—" No ; my heart is too full: I do not want any dinner."

That afternoon the second native lovefeast was held : about two hundred were present. Half of them spoke briefly, simply, and well ; the king first, then all the chiefs, in the order of their rank. When the speaking flagged, the king urged the people to speak freely, and not be afraid,—to speak the truth, and nothing but the truth. Several steady and sincere men ardently desired " to become wise, that they might be employed in instructing others."

On the Tuesday Mr. Turner started in a large canoe for the island of Eua, to ascertain whether the chief there would receive two or three Tongan teachers. He was becalmed the whole day, and spent the night at Hahaki. An old chief named Nuku and his people paid deep attention as he addressed them. He also visited another village inland. Its chief was " the god of winds and rains." He had lately received many offerings of yams, pigs, and native cloth, to induce him to arrest the famine threatened by a long continued drought. Mr. Turner observed with pleasure the influence of the native converts. Wherever they had gone, they had witnessed for Jehovah by morning and evening prayer, and by asking God's blessing upon their meals. The wind and weather being very rough and contrary, he did not get to Eua.

The protracted drought became serious, and called out the faith of the converts. There was the prospect of a general famine, and fear reigned. One morning the Missionaries were visited early by a few of their best praying men. They had come after consultation to inquire whether it would not be right to have a day set apart for special prayer for rain. To support their plea they told of the costly offerings their heathen neighbours had been making to their gods on the same behalf. A day was appointed. At the nine o'clock service there was a numerous gathering of praying men. The Missionaries read appropriate portions of Scripture which they had translated for the purpose of guiding and stimulating their faith. Throughout a solemn service, all laboured hard to take hold on God. On leaving the chapel every eye looked for an immediate answer, but the still dry blue sky was unmarked by any cloud, even as " little as a human hand." Disappointment shaded every face. " *Kataki*,"—" Wait," said the Missionaries, " and God will assuredly answer." At three P.M. there was another service, at which there was still more mighty wrestling with the God of Elijah. Like another patriarch pleading for Sodom, a fine old chief knelt erect in the middle of the prostrate group, and in solemn reverent earnestness argued his plea with " the God of the whole earth." His name was Shem, but Mr. Turner thought of Abraham. " O Lord," he said, " Thou knowest that we have set apart this day to pray to Thee for rain. Our doings of to-day will soon be known throughout the land, and if Thou dost not soon answer our prayer, Thy servants will be mocked, Thy Word will be rejected, Thy Name will be dishonoured, and Thy cause will sink in the land. O Lord, for Thy great Name's sake,

haste and send us rain!" That evening the clouds
gathered and burst; and on the following days there was
abundance of rain. Then the heathen said, "Jehovah is
the God that sendeth rain upon the earth."

This answer to prayer so stimulated the confidence of the
native Christians that they far exceeded their former zeal
in instructing the ignorant and in befriending the sick.
Such was their faith in the power of prayer, that they even
led a number of diseased and dying persons to the Mission
station, that they might be healed. One of these was a
chief of rank, from Houma. They thought him to be
dying, and brought him to Mr. Turner. Abraham said:—
"Mr. Turner, this is a great chief: he has been a long time
sick, and his friends have presented many offerings to their
foolish gods on his behalf. They have carried him from
one god's house to another, but he has only grown worse,
and now we have induced them to bring him to you, that
Jehovah might heal him. He is a great chief, and if he
be restored, it will be a great thing in favour of the *lotu*
among his heathen people. You must do all you can to
heal his body, and we will pray to our God to save his soul."
Mr. Turner sought Divine counsel, and then bled the man
and administered medicine : he slowly but fully recovered.
The converts triumphed, and the enthusiastic Abraham
resolved on making the event serve the cause of the *lotu*. At
an hour when the restored chief's people were all together,
he accompanied the man back, and exhibited him as a
trophy of Jehovah's power and goodness. In the form of
his glorying he proceeded to ridicule the heathen deities,
and then challenged them, if they had any existence or
power, to slay him on the spot. On his way home Abraham
was sunstruck. As he lay dangerously ill, the Christian
converts became concerned lest the heathen should claim
his sickness as a judgment by their gods for his impiety.

Again medical skill was used, and the converts' "prayer of faith saved the sick."

The young Tongan Christians were loth to give up their custom of night dances. At these sports they were often very imprudent. While their blood was hot from dancing, they would throw themselves on the wet grass, and lie there under a heavy dew, and thus bring on acute rheumatism or sciatica. A case of this kind was brought to Mr. Turner, and he resolved on effecting, if possible, a double cure. He got the parents' consent to his proposed treatment, and then applied such a blister as cured the leg and its owner's love of night dancing too.

Under date of December 31st, 1830, there is this entry:— "A year of great and substantial prosperity to our Mission. The statistics of our District Meeting show that we have more than doubled our church members, and that more than a thousand are under daily instruction in our schools. We have received the joyful news that three brethren and sisters have left England to join our Mission. Gratitude and praise ought to flow from us, for God's abounding goodness to me and mine through another year. Nevertheless I have cause to humble myself before the Lord. Much infirmity has attached to my proceedings. At times great have been my physical weakness and suffering. At our late District Meeting my brethren came to the same conclusion as myself, that I shall soon be compelled to leave Tonga for a more healthy clime, or sink into the grave. I greatly love my work and people; but when I think of my dear wife and six children, and my health so sensibly failing, my heart would sink within me. But in my God is my hope, and my times are in His hand. O, may I be ready for all His righteous will!"

The Lord's Supper was administered at the evening service of the first Sabbath of 1831, to about two hundred members. Mr. Cross assisted, but the exertion proved too much for Mr. Turner, and his strength was exhausted before the meeting closed. The 10th of January, the fourth anniversary of their being driven away with but their bare lives by the savages of Wangaroa, was observed at the Mission house with special devotion. Mr. Turner's entry is : " For this I now thank God, as it proved the way in which He brought me to see His glory here. O, what have I seen since then ! Hundreds converted from dumb idols to ' serve the living and true God.' "

Supports in battle were never more joyfully hailed than was the reinforcement of Missionaries in Tonga on the 10th of March. The " Floyd " had stood in the offing for some days, the wind being contrary : at last the captain allowed his passengers to finish their voyage in a whale-boat. Messrs. Turner and Cross gave them a right hearty welcome at the beach ; and the first evening passed in sacred converse, prayer, and song. The entry is as follows : —" Brother Peter Turner is from Macclesfield, in my own beloved Cheshire. In vain we sought to find any nearer relationship, but in Jesus we are one. Both he and his good wife appear truly alive to God, and endued with a Missionary soul. Brother Watkin is from Manchester, and appears a clear-headed, active-minded man. He will soon get the language. His little wife is niece to the holy Joseph Entwisle, one of the most eminent fathers of the Wesleyan body. Brother and sister Woon * are from Cornwall : they will soon win the confidence and affection

* The Rev. William Woon was born in Truro, and converted to God in early life. When twenty-six years of age he entered the ministry, and proceeded to the Friendly Islands, where he remained for four years. Sometime afterwards he laboured in New Zealand, on the Mungungu and Taranaki stations. In 1853 his health failed, and he became a supernumerary. He resided for five years at Wanganui, acceptably serving the church and cause of God as he was able. On September 22nd, 1858, he died in the Lord. His latest words were, " Give my love to all my brethren ; I am going to heaven."

of the people, to whom they have devoted their lives. Brother Woon is our Missionary printer; he has brought a press and a good supply of material. Thank God, this will not only lessen our toils, (who have hitherto provided all with our pens,) but it will supply thousands of hungry souls with heavenly food."

On witnessing the native services on the Sabbath, the new brethren were filled with delight, and exclaimed, "The half has not been told." In the evening Mr. Watkin preached a good sermon in English. On their third Sabbath, the new Missionaries witnessed the public baptism of nearly seventy adults, and the marriage of about twenty couples.

They had scarcely got their sea legs adjusted to land life, when they were in the midst of a hurricane. The night was indescribably fearful. Mr. Turner's house was lashed with ropes to the trunks of cocoa-nut trees close at hand, and yet it rocked like a cradle; and for many hours its inmates feared every moment it would be carried away bodily, or that they would be crushed under its ruins. To the shipping the storm was most disastrous. Between two and three in the morning the Spanish brig "Candida" parted from her anchor, and was carried broadside on to a perpendicular reef, where she bilged and went down. Her owner, a French gentleman, named Lefevre, and the sailing-master and crew, were all providentially drifted ashore alive. At daybreak they went to the station in a most pitiable condition of body and mind. "Yesterday," said Lefevre, " I was worth six thousand pounds,—now I am a poor man; all is gone." The Missionaries hastened to render what assistance they could, but they found the disasters beyond remedy. There were six dead bodies lying on the beach mangled and lacerated; the brig was hopelessly wrecked, showing only her topmast out of water, and the two other vessels were quivering and straining at the

gates of destruction. The Christian natives regarded the
" Floyd " and " The Bee " as Jehovah's ships, the one having brought Missionaries, and the other Mission supplies,
and ascribed their preservation so far to the special providence of God. They earnestly said to the Missionaries,
" Do pray that they may not be wrecked : we have been
praying till we are tired." It was not so easy even for
Missionaries to pray, while sand and shell were cutting
into their faces with hurricane fury. It was evening when
the storm abated ; and then they looked out upon houses,
trees, fences, and plantations, levelled in common ruin.
The sun was setting, when the captain and crew of " The
Bee " got safely rafted ashore ; but it was some hours
before " Lincoln Bill," the skipper, got well over his fright.
He confessed himself "a miserable sinner," and vowed,
" If the Lord will only spare my vessel to me, I will never
beat my wife again." He and his vessel were spared. As
he sailed out of port, he knowingly took away the property
of those who had succoured him. Whether his wife had
any benefit from his tender vow, I do not know. He again
left the port of Sydney, but neither he nor his ship was
heard of more. The Tongans ascribed the wreck of the
" Candida " to the judgment of God upon her crew, for
wooding and watering on the Lord's day.

The last month in Tonga had too much to be done in it.
What with adapting premises for the press, and arranging
materials for its being worked, getting his namesake to
Haabai, and preparing for the removal of his own family
in readiness for any casual opportunity, Mr. Turner had
more on hand than his strength would bear, and became
very low in health.

The sloop of war " Comet," and the colonial government
brig " Lucy Ann," after removing the Pitcairn Islanders to
Tahiti, called in at Tonga upon their return voyage to
Sydney. Mr. Turner applied to Captain Sutherland, of " The

Comet," for a passage for his family by the brig, which also was under his charge. The commander acceded to his request, but stipulated that he must be ready in two days. The vessels, which had arrived on the Sunday, were to leave on the Wednesday. Tuesday was devoted to packing, but they could hardly get on for the constant demonstrations of the affection of the natives. Their tears and endearing expressions were, however, a rich comfort and reward, after years of toil for their welfare. " Father," some said, " if you had not come to our land, we would have lived in sin as our forefathers have done ; but now the light has beamed on us, and some of our relatives have gone to the world of glory."

When the excitement of the day had passed, the subjoined reflections were entered : " When I look at the mysterious way in which the Lord led me to Tonga, and the gloomy state of things in reference to our cause at that time, and compare it with the present, I cannot but wonder and adore : to God alone be praise. During my seasons of weakness and affliction, it was my ardent desire to be spared to see the arrival of a press and a printer. Thank God, I have not only been spared to see this, but to witness the press in full operation, and to carry with me specimens of its first productions. I will forward a few of them to the Committee."

At the time of parting, the children could with reluctance be induced to go. The family were attended by their Missionary friends * and a number of Christian natives to the boat. At the beach Mr. Turner was quite unmanned ;

* The Rev. William Cross was in later years connected with the Fiji Mission. While chairman of that District, and in the sixteenth year of his Missionary labours, he died at Somosomo on October 15th, 1842. Throughout his career he had been distinguished by ardent zeal for the work ; and when upon his last station he found it very unhealthy, he was unwilling to remove from it so long as he could do anything for his Saviour, or could encourage his brethren.

for " they all wept sore, sorrowing most of all for the words which he spake, that they should see his face no more. And they accompanied him unto the ship."

When at sea, he thus wrote to the Committee :—

" My grief would have been greater on leaving them, had they not been provided with those who will gladly watch over them to do them good. More than two thousand copies of a First School Book of four pages had been printed before I left. Two thirds of a Second Book of twelve pages had been composed, and sixty hymns prepared. A Third School Book of twenty pages had been agreed upon. I hope the Scriptures will soon follow, a good portion being already in a forward state. In Nukunuku, between Tonga and Hihifo, a new chapel has been opened, a society formed, and a school established. It is a great consolation to me to know that I have left the Mission in a very prosperous state, with every prospect of still greater success. A little before we left, Mr. Thomas sent me a most encouraging account of the state of things with them. They had just opened a new chapel at Lifuka, longer than one at Nukualofa : upwards of two thousand persons were present at the opening services. Nine classes had been formed, with constant additions. More than five hundred persons are now meeting as members with us. What hath God wrought ! and what may we not soon expect ? I sincerely hope your friends will soon allow you to send additional help to the Tonga Mission. In the event of all Tonga embracing the Gospel, five Missionaries at the least will be absolutely necessary for that island. Two I hope may do for the Haabais, and two for Vavau.

" There is certainly an important Missionary field among the Fijis, and I think you will do well to make a beginning there."

As far as I have been able to ascertain, it appears to be among the honours of Mr. Turner as a Missionary, that he was the first who specially recommended to the Committee the Fiji Islands as a sphere of Mission labour. That field, however, was not occupied for some years afterwards.

The voyage to Sydney takes usually about fifteen days; but the vessel being light and the winds contrary, it was a long passage. Fortunately Mr. Turner was a good sailor, and the protracted voyage, which in some respects was " uncomfortable enough," proved of great benefit to his health. The vessel twice ran short of supplies. She sent boats ashore on the coast of New Holland for fire-wood, and then had to call in at Port Stephens for food. They reached Sydney after six weeks, Mrs. Turner being much enfeebled through sea-sickness.

CHAPTER XII.

1831–1835.

While Mr. Turner had been in Tonga, a variety of untoward circumstances had militated seriously against Methodism in New South Wales. He wrote of it as follows:— "The Rev. William Walker, a talented man, had not only ceased to prosecute his Mission among the poor aborigines, but to be a minister among us. Another excellent and gifted brother, the Rev. Ralph Mansfield, had been induced, under circumstances of peculiar trial, to relinquish his ministry, and enter upon secular engagements. The Rev. William Horton had returned to England. Mr. Leigh, who was stationed at Parramatta, had lately followed the remains of his dear wife to the tomb, was reduced to great weakness both of body and mind, and was utterly unfit for any ministerial duty. Poor Mr. Erskine was quite incapacitated by severe asthma for his charge in Sydney. Our church in New South Wales was now a wreck, and the few faithful in our Israel mourned the desolations of Zion. Windsor was left without any one to conduct the services of the sanctuary."

In this state of things the arrival of an earnest minister, able to work, was welcomed in the colony. As there was a vacant house furnished in Parramatta, it was deemed best that Mr. Turner should reside there, and labour chiefly in that Circuit, until he should receive from Conference a definite appointment. His previous brief residence there had made him many friends, and, in their midst, he entered heartily upon the Lord's work.

He found " much, very much, to discourage, and some things at which his heart sickened."......Nevertheless there were a few who cheerfully united with him in crying, " Come, O breath, and breathe upon these slain, that they may live." A heavenly influence attended the word. The congregations increased, and sinners were converted. To the few then in church fellowship this was as life from the dead.

On the 31st of August, the brethren Manton and Simpson arrived in Sydney, for the colonial work : at the same time Mr. Turner received his Conference appointment to Hobart Town. Mr. Manton relieved him at Parramatta ; but he was several weeks detained by family affliction. His infant child, through Mrs. Turner's hardship and sickness during the six weeks' voyage from Tonga, lay dangerously ill. When he had been released from his sufferings, his parents received grace to say, " The Lord gave, and the Lord hath taken away : blessed be the Name of the Lord." His dust rests in the same tomb with that of Mrs. Leigh, in the Episcopal Church burial ground.

A voyage of nine days in the brig " Argo " was completed on the 24th of November, and the Mission family were in Hobart Town again. Their welcome was worthy of the friends Mr. Turner had left ten years before. With Messrs. Chapman, sen., Hiddlestone, Hopkins, Mather, Dunn, Barrett, Sherwin, and others, he was at once at home. Their Christian confidence and fellowship were a deep pleasure after the solitariness of several years on Mission stations.

Thrice formerly he had laboured in the colonies, but only as a passing visitor. He now entered upon a tour of Circuit labour. To appreciate the character of his work, it will be advantageous to glance at the social and moral condition of the people, and at the position of Methodism at the time; at least, at such features of Van Diemen's

Land life as called for distinctive qualities in a Methodist preacher.

The population of Hobart Town had increased during the ten years from two thousand seven hundred to from six to eight thousand, the increase having been distributed among all classes. It was not an ordinary British population. The island having been selected as a home for the crime of England, a large part of the residents were convicts. In different parts of the island there were then about thirteen thousand of that class. By far the larger number of these had been the victims of ignorance and vice, and had, by their compulsory removal from the old country, lightened its moral atmosphere. But there were not a few from another class. From the crimes for which some had been expatriated, it could not be inferred that their home education had been meagre, or their surroundings those of vulgar vice. The courted ranks of fashion, and of exclusive social culture, had contributed not a few of the voyagers under the penal system.

The transportation system has been so written about from a political standpoint, as to have been made to appear an admirable arrangement for meeting the difficulty of England's crime; and, really, a stranger to ocular demonstration of its working, and to correct knowledge of its results, on reading some of the calmly prepared statements of the system and its regulations, might be disposed to suspend any preconceived unfavourable judgment. But facts in all social questions should command their value. Simultaneously with the labours of Mr. Turner, to be chronicled in this chapter, the philanthropic James Backhouse and George Washington Walker evinced a practical Christian interest in the unhappy class referred to. Their visits among them afforded those gentlemen ample opportunities of seeing the shadows of the system; and I now append their summary notice of it, published in 1862.

" It may be helpful to the reader, to state in precise terms the conditions which belonged to the sentence of transportation in Tasmania ; conditions designed to benefit the free settlers and subserve the interest of the colony, as well as to extend a moral reformation in the convict. The system, with all its merits and all its defects, belongs now only to the past. It was abandoned a few years since, and no convicts have latterly been sent to Tasmania or New South Wales, or any other Australian colony, except Western Australia.

" Convicts, on arrival in Tasmania, were assigned as servants to the settlers, from whom they received, in return for their labour, lodging, food, and coarse clothing, but no money. If they committed offences during servitude, they were punished by imprisonment in the gaols or penitentiaries ; by flogging ; by being sent to labour in the public works in a road party, or in a chain gang ; or, lastly, by being re-transported, as it were, to a penal settlement. The chain gang was a step more severe than the road party, as the prisoners had to work in irons, and wear a most degrading costume, and were guarded by armed soldiers instead of convict overseers. From the wretched character of the huts provided for their lodging, the exposure and hard labour to which they were subjected, and their scanty fare, both these punishments were extremely severe. The penal settlement was reserved for the most hardened offenders. The term of servitude for the assigned convict varied according to his sentence of transportation : if the sentence was for seven years, he had to serve four before he could have a ticket of leave for good conduct ; if for fourteen, six ; and eight years, if his sentence was for life. The ticket of leave in a great measure returned convicts to the condition of free men. They could hire out their labour for wages, or enter into business on their own account ; but they were not allowed to go beyond their own

district of the island, and were obliged to attend public
worship once in the week, and a general muster before the
magistrates once a month.   At the expiration of their term,
or earlier, if their conduct was satisfactory, a conditional
pardon was granted; and continued good conduct was
somtimes followed by a full pardon, which restored them
to all the rights of free men.   If the assigned prisoner was
convicted of any offence during the term of his servitude,
he forfeited the time that had elapsed, and had to commence anew; and the first conviction of the ticket-of-leave
man exposed its possessor to forfeit it, and to be returned
to that state of bondage from which he had been released.

"Macquarie Harbour, the seat in 1832 of a noted penal
settlement, is situated about the middle of the west coast.
Though in itself a magnificent haven, it is of most difficult
access, for which indeed it was chosen, as being more completely isolated from the rest of the world.   What with the
perilous passage of the bar, the nature of the winds which
prevail along that coast, and the dangers of the shore, it
would be difficult to conceive a spot more inaccessible on
the habitable globe; and in 1833, wearied with the difficulties of the situation, the government abandoned it, and
transferred the settlement to Port Arthur."

Messrs. Backhouse and Walker's several religious tours
by government permission favoured them in arriving at a
correct estimate of the working of the system; and one of
their reports, prepared at Governor Arthur's request, dated
June, 1834, comprehensively exhibits the general state of
the prisoner population of the colony, in their view of its
moral aspect.   That paper, which treats specially on prison
discipline, points out that the abuses were serious, and that
the modes of punishment were degrading, and induced
deplorable consequences.   They say,—

"It would not appear that the prevention of crime is to
be expected in any great degree from the dread of punish-

ment, but rather from counteracting the causes which lead to the commission of crime. By extending the means of education, by discouraging the sale and use of ardent spirits, by removing juvenile thieves as well as older adepts, by stimulating magistrates to suppress houses of ill fame, and to remove profligate women from the streets, by promoting a due observance of the Sabbath, by discountenancing every species of gaming, and by remedying those evils by which the labouring poor are oppressed in their wages, the principal avenues to vice would be closed, and the benefit would be incalculable in the prevention of crime."

Most prisoners have a dread of flagellation and of road parties and chain gangs, till they have once suffered such punishments: after this the generality of them exhibit a decided deterioration of character. Flagellation especially is degrading and excites revengeful feelings. The practice of sentencing men to work in chains as a punishment, apart from the mere purpose of restraint, appears to be contrary to sound principles of penal discipline. It is calculated to increase desperation of character; it is a part of that system of abstract vengeance which man is not authorized to inflict upon his fellow man.

In hundreds of instances, the early and natural effect of a blind and vengeful oppression of spirit and of everything precious in man, under the sanctions of irresistible authority, was a state of mind nearly approaching abject disbelief in future rewards and punishments. Indeed, very often such disbelief was avowed with too much evidence of sincerity in its unhappy subject. All this should be kept in mind in estimating the necessity, the difficulty, and the value of those befitting religious efforts for their spiritual emancipation, which Nathaniel Turner and other true-hearted servants of God were wont to make.

The British settlers of the day were a very mixed community. The government officials, though representing many families of station and culture, were as a whole an unlikely class to raise, or even maintain at its then standard, the morality of the land. The associations in nava or military life of many of them had but been exchanged in their Van Diemen's Land appointments for others even less friendly to private and social virtue. Many honourable and worthy exceptions there were, but they were not enough to exert more than a feeble influence. Another class of colonists were respectable families from India, who had been induced, by the attractions of climate and of prospective family advantages, to make the island their home. The agricultural settlers were numerous; but as the large majority of those of them who had immigrated in the earliest years of the colony had been of a very uneducated class, there had not existed any freedom of intercourse between them and the officers of the civil service and of the military. And although more recently a number of settlers of superior character and claims had established themselves, trusting to personal labour for their fortunes, they had not succeeded in breaking down the barriers of caste, which, so long as the representatives of the world's Saviour were so few, made seriously against the success of evangelistic effort. The pastoral occupation of the country had already commended itself, and there were numerous holders of flocks and herds scattered through the land.

Red coats and blue jackets were very conspicuous amongst those of yellow and grey. They were from the regiments of soldiers stationed in the city or distributed in inland towns, and from the numerous vessels detained for long periods in the harbour. Too intimately associated with these were many of the government police, who were themselves of the prisoner class, and who often shamelessly abetted the vices they were employed to expose.

Mr. Turner perceived, however, that the condition of things during his nine years' absence had considerably improved. In commerce, the sixpenny order and the rum-bottle had given place, as a circulating medium, to specie and the notes of incorporated banks; in law, the fiercest tyranny had been superseded by trial by jury; religious and public libraries had been instituted, and Sabbath school operations extended. Nevertheless, he found himself among a community whose general character was unlovely and unclean.

One chief reason of his satisfaction in being appointed to Hobart Town was its salubrity. He believed he would there be strong to labour. The anxieties, toils, and exposure of his career in New Zealand, and the enfeebling heats of Tonga, had so reduced his physical tone, as to have rendered such a climate almost a necessity. For the benefit of all concerned, and for the commendation of my native land, I will say a word as to its climate. It is peculiarly adapted to those who have long resided in a hot country. The cold is never severe, nor so great but that one may attend to outdoor duties during the day with comfort: the heat is so inconsiderable that in the height of summer harvesting is carried on throughout the day without injury or risk to health. Hot winds are very unusual; never lasting for more than two or three days in the year. The nights are always cool. From the surrounding expanse of ocean, there are frequent atmospheric changes, but the air is peculiarly dry and elastic. The tables of mortality compare favourably with those of any part of the world. Frosts are slight; snow seldom lies on the ground for more than a few hours. Two winters before Mr. Turner's going to Van Diemen's Land, snow had lain for a week at Oatlands, the highest land in the colony at that time settled ; but that was considered something extraordinary.

Ten years previously he had helped with his own hand

to dig a foundation for a Wesleyan chapel in Melville Street, and he now found upon the spot " a delightful place of worship, and its assemblies generally very good." Beside it was a Minister's house in course of erection. A gracious revival of religion had taken place some months before, and there was now a flourishing Sabbath school. His satisfaction with these features of the Circuit was increased by the arrival of several excellent Wesleyan families from England : among these were three valuable Local Preachers, Messrs. Wilkinson, Lovell, and Leach. All this was encouraging.   There was, however, a serious difficulty, which grieved him much, and hindered his work. A spirit of disaffection, unreasonable and injurious, resisted all efforts which hitherto had been made to allay it.   It had arisen thus :—Mr. Turner's predecessor, while enjoying the church favour which a warm affectionate disposition and pulpit gifts secure, had given up the ministry, and accepted a secular appointment.   Many of his friends conceived that in the circumstances which had led to his taking this step, he had been harshly treated by his ministerial brethren, and, in consequence, withdrew from Wesleyan fellowship and worship.   Although they gave to Mr. Turner personally a most cordial welcome, they held themselves off from the church in a factious spirit.

The Melville Street congregation was found large and comparatively intelligent.   Nine years' use of foreign languages had not favoured him as an English speaker, and Mr. Turner entered upon his work under a deep sense of his insufficiency.   However, with a mind richly imbued with Divine truth, and his heart full of love, he soon made full proof of his ministry.   The Lord gave him favour, and he believed himself in his right place.

On the 7th of December he welcomed from England the Rev. Joseph Orton,* appointed Chairman of the New South

* The Rev. Joseph Orton was born in Hull.   In 1826 he went to

Wales District, in place of the Rev. George Erskine, whose health had failed. The discharge of the " Auriga's " cargo occupying several weeks, Mr. Orton was detained in Hobart Town, and often preached there. His presence was opportune for the Annual Missionary Meeting, at which he gave an account of his persecutions and sufferings in Jamaica.

The new Chairman desired Mr. Turner's presence and aid at a special District Meeting, which it was needful he should hold in Sydney upon his arrival there. The call of duty appeared to come inopportunely; for he had lately had two voyages, and had but just entered upon an important Circuit, at a time when it required a vigilant and working presence. However, with him, Solomon's advice was a rule of life: "Whatsoever thy hand findeth to do, do it." He commended his loved ones and his Circuit to God, and was again afloat. In six days he reached Port Jackson. The Rev. Samuel Leigh had sailed for England the day before their arrival.* With the business-like despatch for

Jamaica, under appointment by the British Conference, as a Wesleyan Missionary. His earnest labours there for the welfare of the slaves so provoked the local government, that he was subjected to much persecution. After enduring imprisonment in a miserably foul gaol, and other hardships, he returned to England in 1829, much enfeebled. His known fitness to be entrusted with official responsibility influenced the Conference to appoint him Chairman of the New South Wales District. From the beginning of 1832, he laboured for about four years in Sydney, where he was much esteemed. Thence he removed to Hobart Town. He was the first Wesleyan Minister who preached the Gospel at Port Phillip, in Victoria. This was on Sunday, April the 24th, 1836. In March, 1842, he embarked on board the " Briton " for London. When doubling Cape Horn, he was seized with bronchitis, and from the effects of this attack his valuable life was terminated at the early age of forty-six years, on April the 30th. He died in great peace, expressing his assured trust in Christ.

* After his return to England in 1831, the Rev. Samuel Leigh was made Supernumerary, on account of his physical weakness. The re-

which Mr. Orton afterwards became well known, the brethren were called together. The following is from Mr. Turner's notice of the meeting.

" I was greatly pleased with the spirit and wisdom with which Mr. Orton conducted the meeting, but much pained by the disclosures made in answer to the searching inquiries as to moral character, and the proper exercise of discipline. The new Chairman wept like a child in deep sympathy for those concerned ; and, poor man, after all his pity and tenderness, he was called to much suffering in consequence of the faithful discharge of his duty. I, too, shared in the reproaches of the misinformed in these matters, because I had been faithful to my conscience and my God in the information it behoved me to give. How true the saying of the wise man, ' One sinner destroyeth much good ! ' "

During his six weeks' absence, the Hobart Town pulpit was supplied by the Local Preachers. Concerning some of the hearers, (and there are many more of the same sort,) there is this entry in Mr. Turner's diary : " Lord, have mercy upon such souls as cannot feed upon Thy word, when delivered in so plain and faithful a manner." Though the Sabbath congregations were thin, the Lord was present. In one week three sinners found the Saviour. The class-meetings were lively. At several of the prayer-meetings the new converts pleaded most earnestly for the salvation of their friends.

Upon his return by the same vessel, Mr. Turner was tirement was of benefit to him ; and the Conference of 1833 again placed him in the itinerancy, and stationed him at Gravesend. Here and elsewhere in England he had Circuit work till 1844. The following year he settled as a Supernumerary in Reading. He continued, however, to take numerous journeys, to advocate the cause of the heathen at Missionary meetings. On Monday, November 24th, 1851, when making a Missionary speech at Blackwater, he had premonitory symptoms of paralysis, and on Sunday, May 2nd, 1852, he slept in Jesus.

accompanied by Miss Rothwell, who, as Mrs. T. J. Crouch of Hobart Town, has for many years been a devoted and much beloved servant of God, and of His church.

His spiritual life had been maintained, and, upon his resuming Circuit labour, he was in the full strength of grace. There were many towns and settlements accessible by Methodist agency, but too distant to be reached by the Circuit Minister; so, with the approval of the District Meeting, Mr. John Leach was engaged as a hired Local Preacher for the Circuit. He was a thorough Yorkshire Methodist, and very zealous. God had lately honoured him: many of the vilest offenders had turned and found grace under his preaching. The range of country allotted him comprised New Norfolk, The Ouse, Bothwell, Hamilton, Green Ponds, and adjacent neighbourhoods. Mr. Leach's zeal and work proved too much for his constitution, and after a few rounds of labour he was compelled to desist. By this beginning, however, Mr. Turner's labours were much increased; for, these few visits having created a desire for Wesleyan ministrations, several of the places could not be abandoned, and were at once put on the Circuit plan.

The March quarterly visitation was very encouraging. Mr. Turner's conciliatory spirit and manifest singleminded-ness had left party feeling nothing to feed upon, and peace had been fully restored. Many flocked to Melville Street chapel, and to numbers the Gospel came, not in word only; so that believers, "walking in the fear of God, and in the comfort of the Holy Ghost, were multiplied." The whole band of Local Preachers entered heartily into every plan for extending the work.

At a social meeting at the Mission house, over which Mr. Turner presided, it was resolved to have a Sabbath school out-door festival. The occasion is remembered with lively satisfaction, as having given rise to the delight-ful annual gathering of the Sabbath scholars, now numbering two thousand, in whose welfare the Christian churches of Hobart Town take much interest.

Through the influence of the Rev. Benjamin Carvosso, Sir George Arthur had some years before applied and arranged for a Wesleyan Missionary to be sent to Macquarie Harbour, then the penal settlement of the colony. The Rev. William Schofield had been appointed, and had been signally blessed in his labours. A change of station was now being effected between Mr. Manton of New South Wales and Mr. Schofield; and, in connexion with their removal, Mr. Turner had, for a short time, association with each of these Ministers.

The town of Launceston, second in importance to Hobart Town, had a population of more than a thousand; and Mr. Turner and Mr. Manton arranged for a hurried evangelistic visit, in the hope that it might lead to the effective re-occupancy of that town as a missionary station. They travelled one hundred and twenty-one miles there, and the same distance in return, on horseback. Mr. Turner rode a young animal, newly broken in, with paces admirably adapted to mortify the flesh. He found the motion somewhat different from that of a Maori wherry, or of a Tonga canoe; and, at the end of each day's travel, "could scarcely sit, stand, or walk." But he was no worse off than his friend. Mr. Manton had a lively recollection ever afterwards of Mr. Hiddlestone's Timor. It was a long time before he got rid of the soreness at his chest and shoulders, caused by the strain of pulling him in for the greater part of two hundred and forty-two miles. They preached at Mr. Johnson's, at Green Ponds, and at Captain Horton's, at Ross, to small but interested congregations. In Launceston they were cordially received by Mr. Isaac Sherwin, a cousin of Mrs. Turner, and by his young bride. Their visit was made a great blessing to both host and hostess, who then received impressions under the influence of which they afterwards both gave their hearts to God, and their lives to His church.

They spent Friday and part of Saturday in visiting. On the Sabbath they held three services in the court house. Many heard the word, which was attended, on each occasion, by gracious influences. It was made spirit and life to several souls. The sermon Mr. Turner preached on the value of the soul was specially owned by God as the means of salvation. The Lord gave His servants favour with the people. Many of the principal townspeople called, and invited them to their homes ; and, among the number, the Episcopal clergyman. General regret and complaint were expressed that the Missionary Committee had, some years before, withdrawn a Minister from Launceston, after a favourable beginning had been made there. The cause had been want of funds to sustain older and established stations. The Missionary visitors were of opinion that, as soon as possible, a Minister should be obtained. Mr. Turner promised them another visit shortly. On Monday morning horse and pony were remounted. At Ross and at Green Ponds the word of life was again preached, and on the third day they finished their journey.

At the six o'clock prayer-meeting on the quarterly fast day, the vestry was more than crowded, and the people had to go into the chapel. So at the noon-day service, several who had lately been brought from the very gate of destruction into Gospel liberty, gave up their employment for the day, and spent the whole of the forenoon in the schoolroom, in prayer and praise. On the Monday morning following, at six o'clock, a special prayer-meeting for the outpouring of the Spirit was held, and a blessed influence prevailed.

Mr. Turner held many toilsome services among the poor prisoners of all classes. He was full of sympathy for them, and occasionally addressed hundreds of them in the barracks, after their day's duties were over. He knew the Healer of hearts, and how to lead men to Him. In these services he laboured hard, but with much tenderness towards his hearers ; and it was one of the greatest encouragements to know that this kind of labour was by no means in vain.

Sir George Arthur had from the beginning of his vice-regency evinced a desire for social and moral reform in the land he governed, and his personal character and domestic arrangements were on the side of religion. The abettors of social laxity were reproved, if not restrained, by the example of family piety at Government House. The obvious disinterestedness and earnestness of Mr. Turner's life and labours gained him the Governor's confidence and hearty good-will. All superintendents of road gangs were instructed to suspend labour, and muster the men for worship, on every occasion when he might desire to address them. This advantage was freely but judiciously made use of. Often during a long day's ride he would pull up, and while his horse stood tied to a fence, or was being held by one of his hearers, he would kindly but faithfully address some scores of unhappy men. In exhibiting the hope set before them in the Gospel, he would mingle his tears and prayers with theirs. This kind of service occupied a short half hour, and he not unfrequently held several such during the same day. By this means many a prodigal was led to say, " I will arise, and go to my Father."

To the poor men, heart-sore, and almost hopeless of peace, how much more welcome must have been such services, than were the ordinary official Sabbath utterances of a paid magistrate ! The subjoined discourse of one of this latter class was impressed on the memory of the relator by its frequent delivery. It is taken from " The History of Tasmania," by the Rev. John West :— " Now, my men, listen to me. I want you all to get on. I was once a poor man like you ; but I used to work perseveringly, and do things diligently, and as such was taken notice of, until I became a captain of the 46th. Now I want you to work perseveringly, and do things diligently, and that will make you comfortable ; and I will assist you, that you may have houses for yourselves, and rise up to be equal to me."

About this time Mr. Turner formed the acquaintance of Mr. Philip Oakden, who had recently arrived in the colony and settled in Launceston. For some years Mr. Oakden had been a merchant in Hamburg, but more recently in England, where he had become a member of the Wesleyan Church. He had at once joined himself in Christian fellowship with the few converts lately formed into a class in Launceston, and whose first meeting place was Mr. Knowles's wool shed. Mr. Turner's second journey across the island was in company with Mr. Oakden. He was delighted with his spirit and with the prospective advantage to the cause of God by the timely arrival of one of his matured intelligence, piety, and zeal. His humility and meekness impressed the whole class and its leader, as on the second night after Mr. Turner's arrival he received his ticket of membership in their humble meeting place. [Mr. Oakden became a prosperous merchant, and enjoyed the confidence and profit of a very extensive commercial connexion. In 1837, the Union Bank of Australia, which has since been one of the largest commercial institutions in the Southern World, was founded in England, under his auspices. The undertaking, launched at his instance, commanded such favour that the whole capital, one million of money, was subscribed in a single day. Religion shone in his beautiful character, and Launceston Methodism ever benefitted by it.]

That visit was of great advantage. The little church was organized, and its members were strengthened by the addition of several persons of more than ordinary influence. Though Mr. Turner had plenty to do at Hobart Town, he felt it his duty to promise a quarterly visit until a Minister

should be appointed. He returned home thankful that the
Lord had opened so great and effectual a door. Upon the
journey each way he preached every evening.

"Our June quarterly visitation was, I believe, the best
our society ever knew in this part of the world. Glory be
to God! At our quarterly fast the power of the
Spirit came down so that many were led to cry aloud for
mercy. Several souls found peace with God. The spirit
of prayer was given in an extraordinary degree. Such
wrestling and pleading with God I never beheld in these
regions. I could almost have believed myself carried
back to one of our revival meetings in England, at one of
which I remember nearly one hundred souls professed to
have received forgiveness of their sins. Our people seem
all on fire. At most of our prayer-meetings, which are
numerously attended, souls are crying out for mercy. At
one meeting a man and his wife were kneeling side by side.
The man was made happy, and immediately prayed aloud
for his wife. She too found the Saviour."

Meanwhile, the Minister's wife who wrote the above, had
much to endure in home life. Education was expensive,—
from three to five pounds per quarter for a day scholar.
Clothing and food were very dear; so much so that the ministerial allowances were not sufficient by one third for household necessaries. More than one Missionary had retired from
the work, assigning as a reason that the Committee would
not allow them a maintenance, and another was in trouble
for having dipped into business under the same kind of
pressure. Under these circumstances it is not improbable
that another feeling mingled with the thankfulness with
which she received the loan of two tables and some chairs
for family use in her half-furnished house. All this kind of
trouble, however, was but slight in comparison with that
occasioned by forced association with so much that was
morally distasteful and injurious. In families needing

servants, domestic comfort was scarcely known. As a rule the assigned servants were most insolent and provoking: nor did the numerous homes in which the power of kindness was employed modify the evil. The forfeiture of liberty was regarded by almost every one of this class, after a short association with fellow prisoners, as almost hopelessly necessitating the permanent loss of character. Their wilfulness or the temptation by which they would absent themselves from their employer's house neutralized the good which otherwise Christian effort would have done them. The perverseness of the servant at the Mission house obtained for her from the magistrate "six days' solitary confinement." This of course meant six days' extra toil and confusion for her mistress.

The amount of drunkenness in the town was something awful. Thirty inquests were held in rapid succession, and it was ascertained that twenty-eight of the untimely deaths had been caused by drinking. Both parents deeply felt for their children having to breathe such tainted air. On either side of their residence, close by, was a public house ; and from different parts of the town, as well as from the immediate vicinity, they often heard the cry of "Murder! Murder!" proceeding from the wretched victims of drunken broils. The parents feared for their children, who saw more vice in a week than they had known in all their lives.

The moral necessities without and the constraining love of God within the church developed many active charities. A temperance movement, in originating which Messrs. Backhouse and Walker had taken a prominent part, was sustained with much spirit. Mr. Turner had no hesitation in giving it all the influence of his example and advocacy : he preached in its favour from the pulpit. The Bible and Tract Societies, as well as the Benevolent Society, all received a quickening impulse, and the Sabbath schools prospered.   A weekly prayer-meeting for women was made a great blessing, and in the Teachers' prayer-meetings there was power with God.

Messrs. Backhouse and Walker had now spent some six months in Hobart Town, and in visiting different parts of the island.   Through the kindly favour of the Governor they had had many advantages in prosecuting this chosen mission.   Their conversations in the cottages of the poor and in the resorts of sailors were welcomed and made useful.   The chain gangs and other portions of the government population had much of their Christian sympathy; and indeed the reports they felt it their duty to submit to the Governor, had an influence upon the moral welfare of the class concerned, in modifying official abuses, and otherwise.   With much toil and fatigue they visited numerous scattered settlers in out-of-the-way places; and with the best results.   A chief part of their Mission was to do their utmost to redeem the community from the scourge of intemperance.   They also made great efforts to secure provision for the religious care of the aborigines, of whom at that time there were considerable numbers.

Mr. Turner shared the general feeling of esteem in which the Christian people of Hobart Town held those gentlemen, who naturally enough found themselves much thrown among the Wesleyans.   Their friendship and somewhat free co-operation with the church, however, had an undesirable effect not anticipated at the time, but which has since had its correspondences elsewhere, where intelligent Quakerism has been established.   Some worthy heads of families suffered their attachment to Methodism to be weakened by the peculiar views they adopted from the Quakers, and have since remained its friends outside the pale.

A letter, dated October, addressed to the Committee, tells of success and of hope.   The observance of the quarterly fast days with prayer, and of the weekly band-meetings, is named as the occasion of increased spiritual life: for many months these special meetings had been seasons of special blessing. It reports Mr. Leach's failure of health. Colonel Arthur had given him a passage to Launceston. While there, he had been the means of saving souls, and stirring up the church. He had been appointed Catechist to a road gang in the North. At a later date he was appointed Chaplain to the convicts at Norfolk Island. His dust rests in that lonely isle, awaiting the resurrection unto life.

The church accommodation in Melville Street had of late been insufficient, and now considerable enlargements were resolved upon. The additions to the church, and erection of spacious school-rooms and vestries, proved more expensive than had been anticipated, and there was no Chapel Building Fund or Loan Fund to help. Mr. Turner was aware that the New South Wales Government had made a loan to the Trustees of the Macquarie Street chapel, and, upon this precedent, applied to Governor Arthur for a similar favour. His Excellency recommended that the application be made to the Executive Council. On its being considered, a Church dignitary who had a seat in the Cabinet, objected strongly to its being granted. He represented that some of the rooms specified as school-rooms would be used for class meetings, which had an "injurious tendency." The Governor pleaded for the applicant, and pointed at the near relationship of the Wesleyans to the Church of England. "They are the more to be dreaded on that account," was the reply. His Excellency reluctantly informed Mr. Turner of the unfavourable result of his application, and of the occasion of it; but added that he had power independent of the Council to lend the money, subject to the Secretary of State. He then inspected the rooms, and carefully inquired into their proposed uses, and without further hesitation granted the loan. Thus bigotry was defeated. The amount was lent without interest, and ultimately the principal was given.

On the 17th of October, the writer of this Memoir was dedicated to God and His church in baptism, by his father, in the Melville Street Wesleyan church. The earnest prayer of both parents that their first son born after their return from a Mission field should be devoted to the missionary work is not exactly realized, though from his early call he has been labouring in the Methodist ministry.

September, and the two following months, was a season of much suffering. Mr. Turner was almost a martyr to neuralgia; his whole system succumbed to its tortures, and for a time he had serious fears as to the issue. However, with the return of warm weather the malady left him. The last public service of the year was the Annual Missionary Meeting, when the recital of experiences in Maori-land and Tonga produced the best collection at that time reached at a Hobart Town Missionary Anniversary.

With the beginning of the new year came an affecting presentiment that it was to be his last year, and his first sermon was prefaced with an announcement to that effect. A large number responded to the invitation, " Come and let us join ourselves unto the Lord in a perpetual covenant."

The enlargement of the chapel afforded additional sitting room for a hundred hearers, and the new school-room for two hundred scholars, besides convenient rooms for library, classes, and prayer-meetings. The library had been established some years, its first officers having been Mr. Hiddlestone and Mr. T. J. Crouch. By this time it comprised a thousand volumes, and was much appreciated by the congregation. After the re-opening the Sabbath services were increasingly well attended, and on Monday evenings, at the prayer-meetings, the large upper school-room was uncomfortably filled,

It suited Mr. Turner's health and heart to be at the early Sabbath morning prayer-meetings. Though prudence restrained him from anticipating the calls upon his own physical strength, he found his spiritual powers quickened for the public engagements of the day: not, I imagine, by all he heard. A simple-minded bachelor brother used to pray, " Lord, convert the women, that we may have suitable companions on the way to heaven."

His sympathies with the church and the world did not begin outside his home. Some family manuscript before me shows that the unconverted state of their servant at the time gave much concern. She had been with them " more than twenty months, during the whole of which time all likely means her master and mistress could think of were employed to lead her to God, but as yet in vain."

Many of the soldiers stationed in Hobart Town were favourably inclined towards him, and were impressed by his preaching. A distinct class was formed for their benefit, which he conducted on Monday evenings, from six to seven o'clock. He was greatly delighted with their sincere and fervent piety. They soon grew into a large class, comprising privates, bandsmen, corporals, and sergeants. Most of them were comparatively young. One of them, known as " the little drummer," had been a sad scapegrace. His company had felt themselves degraded by his drunkenness and profanity, but in a short time they all admitted that " God had made him into another man through the Methodists."

The Lord sent upon the people " power from on high."' Many young persons, some of them of influence, joined the church. Their preacher was in labours more abundant. A full Sabbath's labour was three times preaching, two prayer-meetings, travelling, and short intervals among the sick and those in bonds.

Early in April he took his third journey to Launceston.

He found the Society prospering under the care of Mr. Leach and Mr. G. Stephenson, a Local Preacher recently from England. Among the services Mr. Turner held was a love-feast in Mr. Sherwin's parlour. At its close the members partook of the memorials of Christ's death. It was a time never to be forgotten. In 1859 Mr. Turner wrote:—"If my memory serves me right, it was at the close of that blessed Sabbath, after specially pleading with the Lord for them at the family altar, that my dear friends, the Sherwins, decided to become members of our church. They did so without delay, and have adorned it to this day. He is a very useful Local Preacher, Leader, and Steward, and Mrs. Sherwin has been a Leader for many years." The first Wesleyan baptism was during this visit. The subject of it has since died in Jesus.

On the return journey Norfolk Plains was visited for the first time. When fording the South Esk river while it was " in fresh," he narrowly escaped being drowned. He and Mr. Stephenson were encouraged by a man on the opposite bank to attempt the ford. Their horses were taken off their feet, and carried some distance down by the current, to within two yards of a position from which, had they gone so far, they could not have been saved. Providentially they gained footing just in time. Several had lost their lives in the same place under similar attempts. At Campbell Town, Ross, and Green Ponds, where he preached on both journeys, he was glad to find an increasing interest in the services.

It was scarcely to be expected that a Minister whose whole sympathies and power were given for the moral welfare of the community would quite escape calumny. An ecclesiastic in authority sought to lower the esteem in which the governor held him, and to restrict his access to the prison population. Mr. Turner missed the road party one morning from the service they had been used to attend at the O'Brien's Bridge chapel. He sought an interview with Sir George Arthur, and ascertained that it had been represented that he had authorized immoral persons to preach, and that Wesleyan ministrations were baneful in their influences upon the prisoners. He indignantly begged for the name of his informant. It was given. Now a good word for our kind friends the Quakers. Upon hearing of this scandal, which they knew to be such, in their own quiet way they volunteered their offices in the interests of truth, and, as they felt, of the prisoners. Upon their return from a long tour through the length and breadth of the land among the prison gangs, they presented to His Excellency a schedule of those whom they regarded as truly converted or reformed persons, specifying in each case the name, time of arrival in the colony, and place of employment, but especially the date and acknowledged agent in his conversion. The number of names submitted was between seventy and eighty, fully sixty of whom ascribed their change under God to Wesleyan ministrations. With his eyes thus opened by disinterested and competent witnesses, the Governor made further inquiry, and afterwards declared, before the whole Council, that the Wesleyans were doing more good among the prisoners than all the other denominations put together. The mouths of gainsayers were stopped, the clerical informant became a victim to his envy, and Methodism stood better than before in the esteem of the Governor. But bigotry dies hard, and the foolish gentleman was not cured. A condemned man expected to die upon the scaffold within a few days, and was glad of the Wesleyan Minister's conversation and prayers. Late on the Saturday he was sentenced to be hanged on the Tuesday forenoon. On Sabbath morning Mr. Turner was apprised of this decision, and of the poor man's desire to see him. He went, but at the gaol door was informed, to his surprise, that none but the chaplain would be admitted.

An application to the Governor, however, soon obtained him free access to the man, and to all others who desired his ministrations.

The visitation of classes in the June quarter showed an increase of members. Tidings came that in the Friendly Islands thousands had cast away their idols. The news fired the Missionary's soul. Men were wanted, and I do not wonder to find, from private journal entries, that his love to Tonga well nigh constrained him to offer for a re-appointment. The eight children and their education were considered, and the former breaking down of health was noted. Indeed, it would seem that all the *pros* and *cons* were talked over seriously; and the result was, that though neither Mrs. Turner nor he saw the hand of God indicating a removal to Tonga, both were willing to go, should it appear the call of duty.

On July the 20th, at a band-meeting, " several testified to the cleansing efficacy of the blood of Christ." The above is the only record I have of any event connected with the ministerial labour of that quarter; but it is enough. O! if all Ministers of God's word could, early in any quarter, secure a blessed testimony by several of their church that they had been filled with the Spirit of Holiness, there would be needed no pen to chronicle the results of the next four months' work. Would there not be " living epistles ? "

September 10th brought the English mail. One of Mr. Turner's brothers had been taken off by cholera. He had lived to God, and was " ready " when His messenger came. The morning before his attack saw him pursuing his daily custom of reading his Bible alone in a retired sequestered spot. The same post announced the deaths of several other relatives ; but of all of them the bereaved were able to say, " Blessed are the dead which die in the Lord."

As I have no record of the September quarter's labours, I extract a few lines from my dear mother's diary, begging to be excused by all for so doing. " I am tried at times with our servants......The children are a great charge. Our two eldest boys are rather refractory, and often, when returning from the means of grace, I feel so tried with the children and servants, that I seem to lose all the good at once. I have now had two female classes for a long time, and almost every class-day when I come home something is wrong."

On the 31st of December, Sabbath, Mr. Turner sailed by the brig "Neptune" for Sydney, to attend the District Meeting. She had a large number of passengers from London, who all attended morning service. In the evening he preached to them again, his subject being " The Ten Virgins." About midnight a passenger went to his berth, and requested him to pray to God for a pious sister of his, who, he said, would be praying for him at that hour in a watchnight service in England. The man felt that he could not pray. He had been a deist, but had had his conscience pricked under the sermon. Of that voyage Mr. Turner wrote, " I held service every night until we anchored in Sydney Cove. The captain manifested deep concern about his soul, and others, I believe, were savingly impressed by the truth. This was my happiest and most useful little sea trip."

The District Meeting was "harmonious, but long and tiresome." His return voyage was in a government brig, which for filth and discomfort exceeded all he had ever seen. She literally swarmed with vermin. The first night was wet, and he spent it on deck, standing under an umbrella, but preferred his lonely vigil there to the worse alternative offered in the cabin. On the 8th of February,. he regained his home in good health, and fully alive to God. His absence had been reluctantly submitted to, as neither his church nor his wife had been able to see that the ordinary business of a District Meeting should require such an expenditure of time and of money. Whooping cough had prevailed in the family, and their mother had been unwell.

The report presented to that District Meeting showed a considerable increase of members, mostly gathered from the world. His zeal inspirited his working band, lately increased by arrivals from England. Open-air services were resolved on. On the first three occasions, Mr. Turner preached to between two and three hundred. He was now able to visit the country places somewhat more frequently. Several interesting young persons were converted. They filled the ranks vacated by some who joined the church above. Their death scenes were of holy triumph. Among the most remarkable was that of Mrs. Rachel Lovell, a notice of whom appeared in the "Wesleyan Magazine" for 1836.

The periodical visits to Launceston were increasingly useful. After much effort, and some trial with the government, Mr. Turner obtained a grant for church purposes of an acre of land in Patterson Street, the site of our valuable church property there. The following reminiscence is given to the honour of the Hearer of prayer. "During one of my last tours to Launceston, a memorable circumstance occurred, which ought to be recorded to the glory of God. Captain Horton,* of Ross, had for a long time been in a declining state of health, from an affection of the throat, which up to that time had baffled all medical skill.

---

* Samuel Horton, Esq., was born at North Somercotes, Lincolnshire, on the 15th of May, 1796. From representations by the Rev. William Horton, his cousin, he was induced to settle in Van Diemen's Land, where he secured an estate near Ross. The reading of Wesley's Works was blessed to his spiritual welfare, and under the influence of Mr. and Mrs. Turner he joined the Wesleyan church. The grounds of Horton College, and a handsome donation towards the founding of the Institution, were his generous gift to Methodism. He died on the 10th of November, 1867.

On my arrival, I found him apparently near life's closing scene, and his wife in deep distress. The best skill had failed, and his case was deemed hopeless. We entreated Heaven fervently and importunately for his recovery, and, thank God, not in vain. On my return from Launceston, I found him greatly improved, and was assured that the change for life had commenced shortly after I had left. Captain Horton was spared to honour God with his substance."

The Conference of 1834 appointed the Rev. William Butters to Port Arthur, and the Rev. J. A. Manton to Launceston, where the warm-hearted friends were taking steps to build. By the same Station List, Mr. Turner was to remove at the end of the year to Sydney, but on account of Mr. Orton's family circumstances this was inexpedient; and it was therefore arranged for him to remain in Hobart Town another year. This was satisfactory, especially as Mr. Manton's appointment to Launceston would effectually serve the cause there, and leave him free for concentrated attention to his Circuit proper.

I am unable to chronicle the events of that year. The Rev. Stephen Rabone, the present esteemed General Secretary of our Missions, arrived in August, and remained for some months. His pulpit labours were very acceptable to the church, and were greatly owned of God. His intercourse with Mr. Turner laid the foundation of a lifelong warm friendship. The Melville Street chapel was ordinarily crowded on Sabbath evenings, and special efforts were put forth to secure a more copious outpouring of the Holy Spirit. Under the preaching on the first Sabbath evening in September many were awakened; and at the prayer-meeting eight or ten found peace with God. Throughout Van Diemen's Land there was a good work at that time. At Glenorchy, the darkness of many was turned to day. At New Norfolk, where for six months

public worship had been held in the Court House, steps
were taken to build a chapel.   Mr. Butters wrote from Port
Arthur that more than twenty had begun to seek salvation.
At Launceston, Mr. Manton was meeting with encouraging
success.

By personal conversation with the unconverted, Mr.
Turner secured many triumphs in Christ.   One day he
received a note from a stranger, a Mr. Struth, desiring a
visit.   On his entering the sick room, Mr. Struth said to
him, " I have sent for you, believing you will show me how
my soul may be saved."   He had known Mr. Turner by
sight and by reputation only.   He was a strong-minded
Scotchman of religious connexions, but had forsaken the
law of his mother, and had become the companion of
infidels.   God's light entered his mind with the instruction offered, and he was soon comforted and saved in
Christ.   By this case Mr. Turner was much cheered.

In December he closed his four years' term in Hobart
Town, amid the tears and prayers of a united, prosperous
church.   The sorrow of parting was relieved by the consciousness that he had been owned of God, not merely in
turning many to righteousness, but in permanently establishing Zion in various places.   The influence of those
four years' labour has been often acknowledged by his
successors, as they have witnessed the beautiful exhibitions
of Christian life on the part of many who were at that time
taught by the Spirit of God, under his preaching and
example.

MANY of the passengers by the ship " Brothers," bound
to Sydney, were gay and pleasure-loving. The prospect of
Mr. Turner's company from Hobart Town did not suit
their taste, and they told the captain that they objected to
his joining them. However, once among them, he immediately secured their respect, and before Sunday came they
requested him to conduct Divine service. He did so twice;
and at the end of the voyage received numerous expressions of gratitude. In Sydney his family were for several
weeks domiciled among friends.

Australasian Methodism has numbered many Ministers
to whom God has committed the talent of strong lungs and
fine voices ; but I venture to think no two out-door
associates in the preaching of the Gospel have excelled
Stephen Rabone and Nathaniel Turner when strong to
labour. Mr. Rabone's voice has yielded considerably under
the influence of a tropical climate and many years of hard
labour; but for a quarter of a century of his service in
these parts it was of marvellous compass and expression,
and very powerful withal. That of his friend Mr. Turner
was equally clear and commanding. The President of
Conference this year, the Rev. John Watsford, distinctly
heard the latter when preaching out of doors at Parramatta
at a distance from him of scarcely less than a mile. Mr.
Rabone spent a short time in Sydney on his way to Tonga,
and these Sons of Thunder aroused the city by the unaccus-
tomed services they held in the open air, in season and out

of season. The chapels were soon filled, and better still, many souls were saved.

The District Meeting passed over "comfortably." The Rev. Joseph Orton delivered up his charge, and Mr. Turner began a term of ministerial success in Sydney, which he anticipated would be for some years.

But it might not so be. The New Zealand Mission had become sadly disordered, and Mr. Turner had been appointed to proceed thither and direct its affairs as Chairman. This was a severe trial, especially as he had a large family, for whom New Zealand could not supply the education they needed. The Committee, however, had written to him in the kindest manner, expressing regret that they had felt compelled to lay such a burden on him, yet hoping for his compliance, if only for two or three years, until the affairs of the Mission should be brought into a better state.

The Rev. John M'Kenny was appointed his successor, and Mr. Turner prepared to remove so soon as Mr. M'Kenny should arrive. He could not leave any of his children as boarders in Sydney, and parental anxiety was considerable. A kind providence, however, relieved his difficulty. At that juncture Mr. James Buller, an intelligent young married man, with good credentials as a Local Preacher, arrived from England, and Mr. Turner engaged him as tutor to his family in New Zealand for two years. That arrangement was ever looked back upon with much mutual satisfaction. Mr. Buller had come out to settle in New South Wales, under the hope and impression that it would in some way lead him to the work of a Missionary, to which his heart was drawn; and so the event proved. While kindly and efficiently fulfilling his engagement, he evinced more than ordinary intelligence, as well as aptitude and zeal for the Mission work. This led to his being recommended to the Conference, and received as a Missionary. Since that date he has uninterruptedly laboured hard in

New Zealand, with much success and honour, as well among the colonists as the Maoris. In 1864 he was honoured with the President's chair, and pleasingly sustained the confidence of the Australasian ministry and church. So much for my first teacher.

April the 3rd was Mr. Turner's last Sunday in New South Wales, before resuming Mission work. He had been unwell during the week, but yielded to persuasion to preach in the evening. As he walked up to Macquarie Street chapel, the harbour view was enlivened by the inward course of a London ship. While he was preaching on the joy of angels over one sinner that repenteth, several Ministers holding God's commission to preach the same joyful truth entered the chapel. After sermon they surrounded the table of the Lord, and the Sacramental Supper proved a bond of love in that service of missionary farewell and missionary welcome. The six Missionaries by the "Bencoolen," of whom five were at the service, were the Revs. John M'Kenny, W. A. Brooks, John Spinney, Matthew Wilson, D. J. Draper, and Frederick Lewis. They were a valuable addition to the laborious and excellent brethren of the day. All, save one, have finished their course; the Rev. Matthew Wilson is an esteemed Supernumerary Minister residing at Adelaide.

On Friday, Messrs. Rabone, M'Kenny, and Draper accompanied the Mission family to the ship, and commended them to God. Wind failing, "The Patriot" anchored in Watson's Bay. On Sunday morning they put out with a fair gentle breeze and a smooth sea. At eleven o'clock Mr. Turner preached to the ship's company from, "The Lord preserveth all them that love Him : but all the wicked will He destroy." (Psalm cxlv.) The next Sabbath was " one of the best he ever spent at sea." On the 23rd, when in sight of port, they were boarded by the Rev. William White from a schooner, by which he had just started on a

visit to the southern stations. There came on a gale,
however, which drove them far south; so that they did not
reach their anchorage within the Heads for several days,
having been three weeks on board. They were soon surrounded with Maoris in their canoes, with fresh fish and
kits of potatoes, for sale in exchange for tobacco. On the
shore, meanwhile, were seen numbers of them squatting
on their haunches, wearing a native garment of coarse flax,
which, as it fell over their broad shoulders, made them look
like so many thatched beehives. Those who came on board
were very civil, though noisy,—the men of fine physique.
Their faces and bodies were tattooed. Some wore a
blanket, others a Maori mat around the loins. The next
day with flood tide the vessel went up the river, and at five
P.M. anchored off the Mission station, twenty-two miles from
the Heads. It was well called "Mangungu," which means
" broken to pieces." The scenery around was very bold.
It seemed as though nature in some fantastic mood had
moulded the country into all rugged forms. On every side,
as far as the eye could reach, lofty hills succeeded each other,
range upon range,—those distant from the bleak coast
being covered with forests of fine timber. The old Maori
legend seemed realized. It says that when Maui fished up
New Zealand from the bottom of the sea, his brothers,
afraid of the huge marine monster, fell to with their
paddles, and sliced up his back into hollows and ridges;
and hence the broken surface of the country. Several
large tributaries flowed into the main river, meandering, as
was afterwards found, through luxuriant valleys of rich
alluvial deposit.

The occasion and results of Mr. Turner's second appointment to New Zealand are alluded to as follows, by one of
the senior Missionaries, who was associated with him
during that term,—the Rev. James Wallis.

"The state of the New Zealand Mission requiring the

immediate inspection and oversight of some one, who, regardless of human favour or power, and indifferent to any degree of obloquy that might be cast upon him in the discharge of his duty, would prove himself a servant of God, Mr. Turner was appointed by the Missionary Committee in London to take the superintendency of the Mission. At the sacrifice of much personal and family convenience, he cheerfully returned to this country, and was welcomed by the Missionaries already in the land, as the very man they needed to counsel and guide them in the circumstances of difficulty and perplexity by which they found themselves overtaken. The confidence they reposed in him was not misplaced; but, on the contrary, was soon rewarded with all their hearts could desire in the improved position of the Mission, and in the cheering prospect of increasing usefulness in various directions."

At public worship on the first Sabbath, two hundred devout New Zealanders were present; their demeanour contrasting most favourably with what Mr. Turner had been accustomed to see eight years before at Whangaroa. In the afternoon, the English congregation numbered fully twenty, including the Mission families. In the evening he was delighted with a native youth, named Timothy, preaching on the parable of " The Sower."

Much had been done by the Missionaries. The manners of the people had been softened, and Christianity was becoming popular. The Missionaries of the Church and Wesleyan Societies had co-operated in brotherly love, and their printing presses had been mutually helpful. The Sabbath was observed, the Scriptures were read, and knowledge was increasing: indeed, " the fields were white unto the harvest."

On the Tuesday, Mr. Turner was politely received by the British Resident, Mr. Busby, and in the evening held the first English prayer-meeting. At this means of grace he was consciously strengthened for painful trials. Next Sabbath morning he read prayers at the public native service. In the afternoon he heard nearly seventy Maories speak at a lovefeast, at which two hundred were present. The testimony of several was very pleasing. The day after, one of his fellow voyagers, brother of the Rev. J. Wallis, was drowned. He had gone from the colony on purpose to see his brother, but had found a watery grave before that brother could arrive from his station.

Pursuant to an arrangement, made between the London Committees of the Church and the Wesleyan Missionary Societies, as to territorial limits of church operations, it had been determined to withdraw our agents from Kawhia and Waikato, and to concentrate our labours by forming two new stations near Mangungu; and Mr. Turner received peremptory instructions to that effect. In selecting sites he sought earnestly the guidance of God. In company with Mr. Woon, he visited the entire neighbourhood of the Heads of the Hokianga River, and purchased a suitable area from Woetara, a principal chief.

During the next week he visited the Church Mission families at the Bay of Islands. On his way he was overtaken by darkness and rain, and had to shelter for the night in a native hut. He was pleased to find that the occupant had been baptized into the church of Christ, and was accustomed to read among his people the Word of God. Renewed friendship with the Revs. H. and W. Williams he much enjoyed, and wrote : " Had much profitable intercourse with them on missionary operations in New Zealand. They are most valuable men, and God has crowned their labours with considerable success in the temporal and spiritual welfare of many around them." On leaving he passed a number of natives who had been encamped by the wayside for the night. Having just arisen, they had met together to offer their morning sacrifice to God, of whom till lately they had not heard. One, who appeared to be the head of the party, was reading a chapter from St. Luke, as their morning lesson. Journeying on, he saw a number more, just separating from morning worship in their chapel. He halted at the homestead of a Christian Maori chief, whom he had known as a heathen. He was now a successful dairy and agricultural farmer. The villages he passed through were Christian. Each of them had its school-chapel, regularly used for a school and for public worship.

Mr. Turner had now to endure severe personal affliction. While suffering from a cold, he left home for the Heads, to give directions for the building of a temporary Mission house at the new station. His cold was seriously increased by undue exposure on the water. This brought on fever, under which he lay delirious for some days. In this state he was conveyed home in Captain Young's boat. Dr. Smith was called to him, and also the Rev. William Williams, of the Church Mission, who kindly spent several days with him. By God's blessing on their united efforts, the fever was overcome; reason returned, and Mr. Turner recovered. It was many weeks, however, before he regained his usual vigour. After his recovery he distinctly remembered two circumstances by which his mind had been affected during delirium. The first was a powerful temptation or inclination to drown himself in the river, while on his passage home in the boat. From this fearful act he had been mercifully withheld by the interposition of his eldest son, who providentially was with him at the time. The second was a persuasion that reason would never return, and that thenceforth he would be an inmate of the Lunatic Asylum, in New Norfolk, Tasmania. In this, however, he took comfort in the thought that his old friend Dr. Officer had charge of the institution, and that he would treat him well. It was felt to have been the kind hand of God which saved his family from bereavement.

On Friday, the 17th of June, the brethren Whiteley and Wallis arrived from the southward, pursuant to an arrangement above noted. Their presence was a great comfort to Mr. Turner in his then weakly state. On the 26th, he again joined in the public worship, hearing Mr. Whiteley * preach. In July and August his official duties brought him

* The Rev. John Whiteley was born of pious parents at Kneesal, Nottinghamshire, England, on July 20th, 1806. From childhood he feared the Lord, but he was in his twentieth year when he obtained a satisfactory assurance of his acceptance with God. At this period he was connected with an Independent church. Soon after his conversion he removed to the vicinity of Newark, where he became a Local Preacher in the Wesleyan Methodist Society. In 1831 he was accepted as a candidate for the missionary work, to which he believed himself called by the Holy Ghost. He received an appointment to New Zealand, whither he went in 1832. He entered upon his important work in the spirit of self-sacrifice. As a Missionary he was in labours more abundant, being unremitting in attention to their wants, both temporal and spiritual. He was eminently a man of peace, and often exposed himself to great danger in attempting to effect a reconciliation between hostile and contending tribes. He had the unbounded confidence of the natives, who regarded him as their counsellor and friend. The British authorities also consulted him in their efforts to adjust the differences that had unhappily arisen between the two races in the Taranaki part of the island. In consequence of the rebellion of the natives against British rule, portions of their lands were confiscated, and were given to Europeans as a compensation for losses sustained by them in the war. The spiritual wants of the settlers located on these lands were regularly ministered to by Mr. Whiteley, and it was while on one of those errands of mercy he met his death. He left his home on the morning of Saturday, February 13th, 1869, intending to ride upwards of thirty miles to a settlement, where he was to pass the night, so as to be in readiness to begin his Sabbath work. When within a short distance of his journey's end, he was waylaid and shot down by murderous savages. He died in the sixty-third year of his age, and the thirty-eighth of his ministry.—From the Minutes of the Australasian Conference, 1870.

much trial. The latter part of August was spent in missionary work among the natives, in places somewhat distant from the station. He was much delighted with the Wacina valley. He found Tanhia, the principal chief, a shrewd, active man, and concerned for the religious welfare of his people. Among those to whom he ministered the word of life were five venerable men, each of them over threescore years and ten. Their earlier years had been spent in cannibalism, war, and every heathen abomination ; and it was delightful now to find them sitting at the Saviour's feet and enjoying His peace. Their chief had particularly wished that the Missionaries would spend some time with them, and Mr. Whiteley conversed with them till after midnight.

From various causes Mr. Turner did not, for some time after his arrival, attempt to preach in Maori. He had at first conceived himself unable, having been out of practice for nine years, during four of which he had been in the habitual use of another foreign tongue. Besides this, there had been no necessity, as other Missionaries sufficient for the work were on the spot ; and indeed lately his illness had unfitted him for public duty. However, on the 4th of September he made his first attempt, and was encouraged by the result.

If the estimate of New Zealand Missionaries, and of the Maoris themselves, is worth anything, Mr. Turner became one of the most effective speakers of that language our Missions have known. He not only understood well idiomatic Maori, but he had in a high degree the faculty of adaptation, so that as a preacher he could be " all things to all men." Understanding well their favourite proverbs, parables, and similitudes, he could select telling figures of speech, and with the utmost facility employ them with convincing effect. He was much helped by the fire of his eye, and the life of his voice and manner,—characteristics of which his native friends often spoke with admiration.

The Spirit of the Lord and of His work took hold of the missionary band. The English class and prayer-meetings were times of refreshing. On Saturday, the 17th, Messrs. Turner and Woon visited the tribes at the head of the Mangamuda river. A West India hoe did duty for a bell, and they held service. After Mr. Woon had preached, tickets of membership were given for the first time to those who had been meeting in class. This being a new thing, the natives did not at first appreciate it. After a while the token came to be valued. At early Sabbath-morning worship fully two hundred were present. Mr. Turner preached from " The Rich Man and Lazarus," and then met for instruction a number of candidates for baptism.

The subjoined entry shows an interesting variety of engagements for a single Sabbath.

" Sunday, 25th.—Our native congregations were very good. Captain M'Donnell and three other Europeans were present. After service I united in marriage Samuel Davenport and Mary Anne Perry, our servant ; afterwards met a number of candidates for baptism, with most of whom I was pleased. Our English service at three was better attended than usual. Captain Gedney, of the ' James Laing,' and six of his crew, were present. After service baptized James Martin, Mr. Buller's infant son. ' May the Angel of the Covenant bless the lad ! ' Held a meeting in the evening with our native Leaders and principal members, to set a few crooked things straight. We required that each baptized person should retain his native surname. Some who had not been taught the propriety of this strongly objected. It transpired that the chief objectors were those whose native name was ugly, or had an evil meaning. Then we proposed that all such should be allowed to exchange their old name for another. The difficulty vanished."

A month later the services of a memorable Sabbath were recorded. The chapel was overflowing. Mr. Wallis read the Liturgy, and addressed the congregation on baptism. Mr. Turner counselled the candidates ; Mr. Whiteley read the service for the occasion ; after which more than one hundred adults were baptized. Many of them were of hoary hairs, and three were chiefs of rank. They were true triumphs of the Cross. After the English service in the afternoon twenty-seven couples, part of those baptized in the morning, were married. In one case Mr. Turner felt special interest. Moses Tawhai, the chief of Waima, in his heathen state had had two wives, the elder of whom he loved the better, though she was childless : the other was the mother of his children. It had been a long and hard struggle with him whom to marry. At length he chose his children's mother. She was the slave girl whom Mr. and Mrs. Turner had redeemed at Whangaroa, but who had afterwards been forcibly taken from them. Old Moses Tawhai, who was then an elderly man, is still alive and active. In his youth one of the most renowned warriors of his day, he has now been a soldier of Christ for more than thirty years. He is described as having an eye of fire, sinews of steel, and the tongue of an orator ; his natural force is not abated.

The first regular District Meeting held in New Zealand closed on the 25th of October. It was one of harmony. Certain events of the previous year occasioned much pain, and the heavy expenditure, though unavoidable so far as he had been concerned, depressed the Chairman. On Sunday many of the children of those lately received as church members were baptized, and at the same service Mary Fletcher Whiteley and Edwin Turner Woon were also dedicated to God. In the evening more than one hundred

New Zealanders were admitted to the Lord's Supper. They approached the table with greater reverence and solemnity than could have been expected. The native Leaders had evinced scrupulous care that no improper person should be admitted.

On Monday morning Mr. Turner went to Mangamuka to visit an European, who was alarmingly ill. The same day he began a journey to Kaipara, in company with Mr. Whiteley. At night they reached Captain Young's, at the Heads. By early and continuous travel next day, they gained at nightfall the usual halting-place. Here they rested on beds of fern. Their third morning's journey was through one of the roughest woods ever travelled. By noon they made Kaihu, in the Kaipara district, situated in the centre of a magnificent valley. In the evening Mr. and Mrs. Wallis welcomed them to their temporary abode at Wairoa.

The Kaipara district had been decided on as the sphere of Mr. Wallis's labours ; and on the 3rd of November the three Missionaries started to search for a suitable site for the intended station. They travelled during very unfavourable weather by boat, pulling forty miles against the Wairoa stream, intending to search Mangakaihia. Night coming on, they stopped at a small village, and were glad to shelter from the rain in an old potato house. The chief Tirarau had been made aware of their visit and its object ; he met them at this village, and cordially furthered their purpose. He conducted them to the site he thought best ; they approved of his choice, and, without much difficulty, " purchased the land required for forty pounds,—half cash, the other half in articles of barter." The prospects of the Mission seemed pleasing, but Mr. and Mrs. Wallis would have a lonely time of it. The return journey was hazardous, as the swollen rivers could only be passed at much risk. Mr. Turner reached home just in time to attend the funeral of Mr. Mitchell, who had died the previous day. At the grave-side more Europeans were present than had been seen together before. A deep solemnity prevailed as he addressed them on the words, " Set thine house in order; for thou shalt die, and not live."

There were white heathen in those days at Hokianga. One Sunday word was brought that a European neighbour some miles up the river had been robbed, and that the ruffianly perpetrators had intimidated others. He acquainted the chief, and in fifteen minutes a competent number started in company with the Missionaries to give an account of them. November 26th.—" There have been serious disturbances on the river, and but for the providential interference of Mr. Whiteley, blood would have been shed. All were armed, and wrought up to desperation. We are surrounded by an awful set of desperately wicked fellows. Satan is making vigorous efforts to scatter, slay, and tear our little flock, gathered from among the heathen people. But the Lord reigneth, and can turn to foolishness the counsel of every Ahithophel."

Early December brought letters from the colonies, and glad tidings of the Lord's work in Tonga. Mr. Turner wrote :—" It does us good to know that we have the sympathies and prayers of the Lord's people in many lands. On the 3rd we committed to the dust the remains of Samuel Butler, the son of one of the first Church Missionaries in New Zealand. He had been drowned in the river : his widow and children were for some time under the care of the Mission." On Christmas morning an English service was conducted by the Rev. Mr. Bobart of the Church Mission. In the afternoon and evening Mr. Turner preached, also in English,—three sermons on Christmas Day !

The renewal of tickets that quarter was a pleasurable toil, and the watch-night service a season of grace and power.

His diary for the year closed with appropriate expressions of gratitude and renewed consecration.

On the first Sabbath in 1837, the natives manifested deep excitement under a sermon on the barren fig-tree. In the afternoon he met ninety candidates for baptism. Later in the day he preached again, and at the Covenant Service joined his Christian associates at the table of the Lord. On the same evening, Mr. Whiteley baptized Mr. Turner's infant child, who was named, in affectionate memory of a dear Hobart Town friend, " Sarah Eliza Hopkins."

The settlement was startled on Sabbath morning by intelligence that two native teachers had been shot dead by a small heathen tribe, to whom they had gone with the message of salvation. The Missionaries pulled up the river with all speed, and found the native Christians in great excitement awaiting their counsel. The occasion was as follows:— Three young men, Matthew, Rihimona, and Wiremu Patene, (William Barton,) a young chief of the first rank and of great promise, had often gone to visit a small tribe, to induce them to abandon heathenism. The tribe had rejected their message, and had warned them that evil would result if they repeated their visit. Without acquainting the Missionaries of this threat they went again, repeating to some of their friends, who suspected danger, their Saviour's words, " Fear not them which kill the body." The chief among the heathen villagers was named Kaitoke (Worm-eater). He was a ferocious fellow ; and as soon as Matthew and the others got within musket range, he and his men fired upon them. Matthew fell dead, and Rihimona mortally wounded. William Barton was unhurt, although three balls passed through his blanket. When the Missionaries arrived near the scene of blood, the principal men almost clamoured to be told at once what to do to the murderers. Said they, " We cannot, now that we have become Christians, treat our enemies like the New Zealand men do : we therefore look to you as our Christian fathers to guide us aright." This, however, was not the feeling of all. Many burned for blood-revenge. The Missionaries were in some difficulty. Retaliatory war would be un-Christian, and would lead to seriously hurtful results upon the native mind, and ruin the Mission. They reminded them of Christ's spirit towards His enemies. " But," replied the natives, " if these murderers go unpunished, it will only embolden all such like men to similar deeds."

The Missionaries returned late to their station, and together sought a few hours' rest on their chapel floor. On Monday morning early they joined their people in devo- tional exercise, thus beginning a day of still greater excite- ment. Maori couriers had gone in every direction, and by ten o'clock nearly six hundred people had assembled. Among them were all the principal chiefs. Many speeches were made,—some advising summary punishment. Mr. Whiteley and Mr. Turner proposed to accompany two or three of the chiefs to the murderers' village, to reason with the offenders. The people, however, knew Kaitoke, and replied that he would shoot them too. At this moment several musket shots were heard in the direction of the murderers' pa. The natives imagined that some of their friends had gone to reconnoitre, and been shot, and imme- diately rushed off towards the pa. Just when they got in sight of their pa, which was simply a trench dug in a con- venient spot, they received a succession of musket balls : one chief fell dead, and another seriously wounded. After the third shot, the Christian natives fired. Then the balls flew thick, some whizzing close by the Missionaries, who had followed to restrain them if possible from violence. Mediation just then was hopeless, and with reluctance they left the place.

Early on Tuesday morning they again left their homes,

to relieve the wounded and serve God as occasion might arise. Up the river they met their people returning, and found that after they had left them on the previous day, they had stormed the pa, put twelve to death, and taken the rest prisoners. Among the latter was Kaitoke himself, who had received a ball through his ankle. Several Christian natives had been wounded, but no others killed than those named. The affair illustrated the influence of the Gospel. After they had overpowered their enemies in the trench, not another blow was struck ; and, instead of enslaving their prisoners, they at once liberated them, and then brought their wounded down to the Mission station for medical care and attention. By this unhappy business seventeen lives were lost, many persons were wounded, and insecurity was generally felt among the tribes ; for at any hour a serious tribal war might now break out. The New Testament truly connects murder with covetousness. It was ascertained that the original cause of the murder was not so much hatred to Christianity as a dispute about a Kauri pine forest.

Mungungu was all life next day. Christian families, bringing with them their earthly belongings, poured in from every direction, that they might be shielded from their enemies by missionary influence. On the Sunday the chapel could not hold the crowd. Mr. Whiteley preached on Jesus weeping. After service a Leaders' Meeting appointed two new Leaders in place of the martyr Matthew, and one named Apollos, then

> " Passing through the watery flood,
> Leaning on the arm of God."

He and Robinson died next day.

" As iron sharpeneth iron, so doth the countenance of a man his friend." The Rev. Samuel Marsden visited Hokianga on the 23rd of February. He had arrived in the

" Pyramus," in company with his daughter Martha, the Rev. F. Wilkinson, a colonial Chaplain, and his family. On the Lord's day many assembled to see the founder of New Zealand Missions. After Mr. Turner had read prayers, the venerable servant of God addressed the multitude, Mr. Turner interpreting. The occasion could not but awaken general religious sympathy. There were the representatives of a nation, redeemed and raised from hellish horrors, gathered in a Christian sanctuary on the Lord's day, and lovingly addressed by the two men to whom, under God, more than to others, they owed eternal peace. Is it any wonder that the grey-headed chieftains and their rising descendants were moved to tears ? The same afternoon Mr. Marsden preached in English from, " Lord, what wilt Thou have me to do ? " It was a plain, profiting sermon. On the next Sabbath evening he administered the Lord's Supper, when the missionary friends, as united members of Christ's body, rejoiced together. When the visitors had left for the Bay of Islands, the prayer was penned, " May the Divine blessing rest upon them,—on His aged servant especially."

During the stay of the " Pyramus," loading spars for England, Mr. Turner often preached on board, by the captain's special request. Under his first sermon, one of the sailors was brought to concern for his soul.

Soon after a double murder was reported. It was not far from the station, and the Missionary hastened to the scene. He found that one of his Christian natives, while carrying his young child on his back, had been suddenly attacked by some unknown person, and literally cut to pieces with a hatchet, and that his body had been scalped with the same weapon. The murderer was a slave belonging to Pi, chief of Waima. Mr. Turner went over, to endeavour to secure a trial according to English usage. He learned that the man had already been taken by two Christian natives,

Moses and Andrew. While Andrew had gone to inform his master, Moses had sought, by talking with him of Christ and praying with him, to prepare the poor sinner for the death which he knew awaited him. Pi returned with Andrew, and shot him dead upon the spot. The occasion of the murder was a domestic broil. The man had quarrelled with his wife, and would have killed her, had he not been prevented. He left his home in a rage, saying, "A man shall be my payment," and slew the first he met.

On the 23rd of March a Sabbath school was commenced, at which about one hundred and fifty children were present. The talent required in the missionary teachers was temper. On the same day Mr. Turner preached to about seven hundred, on "The Prodigal Son." They appeared to devour the moral. Five hundred attended the lovefeast in the evening. Many spoke with freedom, and some with good effect, evidencing that the Spirit of God was their teacher. On the following Lord's day Mr. Buller for the first time preached in the Maori language. He had just been twelve months in the land, and acquitted himself with credit.

The European residents did not improve in character as time wore on. Most of them were sailors, sawyers, or timber dealers. They had only one interest in common,— spirit-drinking. During a fight between two timber dealers, at a Sabbath carousal, a man received mortal injuries. For several days Mr. Turner's time was much occupied with him. There were some spirits on his premises, which he feared would occasion more mischief after the man's death; so he begged him to have them destroyed. The death-bed penitent called to a young man, and directed him to knock in the head of the cask; which was done. At the grave-side of poor Styles, Mr. Turner addressed a warning voice to about forty Europeans. During the same month he interred the part remains of a poor suicide.

He had been a spirit-trading captain, had led two or three others to an untimely end, and had finished a miserable career by drowning himself. The sharks had partly devoured his body.

In pleasing contrast was the peaceful end of a pious New Zealand woman, the wife of the principal chief, Thomas Walker. "Jesus is my Keeper!" were among her last words. She was the first entombed in the new Mission burial-ground.

June and July appear to have been comfortless months. Many of the Mission party, and Mr. Turner among them, were unwell. One of his mottoes, however, was, "Labour is rest;" and his diary has notes of chimney-building, farming, gardening, hymn-making, and translating a Tongan tract.

"Saturday, July 15th.—A week of hard labour, assisted by my brethren and the natives in sowing and covering in wheat. If favoured with a crop, we shall have as much another year as will supply us with bread."

The glory of heathen Maoridom was fighting, and the tidings of it, or prospect of it, was often a temptation to the Christian natives, so much so that it took all the wisdom and care of the Missionaries to keep them from being involved in it. In general, they succeeded by the help of God. The Bay of Islands tribes were engaged in serious war with one another. Pi, the head of a small heathen tribe, with whom Mr. Turner was friendly, sought his advice as to going to war, but would not accept it. At the close of the conversation, he said to him, "Well, Pi, if you will go, take your coffin with you." He went, and in a day or two was shot dead. Messages were sent from the seat of war to obtain the mediation of the Christian chiefs; for, although a reconciliation was desired, the tribes concerned were not able to effect it. The Missionaries cautioned their chiefs that if they went, they would not be able to resist the temptation to enter into the fight. Under this apprehension it was agreed, that Mr. Turner and Mr. Whiteley should accompany them, as counsellors. This business occasioned them much exposure and discomfort, and kept them from their families for ten days. They were, however, amply repaid by complete success. Their Church brethren had tried their best, but had failed. The behaviour, on that occasion, of the Christian natives gave proof of the transforming power of the Gospel: a few years before, every one of them would have hasted for his brother's blood.

At the station the Missionaries were instructing a large number of candidates for baptism, and on the 29th one hundred and twenty-nine were admitted into the church of Christ.

The Christian people having come in from the out-station, there were not less than seven hundred adults at Mangungu. The native prayer-meeting at seven A.M. was attended by three hundred persons. It was soul-reviving to be associated with so many sons and daughters of once cannibal New Zealand, thus early at the house of prayer. At nine, Mr. Turner catechized the candidates, and solemnly charged any who might be living in sin, or were not sincere before God, not on any account to be baptized, even although they might have been approved of by him or his brethren. They were placed for baptism a little before eleven. Then the congregation were admitted, that is, as many as could crowd into the chapel. Happily for the large number compelled to remain outside, the day was fine. Heart and voice were in the first hymn, " Hear the sounding word from Calvary." The responses of so many hundreds of Maori voices in the morning service were most affecting. With wonder and delight, the Missionary stood before that large assembly, representative of the nation, with the promise of the Holy Ghost upon his lips, " He shall baptize you with the Holy Ghost, and with fire." The promise was fulfilled, and many wept with joy. Then there rushed unbidden upon his mind the scenes of early days,—lust, war, infanticide, man-eating,—and, amid it all, his own life-perils, when almost a solitary witness for God. As one noble chief after another, in the presence of his children, his people, and their friends, stood up, and reverentially presented himself to "Jehovah, the great God, the King of heaven, and the King of earth," Mr. Turner bowed in spirit, and cried, "Who are we, O Lord God, and what is our house, that Thou hast brought us hitherto? For Thy word's sake and according to Thine own heart hast Thou done all these great things, to make Thy servants know them." The candidates then answered appropriate questions, and received the symbol of the Spirit's grace. in the name of the Three-One God. They comprised men of hoary hairs and children of tender years, base-born slaves, captives of war, and chiefs of first rank. The solemnities of a blessed Sabbath closed with the Lord's Supper.

The social condition of the natives was sad in time of general sickness. Influenza prevailed for many weeks, whites and Maoris alike suffering. Mr. Turner wrote:— "Our domestics are laid up, and we ourselves are very poorly. Many of the poor natives are in a wretched state, all but starving for food, and with but little to cover them from the wet and cold. Our means of affording them any relief, except by medicine, are very scanty. We have sought to comfort them by dwelling on the sympathies of Jesus, and by directing their hopes to the land where affliction is unknown."

On the 27th, Mr. Butler and Mr. Turner visited the villages at Mangamuka, and administered medicine to more than forty persons, eighteen of whom they bled. His own physical weakness was an occasion of religious trial. On September 2nd, he wrote: "This has been a painfully trying week, from various causes, but principally from my giving way to

undue warmth of temper, and using unguarded expressions,
by which the Spirit of God has been grieved, and darkness
spread over my mind.   I have longed to go out visiting our
people at their different settlements, but the weather has
not allowed, and my frame is too feeble to be exposed to
much rain."

The following entry is copied in honourable compliment to the grand old chief reverenced in later years for
his loyalty to the British Crown.

"Thursday, 28th.—Have this day committed to the dust
the remains of Ane Patene, (Ann Barton,) daughter and
only child of our principal chief, Thomas Walker Nene.
She has for some time been wasting by consumption.   I
have not felt so great anxiety for any native as for her, but
the Lord has seen good to remove her hence ; and I doubt
not, her sacred spirit has overtaken in the skies that of her
pious mother, who died six months ago.   Her excellent
father, now childless, and a widower, is left to sorrow alone."

On Sundays, 1st and 8th of October, he preached to
attentive congregations on board the "John Barry."   The
District Meeting was held in the succeeding week.   The
Missionaries lost no time in carrying into effect their decisions.   On the 17th, they went to Waima to fix on the
site of a new station.   Mr. Turner was somewhat astonished
to find that the only spot which the natives would part with,
was the only piece of land he had considered eligible.   He
wrote :—

"A leading chief, Moka, son and successor of Pi, strongly
objected to any land being disposed of to us, because our
Church Missionary friends had bought up nearly all the
land at one of their stations, the Waimate.   He said, that
if we got a little, we would tempt them to sell us more ; that
we would bring cattle and destroy their plantations, and
thus drive the people away from their present homes.   When
we had assured him that we had no such objects in view,

but merely wanted enough for the Mission premises, he consented to our repurchasing this said land from the European to whom it had been sold by his late father. After some trouble, we secured the site."

Early in November, a second deputation of natives from Waikato appealed to the Missionaries at Mangungu to take them again under their care. When the Committee at home had resolved on the withdrawal of the brethren Whiteley and Wallis from two important stations in that district, it had been on the understanding that the people would be supplied by the Church Mission. The New Zealand Wesleyan Missionaries all felt that a great mistake had been made ; and now that God was so evidently working among the people, although deprived of proper ministerial care, they decided to send them some native teachers, until the mind of the Committee could be known. At the same time they apprised their friends of the Church Mission of this step.

The community were now somewhat startled by the arrival of an unknown gentleman of large pretensions, accompanied by a considerable number of men, to settle in the neighbourhood. He laid claim to a large portion of the Hokianga district, which, he averred, had been bought for him many years before, and for which, he said, several dozen axes had been paid. The chiefs utterly repudiated any such transaction, and Mr. Turner became interpreter in the difficulty. The claim was openly and clearly disproved by the very chiefs who were said to have sold the land. Truth and right were on their side, and the deluded Baron was crestfallen. Well he might be, with his wife and a train of seventy Europeans, and without any prospect of a single rod of ground on which to erect a shelter.

In this case the Maoris exhibited true Christian principle. Though they were averse to parting with their land, as we have seen, the Christians among them were not ungenerous. It appearing to Thomas Walker Nene that

the European adventurer had been deluded, and that his
case was one for consideration, he magnanimously presented him with a large tract of excellent land, and
requested Mr. Turner to go with him to see it. Taunui,
another chief concerned, also made him a present of another
large portion. Mr. Turner wrote : " The Baron, although
a gentleman, will I fear be of no real benefit to the New
Zealanders, or to our Mission among them. His airy
schemes will come to nought."

A strange man was this Charles Baron de Thierry. He
was the son of a French emigrant to England, and in his
early days had been a teacher of music. While thus
engaged, he secured the affections and hand of the
daughter of Archdeacon Rudges. He was presented to the
Bishop of Norwich for admission into the Church, but was
rejected. He met the Chiefs Hongi and Waikato in
England in 1825, and gave to Mr. Kendall, who was in
England the same year, the value of a dozen axes, to purchase for him some land at Hokianga. About twelve years
later, he conceived the idea of establishing himself as
Sovereign-in-Chief of New Zealand, and left England with
that purpose. In Sydney, those upon whose influence he
had counted smiled upon him in ridicule. Still jubilant as
the imagined possessor of a vast territory, he appointed his
secretary, master of stores, and other officers ; and, after
publishing a printed proclamation of his authority, proceeded to New Zealand. The noble generosity of Thomas
Walker, as above related, saved him from beggary ; but
his experiences did not cure his impudence. He wrote to
the Church Missionaries at the Bay, advising them to
establish themselves as an independent state ; and cha-
racteristically suggested himself as the head of it, if no one
more suitable could be found. Of course they smiled at his
letter. It transpired that he had previously written to the
French Government, transferring his chieftainship. That

power accepted the transfer, and promptly sent out Commodore Laborde to the Bay of Islands, to take and to settle the country around. They were too late. Representations to the British Government had anticipated De Thierry; and when Laborde arrived, he found that the treaty of Waitangi had been signed a few days before. It is said that France supported his claims notwithstanding, and invited him home as the guest of the country. He did not go, but afterwards became a teacher of music in Auckland. Thence he went to California with one of his sons. After his return, he attempted in 1857 to get up a flax company; but though he raised large subscriptions, his project failed. French vessels calling at Auckland always paid him marked respect; it is said, under instructions. He died at the age of seventy-one, on July 8th, 1864, in indigent circumstances.*

To resume our biographical narrative: on the 12th, Mr. Turner preached at Horeke to the Baron's household and people, from the prayer of Jabez; assuring them that, unless like Jabez they sought counsel and help from God, their hopes and efforts would be blasted. Many felt their position, and some wept at their disappointment. The same evening he addressed a European congregation on board the "John Barry."

From Mangungu sounded forth the Word of Life. The native teachers were very successful in distant places. Such was the eagerness for the Gospel, that many travelled distances of nearly fifty miles to the Mission station to attend the worship of God, and this very frequently. On the 17th, Messrs. Whiteley and Turner set out to visit Honruru and other places on the eastern coast, where a good work had begun. By seven P.M. they reached the foot of Mount Tauiwa. The camping-ground of native

* See "New Zealand, Past, Present, and Future," by Rev. Richard Taylor, M.A., F.G.S. 1868.

travellers was a kind of half shed. They made a break-wind of Nikau branches, and after a cup of tea had prayer with their attendants, wrapped their blankets around them, and slept soundly. By sunrise they were on top of the Mount, a remarkable cone, capping a high range of hills. The beauty of nature in its grandeur repaid their toil in climbing. At an immense depth just below them were silvery rivers, lighting up the primal forests and vales. On the east coast, skirted by a low thick fog, was the noble Whangaroa Bay, with its bold cliffs, and the island guardian of its ocean gate; and on the west, beaming its welcome to the sunrise, their own lovely Hokianga. Far reaching in the distance beyond their sight was the Northern Cape of their sea-girt home. They saw the coast-line of cliffs, and sands, and crags, laved by old ocean, rolling in his majesty; and in spirit they heard the grand harmonious anthem of the waves, east and west, " Great is the Lord, and of great power." Here they tarried for half an hour, and indulged thoughts of New Zealand worthy of Christian Missionaries. How I wish I could record their conversation, or their prayer, or even the guesses at their thoughts by their fellow-travellers,—those redeemed children of the land !

They descended by the eastern side, and " travelled hard " over hill and dale, crossing one serpentine stream nearly twenty times. They reached the first native village in the Honruru valley an hour before noon. The people, thirty or forty in number, including children, were busy in their plantations, and much surprised by their visit. Shaded by a copse in the sequestered dell, the whole tribe assembled for worship, and " Jacob's God was there." A youth named Matthew, whom Mr. Turner had baptized at Man-gungu twelve months before, had been their teacher; and it was richly assuring to find that hearts hardened by three-score years of heathenism had been subdued by the Spirit,

under the teaching and prayers of the babe in Christ.
Matthew received a few books, and was much encouraged
for further labour. Having halted for two hours, they travelled on up the lovely valley, observing as they went
traces of a large population in former days.

The Missionaries next tarried at a village whose chief
had lately been baptized by the name of Joseph Orton. Mr.
Whiteley was remarkable as a pedestrian. Few English-
men, even renowned explorers, could excel him; but his
companion in travel was tired out, not having before
walked so many miles in one day. Though they had
planned a further journey, they rested and were thankful.
Their wash from a calabash, and a cup of tea, were very
refreshing. They then conversed till evening with the
people. Mr. Turner preached to about seventy persons on
a traveller's theme, Philip and the Eunuch. Several native
helpers had lately gone among this people, and had led
many of them to God; and now they earnestly desired the
appointment of a Missionary. It was the very spot where
Samuel Leigh had thought of beginning his labours; and
was, in some respects, a most eligible and commanding
position. But the people were now too few to have their
wish gratified. A bed of fern in Joseph Orton's verandah
afforded rest till daybreak.

After five o'clock morning prayers, they resumed their
travels. The roads being muddy, and the rain falling
heavily, they were four hours instead of two reaching
Kohumaolu. As they approached the village, they heard
the bell for worship. The people had not been aware of
their coming, and gladly deferred service till they had
changed their clothing and refreshed themselves. Forty
persons were present, in whose hearts desires for salvation
had been begotten by the agency of native teachers. The
Missionaries were storm-stayed, and held another service in
the evening.

True-hearted Methodist Preachers are happy men. I remember one honoured Minister of the Irish Methodist Conference, telling of his joy in successful Mission toil among Erin's poorest families. He had had a hard day's travel, and a blessed evening service. Then he was entertained for the night, with his host and family, and pig and calf, upon the same floor, and in uncomfortable proximity to his bed. The whole company no doubt were happy, but he alone was wakeful; and in the middle of the night he broke out singing,—

"How do Thy mercies close me round!"

Not dissimilar from his were the mingled causes of wakefulness and joy from which, unrested and unrefreshed, Mr. Turner arose to pursue his journey. The untravelled in Maoridom should know that a New Zealander's hut, infested by fleas in summer, can supply no easy bed.

They sought the road at six o'clock, and by eleven arrived at Mr. M'Lever's, three miles from Whangaroa. That gentleman, who had been accustomed to sit under Mr. Turner's ministry in Hobart Town, received them with much pleasure. After refreshment, he took Mr. Turner in his boat to visit his first New Zealand home. The journey of three hours was amidst the familiar scenes of former years; and a rush of mercies and trials, dangers and deliverances, filled his mind.

Wesley Vale had suffered nothing by the lapse of time. Indeed, its native loveliness had been somewhat increased by the growth of scented groves of sweet-brier here and there upon the rich valley; and, with the beautiful river flowing past, it would have charmed an artist. But as the servant of God stood once more on ground hallowed by toil, by suffering, by prayer, and by a tender consecration, the silent air seemed weighted with melancholy. At his feet was all that remained of his own manual work,—a few broken bricks. He looked to the right and the left as if for those he had known; but there were no family groups circling round their fires, nor children sporting in the bushes, and he felt the desolation. He sought the spot where his first-gone child had lain. The soil was sunken and disturbed, and told of despoilers' hands. The little one's sepulchre had been in a garden: his own hands, when younger, had planted and had trained its trees. Though now all traces of any enclosure had disappeared, there were lovely flowers and fruits. He gathered some roses to carry home, for there were other sympathies with that silent spot;—he plucked them as God's own emblems.

The valley had been harvested. Sin, war, and disease, had been the reapers! Though for three hours he travelled the familiar walks, now covered with grass, he saw but a small remnant of the tribes. Of those whom he had known ten years before, only two old people remained.

Heavy rains detained them till noon next day. Their course homeward lay through the Otangaroa, which they found in high flood. The natives tested the stream-depth here and there till they found footing with their heads above water: then they conveyed their Missionaries across. Two Maoris took hold of Mr. Turner's arms, other two of his legs, and, with the water supporting his weight as he lay upon it between the two couples of bearers, he was partly carried and partly floated over. His companion was bridged over in the same way. They made slow progress through a country almost untravelled, and overgrown with bushes and fern; and at length lost their way, and got benighted. With their clothing drenched, "every tree and bush dripping, the ground deluged by the down-pour of many hours, and without shelter, or the apparent means of procuring it, they were more than weary in their evening discomfort." They set to, however, to make the best of it. All hands gathered bushes, and within an hour they had constructed a partial shelter. The natives got two dry pieces of wood from a hollow tree, and by rubbing them together obtained a fire. The Missionaries dried their clothes, reduced their discomfort as much as they could, and by the light of their camp-fire at midnight read God's holy word. They then, in that dense wild forest, rested "beneath the Almighty's shade," and rose unharmed.

It took an hour to regain the overgrown path, a circumstance not unusual in Mission travel in New Zealand. Upon a hill top, they passed one of the big guns of the ship "Boyd." Years before some Hokianga natives had conceived the bright idea of securing it for their great pa, to be used as an arm of defence in time of war. They had dragged it over hill and dale and through water streams, until, food and courage failing, they had abandoned it. It remained a witness of their folly. Travelling down the mountains, they crossed one stream sixty times. Mr. Turner was curious enough to count. At four o'clock they sighted their boat at Mangamuka, and by twilight reached their homes, thankful for the travelling mercies of six days.

In reference to this and other Missionary journeys in which they were associated, Mr. Whiteley wrote of his companion: " He was always happy, always cheerful, always pressing onward in the great work." Some of the missionary journeys frequently taken were far more laborious and dangerous than that above noticed, especially one between Waikato and Taranaki.

The Mission premises in which he lived in the Southern World he always tried to improve as time and circumstances would allow. The orderly fences and neat and productive gardens of his colonial homes would have been equalled at Hokianga, could it possibly have been managed ;

for he regarded the non-improvement of the surroundings of Mission premises as almost equally discreditable with their dilapidation through neglect. The stumping, fencing, draining, and levelling at Mangungu, however, required more time and energy than he felt free to give. Yet he sought by example to create among the Maories a taste for order, cleanliness, and comfort in domestic life. He often talked anxiously with the chiefs upon their social condition, and repeatedly tried to induce them to form a regular village near the Mission premises, with a view to the better oversight and education of their families; but in vain.

December 31st was a profitable Sabbath. Soon after five in the morning three hundred were at the prayer-meeting; one hundred were at the Sunday school. As was the custom, Mr. Turner's eldest son led the children in their repetitions. The morning public service was crowded. Mr. Buller preached in the afternoon in English. Then a lovefeast was held, when it was found impossible to control the emotion of the native members. The watchnight service was in part conducted by the chiefs. The fruitful year passed away amid the holy vows and joys of consecration.

The review was cheering. Hundreds had been received into the church. Several chiefs had been appointed teachers, and some were actively and usefully employed in preaching the Gospel. The press had done a good work. The issues were,—First Small Book, one thousand; Harmony of the Gospels, and Lessons from the Acts of the Apostles, one hundred and twenty pages, one thousand; the Liturgy, twelve pages, one thousand; First Part of Conference Catechism and Scripture Names, twelve pages, one thousand; Compendium of Gospel Doctrines and Ordinances, one thousand; Rules of Society, one thousand. While many of the above were being circulated, a

new Book of Old Testament Lessons was being prepared.

We could scarcely over-estimate the advantage which
the Maori nation reaped from the early issues of the religious
press by the Church and Wesleyan Missionary Societies.
The natives felt their value. They raised the level of
general intelligence, moulded the principles and for many
years guided the lives of thousands. The Scripture
selections were their companions in travel, and by many a
firelight in the forest, or in a rude hut, afforded comfort
and courage. They not only supplied instruction in their
family groups, but in untold instances laid the foundation of
Christian tenderness, truth, and fortitude, which have
commanded the admiration of devoted Christians from
other lands. As thus mightily grew the Word of God and
prevailed, the united labourers in the Mission field rejoiced
together.

On the first Sabbath in 1838, the Rev. William R. Wade,
of the Church Mission, on a visit to Mangungu, preached
in English and in native. But that Sabbath of happy
Christian union proved a dark day for New Zealand.
Among the passengers of the schooner " Raiatea " were a
French Roman Catholic Bishop and several priests,
appointed to begin a Mission in that neighbourhood. Mr.
Turner had of late paid special attention to the Europeans
accessible. Among his arrangements was the holding a
regular service at the house of one Poynton, an Irish
Catholic. The Roman emissaries took up their abode at
Poynton's house, and of course closed the door against
Protestant influence.

Papist zeal did not slumber. On the Saturday after the
Bishop's arrival, as the Mangamuka natives were
travelling towards Mangungu to enjoy the privileges of the
Sabbath, they were met by Poynton opposite his house,
and introduced to his new acquaintances. The Missionary

Prelate upon this occasion began his public labours, and "astonished the natives." Dressed in gaudy vestments, and surrounded by his priests, he stood solemnly in the still air of the morning, mysteriously lifting up a large crucifix, and an image of a woman and infant child. Poynton acted the interpreter, and the Maoris' wonder increased as the Bishop addressed them. In open view was a large tree with spreading branches. He pointed to its grand old trunk, and said it represented the Church of Rome, which had withstood so many storms. The large arms were the Church of England, and the small decaying boughs the Wesleyan Church. With unmingled wonder and anger at what they had heard, the natives sought their religious teachers. The first impulse of the chiefs was to have the new arrivals expelled from the land. Mr. Turner's text the next morning was, " And when the woman saw that the tree was good for food," &c. He had Divine help in preparing the native mind against soul-destroying errors.

Meanwhile a number of villanous settlers were traducing Mr. Turner's character, in respect of some native grievances brought to him in land disputes. Happily, however, he so lived as not to need to take care of his character: it always took care of him. The ungodly European Catholics often threatened his life for exposing their errors. Several were monsters of iniquity ; and prominent among them was a reprobate who had spent many years with the heathen Maoris, and had joined in their wars, and even in their cannibal feasts. But Mr. Turner was not the man to fear. While these threats were most violent, he interfered and prevented a baptized son of Christian parents being taken to a Catholic meeting-house, where it had been arranged he should be re-baptized.

These priests, who were all Frenchmen, soon became known as subjects of another government. The tribes who

had refused the teaching of the Missionaries were easily
induced under cover of a hostile party to join them. The
Bishop was sanguine, and soon filled the land with priests,
who laboured hard, distributing images and teaching their
doctrines with zeal and self-denial. As religious teachers
they never obtained a firm hold of the native mind. The
Gospel had been there before them.

The Rev. John Hobbs was proceeding from the Friendly
Islands to Hobart Town, pursuant to the recommendation
of his District Meeting. Upon his visiting his brethren at
Hokianga, they united in persuading him to remain with
them, at least until the mind of the Committee could be
known. They did this because the rapid growth of the
work needed additional labourers, and Mr. Hobbs, having
already spent several years in New Zealand, was proficient
in the language. On his first Sunday he preached to
about seven hundred persons with such ease and fluency as
surprised his brethren. After the sermon, one hundred and
twenty adults were baptized, and in the afternoon forty
children. On March 23rd he brought over his family, who
had been detained some days at the Waimate, through the
sickness and death of the youngest child.

The Church Missionaries had instituted a school at the
Waimate for the education of their sons. It was under
the care of the Rev. Henry Williams. A kind providence
timely offered its advantages to Mr. Turner's two eldest
sons, and on May 1st they left home for school. This
kindness of the Church Missionaries was gratefully appreciated.

Some Waikato Christian natives travelled two hundred
miles to consult the Missionaries upon a case which had
caused them much grief. Some of their tribe had plundered
a trader in Whangaroa Bay. Three only of the number
had been professors of religion. The other Christian
natives had all acted most honourably. One native

Christian, a chief, had voluntarily made the captain handsome restitution for what the heathens of his tribe had stolen from him.

Subjoined is the history of the first execution of a Maori for the murder of a white man. On the 15th of April, a European surveyor was missing, under suspicious circumstances. After consulting the chiefs, Mr. Turner went. to Wairinaki, the town of the suspected man, who was a slave. The chiefs there having endorsed the suspicion as to the murderer, he spent four hours trying to persuade them to secure him until further investigation could be held. They offered to surrender him to Mr. Turner, but from prudential motives he declined to receive him. Later in the evening, at his suggestion, Walker Nene went and induced them to bind the man, and hold him over for trial. On the third day the body of the missing man was found, twelve miles from where he had lost his life. Medical examination confirmed suspicion. Mr. Turner buried him in the presence of some sixty Europeans. Next morning a formal trial was instituted in the chapel, by the British resident, Mr. Basby. He had no power to impanel a jury, but had the moral support in his action of the numerous Europeans and chiefs who attended. By five in the afternoon the evidence was concluded, and the majority present gave a verdict, " Guilty of wilful murder." Mr. Turner's opinion was, that the man had been guilty only of manslaughter. It was agreed among the chiefs to put the man to death. The Missionaries visited him on the Sabbath, and Mr. Hobbs attended him to the last, and had hope in his death. He was taken on the Monday morning to a small island near the station, in view of it, and was there shot. The whole circumstances caused general excitement.

The purchase of lands from natives on Mission fields by those sent among them on Gospel errands has ever been justly restricted, and, in later years, has been forbidden by our Missionary Committee. Many of the difficulties in adjusting the New Zealand colonization enterprises originated in the agents of another Missionary Society acquiring considerable tracts of land, which they held for the future interests of their children. Of this custom, as it then existed, Mr. Turner disapproved. No doubt in those days equally good men held widely differing views as to what was right or equitable. But though he had a large family growing up, and had as clear an idea of the bright future of New Zealand as had most, and though few friends of the Maories at that time could have more securely benefitted their families than he, happily he experienced no temptation of the kind. If he did, there is no record of it. It must therefore be believed that it was hard for him to bear, even for a short time, the odium of an ugly rumour of this kind; and I feel it right to append his personal narration of a circumstance which much annoyed him. Subjoined is the copy of an original manuscript entry, which, singularly enough, speaks in thankful commendation of Dr. Harris's very searching volume on Covetousness, and, in immediate connexion with it, of the purchase which had occasioned prejudicial remark.

"Saturday, June 2nd. On Monday and Tuesday was busily assisted by about twenty of our natives in putting in part of our wheat, and since then have been attending to various duties connected with the station. Have been much edified reading 'Mammon,' one of the best written works I ever read. It has thrown fresh light into my mind, and discovered the selfishness of my nature as I never before saw it. How thoroughly depraved is the human heart! Have this week made a purchase of some land, which I intend for the benefit of my children, should Providence lead to their permanent abode in New Zealand. This has caused my mind considerable exercise; for I fear lest I should have done wrong in this matter."

In his manuscript autobiography, written for his family in the year 1858, he thus alludes to the circumstances :— " This purchase afterwards occasioned much anxiety of mind, because it exposed me to painful reflection by the Committee and others, as if I had been guilty with the many who at that period purchased land from the natives to a great extent, at a merely nominal value. I think it right, therefore, to place on record here the circumstances of the case, that my character may not be handed down to posterity as tarnished by my having sought to enrich myself at the expense of the natives. Dr. Ross, a respectable medical gentleman whom I had formerly known in Sydney, purchased this property from a former proprietor, a Captain Clarke, and came to reside upon it. Shortly after this he became very ill, and sent for me to visit him. I attended him, with others of my brethren, until he died. As he approached the grave, observing his mind under deep depression, I asked him, in the presence of one of my brethren, to tell me fully his grief, promising that as far as possible I would bear his burden. He told me, that he was distressed at the thought of his wife being unprotected and unprovided for in so barbarous a land, and added, ' The only property I possess in the world is this on which I lie ; if I could dispose of this for cash before I die, I could die in peace, for she would then have the means of getting back to her friends.' I promised at once, in case of his death, to take Mrs. Ross into my own family, until she could do better for herself, or join her friends in the colonies, and that I would try to dispose of the land for him. I took his papers and examined them ; and finding that the property had been fairly purchased from the natives many years before, that they now laid no claim to it, and that his title was good, I was induced for various reasons, after consulting with my brethren, to purchase the land myself. I paid Mrs. Ross one hundred and fifty pounds for it, the

utmost value the Doctor placed upon it.   Shortly after the
purchase, Mr. Russell, a timber merchant, who was rent-
ing a small portion of it, claimed the prior right of purchase,
one ground of which was the Doctor's promise.   I allowed
him to take the portion of it he desired, for half the amount,
and afterwards, through Mr. Hobbs, sold the remainder to
Mr. Mariner for the original cost.   Having thus given a
statement of the only land I ever possessed, while among
the heathen, I leave my children to judge how far their
father was deserving of blame.   The good which resulted
through the conversion of Mrs. Ross to Christ while under
my roof, eternity alone will tell.   In after years, through
her instrumentality, in New South Wales, many were
blessed indeed."

Like her husband, Mrs. Ross had been brought up a
Presbyterian.   When subdued by sorrow and bereavement,
and an inmate of Mr. Turner's house, she soon lost the
prejudices which, up to that ·time, she had entertained
against some of the doctrines of the Wesleyans.   During
a long and severe illness with which Mrs. Turner was
visited, she read much to her, and among other books,
"The Life of Mrs. Fletcher."   The biography of that
saintly woman was blessed to her salvation.   One Wednesday evening she joined the English class, which met in the
Mission house, and distinctly stated, " Now I know that
God does on earth forgive sins ; for He has pardoned me."
In August, 1839, she removed with Mr. Turner's family to
Sydney.   During the progress of a revival in that city, she
invited her sister, Miss Willis, to hear Mr. Turner preach.
That lady became convinced of sin, but, having cherished So-
cinian views, was in a hopeless state of mind.   In deep agony
she prayed, " O Lord ! if Jesus be Thy Son, make me willing
to believe it."   Light shone on the New Testament page, and
she, too, found that "the Son of man hath power on earth to
forgive sins."   Miss Willis afterwards became the wife of

the Rev. Frederick Lewis. Mrs. Ross was an eminently holy and zealous woman. She accompanied her sister and brother-in-law from Circuit to Circuit for many years, ever devoting her energies to the services of Christ. She still pursues a course of Christian usefulness in the neighbourhood of her residence in London.

One Saturday, while reading letters from beloved friends in Tasmania, Mrs. Turner was suddenly seized with an attack of pleurisy. High fever set in, and though the usual remedies were applied, they had no beneficial effect. The illness was serious, and was attended by much pain for ten weeks. Mr. Turner's anxiety proved an almost equal affliction to him. The constant attendance of three medical gentlemen, one from a distance, served but to keep hope and fear in constant alternation. The weekly entries noting the progress and changing features of her affliction remark her power of faith, and Mr. Turner's comfort in prayer.

On Tuesday, the 19th, he received letters from Messrs. M'Kenny and Watkins, "breathing a most affectionate spirit, and giving important intelligence." Mr. Watkins had been appointed to New Zealand by the Home Committee. Four days later he heard from the Mission House, that so soon as a suitable successor could be found, he would be allowed to remove to one of the colonies for the benefit of his family. Early in August he received gratifying intelligence from his friends in Van Diemen's Land, among whom the Lord's work was prospering. Apart from the prosperity of his work, he had in New Zealand few sources of greater gratification than his Van Diemen's Land correspondence. After long-continued waiting upon the invalid indoors, Mr. Turner was glad to be able at length to resume his customary labours among his people.

The extracts freely given hitherto in this memoir have

been collated from the Missionary Magazines, or other authentic transcripts. For the first fourteen years of his missionary life Mr. Turner had regularly made journal entries. And in later years it was a matter of grief to him and of regret to his friends, that anything should have occurred by which nearly the whole of them had been lost. But for that untoward event the memorials of his life would have been published much earlier, and would have comprised many incidents of missionary interest, now lost to the Church. As his biographer I specially regret that by the same cause I am deprived of the notes of his spiritual life and communion with God, which, to those who knew him best, were the chief excellence of his harmonious character. After that occurrence he ceased to be systematic in keeping a diary of events ; for he had lost all heart for it. His subsequent correspondence with the Committee was more general ; and for the remainder of his public life I am indebted for material, in great part, to general and family correspondence, and other family manuscripts. I now append the last entry in the journals of fourteen years' experiences.

"Thanks to my Heavenly Father for His abounding mercy to me and mine. After ten weeks' confinement to a bed of affliction, my dear wife has been enabled by my assistance to move into the parlour, and just set her foot inside the door. As the weather is becoming more settled, I hope she will rapidly gather strength, and be able to attend to her family. I here record the great kindness of our brethren and sisters to us during the long night of affliction, and especially that of our pious neighbour, Mrs. Monk, who has been unwearied in her kind attentions to my dear afflicted wife. May she be rewarded at the resurrection of the just ! "

After penning the above on Saturday night, the 18th of August, Mr. Turner retired to rest with a mind more than usually tranquil and composed. It had been a preparation day, and he rested in hope of a blessed Sabbath. But not for long. Before daylight the family's home and property were burnt to ashes. About two in the morning, on being awakened by a crackling noise, he went to the sitting-room and found it full of smoke and flame. He alarmed the household, and then tried to re-enter the room, but was almost suffocated, and was driven back with his feet dreadfully burned. The settlement was aroused by the chapel bell. Messrs. Hobbs and Woon and hundreds of natives were on the spot in a few minutes. The flames rapidly bursting through the roof, every effort was made to save whatever could be got out of the house. Mrs. Turner had scarcely left her room for ten weeks, but had strength given her to get the children and herself outside the burning building. When she had done this, she fell from feebleness, and bruised herself seriously. A native youth threw a blanket around her, and carried her to Mr. Hobbs's house, a few yards distant. Flakes of fire were already falling on its rush roof, and a few minutes might see it also sheeted in flame. The children, with their mother, were now being carried in the arms of willing natives to Mr. Woon's house, out of the reach of danger, when Mrs. Turner would have them stop, that the children might be counted. In counting by the flamelight from the burning building that group of the large families of children in their night-dresses, it would have been easy to have made a mistake; but they were counted by a mother's eye. One was missing, but it was not known from which family. Instant search was made in both houses, and in a bedroom on fire a little boy was found. He who now writes this record of God's mercy is in more senses than one a brand plucked from the burning. He well remembers their wild excitement as he ran to the rest upon the open green. Then a grateful mother offered praise to God.

There was one thing the fire did not consume. The firmest thing in the universe is Christian confidence ; and I connect with the latest entry in the book saved from the fire the first made after it. Mr. Turner wrote :—" Much of our personal property as well as that of the Mission was destroyed. Much wearing apparel was consumed, together with many of my most valuable books, and my private journal for fourteen years, including a brief narrative of my early life, conversion to God, and call to the missionary work. This part of my loss I deeply feel, as I know it cannot be retrieved. All my public and private letters and documents of every kind have also been destroyed. But I would not, I do not complain. Blessed for ever be my Great Deliverer's Name. My life has been spared, and my wife and children are with me, the living, the living to praise our God. This calamity I am satisfied is designed of Heaven for our good, and I see and feel that the bitter cup has been mingled in mercy. Had the fire occurred a few weeks sooner, in all probability the shock would have killed my poor wife, then to all appearance at the point of death. Through mercy, however, she appears not to have sustained any material injury, and her grateful spirit magnifies her Heavenly Father. Though many were on the spot, and it was in the dead of night, we are not aware that a single article was pilfered. What a contrast between the conduct of the natives in this instance, and that of our people at Whangaroa in 1827 ! Glory to God for the change wrought ! Then we were stripped of everything, and our people were amongst the greatest plunderers."

Surely it was in the beautiful simplicity of holiness, that he wrote that evening,—" This has been a painful Sabbath to me. Although conscious of the mercy and goodness of God to me and mine, and grateful for our deliverance, I could not keep my mind from dwelling upon the burning scene. But God is good; He knows our weakness, and pities the infirmities of His children."

The Missionaries acknowledged a special Providence that night. When the flames were at their highest, and flakes were being carried towards Mr. Hobbs's house, the printing office, and the chapel, the wind quite suddenly veered round, and carried the burning pieces into the river. " He holdeth the winds in His fists."

Chiefs and people exhibited the utmost sympathy. As a special favour, Thomas Walker,* who was highly esteemed, was allowed to visit Mrs. Turner, to offer condolence. He had known the chastening hand, and his sympathy was welcome. " O, mother," he said, " do not let thy heart be very much distressed ; for though thy home and property are destroyed, thy life, thy husband, and thy children are spared. I have no European garments to give for your children, but they shall have pork and potatoes to eat, and such things as we have."

The entire loss, public and private, including the buildings, was estimated at about eight hundred pounds. How much of this was private I do not know, but the Committee probably made a compensatory grant on account of personal loss.

The calamity was supposed by some to have originated in the room taking fire by the rolling down of a piece of burning wood which had been left standing in the fireplace when the family retired. Mr. Turner wrote as follows :—" It is possible, however, to have been the work of an incendiary. It is well known that John Marmon, a most wicked Irish Catholic, now the interpreter and most active agent of the Romish Bishop, had threatened to make Mangungu smoke ; and this Marmon was on the

* Thomas Walker Nene is now nearly ninety years old, and a fine specimen of a New Zealand chieftain. He is one of the few deserving pensioners of the British Government.

station yesterday." And at a later date :—" A few days after the fire, I met him, when he said to me, ' I hope, Mr. Turner, you don't think it was I who set your house on fire.' " Had British rule obtained in those parts, Marmon would most assuredly have been arrested on suspicion.

On the Monday, the brethren resolved that a good permanent house should be at once built, that during its erection Mr. Turner should have Mr. Buller's residence, and that meanwhile Mr. Buller should reside at Newark, with Mr. Whiteley. This arrangement, it was thought, would suit the families concerned, and at the same time would offer to Mr. Buller an opportunity of supplying religious instruction to some tribes on the north side of the river, near the Heads, who much desired it. The whole of the available time that week was devoted to reproducing, as far as possible, public accounts, and sundry business papers of importance. As may be imagined, it was a difficult and vexatious business, but it was one which blistered feet did not impede.

" These are they which came out of great tribulation," was his text on the next Sabbath morning. As soon as able, he travelled to the Waimate, and during a profitable evening with his old friends received much sympathy. He wrote : " Found my two boys well, and glad to see their father. Poor lads, they had many inquiries to make about the fire." September 10th :—" Letters from the Committee, and from friends in the colony. Nothing but expression of sympathy and kindness from the Committee toward myself, for which I praise God. Poor Sydney is still very low, I learn, and without much prospect of seeing better days at present."

On Sabbath, at Waikow, about a hundred praying natives assembled. He commented on the last chapter in the New Testament, and hoped that what he said would " abide with them and do them good all their days." He then spent three hours with Baron de Thierry and his household, with whom he read and prayed.

The District Meeting had just opened on the 3rd of October, when the brethren received important communication from the Committee. "Our hearts were ready to dance with joy when we heard that we were at full liberty to re-occupy our stations at the south, and that three additional brethren were about to be sent to our assistance. Glory to God for this soul-reviving intelligence." That Meeting unanimously petitioned the Committee to send ten more Missionaries to enable them to take up the whole line of coast to Cook's Straits.

Mr. Turner's relations with the Church Mission continued most friendly. During this month he preached one Sabbath afternoon to the sons of the prophets at the Waimate. On the 18th, a deputation of three of their Missionaries visited Mangungu, to confer with the Wesleyan brethren as to the best modes of harmonious operation, and as to the boundaries of their Society's labours in the Waikati district. From the result of that conference, Mr. Turner anticipated increased efficiency in the operations of the two Societies. The kindly feeling of the Church brethren towards their old friend expressed itself in an affectionate letter from the Rev. Henry Williams, enclosing a draft for forty pounds from himself and his brethren, towards making good the loss he had sustained by the late fire. The letter expressed a hope that Mr. Turner's own Society would fully make up what he had been called to lose. That hope was but partially realized. I suppose it was a year of deficient income at the Mission House.

On Sunday, November 18th, there were a thousand worshippers at the Mission station. Many had come from afar to bow for the first time before Jehovah. The chapel was more than filled. From end to end, from side to side, it was crowded. The window sills were thronged,.

and every rising slope close by was taken up. Moses Tauhai and others had induced the Christians of the settlement to give place to strangers. With the utmost good will and decorum this had been done. After Mr. Hobbs had preached from, "Go ye into all the world," &c., one hundred and thirty-eight adults and forty-six children were admitted into the Church. Several of these were of the first rank, and some had for years, until lately, stood out against the truth in every form that Christian zeal could employ. Others were from Whangaroa, and had been among those who had spurned the Gospel at the lips of the same Missionaries in former years. It had transpired, however, prior to their baptism, that impressions had been made at Wesley Vale which had never been erased. One instance was Hongi, eldest son of Te Puhi, a principal chief of Whangaroa. Another was his wife, who had been Mrs. Turner's servant there. The after services of the day were seasons of blessing. The strangers were instructed and encouraged ; and returned home resolved to do their utmost for Christ, and for the heathen around them.

The day and Sabbath schools were now well attended, and excited much interest. The word of God disseminated by their means resisted the encroachments of Popery, now spreading delusion somewhat rapidly. Some of the half enlightened had been entangled by the Bishop's free distribution of medals and of crosses. The brethren put forth special effort to diffuse Bible truth and useful knowledge. They purchased one thousand copies of the New Testament from the Church Mission. In sending half of these to England to be bound, they requested that a few thousands more be printed. "Had we," they wrote, "the whole one thousand copies now, they would soon be all gone ; then what should we do for the thousands who, we have every reason to believe, will be soon gathered into the fold from the southward ? Would not the Bible Society do this for us, if applied to ? In no part of the world would their liberality be crowned with the blessing of Heaven more abundantly than here. And our press cannot, for a long time to come, be better employed than it is in printing elementary books, hymns, tracts, &c. Besides, if we could print the Testament, we have neither the ability nor the time to bind the copies printed......No book will counteract the errors of Popery like the New Testament of the Lord Jesus."

The year closed amid general affliction ; young and old were laid up with influenza. A public watch-night service was impracticable. A few, however, met at Mr. Turner's house for prayer.

On New Year's Day, 1839, he received a letter from a native, acquainting him with the death of a Christian chief of rank, Haimona Pita Matanfi of Utakura. Mr. Turner thus referred to him :—" His conduct in general has been very circumspect since I have known him, and while talking and praying with him, I have often had my spirit refreshed. When I parted with him yesterday, he was affected to tears, but I did not then apprehend he was so near his heavenly home. He has, without doubt, triumphantly passed to heaven. His family, and the class of which he had been Leader for some years, will greatly feel their loss. With no other New Zealander did I hold so intimate and frequent intercourse on religious subjects in general. One of my last interviews was most affecting. I had generally asked the Lord to be pleased to spare his life. This I had done on account of his usefulness. But at the time referred to, as I was going away, he said, ' Mr. Turner, I have a favour to ask of you. Don't ask the Lord to keep me here any longer. I have taken leave of my children and people. My heart is in heaven, and I long to depart, and go there. Such was the closing scene of one formerly a terrible warrior, and an awful cannibal. Such wonders Love can do, such conquests the Gospel can achieve." The shafts of death were many. Before the month closed, another chief of first rank, Wiramu Wunu, (William Woon,) was taken home to God. He was of such a mild and peaceful spirit as is rarely found among the natives. His life had been that of a sincere Christian, and he died well,—the third of his rank called away within a few weeks.

A deputation from the Waikato tribes having asked for religious instructors, Mr. Turner consulted the native Christians, and resolved to send forthwith some of the best men who could be found. He fixed upon a valuable Local Preacher and Leader at Mangamuku, named Haere Tepene (Charles Stephens). When young he had been taken captive in war, and had become the slave of Wiramu Wunu. But when that chief had embraced Christianity, he had liberated his slaves, and allowed Charles to marry into his family. On visiting Mangungu, Charles listened attentively to Mr. Turner's request, and then significantly shook his head, and said, " I am not able to go, for I am fast bound with a chain." Mr. Turner answered, " Haere, tell me what is your chain." He replied, " You know, Mr. Turner, my chief, Ko-te-Wunu, has lately died. When dying, he sent for me and said, ' Charlie, I am dying, and I am dying in the dark. My mind is sore troubled. You know that a short time ago I received from Captain ——— so many blankets, spades, axes, &c., on credit, for which I was to get out of the bush so many spars as payment. The property has all been distributed among my people and friends, and sickness has come upon me before I have been able to fulfil my agreement; and now I am dying in debt, and therefore cannot die in peace.' Charlie then added, ' I said to him, Die thou in peace: be upon me thy burden; I will pay thy debts !' Now this is the chain that binds me fast; and, but for this, I would gladly go to

Waikato, and teach my countrymen about Jesus Christ, that they may be saved."

On Thursday, Mr. Turner committed to the grave the remains of the commander of the London ship "Coromandel," then in harbour. He preached on board each of the three following Sabbath evenings, and was favoured with special freedom in doing so.

An intelligent Irish Methodist, Dr. Day, visiting New Zealand, was so pleased with the country, that he projected bringing out a number of pious families from his native land as permanent settlers. He was with Mr. Turner for a fortnight travelling among the tribes. The following extract, if lengthy, is not without interest:—

"Left home on Monday, 18th, with Dr. Day and a Mr. Uler, for Kaipara, where we arrived on Thursday, just in time to accompany Brother and Sister Wallis down to the 'Elizabeth,' bound for Whangaroa. The wind being unfavourable, we remained on board until Sunday. Sailed across the Great Wairoa, twenty miles up the Oruawara, to visit a part of Parore's people; who, with Mr. Stephenson, accompanied us down. Had a most interesting time with about sixty people. The big tears rolled down many cheeks as I addressed them from, 'Lord, remember me when Thou comest into Thy kingdom.' Had much conversation with them, and retired encouraged in spirit. On Monday addressed them again, and baptized three children. Was highly delighted with the country. We passed many beautiful spots very eligible for farms, and others for towns. Spent a short time with a few natives at another settlement of the Pakanar tribe. The wind being dead against us, we did not enter the Otamatea River before dark. We fortunately, however, came up with Tuiraru's tribe seven miles up, and encamped with them for the night. We had neither hut nor tent, but the lads made a breakwind of the boat-sail, and we rested pretty well.

Next morning returned with Tirarau, the chief. Was pleasingly surprised to find the Otamatea so fine a river. The country is superior to most parts of New Zealand which I have seen. The wind being unfavourable, we only got about thirty miles up the stream. Here we encamped again, sheltered by a boat-sail. By one next day we reached Mr. Stephenson's, and then enjoyed the luxury of a change of clothing. At seven P.M. set off with the flowing tide for Mr. Buller's Mission station, where we received a welcome at midnight. Spent Thursday most agreeably, and were joined in the evening by the Rev. H. Williams, who had left home to visit the neighbouring settlements. He had come this much out of his way to see Tirarau, who has been much tried by some of his people listening to the Catholic Bishop. On Friday, Messrs. Buller and Williams went with me to Mr. Stephenson's. In the evening had my soul quickened and comforted at the throne of grace. God was very gracious. On Saturday reached Kaihu, one of the most delightful valleys I ever saw. My good friend Dr. Day has resolved on making it his future abode. He has agreed with Parore, the chief, for an extensive portion in the valley, intending to go home and return with several of his Wesleyan friends to settle. I shall feel thankful if the scheme succeed, believing it will do much good in the land. On Sunday, the attention of the people at Kaihu was fixed, morning and evening. In the afternoon I catechized them, and heard many testify what the Lord was doing for their souls. Indeed, I had scarcely a moment's leisure from morning till night. I retired quite wearied in body, but rejoicing in God my Saviour."

The little scheme of Christian colonization was followed up, but it had a mournful issue. Dr. Day went to Ireland, and made the voyage out again with several pious families. But while entering the Kaipara Heads, the vessel was wrecked, and nearly the whole company found a watery grave. " His ways are past finding out."

The reinforcement of Missionaries arrived on Tuesday, the 19th of March, 1839. They were the Rev. J. H. Bumby, who was accompanied by his sister, Miss Bumby, and the Revs. Samuel Ironside and Charles Creed, with their wives. The Rev. James Warren had been of the party, but had been detained at Hobart Town in lieu of the Rev. John Hobbs. The new brethren at once found favour on the station as "proper Missionary spirits, adapted to the labours and trials of the New Zealand work." Mr. Turner received several letters from the Mission House expressive of the Committee's approval of his proceedings while guiding the Mission. Of one of these I subjoin a copy :—

" LONDON, WESLEYAN MISSION HOUSE,
" *April 19th*, 1838.

" MY DEAR BROTHER,

" You will learn from the general letters what are the arrangements we have made for New Zealand. One of the three we have resolved to send is intended to relieve you, in order that you may, according to your wish, return to the colony. If you could remain some six months after he arrives, in order to make him fully acquainted with your views and plans, it would be extremely desirable ; but we must not press you further than a sense of your duty to your family will allow you to go, on behalf of New Zealand. The Committee feel under great obligation to you for your services there ; and it must be a great consolation to you to have been permitted to witness the scene of your early labours and sufferings rise to such importance and interest, during your second appointment there.

" I remain, my dear Brother,
" Yours affectionately,
(Signed) " JOHN BEECHAM."

The "James" conveyed also many pleasing letters from friends in Hobart Town, who desired his return to labour amongst them. Their grateful memory of his labours, and affectionate interest in his welfare, were a comfort to him.

Saturday's entry is as follows :—" Busy all the week with the new brethren getting on shore luggage and Mission stores. Have been kept in a holy, happy state of mind. Very much blessed at class last evening. Mr. Bumby led the meeting, and I could not but admire his talents, and glorify the grace of God in him. Have given tickets to six classes to-day, besides other engagements. My physical nature seems ready to sink, but the Lord gives me strength for all my work."

On their first Sabbath the new Missionaries witnessed a fine illustration of the power of the Gospel.

" Sunday, 24th.—Had a large attendance of natives at the early prayer-meeting. Never did I hear more appropriate addresses to the throne of mercy than from several natives recently converted from heathenism. An overflowing congregation at eleven. I read prayers, and Mr. Hobbs preached a good sermon on the Lord's Supper. The notorious Kai Toke ('worm-eater') was present for the first time. At the close of the service I requested Wiramu Patene (William Barton) to pray. In his prayer he particularly remembered Kai Toke, and earnestly entreated the Lord to give him a new heart. Here was literally a converted heathen praying for his enemy; for Kai Toke had a short time before shot two of Barton's praying companions, and had sent three bullets through the blanket he had worn at the time. The English service was well attended. Mr. Bumby preached a most excellent sermon from, ' I have learned in whatsoever state I am therewith to be content.' After the native sermon in the evening, the Lord's Supper was administered to more than two hundred communicants, the newly-arrived brethren and sisters partaking with them. The conduct of the natives was very becoming. It has afforded me satisfaction to hear Mr. Bumby say frequently, the natives are far in advance of what he had expected."

Captain Todd was unwilling to go to Cook's Straits, and there was some difficulty as to locating the newly-arrived Missionaries; the more so as the winter season, adverse to travellers, was coming on. While very anxious on this matter, Mr. Turner was seized with a severe inflammatory attack. Its agonies lasted some eight or ten hours, and it was fully a week before he recovered his tone of health. His family removed into their new house on the 13th of April.

The next day, Sunday, he paid an apparently fruitless visit to a hardened chief, named Nau. In the afternoon Mr. Bumby preached from, " And He led them by a right way, that He might bring them to a city of habitation." The same evening Mr. Turner consecrated his new home, by preaching in it to a room-full of people. On Tuesday the Missionaries took counsel as to the founding of new stations. The natives objected to journey by land at that season of the year, and it was resolved to charter a small vessel, by which Mr. Hobbs and Mr. Bumby might proceed on a cruise of inquiry and observation. The first week in May, Mr. Turner was called away to the Waimate to see his eldest son, who had met with a serious accident.

Messengers arrived in July giving most cheering accounts of the progress of the truth, and the general desire among the natives for the Word of God. In many villages they had erected chapels, in which they were most anxious to place one of "Jehovah's Books." Where they had not been able to secure a New Testament for each sanctuary, they had divided one, and from it furnished a few leaves for each of several chapels.

He arranged to leave everything in business-like order for his successor. There being a barque in port bound for Sydney, and Mr. Bumby's return being almost daily expected, he made up his mind to leave by her, *en route* for Hobart Town. To prepare a family of twelve for a sea voyage was no easy matter.

The missionary explorers returned on the 17th, having been absent fourteen weeks. They had had many difficulties by land and by sea, but had been shielded by their Master's presence. They reported favourable prospects, and had decided on Port Nicholson as the best site for their southern station.

On the next day, Sunday, Mr. Turner gave his farewell address to the native church and congregation, and was much affected while doing so. They had been his thought and care and burden through several eventful years, and the one public service among them which remained to him was made use of for their good. One can scarcely recall the perils of his first term, and the successes of that now closing, without admiring his self-suppression and self-hiding in his chosen theme. And, indeed, what could he have better chosen to say to them than, "Only let your conversation be such as becometh the Gospel of Christ"? Similarly his spirit prevailed when, in the evening, his parting counsels to his missionary brethren were from the words, "Therefore, my beloved brethren, be ye steadfast, unmovable, always abounding in the work of the Lord, forasmuch as ye know that your labour is not in vain in the Lord."

Four extremely hard days' work in packing was relieved by helpful hands; and on Friday evening, the 23rd, Mr. Turner's family had their last row in their old favourite boat "Missionary." The children were amused at seeing for the first time the use, over a ship's side, of a chair for taking on board lady passengers. On Saturday morning early their vessel crossed the bar with a fair wind. As the coast-line receded behind the distant billows, a fellow-passenger who had joined the ship at the Heads paced the deck, singing to the old tune " Deritend,"—

> " God moves in a mysterious way
>   His wonders to perform ;
> He plants His footsteps in the sea,
>   And rides upon the storm."

The following is an extract from a letter to the Committee :—

> " AT SEA, ON BOARD THE ' FRANCIS SPAIGHT,'
>   " *August* 28*th*, 1839.

" IT is painful to me to put the Committee to additional expense by going by way of Sydney. There was, however, no alternative, except my remaining many months longer at Mangungu. I have not left the New Zealand Mission without considerable regret. For some months I have experienced a growing affection for the natives, and delight in the work amongst them. As my knowledge of their language and ability to preach in it have increased, my attachment to their cause has greatly strengthened,— of late, especially, while I have beheld hundreds hanging on my lips with deathlike silence and interest, as I have impressed the truths of eternity upon them. I must confess that as the parting drew nigh, had it not been for the paramount claims of my family, I would have been ready to say, ' Here let me lie, here let me labour, here let me die.' Another cause of sorrow is the great need there is just now of more vigorous help. I cannot but regret that in conjunction with my brethren, I have not been able to achieve more; yet I cannot but be grateful to the great Head of the Church for the improved circumstances in which I have left the Mission. I rejoice in the recollection that I have laboured in love and harmony with my brethren; that I have not had a serious misunderstanding with either natives or Europeans; and that I have left, followed by the blessings and prayers of all. May God in mercy still direct my steps, and make me a greater blessing in the colony to which I am appointed."

Three times Mr. Turner conducted public worship on board, and family devotion twice each day. After a seventeen days' voyage, he was welcomed in Sydney by Messrs. M'Kenny, Orton, and Watkin.

CHAPTER XIV.

NEW ZEALAND PAST AND PRESENT.

SOME interest attaches to the subsequent religious history of the tribes among whom Mr. Turner laboured, and to their present condition. Though the whole career of the Mission is bright with illustrations of Christian devotedness on the part of the holy men who have succeeded him, and of the saving power of the Gospel, the story is a painful one, in many particulars. The final issue, however, is not to be read in the light of present events, but awaits the revealing light at the end of the days.

At Wangaroa, in the vicinity of Wesley Vale, the natives have but exchanged one set of vices for another. The revolting barbarities of savage life have given place to the evils of a corrupt civilization. But they are without excuse. While sober settlers are creating happy homesteads in their beautiful valley, the infatuated tribes are disappearing through self-neglect and vice. In the small court house a Sabbath school is held, and religious services are statedly attended. On the very site where Mr. Turner's house stood, a neat wooden church has lately been built; so that the spot consecrated by prayers, tears, and sufferings, is still sacred to the God of Missionaries. Near this sanctuary nearly a score of European families reside, and among them a worthy Irish Methodist, Mr. Hare, who leads a class, and conducts Sabbath service. Till recently, there was a little wooden building near, in which native worship was held. But few attended. The Maoris are visited by the Missionary from Waima. Formerly, the

natives were very numerous, but now there are scarcely
three hundred in the whole district, and these are scattered
in small companies, demoralized by drink. The Keri
Keri, too, was very populous; now there is not a solitary
native within twelve miles of Mr. Kemp's residence; for
the old gentleman still lives at the same spot. At the
Waimate, the natives have diminished in number from one
thousand to two hundred. They earn much money by
digging for gum, but spend it in drink and gambling.
The only Missionary is the Rev. Mr. Clark, one of the
sons of Mr. Turner's contemporary. There are about
twenty English families around, most of them connected
with the Missionary pioneers.

Mr. Turner's subsequent New Zealand station presents
another picture of similar desolation. The old residences
of the Missionaries are almost lost to view amid the wild
growth, for years, of grass, fruit trees, and shrubs. No
chapel bell is heard, but the building within which seven
hundred Christian natives have often crowded to worship
God stands amid the silence of nature, as a solemn remembrance of the glory departed. The broad stream, and its
many tributaries, upon the bosom of which fleets of canoes
bore their joyful crowds towards the house of prayer, flow
on and on, but the most that may now be seen is here and
there a solitary native propelling an old canoe, a relic of
former days. In the extensive district drained by the
several rivers flowing into the Hokianga, there is a sparse
population of not more than two thousand, old and young.
Though the law prohibits the sale of intoxicating liquors
among them, the collector of customs received last year
not less than £2,000 duty for their share of the local consumption of spirits. The settlers around are fewer than
in Mr. Turner's day, but are of a more respectable class.
Mr. Bushby, the first British resident, is the head of an
esteemed Christian family, and still occupies the estate

of ten thousand acres, delightfully situated. The aged Christian chieftain, Te Otene, (Orton,) still enjoys a peaceful life at the foot of the lofty Manuga Tawhia, at the head of the Mangamuka valley. The prosperous condition of his people, with their farms and homes, betokens the comfort possible to Maoris, which too many, unhappily, have refused to seek.

At Newark, a station first occupied by Mr. Whiteley, two Norfolk Island pines stand as the only memorials of the Mission. Waima, also founded by Mr. Turner, is still occupied. There are about three hundred natives in the valley, and through a prohibitory law, as it respects spirits, they are comparatively prosperous, owning numerous sheep, cattle, and industrial farms. The excellent Mr. Rowe is the stationed Missionary, and he has no European neighbour within twelve miles. The chapel, which will hold nearly two hundred, is pretty well filled on the Sabbath with natives in European costume. Separated the one from another by several ranges of hills, are the parallel valleys, Omaura, Wirinaki, and Pakanai, each sending its stream, as does the Waima, into the Hokianga. In each vale Mr. Rowe ministers to a few natives. Love of strong drink has reduced them to but a remnant, and their appearance at the house of God presents a marked contrast with that of their neighbours of Waima.

The station formed in Mr. Turner's time on the Upper Wairoa, by the Rev. J. Wallis, under the patronage of Te Tirarau, was for sixteen years occupied by the Rev. James Buller. It became one of the most promising in the land. The Rev. William Gittos at present labours among the people. He is a gifted Missionary, and has great influence with them. His Mission premises are at Rangiora, the Maoris having moved thitherward. All the natives of this station have remained steadfastly loyal to the British crown.

On Mr. Turner's leaving Hokianga in 1839, the Mission had stations at Waingaroa and Kawhia, (Raglan,) and preparations were about completed for the establishment of others at Waipa, Aotea, Mokau, Taranaki, Port Nicholson, and elsewhere. These stations are all now represented by a single Missionary, the Rev. Cort H. Schnackenberg, who resides at Raglan, and is in "labours more abundant." The well known King movement had its seat within his Circuit. Within three days' journey six flourishing stations were abandoned in consequence of the war; viz., Waikato, Taupiri, and Te Awamutu, of the Episcopalian Church, and Waipa, Aotea, and Kawhia, of the Wesleyan. Not one of these has been resumed. In no part of the land did the Mission work seem more successful. Day and boarding schools were flourishing; religious ordinances were valued; the natives were cheerfully engaged in industrial pursuits, supplying considerable quantities of flour from their own mills to the Auckland market. From Kawhia alone they exported sixty thousand bushels of wheat to Sydney in one year. They were, moreover, very anxious for some legislative action by which intemperance might be suppressed, and order maintained. Indeed, it was this desire which brought about the Maori King agitation. The feebleness of the Colonial Government suggested to them action of their own. The sequel is but too well known, —hostile collision with British troops, the confiscation of native lands, and the consequent arousing of a spirit of native rebellion, which only death can quell. The tribes, after sustaining heavy losses, fell back into sullen solitude. Remaining beyond the boundary in armed neutrality, they have resisted every attempt at peacemaking. These tribes, it should be known, have taken no part with the savage Te Koote, but yet they will not allow him to be pursued within their territory.

An interesting feature in Mr. Schnackenberg's sphere of

labour is the prosperity of three native schools maintained in part by the government. They are at Kawhia, Aotea, and Karakaski. The scholars acquire the English language and habits, with considerable rudimentary knowledge. The war broke up several similar schools, besides an important institution at the Three Kings, which for many years had supplied a good education to the Maori youth.

We are not prepared, however, to admit that Christian Missions in New Zealand have been a failure. If, after the toil and sacrifice of half a century, there are at this moment found comparatively few Maories in the fellowship of the Church of Christ, and evidencing a work of saving grace, we must not undervalue these few. But we are not willing to overlook the large numbers who in their day gave scriptural evidence of a change of heart, and who died rejoicing in the Lord. It is sad to know that missionary life has been sacrificed there. The Rev. C. S. Volkner, of the Church of England, and the Rev. John Whiteley, of the Wesleyan Church, have fallen by the violence of the race they lived to bless. But they had themselves saved many from death, and in the resurrection morning will be attended to the skies by a cloud of redeemed New Zealanders. The money cost of the Mission has indeed been large. Nearly £200,000 on the part of the Wesleyan Mission from first to last, and considerably more by the Church Society, have been expended. But what Christian dares weigh this money against the unfading trophies which gem his Redeemer's crown? Or what British statesman, or patriot, would grudge half a million of money for the national advantages arising from the settlement of New Zealand? For it must be distinctly acknowledged, that at no time could New Zealand have been safely colonized before the way had been prepared by missionary influence. Many illustrations might be given in proof of this. I cite one,—the colonization scheme by Captain Herd in 1826. That gentleman secured

land at Hokianga, and at the Thames, and introduced sixty
immigrants; but after expending £20,000, his company
were obliged to abandon their project, solely through the
ferocity of the natives. When, however, the tribes had
experienced the goodwill of Christian Missionaries, and
from them had learned the secret of Britain's greatness,
their passions and prejudices gave place to a desire for
national elevation, and their opposition to British settlement ceased. The result is the addition to the British
crown of one of its most valuable possessions.

The race has been diminished during the last fifty years
by war, improvidence, and vice. This is a sad spectacle.
It is, however, one on beholding which no one can feel
so deeply as does the New Zealander himself. The
Maoris, who are distinguished for being accurate observers
of all circumstances relating to natural history, have
remarked that some of the small native birds are gradually disappearing, and allege that these little birds are in
the habit of gathering their food by dipping their long
tongues into the blossoms of native trees; but since the
introduction of bees, they have likewise sought the same
blossoms for honey, and, while concealed in the
flower, have stung the tongue of the birds, which has
caused death. The natives compare the condition of these
birds to themselves, and say that while unconscious of the
dangers introduced by civilization, they fall into them, and
become its victims, and, in the same way as the little birds,
they are themselves gradually disappearing. These obser-
vations, while highly interesting and instructive from the
display of intelligence on the part of the Maoris, are yet
tinged with a shade of melancholy, by the reflection that
such a noble and intellectual race is, in the manner so
feelingly and despondingly described by themselves, rapidly
disappearing.

It is an unwelcome task to trace up the state of things

now unhappily existing to its remote causes. But, for the honour of the Church somewhat represented in this biography, a few words must be written. The ten years preceding 1838 had witnessed a marked change in the native mind and character, which the Maoris themselves ascribed to the Word of God and the Missionaries. But with the Romish Bishop and his French priests came an element of discord. Later still, it must in duty be said, arose another disturbing cause, in the exclusive and unmissionary-like policy at first pursued by Bishop Selwyn. Though his talents, zeal, and intrepidity command admiration, it cannot be forgotten that that Missionary Prelate did much to create division among those whose previous union in Christ's work had been a general blessing to the natives. Then came colonization, with its train of vices too powerful to be resisted by the people who (like most persons in professing Christendom of every nation) had little more than the form of religion. At that juncture they were found adhering to the ordinances of the Gospel they had received, everywhere observing the Sabbath, and abhorring drunkenness. Their social condition, however, was perilous by its inexperience, and their national by its friendlessness. Then came the most potent evil of all, bearing their doom in its rapid strides throughout their land,—political discontent. Writing the political history of the New Zealanders is not my business; but it is obvious that if the Government had uniformly acted with integrity and firmness, there would have been no war.

We review the missionary era of New Zealand with mingled feelings, but we are bold to say just this, that notwithstanding the manifold difficulties of the Committee at home, and the ever-changing forms of discouragement their agents encountered in their work, the Wesleyan Mission in that land has from the beginning maintained the spirit and upheld the honour of the Church of Christ. Such at present

is the condition of the remnant scattered through the land,
that the moral conflict of truth with heathenism as a system
may be said to have closed ; and in coming out of the
conflict, the Missionary Church bears with it a stricken,
but an unstained, shield.   The calm self-sacrifice and heroic
devotion of such men as Henry Williams and John Whiteley,
Carl S. Volkner and Nathaniel Turner, and of others not yet
dismissed to their reward, will brighten the most eventful
page of New Zealand history ; for they were God's servants;
they prepared the native race in thousands of instances
for the land where there is no war, and, in doing so, prepared a home for a future Christian nation in the southern
world.

There is every probability that New Zealand will speedily
rise to eminence among the favoured homes of the Anglo-
Saxon race. Claiming as I do its colonization as an indirect
fruit of missionary enterprise, it may not be considered
much out of place if I glance at its climate, resources,
and institutions,—important features in any land inviting
immigration.

The climate is excellent, affording an agreeable variety
between the parallels of $34\frac{1}{4}°$ and $47\frac{1}{2}°$ south latitude.   In
the north snow is never seen, and frost seldom.   In the
extreme south both are common, and in some places
severe.   The English fruits grow to perfection in the
southern island ; and tropical productions flourish in the
northern.   But there are no extremes.   Protracted droughts
and extensive floods are unknown.   It is drier in the
south than in the north.   The mean annual temperature
of the latter is 57°, while that of the former is 52°.   The
nights are about twelve degrees colder than the days.   The
mildness of the temperature at Nelson and Canterbury in
the Middle Island may be known by the fact of sheep
lambing in winter with no greater loss than five or ten per

cent. More rain falls in New Zealand than in London, but less than is known on the west coast of England. The weather is everywhere subject to sudden changes, but nothing can exceed the purity of a clear New Zealand sky. It is certified that the military stationed there enjoyed better health than anywhere else in Her Majesty's dominions.

The Northern Island contains twenty-six million acres, the Middle Island thirty-eight million, and the Southern Island one million. The whole group has nearly the same area as Great Britain, the coast line measuring three thousand one hundred and twenty miles. A lofty range of mountains runs north and south, and in the Northern Island there are many fine harbours and navigable rivers. In the Middle Island there are extensive plains covered with natural pasturage ; but in the north the open country, with but little exception, is clothed with fern. Much of the soil, which seems inferior, greatly improves when brought under cultivation. There are many rich plains and valleys, and in not a few places a strong loam is found to the very tops of high hills. In several districts there is a light volcanic soil, which carries luxuriant grass. The extensive forests afford a variety of woods suitable for ship and house building, and for furnishing. Gum is dug from the soil in the north, and finds a ready market, in large quantities, in England and America. The New Zealand flax bids fair to become an article of extensive export. It will afford a very ready means of profitable industry to persons of small capital. The country abounds in mineral riches. Both in the north and south there are rich deposits of gold. It is " a good land, a land of brooks, of water, of fountains and depths, that spring out of the valleys and hills ; a land of wheat, and barley, and vines, and fig-trees, and pome-granates ; a land of oil olive, and honey ; a land wherein thou shalt eat bread without scarceness, thou shalt not lack anything in it; a land whose stones are iron, and out of whose hills thou mayest dig brass."

The religious, social, and educational institutions resemble those of Australia; and the moral tone of society is at least as good. The colonial population is about two hundred and fifty thousand; the Maoris are estimated at thirty-six thousand. The lamentable war of the last ten years has been the greatest drawback to the colony. But the end of it is near. The political institutions, which are peculiar, are cumbrous and expensive. Besides a general government, embracing two houses of legislature, the colony is divided into nine provinces, each having an organized representative government. Each province controls its own legislation; excepting in the departments of the customs, the post-office, the telegraph, and the Maoris.

The chief towns are Auckland, Wellington, Nelson, Lyttelton, Christchurch, Dunedin, Inver-Cargill, Napier, and New Plymouth. The last-named is an open roadstead. All the rest, save Christchurch, are seaport towns. The revenue for the year 1869-70 amounted to one and a quarter millions. The great wants of the colony are roads, population, and capital; and the tendency of recent legislation is to secure them as speedily as possible. Notwithstanding the incubus of the war, and the ill effects of over-legislation, New Zealand has made rapid progress, as well in religion as in matters social and commercial. There is no state aid, and Methodism, having faithfully served the past race of the Maoris, holds an honourable position, and finds its appropriate work, among the Churches throughout the land. The largest Protestant place of worship in New Zealand is that of the Wesleyan denomination in Christchurch. The statistics of New Zealand Methodism, now seeking self-government under a separate Conference, show 3 Districts, 29 Circuits, 119 churches, 45 Ministers, aided by 181 Local Preachers, 2,658 Church members, 16,000 hearers, and 5,615 Sabbath scholars. These returns show the result of steady progress; for no Wesleyan settlement has been formed, though the Episcopalian, Presbyterian, and Independent bodies have all had their New Zealand Pilgrim Fathers. There is much room for intelligent, enterprising Christian men, and especially for Christian workers.

CHAPTER XV

ON the evening of his arrival, Wednesday, Mr. Turner conducted the service in Macquarie Street chapel. He found " Sydney much enlarged and improved. Many emigrants had arrived, and among them some of the excellent of the earth."

On Sunday afternoon he preached at Princes Street on Christ's ability to save to the uttermost, and had a blessed season at Macquarie Street in the evening. At the prayer-meeting in the vestry afterwards, six souls entered into Gospel liberty. The next evening he conducted a special service in the same chapel, preaching from, " Blessed are they that mourn." Five or six went forward as penitents, and had the promise verified, " They shall be comforted." His eldest daughter was one of the happy number. [During the interval of thirty years she has honoured God in His Church. She is now the wife of the Rev. John Harcourt.]

The new chapel in Macquarie Street, Parramatta, was opened on the following Thursday. The Rev. John M'Kenny, Chairman of the District, preached in the fore-noon from, " Thy kingdom come." The congregation then proceeded to the site of another intended new sanctuary. Here Hannibal M'Arthur, Esq., M.C., gave an appropriate address, and then laid the corner-stone of the Centenary Chapel. The Rev. D. J. Draper also addressed the assembly. In the evening the Rev. Joseph Orton preached an excellent sermon from, " How goodly are thy tents, O Jacob ! "

Next Lord's day Mr. Turner preached in the morning in the newly-opened church. In the afternoon he stood upon the foundation-stone of the Centenary building, and cried, " Neither is there salvation in any other." At night he heard the Rev. James Watkin from, " The redemption of their soul is precious." After sermon he assisted in the administration of the Lord's Supper, when one soul professed to enter into the enjoyment of " perfect love."

Methodist preachers have few holidays. At the instance of the Chairman, he spent the next Sabbath at Maitland, an interesting rising town upon the river Hunter. He was received by Mr. Ladsam, a warm-hearted Irish Methodist lately arrived, and who was a very acceptable Local Preacher. God had so blessed his labours that there was now a promising cause, and a chapel was in course of erection. Mr. Turner preached twice to a good congregation in the billiard room, gave tickets to the members, and administered the Lord's Supper to the Society and to a few other pious persons. His notes of the Maitland district close thus : " A more beautiful and fertile country I never saw in all my travels."

His sojourn in Sydney was extended longer than he had anticipated. But it was well, for his ministrations were much owned of God. He was not sorry, however, when the time came for his departure ; for Sydney was a place he never loved, except as it offered a sphere of usefulness.

Having been re-appointed to Hobart Town, and made Chairman of the Van Diemen's Land District, he sailed on the 3rd of November, in the " Lord Glenelg." It was Sabbath morning ; and, when the brig had cleared the Heads, he held Divine service on the quarter-deck. He found his fellow passengers, the Rev. Peter Campbell and family, of the Presbyterian Church, " very intelligent and agreeable people." On the ninth day, Tuesday, they were again in their old Melville Street home. It was soon besieged by kind friends who hastened to offer their welcome. The same evening he was greeted by a large congregation in the chapel. For once he was unmanned. His over-excitement had put preaching out of the question. He could but express his thankfulness to God, and say a few words to those assembled. His feelings had been increased by the unexpected appearance in the congregation of about twenty New Zealanders, who had made their way to the church to look upon the friend of their race and country. As he addressed them warmly in their own language, they listened with liveliest demonstrations of pleasure. This episode of the evening created much interest. The service closed by prayer, in English, offered by the Rev. John Waterhouse, and in Maori by Mr. Turner.

"The Lord God is a Sun and Shield," was the theme of his introductory service next Sabbath. As there were many New Zealanders in port, he announced for a Maori service in the afternoon. About thirty natives attended, and the chapel was filled with an interested congregation. In the evening he preached with much plainness of speech from, "Examine yourselves whether ye be in the faith." Lady Franklin, the Governor's sister, and some military officers were present. Many Maoris attended, and Mr. Turner could not slight the opportunity to give them another short address.

His colleague, the Rev. John Eggleston, was to have gone to Launceston for the succeeding Sabbath, but family circumstances preventing, Mr. Turner went in his stead. The journey occupied from Thursday noon till Saturday evening. He rode sixty miles on the Saturday, but a cordial welcome compensated him for his fatigue. He found "most of the friends prospering in their souls." On the Sabbath he "laboured hard," preaching twice, meeting a class, and administering the Lord's Supper. Monday morning was spent in visiting numerous old friends. In the afternoon he met Mrs. Sherwin's class for tickets, and at night conducted a public prayer-meeting. While he was giving an account of the Lord's doings among the heathen, many were graciously affected, and his own heart softened. The next day he was accompanied by Messrs. Oakden, Reed, and Sherwin, to Westbury, on the occasion of laying the foundation stone of a new chapel there. He found Mr. Reed "flaming with love to precious souls." At Westbury he met the Rev. John Warren, who was about to proceed to New Zealand. In Launceston he preached on Wednesday night, to a chapel full of people.

By sunrise next morning he left for Avoca and Paul's Plains, nearly fifty miles distant, Mr. Gleadow kindly driving him half way. In the afternoon, in company with the Rev. W. Butters, of Ross, he visited Major Grey and family. It was somewhat remarkable that in that neighbourhood three related families of the same name, "Grey," had lately suffered bereavement by the sudden death of the eldest son. Two of the young men had been drowned. The other had been killed by a horse bolting, and dashing his rider's head against a tree. The visit, which was one of condolence, was kindly received. He preached in the local court-house to a good congregation, on the improvement of time. In the evening he was hospitably entertained by Mr. Simon Lord, to whose family the ministerial visits of the Rev. William Butters had lately been made useful. At nine o'clock next morning he again preached in the court-house. He held service in the afternoon at Campbell Town, and rested at Somercoates, the residence of Captain Horton,—twelve miles further on his journey. Here he found three young men who, though but lately converted, were engaged as exhorters in the neighbourhood. He was at their little prayer-meeting at six on Sunday morning. At half-past nine he preached in the new chapel at Ross, and then rode twenty miles to Oatlands, where, at three and six P.M., he again preached the word of life. His impressions, after meeting the class there, were that the cause at Oatlands was "in a promising state." A new chapel was in the course of erection. On Monday he preached, at noon, at Mr. Johnson's, and late in the evening regained his home in Hobart Town. In ten days he had travelled three hundred miles, and conducted eighteen public services.

During the fortnight which followed, the duties of the Circuit were pressing; yet his mind was much exercised about the New Zealand Mission. There were now many fair flowers and much fruit of the good seed; and he dreaded the blasting breath of Popery. In arranging for the approaching Missionary Anniversary, he appointed a special afternoon service with the Maoris then in the city. The interest of that service induced him to resolve to raise special subscriptions on behalf of that Mission. He personally solicited several friends who were in good means, and was grateful to God for the sum of seventy pounds thus obtained. The Central Missionary Meeting was presided over by Sir John Franklin, and the collection amounted to fifty pounds. The watchnight service was peculiarly interesting and impressive; it was conducted by Messrs. Waterhouse, Eggleston, and Turner.

On the 4th of January Mr. Bumby arrived from New Zealand, to consult the General Superintendent, Mr. Waterhouse, upon Mission matters. Mr. Turner received by him many kind letters from his former missionary associates and native friends. He was much affected by the earnest, loving requests of the latter that he would return, and labour amongst them; for no change ever cooled his affection for that race. In that week's diary he thus wrote of a " sister departed," Mrs. John Barrett, —" A woman greatly beloved by all who knew her, and whose loss will be much felt by many, especially by her family. A more useful member was not found in our Society, or in the colony."

On the New Year's Sabbath morning he preached on spiritual health. Mr. Bumby assisted at the Covenant service, and in the evening preached a telling sermon on, " Watchman ! what of the night ? " Mr. Bumby and he spent most of the week together, visiting friends. On Saturday Mr. Turner wrote, " I seldom find this a profitable way of spending time. O for a closer walk with God ! Lord, draw me, that I may run after Thee ! "

He went to the Brown's River Chapel Anniversary on the Monday, in company with about thirty or forty visitors, whose Christian zeal took the form of a pleasure trip. The wind being dead against them, they were two hours behind time on reaching the chapel. Mr. Bumby preached. On Wednesday he started as a deputation to the Missionary Meetings on the northern side of the island. Of this laborious trip he wrote : " Have attended three Missionary Meetings, at Ross, Launceston, and Longford. They were all interesting meetings, the two former especially. After the Sabbath and Monday services at Launceston, we collected two hundred pounds. Thanks be to God for the change He has wrought in that place, and for the disposition He has given to some of our leading men there to support His cause, and extend its influence in every way they can."

The succeeding entries are as follows :—

" Sunday, 26th.—This has been a day of light. Seldom more at liberty in pressing home the truths of God to the souls of men. But, alas ! no conversions yet. O for saving power ! "

" February 1st.—A week of profitable labour. Have felt the presence of my Master while visiting the poor of our people from house to house. O, this is a blessed and important part of the Christian pastor's duty! This evening re-commenced the public band-meeting, and we had a soul-encouraging time."

He had now an unexpected trial, which he felt was untimely. It was the removal to another Circuit of his fellow labourer, Mr. Eggleston. The Rev. W. Longbottom * having arrived from Adelaide invalided, the General Superintendent arranged for Mr. Eggleston to take his place. Mr. Turner felt that his Circuit would suffer, and that, if Mr. Longbottom did not regain his health, as appeared probable, an additional burden of labour would be cast upon him. Already his energies had been taxed to the utmost, and he keenly felt the altered position. However, he penned, and no doubt appropriated, one of his favourite promises, " As is thy day, so shall thy strength be."

On Sunday, March 2nd, he preached in Mr. Lucas's barn at North West Bay, and next day obtained an acre of land, and numerous promises of money towards the erection of a chapel there. Returned home, he found his New Zealand servant girl in a dying state. That week he accomplished an important object on which he had set his mind,—the purchase of the chapel property from the Association of Friends, several of whom had resolved to return to the Church from which they had seceded. On Saturday morning he " bade farewell to Mr. Eggleston, and prayed

---

* The Rev. William Longbottom, who was born in Bingley, Yorkshire, entered the ministry in 1826, and in 1829 proceeded to Madras. After a short stay at the Cape of Good Hope, he came to the colonies, in 1837. While voyaging from Hobart Town to Swan River, he was shipwrecked near Lacepede Bay. He was providentially led to Adelaide, where, finding a few Wesleyans, he founded the Church there. For about eighteen months he laboured with much success, and then, through failure of health, went to Tasmania. In 1844 he returned to South Australia. Two years later he retired from the active work, and in 1849 he " finished his course." His memory is cherished as that of an amiable and devoted servant of God.

earnestly for his success." The same afternoon he committed to the dust the remains of Parinhia, his New Zealand servant, and recorded his trust that, through the Atonement, she had gone home to God.

Next morning he preached in High Street chapel,—that above alluded to,—and received numerous expressions of satisfaction at his having been able to do so. At the Bethel in the afternoon, and at Melville Street at night, he had much freedom and power. His next records are of labours among the poor, the sick, and the dying.

On April 7th he hailed the arrival of nine Missionaries bound for New Zealand, the Friendly Islands, and Fiji. The "Triton" had been expected, and a short time saw the whole party comfortably domiciled among hospitable Christian friends. Mr. Turner's guests at the Mission house were Mr. and Mrs. Williams and Mr. and Mrs. Turton. The remainder of the party were Messrs. Buddle, Francis Wilson, Kevern, and Skevington, with their wives, and three single brethren, Messrs. Buttle, Aldred, and Smales. Six of the number were appointed to New Zealand, and Messrs. Wilson and Kevern to the Friendly Islands. The appointment of the Rev. Thomas Williams to Fiji completed the first staff of seven Missionaries to that group. The Committee had pledged themselves in terms of promise to Mr. Brackenbury of Raithby Hall, Lincolnshire, to send that number.

Their sojourn of sixteen days afforded much delight to the Hobart Town church. The social public welcome given them, and the monster gathering at the Sunday School Anniversary, called forth the oratory of several, and it was not vainly employed. Two Missionary Meetings were held at O'Brien's Bridge and New Norfolk. Upon re-embarking on the 23rd, they were joined by their esteemed General Superintendent, upon a visit to the several Mission fields.

So large a reinforcement must have helped Mr. Turner's faith for the answer to his prayer,—

"O Jesus, ride on, till all are subdued."

Mr. Longbottom's health did not improve, and almost all the duty of the Circuit devolved on Mr. Turner. The depression from this cause was increased by the grievously unchristian behaviour of several of his members, and by family affliction. During that quarter he did not see the desire of his heart in a general awakening. In August he wrote, "We have at times appeared to be on the eve of a revival; then something has transpired to put an extinguisher upon the gracious flame. Blessed be God, He has drawn me out in strong desire after Himself and the salvation of souls!"

On the 20th he received the unexpected and painful intelligence of the death by drowning of the Rev. J. H. Bumby, and of twelve natives, by the upsetting of their canoe, while crossing the Frith of the Thames river in New Zealand. He wrote, "How painfully mysterious this event! how afflictive to the Church! how distressing to his friends! A finer young man I scarcely ever saw or heard; a polished shaft in the Lord's quiver; a workman that needed not to be ashamed. Though highly gifted and deeply devoted to God and His cause, his missionary career has been short; but he shines above. Perhaps the Lord has in mercy taken him from the evil to come. That day will declare the why and the wherefore. O that I may pray and watch, that I may be found of Him in peace, without spot, and blameless! Lord, help me! Why, Lord, have I so long been spared, while Thy more highly gifted servant has been cut down?"

On September 2nd Mr. Waterhouse returned in "The Triton." With him were the Revs. David Cargill and W. Brooks. Mrs. Cargill had been called away by death, and the widowed husband had brought his four children to where they would less feel their loss. Mr. Brooks' health, and that of his family, had so suffered as that their removal had become a necessity. The wife of the Rev. Francis Wilson had died upon the outward voyage, and her remains had been committed to the deep.

By a letter from James Garland, a Christian native, who had been with Mr. Bumby at the time, and had witnessed his dying struggles with the waves, Mr. Turner learned that six of those who had been drowned were of the choicest youths of Mangungu. Garland himself had but narrowly escaped by swimming a great distance. Mr. Waterhouse improved the event before a crowded congregation in Melville Street, preaching from the words, " Clouds and darkness are round about Him : justice and judgment are the habitation of His throne."

The District Meeting of that year began on October 15th, the General Superintendent presiding. The Hobart Town Circuit Report mentions nearly twenty members having removed to Port Phillip, besides others elsewhere. The change decided on involved Mr. Turner's removal to Launceston, with Mr. Brooks as his colleague, to reside at Longford. The arrangement was quite in harmony with his judgment, and was in every respect agreeable.

The new chapel in Melville Street was so nearly finished that advantage was taken of the presence of the brethren at the District Meeting for the opening services. The erection of that immense and costly sanctuary had been entered upon before Mr. Turner's arrival; and it is right in me to say that, in spite of his love to Hobart Town and the Methodist friends there, he from the first regarded the building as unnecessarily large, and the expenditure as likely to entail difficulty. However, that Centenary Chapel, which, for many years afterwards, was the largest Methodist sanctuary in the Southern World, was formally dedicated to the service of Almighty God on Sabbath, October 18th, 1840. The weather had been unusually wet, but partially cleared up for the celebration. At 11 A.M. the Rev. J. Waterhouse read the

Morning Service, and preached from, "I beseech Thee, O Lord, send now prosperity." It was a good sermon. In the afternoon the Rev. Benjamin Hurst, from Port Phillip, preached a very plain, pointed, useful discourse from, "They that wait upon the Lord shall renew their strength." Sir John and Lady Franklin and other distinguished personages attended the evening service. It was conducted by the Rev. David Cargill, M.A. In an admirable sermon on a part of Solomon's prayer at the dedication of the temple there were some fine bursts of eloquence, and many powerful appeals. The congregations were good; but, in Mr. Turner's judgment, "the collections were not what they ought to have been, considering the numbers and means of those present." The continuation services were of a missionary character. On Monday evening a large meeting was addressed by two Christian natives, the one of Fiji, through Mr. Cargill as interpreter, and the other a Friendly Islander, for whom Mr. Turner rendered that service. The Rev. W. Simpson closed the opening services by preaching on the Tuesday night from the text, "And mine eyes and mine heart shall be there perpetually."

On November 16th Mr. Turner took a Christian farewell of his congregation, and on the next day left Hobart Town. The itinerancy in Methodism causes many family separations; and it was a trial to leave two of his sons in Hobart Town; the eldest in a banking situation, and another at school. On the Wednesday the travellers halted at Somercoates. By previous arrangement with Mr. Butters, Thursday was set apart for the Ross Missionary Meeting. It was presided over by George Palmer Ball, Esq., and the chief speaker was Mr. Cargill. The meeting was of a most delightful character; the collection twenty-eight pounds. On Friday night they were entertained at Mr. Ball's beautiful house at Mountford, and on Saturday afternoon finished their journey to Launceston.

CHAPTER XVI.

1840–1843.

I HAVE heard of some one saying, "These Methodists are worse than the devil,—we do hear of him being cast out of one place, but we never hear this of the Methodists." I suppose we must accept the compliment. Ordinarily, where we take root, we grow and spread. Launceston, however, was an exception. Indeed, its early Methodist history is almost an anomaly, as the subjoined account will show. It is compiled chiefly from a paper read by Mr. Isaac Sherwin * at the Launceston celebration of the Jubilee of Australasian Methodism.

About the year 1827, the Rev. J. Hutchinson was stationed there. A Society was formed, and a chapel and

---

* The Honourable Isaac Sherwin was born in Burslem, in 1804. As a youth he resided in Germany for six years ; and at the age of nineteen accompanied his father to Van Diemen's Land. After a few years he revisited the Continent, and then settled in Tasmania in 1829. During the visit of the Revs. N. Turner and J. A. Manton to Launceston, in 1832, lasting religious impressions were made on his mind, and on that of Mrs. Sherwin,—impressions which deepened until they both found the Saviour. Early in 1835, just six months after he had joined the Church, he began to preach ; and shortly after was appointed a Leader. From that date till the close of life, he held various offices of influence and trust in the Church, fulfilling their duties with humility and faithfulness. In his business relations he was respected for his promptness, conscientiousness, and perseverance,—qualities by which, under the smiles of Providence, he prospered. As a citizen he was highly esteemed for the interest he evinced in the charities and public institutions of the town. Amid the activities of life his Bible was his counsellor, and in his retirement it afforded him light and solace. He died in great peace on June 27th, 1869.

Minister's house were erected. He was succeeded by Mr. Esh Lovell, a hired Local Preacher. The Missionary Committee, by whom the station had been sustained, finding the year 1828 one of great depression, withdrew its aid, and removed its agent. The chapel and house, towards which members and friends had contributed, were sold to the Government; and the original private subscriptions were returned to the donors. To their Christian honour, the subscribers regarded the amounts as still sacred, inasmuch as they had been devoted to God. They held them over until the arrival of the Rev. J. Anderson, and in connexion with his settlement in the town as a Presbyterian Minister, they re-applied them. The Treasurer of the fund so reserved, and one of the Trustees of the property, was Mr. John Pascoe Faukner. So far as is known, the only surviving member is Mrs. Thomas Cox, who at that period was Mrs. French. Mr. Hutchinson retired from the work many years ago. In the year 1832, Mr. Francis French, a Local Preacher from Cornwall, preached in the open air, upon the Windmill Hill. It was at this time, as before narrated, that Mr. Turner and Mr. Manton visited the town in company, spending one Sabbath there. They found no Society, but preached twice in the court-house.

For two years Mr. Turner paid a quarterly visit, preaching many times and with encouraging success. His services were held in the public school-house, the former Wesleyan chapel. The building was more than crowded, and many sincere worshippers who came too late for a seat, were thankful their preacher's voice was so good. Numbers joined the Church. For a brief term, Mr. Leech was employed as Catechist. In 1834, the Rev. J. A. Manton was appointed, and having found a people prepared of the Lord, appropriately took as his first text, Acts xi. 23. The co-operation of the Society was most hearty, and arrangements were entered upon for building a chapel. During one of his apostolic visits, Mr. Turner had fortunately secured the present valuable site in Patterson Street. It had been appropriated as a Government pound for bullocks. But he requested that its reserve for that purpose might be cancelled, and that instead it might be dedicated to the use of the Wesleyan Church, to whom Sir George Arthur was under the promise of a building site. Mr. Manton was honoured of God in the establishment of the infant Church. With such devoted and influential Christian men as Philip Oakden, Henry Reed, J. W. Gleadow, and others like-minded, the funds were speedily provided for the erection of the chapel, and subsequently for the school and class-rooms in the rear. Mr. Manton remained four years, during which term the cause was extended to Perth, Long-ford, Westbury, Wesleydale, and White Hills. His first staff of Local Preachers were Peter Jacobs, John Williams, George Goold, John Smith, John Tongs, Henry Reed, and Isaac Sherwin.

The zeal and liberality of the Launceston Church at that time was soon distinguished among all in those parts. In its first ten years, the Circuit subscribed not less than ten thousand pounds. In this sum was included fourteen hundred pounds, as a thank-offering on the Centenary list. It was expended upon the Minister's residence, which was placed, in the first instance, free from debt, for the use of Mr. Turner's family. The early office-bearers adopted as an axiom in their polity, that every man in the Church must have something to do for the Lord. The improved morals of the town, especially in respect of Sabbath obser-vances, were in a great degree the result of this action. The Rev. W. Simpson, a gifted Minister, followed Mr. Manton ; and after two years was succeeded by Mr. Turner, at the date reached in this biographical record,—Novem-ber, 1840.

After preaching twice on his first Sabbath, he met the

Society in the evening, under a deep feeling of desire for the salvation of souls. For a month he had hard work and much spiritual anxiety, though the cordial co-operation of so many, with a single eye to the glory of God, was very encouraging. His first sacramental service was one of "hallowing power:" and on the next Sabbath morning two precious souls professed to enter into Gospel rest.

On Monday 21st, he went to Wesley Dale,—a ten hours' journey. Messrs. Oakden, Gleadow, and Ferguson accompanied him. He preached at night at Mr. Oakden's farm to forty persons, and gave tickets to about twenty members. Their Leader, William Pitt, was a monument of saving grace. He had been a notoriously wicked man, but was now avenging the Lord's cause. He also preached to about fifty on Mr. Reed's farm. Next day he told ten persons in Westbury chapel, "Ye must be born again," and then met the members. On Thursday, after riding twenty miles, he took tea at home, and then rode out to "The Springs," to give tickets to Mr. Bartley's class. The last Sabbath of the year was spent at Longford, where Mr. Brooks had been called to suffer the loss of his eldest boy, and was now mourning the serious affliction of his wife and surviving child. The year closed with the customary solemnities of Methodism.

New Year's Sabbath is thus alluded to: "January 3rd.— A solemn, sweet, heavenly Sabbath. The sermon this morning appeared to make deep impression. In the afternoon renewed the covenant with the Society. My own soul was deeply humbled and sweetly elevated, and with sincere heart I gave myself afresh to God. In the evening, Mr. Brooks preached from, 'I know Thou wilt bring me to death, and to the house appointed for all living.' The sermon was solemn and impressive; and, poor man! he looked like one dropping into the grave. After sermon we held a prayer-meeting in the school-room, where the Lord made bare His saving arm. About a dozen in deep distress came forward as penitents, that we might pray for them. Nor did we pray in vain. Half the number entered into Gospel liberty. Three of these had been backsliders. Glory to God for His reviving power!" After the Mission prayer-meeting the next evening, at which Mr. Bumby's tour round northern New Zealand was read, three more received the assurance of God's forgiving love.

There was now much sickness in the town. Twenty children were reported to have died in one week. Mr. Turner himself and several of his children were somewhat seriously ill; but the more afflicted state of his colleague and family seemed to forbid his being laid up. On Sunday, 17th, having a heavy cold and sore throat, he rode through the rain to Longford and Cressy, and did a full day's work. The next Thursday, Mr. Brooks' youngest child was buried in the same grave in which his little brother had been interred only a month before,—"In their death they were not divided."

On the 21st, he preached out of doors in Launceston, at a place called St. Giles, to "a large company, who behaved well." He believed that to some the word was "spirit and life." On the 28th, he had three services at Wesley Dale, and on the Sunday after was at the other side of the island, preaching at New Norfolk and Back River. He preached at many villages upon both journeys, and had reason to believe that the seed would be fruitful.

Up to this time the family had lived in a rented, old-fashioned house, as a temporary Circuit arrangement. Subjoined, is the first entry in the study of the Centenary House. "March 22nd.—Removed into the new Mission house to-day, a spacious dwelling, raised by special contributions, and presented to the Conference as the Centenary offering of the Society. The cost, with outer buildings, is about fourteen hundred pounds. It is by far the best house we ever inhabited, and with our large family is a great comfort. Have had some gracious seasons while renewing the tickets the last quarter, but am ready to be discouraged because more souls are not converted to God among us."

At the lovefeast on the 29th, the Lord of hosts was present. The Circuit Quarterly Meeting was one of harmony and peace. Through all his public career Mr. Turner sought to place the financial polity of his Station, Circuit, or District, upon its right basis. Access to a general or public fund was never suffered as an excuse for local indifference. At the official meeting of this date he had the satisfaction of securing an unanimous resolution that the Circuit would support its own Ministers. The brethren present, with a nobleness of mind which did them honour, at once paid up the deficiencies of the past, that they might start clear, and proceed in honourable independence of the Mission fund. It was customary to hold a quarterly watchnight service. . That quarter, Mr. Lassetter preached, and the brethren Crooks and Smith delivered good addresses.

Upon his April visit to Wesley Dale, he found the people alive to God. They "received the word with a ready mind." From this date an undue share of the ministerial labour of the Circuit was thrown on Mr. Turner, and he became much depressed from this cause. Early in August the excellent Mrs. Brooks fell asleep in Jesus, making a glorious end. The case of her widowed, childless survivor, evidently soon to follow, called forth much sympathy from his colleague and friend. The bereavement was, as in many similar instances, sanctified. No order of society (if so they may be spoken of) are more united in the fellowship of love than Methodist Preachers, and the grief of one bereaved family is often healing and life to another.

Early in spring Mr. Turner visited the Nile, a new place in Methodism, some thirty miles from town, and preached on the evening of his arrival at Mr. Glaer's. Before breakfast next morning he preached again at the same gentleman's house, at ten in the forenoon at Mr. Mitchell's, and at one o'clock at Mr. Pike's. He wrote,—"Glory to God! there is a powerful awakening amongst the dwellers in this romantic, secluded spot. Ten have begun to meet in class, and I have resolved to help them all I can."

At the September Quarterly Meeting a considerable increase of members was reported, and, despite great mercantile depression, the finances were in a better state than on any former occasion. This meeting over, he again crossed the island. He found Hobart Town friends kind as ever, and had an agreeable time with the General Superintendent, who had just returned from his second official visit to the islands. Mr. Turner wrote,—"The island Missions are wearing a pleasing aspect, though there are some things to discourage."

The District Meeting that year was held in Launceston. Five days' close application from six in the morning till late at night saw it through. Seventy pounds were collected at the Missionary Anniversary on Sunday and Monday.

"December 31st.—Since my last journal entry I have had to labour hard in consequence of Mr. Brooks' affliction. He has been entirely laid aside for some weeks past. My own health has also been failing for the last few weeks. From weakness and excessive labour I fear being laid aside altogether. Because I cannot do the full work of two men, some of the places are neglected, and the people complain. May it please the Lord to spare me a little longer, and give me strength to labour in His cause! I love my God, I love His work, and wish to live to Him alone. O for a greater conformity to His image and will in all things!"

The Circuit now needed the full labours of two men. Its scattered Societies, forty miles in one direction, and twenty in another, in addition to the claims of the town, called for systematic and laborious service; and now that his colleague was laid aside, it was peculiarly distressing that his strength and energies were sensibly failing. The public labours of the first three Sabbaths of the year were rendered in much feebleness, and he arranged with Mr. Butters for change of air, and other engagements. On the 23rd and 30th, and during the intervening week, he laboured in Ross, Campbell Town, Oatlands, and Green Ponds, Mr. Butters meanwhile working the Launceston Circuit; and then on the Monday travelled down to Hobart Town to see Mr. Waterhouse, who was seriously ill. The afflicted servant of God looked upon his friend and wept; he was too ill to converse. Another call was made with similar results. His bodily sufferings were too great to allow of an interview. It was a sorrowful disappointment: Mr. Turner had taken a long journey on purpose to offer his Christian sympathy. By Friday evening he was again in Launceston.

On the 20th of February, the Sabbath before the races, he preached in the open air, from, "So run that ye may obtain."

"March 21st.—Early in the morning, yesterday, was greatly tried in my family; and having yielded too much to temper, I became much distressed in my mind, and harassed by the devil." That week's diary contains notices of three friends:—a member's child,—George Brentley, a good man, who had been called suddenly to his heavenly home,—and Mr. Daniel Robertson, who had been drowned while out fishing; cut off in the midst of his years and his health. Ten days later he left for Hobart Town, hoping to reach there before Mr. Waterhouse's death, which was daily looked for.

"Saturday, April 2nd, Hobart Town.—Our dear brother Waterhouse quitted this mortal vale on Wednesday night a little before nine o'clock, and of his triumphant entrance into the everlasting kingdom no doubt can be entertained, though the very depressing nature of his affliction forbad his saying much. I waited upon his widow and family, and found them sustaining their bereavement with Christian fortitude and resignation. This afflictive dispensation preys upon my mind, and is exciting universal sympathy in the town. His death will be felt as a public calamity. O, how mysterious the dispensations of Providence! Poor Mr. Bumby, and now Mr. Waterhouse, two of the most likely men for great public usefulness that have been sent to this part of the vineyard, are both gone. Lord! may I be ready for Thy summons!"

On the Tuesday following he conducted the funeral solemnities: there were fourteen Ministers and a large number of friends at the service. Later in the day, he called his ministerial brethren together, when they officially recorded their deep sympathy with the Church in the loss sustained. They also resolved on erecting a memorial tablet in the Melville Street church. The Ministers of the Mission and other Districts joined in this expression of esteem.

Temporarily the duties of the late General Superintendent fell upon Mr. Turner, he being Chairman of the District at the time. The "Triton" returned from the islands on the 18th; and on the 26th Mr. Turner again went over to Hobart Town, to carry through the business necessary to her being again despatched on Mission account. Three or four days sufficed for this work. Upon his return there was introduced to him his fourteenth child, being his eighth son.

Written in the spirit of Christian charity, there is a diary note of a miserable act of clerical bigotry. A Church Clergyman, who, I suppose, held some exclusive privileges at the time in his official relation to the Government, interfered so as to prevent his visiting a young man in the gaol, then lying under sentence of death; although the unhappy youth had expressly sent for him, and the Sheriff's pass had been given him.

The usual visit to Wesley Dale had become a pleasure, though involving much labour. That in June was during severe frosts and biting cold ; but its incidents were those of Gospel joy and success. On Monday, June 20th, after a series of blessed services on the Sabbath, a gracious revival broke out in Launceston. "At the prayer-meeting several were in deep distress, and three or four found peace with God. Many of the old members appeared on full stretch for holiness. May the sacred fire continue to burn, and set us all on a flame !"

The record of one of his country Sabbaths is as follows :—

"Sunday, 25th, Longford.—Here morning and evening. In afternoon at Mr. Ball's prayer-meeting at Mountford, where we had a most lively season. Thank God, here are souls of the right sort ; men of strong faith, and mighty in prayer, whom God is using for His own glory. Colonel Hazelwood, father of Mrs. Ball, a man of nearly eighty years of age, has become the subject of saving grace." At the prayer-meeting the next evening the room was full, and there were many penitents. The lovefeast, Quarterly Meeting, and watchnight service were all seasons of blessing.

Many will remember the interest Mr. Turner evinced in the baptismal services of the Church ; and if in several Circuits he was a favourite Minister with parents desiring this ordinance for their children, it was an appropriate tribute to his fond and fatherly nature. He was not wont to say, with a half apologetic tone for the infliction to be announced, "The sacrament of baptism will be administered," and then hurry through it as an unwelcome addition to the morning duty. Singers had to look out an additional tune, and parents of all ages would evince more than usual liveliness in the service. He knew the heart of a Christian father, and could touch corresponding chords, while he lovingly and faithfully reminded the witnessing congregation of their own obligation to God; and it can in truth be said that, in many instances, the best spiritual results have followed the well-timed addresses upon such occasions.

"Monday, June 18th.—Delightful service yesterday; much of the unction of the Holy One was felt. After morning sermon, baptized the children of Messrs. Oakden and Sherwin, two dear friends and valuable servants of the Church. During this interesting service many felt the Divine influence. The prayer-meeting this evening was the best attended I have seen in Launceston. Large schoolroom all but crowded. At the protracted meeting were many penitents."

The gracious work spread. In different parts of the Circuit believers were sanctified and sinners saved. On August 21st, during the revival season, the Sabbath School Anniversary sermons were preached by Mr. Eggleston, recently returned from Adelaide. On the next Wednesday evening several obtained the "perfect love of God" in a prayer-meeting, after that Minister had preached on, "Is there no balm in Gilead?"

September brought trouble. One of the members grievously slandered Mr. Turner, and another abused him in the press on account of his total abstinence principles. While in the country, he fell from horseback. He suffered from the effects for several weeks. Meanwhile there was light within, and the Church was alive to God. The Quarterly return of members and of finances were highly cheering; but still more so the spirit of the assembled brethren.

"October 20th.—Returned this evening from our District Meeting in Hobart Town. The Lord was graciously present; and a loving feeling was manifested. We parted renewed in spirit, and sacredly pledged to pray daily for each other, and to lay ourselves out for greater usefulness in the Church. Such a District Meeting for brotherly love I never attended. O may God's truth greatly grow in the land, through our instrumentality!"

In December he again crossed the island on business connected with the Mission ship. During the journey he experienced much annoyance by the roving proclivities of a borrowed horse. There are some strange horses lent to Methodist Preachers, and, for the matter of that, some peculiar aids to locomotion by courtesy called "Circuit horses." Mr. Turner's happy Christmas was spent in riding forty miles to Wesley Dale.

The first Sabbath of the New Year and a lovefeast on Monday evening had passed away amid tokens of the Divine presence, when he was called to a painful trial. His infant child, after a lingering illness, breathed his last at nine o'clock on Tuesday night. Those of the family who had not retired, knelt at the bedside around his lifeless clay, and heard the first utterance of the bereaved father, " The Lord gave, and the Lord hath taken away; blessed be the Name of the Lord." His diary notice of the dispensation closes thus :—" Pleasing thought ! three children before the throne of God ! We feel the stroke, yet strive to bow to the will of God. For us our children sicken, and for us they die. O Lord, save me and mine for ever ! "

More fruit. Early in February he wrote, " Thank God, I find my feeble efforts are not in vain. Three souls have entered into liberty, and are rejoicing in God; a few backsliders are being re-awakened." On the 9th he recorded, with grateful satisfaction, the arrival from England of his friend Mr. Henry Reed, and a number of immigrants, some of whom were members. Among them were two Local Preachers. A month later he had " a laborious but successful trip to Wesley Dale. Brother Tongs was enabled to believe for full salvation. Two newly arrived immigrants were in deep distress ; one entered into Gospel liberty."

" April 1st.—Blessed be God, our people are rising in their tone of feeling, and in holy effort. Several have lately believed for and obtained a clean heart. I long to see this in all our members, and to declare it myself from day to day." Holiness is power, and the word preached that month was owned of God in the salvation of sinners.

A District Meeting on special business was held in Hobart Town. It was one of great harmony. May was not all sunshine. One of the Local Preachers had fallen into sin, and another loved brother had imbibed doctrinal errors which Mr. Turner feared would involve his being separated from Methodism. While journeying to a country appointment, he sustained a severe injury, and narrowly escaped with his life. A new Circuit horse he was driving turned restive, kicked and plunged, threw him out of his gig, and dragged the wheel over his body. Providen-tially, he suffered no more serious hurt than some severe bruises.

The latest entries of May notice the happy death of Willy Bartley, a dear boy of twelve years, the son of one of Mr. Turner's friends; and on the same day that of an older friend, under circumstances of special and monitory interest. " On my return home this morning I found my poor old friend, Mr. Alexander C. Lowe, dead in my study. About a fortnight ago he had arrived, in a very ailing state, from Tasmania Peninsula, where he had acted as Catechist for the last two years. I frequently visited him. Some-what improved, as it was thought, he re-embarked for home; but, on his becoming seriously worse, Dr. Pugh brought him to my house. On entering, he said, ' Eight years ago I was converted to God under Mr. Turner's ministry, and now I am come under his roof to die.' After some hours of extreme suffering, he passed away."

Ministerial intercourse with his brethren Messrs. Gaud and Eggleston was much enjoyed. He was delighted with

their services at the Sabbath School Anniversary. The
quarter's return showed prosperity. In September he had
his first interview with Sir Eardley Wilmot, and was
pleased to find that the new Governor was intimately acquainted with Dr. Bunting and other leading men among
the Wesleyans in England, and that he was well disposed
towards Methodism.

Mr. Turner went again to Hobart Town in October, to the
District Meeting. His Circuit schedule again showed
an increase of members. His report says, " We do not
remember a period when the members of our Society were
more athirst for their Saviour's love." The next month
the scarlet fever prevailed in Launceston, and his family
were mostly down with it.

While several of his children were prostrated, Mr. Turner
himself was laid aside with fever of a malignant type, the
inflammation seizing in turn his head, throat, and chest.
Serious consequences were averted by the blessing of God
upon the skill of kind physicians. The enforced silence
and restraint from public labour for six weeks were a heavy
trial. Official duty necessitated his visiting Hobart Town
again, where he closed the year in private devotion. His
records are the experiences of an humbled but grateful
heart. The change of air did him good.

Travellers at that time ran serious risk of robbery or
personal violence. Three notorious bushrangers, named
Cash, Kavanagh, and Jones, were at large, and held the
country in terror. Several of Mr. Turner's friends among
others had been " bailed up " in their homesteads, and their
lives endangered. In all his travels, however, he had but
one trifling experience with bushrangers. A novice at the
business, armed only with a stick, rushed out of the bush,
seized his bridle, and ordered him to dismount. He declined,
and received several blows. In self-defence, he heavily
laid his riding whip across the hands and head of his

assailant, who soon returned to the forest, probably to meditate on " the way of transgressors."

The " Triton's " return brought tidings of the deaths of the Revs. William Cross and David Cargill, two brethren whom Mr. Turner had honoured and loved. Of the former, he wrote :—" Brother Cross was my fellow-labourer in Tonga for nearly four years. He was a pious, devoted, useful Missionary,—a man of one business. His end was eminently peaceful, and his eternal reward is, I doubt not, glorious. He has left a widow and five children to the care of a covenant God, who will watch over and provide for them."

The Circuit Quarterly Meeting held in January was not to his mind. He says :—" Myself and colleague were greatly tried. The spirit and conduct of the office-bearers were very different from what we expected or desired ; but our Maker is our Judge, and we leave our cause with Him." What was the matter I do not know. Paul prayed that he might be delivered from wicked and *unreasonable* men. Most people have a pretty extensive acquaintance with the latter class. The lovefeast and the watchnight service that quarter were spiritually profitable seasons.

Mr. Turner had now laboured in Launceston a little more than three years. His next appointment was to New Norfolk, about twenty miles from Hobart Town.

Among the pleasing incidents of his leave-taking, one was the gift of a Remembrancer, by a number of young men of promise in the Church, to whom God had made him the honoured messenger of reconciliation. Mr. Turner often looked with pleasure at their autographs at the back of the memorial engraving of Wesley's rescue. Several of the names have since been enrolled among the successful Australian workers for Christ, and prominent among them that of Walter Powell, who, at the date of our narrative, was a youth of about eighteen, in Launceston. Upon the death of his eldest sister he had become much impressed, and, under promise to a loved friend, gave up his Sabbath pastimes and irreligious companions. The death by drowning of one of his late associates, during a Sabbath boating excursion, which he had refused to join, and an affliction with which it pleased God to visit him, were the occasion of much seriousness and spiritual anxiety. Mr. Turner had endeared himself to the family with whom he was residing, and soon made special visits on his account. These were made blessed to him. Upon his recovery he joined the Church, and one Monday, in Mr. Turner's study, where he had been engaged in conversation and prayer, during the ordinary dinner hour, he found peace with God. He went home rejoicing, and from that day was an humble servant of Christ. Though in comparatively early life he rose to affluence, he ever retained the charm of high Christian character, humility and love.

CHAPTER XVII.

1844–1846.

THE day after they had taken possession of their new house, Mr. and Mrs. Turner drove to Hobart Town, to say "farewell" to Messrs. Longbottom and Simpson, and families, who also were removing. The following incident, given in the diary of that week, is not a solitary one of its kind in Mr. Turner's life. "We stayed with our esteemed friends, Mr. and Mrs. Perkins. Just as the clock struck four in the morning, Mrs. Turner awoke me under great excitement, caused by the following remarkable dream or vision. She dreamt she was in her old home in Ipstone, Staffordshire, where she saw her father brought home extremely ill: she attended him with medical men and friends during his sickness, heard him say, relative to his soul, 'It is all right,' and then saw him die." Four months afterwards the mail brought intelligence of her father's death, detailing the time and circumstances, just as had been seen in the dream.

The New Norfolk station had been but lately formed, and was in all respects an inconsiderable affair. Viewed as a Circuit, I suppose such a station as it then was, would be found at times a convenience to a Stationing Committee. It would afford a convalescent Minister an excellent climate, agreeable scenery, quietude, and freedom from mental strain. Or if Conference wanted a penal settlement for active but refractory spirits, twelve months on such a station might serve the purpose. Two years at most would teach them wisdom.

Six weeks' experience made not the most pleasant impressions on Mr. Turner's mind. He could find work enough for a man much stronger, but it was on a most sterile soil. The town Society numbered but one person, a woman by whose absence the cause would have been strengthened. There were a small congregation and Sabbath school. At the Back River, two or three miles distant, there was a class, but no Sabbath school. At the Ouse, thirty miles away, several families gladly attended Divine service in their little chapel, whenever they had the opportunity. There were also a few nominal members. Elsewhere in the Circuit occasional services had been held.

Though the spiritual soil seemed sour and barren, Mr. Turner regarded it as part of God's husbandry. He began a class in his own house, and committed the Sabbath school to Mrs. Turner's care. His eldest daughter by personal canvass from house to house gathered a number of children in the Back River settlement, and conducted a Sabbath school in the chapel there. Her pony carried her to and from this service of love for about sixteen months. The relaxation from mental work, and the quietude of a country Parson's life in a salubrious region, soon restored his vigour.

It was granted, however, but for increased toil. In March Mr. Simpson obtained leave to return to England on account of his motherless children. This led to the removal of Mr. Butters, from the Hobart Town Circuit, to Launceston, and left Hobart Town and New Norfolk Circuits to be worked by Messrs. Manton and Turner. While fulfilling his various city engagements under this arrangement, Mr. Turner tried hard to raise a living Church in New Norfolk.

The general population were ignorant and debased. He accepted the office of President of a Total Abstinence Society, and laboured for its success, with good effect. He records a

typal illustration of social and religious reform by its means.
Mr. and Mrs. H., who had known better days, were
wretched drunkards, and in abject misery. Kindly visits
and conversations induced them to sign the pledge. After
a few weeks' hopeful change they both relapsed. Mr.
Turner tried again : they signed once more. Being sober
and a good tradesman, the husband obtained work, and
soon with improved character he acquired position. Before
Mr. Turner left the Circuit they were the owners of a free-
hold property, and were esteemed members of the Church,
enjoying the saving grace of God. Special and regular
attention was given to the inmates of the General Hospital,
and in some instances with pleasing results.

At the District Meeting of that year Mr. John Harcourt
was recommended as a candidate for the Ministry. Among
the financial records is one to the effect, that the debt upon
the Melville Street church stood at £3,875, bearing interest
at 10 per cent.

Early in 1846 Mr. Manton* was seriously unwell, and
for about two months Mr. Turner had charge of his Circuit

* John Allen Manton was converted in early life through the instrumentality of Methodist preaching. In 1830 he was sent as a Missionary to Australia. After a short residence in New South Wales he was
stationed at the penal settlements of Van Diemen's Land, first at
Macquarie Harbour, and afterwards at Port Arthur. Here he was the
sole religious instructor of the condemned men, and his self-sacrificing
labours were owned of God in the conversion of many. He afterwards
laboured with great acceptance and success in Launceston, Hobart
Town, and elsewhere in Van Diemen's Land. His affectionate manner
and clear earnest preaching won for him many souls, and much general
influence. Few Ministers have been more highly esteemed by their
brethren, and he was appointed President of the third Australasian
Conference. He took a special interest in the young people of his
Circuits, and in the interest of the youth of Methodism generally.

The founding of the Wesleyan Colleges in Tasmania and New South
Wales was brought about in a good degree by his zealous efforts for
them. In 1863 he suffered much bodily affliction, and died at Newing-

as well as of his own.   In March a most painful affliction
was permitted, and in recording it I may as well give my
readers some idea of the servant who caused the mischief,
and who, for ideas of propriety and morality, was a fair
specimen of many more.   I was at the time at boarding
school in Hobart Town.   A friend having selected at the
hiring-room a servant for our family, I was sent to attend
her to the New Norfolk steamer.   It seemed a simple
errand, but I was scarcely equal to it.   The young woman
said she had " to call on a friend," and while she did so I
stood at the door.   She spent some ten minutes drinking
spirits and gossiping with two or three somewhat like herself.   Presently she resumed her way, and as I was medi-
tating on the doubtful advantage to our family of her services,
she loudly uttered an oath, and excitedly rushed across the
street towards a woman leaning at the casement of a
butcher's shop.   She gave her a volley of abuse, and a few
blows in the face.   A crowd gathering, she moved on.   My
wonder soon increased.   She recognised some man standing at a street corner with his back to us, and flew towards,
him ; springing up she struck him behind his ear, and the
instant that he turned round spat in his face.   As he
skulked away, she filled the street with violent abusive
language.   I got a policeman to be my substitute.   She
explained to him that the man was her husband, and that
she had last seen him in England.   This virago had been a
week or two in Mrs. Turner's service when through careless-
ness she caused serious trouble.   There were two attic
rooms, and by leaving a candle too near a basket of linen,
she set the outer one on fire.   All the family but three were
at chapel.   Mrs. Turner thought her youngest children
were in the inner attic, and rushed through the blazing

ton College, of which he was President, on September 9th, in the thirty--
fifth year of his ministry, aged fifty-eight.   During his mortal illness he
had much peace of mind.   His latest expression was, " Saved at last ! "

room to rescue them. Providentially they were in another part of the house. The flames spread, and her only possible safety now was to rush down again by the stairs, while they were burning. She had the courage to do this; and though her presence of mind saved her life, she received several severe bruises, and was for a long time in danger, being confined to her bed for many weeks. The incidents of that third fire called forth grateful acknowledgments of the providence of God.

Mr. Turner regarded that at New Norfolk as the least satisfactory of all his terms of labour, because it afforded him the least opportunities of usefulness. However, he succeeded in his work, and wanted nothing.

Thirty years had now passed since the planting of Methodism in the Southern World. Its growth had been great; but its distance from the Committee at home had often been found a cause of embarrassment and confusion. To reduce for the future the risk of wasting public money or ministerial power, which in some degree had hitherto been unavoidable, was now the Committee's problem. With the purpose of establishing and consolidating a better financial system in these parts, the Rev. William Binnington Boyce was appointed General Superintendent. And he had, as was necessary, considerable discretionary privileges and powers. Soon after his arrival in Sydney in 1846. he desired for the general good to effect some changes of appointments among the more experienced Ministers. This embraced the removal of Mr. Draper from Sydney to Adelaide, and Mr. Turner's taking charge of the Sydney Circuit.

Late one calm evening in September, as the good ship "Lord Auckland" slowly dropped down the Derwent, Mr. Turner's children sang from her deck with fondest affection to the home of their childhood, "Isle of beauty, fare thee well." Captain Brown was a fine old English sailor, and made his passengers comfortable. Among them were

the family of the Rev. Joseph Beazley, a gifted and zealous
Congregationalist Minister. On the eighth afternoon the
Five Islands, with the noble Keera and Kembla mountains
of Illawarra, towering on the mainland behind, were in
view, and early next morning they entered Port Jackson.
Just as the pilot had reached the deck, unusual sounds of
joy were heard astern ! We children ran aft, and what was
our surprise to hear our names called out one by one by a
crew of Maoris, in the boat astern! They were of the
Hokianga tribes, and were over delighted at seeing again
their old Missionary and his family.

CHAPTER XVIII.

1846–1849.

THE population of the southern metropolis had much increased since 1839, and numbered now fifty thousand. Methodism, having successfully struggled through a long youth-time of trial, was exhibiting much vigour and purpose. Outwardly represented by the Centenary Church in York Street, it held a leading position among the Protestant denominations. A new chapel had been lately built at Hay Street, then prospectively an important site, and another was in course of erection at Balmain. Meanwhile the old sanctuary at Prince's Street was being enlarged. The laborious services of two Ministers and of many zealous Local Preachers had been applied to the congregations of these places, and of Surrey Hills, Warnley, Chippendale, and Botany. Of late, the Rev. W. B. Boyce, who had no distinct Circuit charge, had rendered valuable assistance by his pulpit services.

On his first Sabbath evening, after hearing Mr. Schofield in the morning, Mr. Turner occupied the pulpit of the York Street church, which was crowded. The full soul of a Methodist Preacher was given with the words,—

> " O for a thousand tongues to sing
> My great Redeemer's praise !

Charmed with the hearty singing of an old favourite tune, " Ebenezer New," he announced the whole eleven verses. He preached under some embarrassment. Captain Brown and some of his officers and crew were present at the service.

There was the effect, too, of a mass of faces nearly all new to him, and with it the deep consciousness of ministerial responsibility. These influences, added to the excitement connected with his taking charge of a new and important Circuit, affected him much. His text indicated his purpose as a preacher : " Who will have all men to be saved, and to come unto the knowledge of the truth."

There were in Sydney several Christian families of other Churches whose esteem and religious friendship he had formerly enjoyed. Their kind welcome added to his early satisfaction with the prospect. He soon found that he had no sinecure. When he had taken a round or two of his Circuit, he recorded his conviction that, though there was a fine sphere of labour, there were great difficulties in the way of his working it to advantage. His was an inventive mind. It was impossible for him not to anticipate. He was troubled by the absence of suitable chapels. However, he accepted the position, and threw his soul into his work. One of the brightest features in the Circuit was the Sabbath school interest, which in different places was succeeding well. With the assistance of his colleague, the Rev. Samuel Wilkinson, he laboured hard to establish and extend the work of God in several outlying places, the walks to and from which were found trying enough. It was early seen that, to make good the position and safely to advance, a third preacher must be had.

Indeed, apart from proper ministerial labour, Mr. Turner had enough to do. There were numerous engagements which the Church regarded as mere matters of course, possibly of recreation, which were harassing and teazing to a great degree. The whole business of the Methodist Book Room for New South Wales and for the Islands was in his hands, and no assistance was provided. The Mission house, too, was a semi-official post-office. Immigration was flowing to the colony, and the English correspondents of Methodist people had adopted the idea of addressing their letters to the care of "the resident Wesleyan Missionary, Sydney." This, however, though by no means a trifle, was a far less tax on his time than were the calls for his assistance by the large numbers of new arrivals. His files were full of letters of introduction. His sympathies with the immigrants were genuine and strong, and no demands upon him for inquiry or counsel were considered too much. He anticipated the arrival of immigrant vessels with more apparent interest than did the intending employers of labour. Very often, soon after the signal staff had shown that such a ship was within the Heads, he took a boat, and boarded her, in order to see and counsel as many as reported themselves Wesleyans. It will be imagined that by such families the kind and intelligent interest he manifested in their welfare was received with the liveliest satisfaction, and that, in hundreds of instances, it is to this day remembered with gratitude and affection. He sometimes canvassed the city from early morning till evening in search of accommodation for Christian friends from beyond the sea, and, in some instances, for employment for them; and, if expostulated with by members of his family, would say, " Ah, well ! if in this way I can but serve my Master, it will be all right." Amid Sydney dust in summer it was often warmer work than was pleasant; however, the persons concerned were benefitted, and the cause of God was aided.

All ministers have not equal tact and willingness for this kind of work; and of late years there has not appeared much occasion for it. But, inasmuch as, before the Australian continent shall be all occupied under the providence of God, immigration may again and again set in as with a flood tide, I make special allusion to this kind of service, in the hope that, in every similar condition of society, timely sympathy will be shown. While it is the duty of all newly-

arrived Wesleyans to lose no time in presenting their credentials of Church connexion, it is the duty of the Australasian Church at such times to seek out her accredited
members as early as possible. Several of our Ministers
have made a specialty of this work, and in it have been, by
much personal sacrifice, helped by lay workers for God ;
and the reward has been great. In almost every Circuit in
which I have travelled I have met with some successful
and pious colonists, who, with grateful emotion, have told
me of the welcome and counsels given them by Mr. Turner,
a few hours after they had entered the harbour, or had
landed.

Of the succeeding years of Mr. Turner's life I have
nothing in the way of diary or journal, excepting notes of
voyages, and, as his biographer, am dependent upon sundry
correspondence and printed notices. But, though the
remainder of the memoir will from this cause be less suc-
cinct, it will not be less correct.

His two eldest sons had been left in Van Diemen's
Land, in banking offices. In his earliest letters to them he
says, " I am extremely busy, and must be here ; but the
people are very kind, and my work will be rewarded. My
chest, from which I was suffering at New Norfolk, is now clear
and strong, though I work very, very hard. Life with me
is only desirable as I can spend it to the glory of God.
There is an excellent spirit of hearing, and we are building
good chapels in every direction."

The era of chapel-building in Sydney began with Mr.
Boyce's arrival, and the works undertaken were much
indebted to his assistance from funds at his discretionary
disposal. On the last Monday in October, 1846, the foundation stone of a chapel, fifty by thirty feet, in Bourke Street,
Surrey Hills, was laid ; and a few weeks later that of one of

a similar size, at Chippendale. Following these enterprises, a few additional pews were put into the York Street
church. The various congregations, classes, and schools
throughout the Circuit increased in number and in life.

One marked feature of the Circuit was the tendency of
the population, Methodists included, towards the suburbs.
Though this was perfectly natural, and spread spiritual
seed corn over new fields, yet the congregations and
interests of the city proper were plied with vigorous
effort, and with satisfactory results. Both the York
Street and Prince's Street chapels were regularly filled,
and each was the centre of organized successful labour
in tract distribution, sick visitation, Sabbath schools, and
Society operations.

The first watchnight and New Year's commemoration
services were of interest. When the service of the renewal
of the Covenant was held, nearly five hundred persons
sealed their vows at the Lord's Supper. The next week,
Mr. Turner preached at Windsor, and otherwise assisted at
the Sabbath school anniversary there.

On the evening of the 18th of March, the Methodists
of Sydney were gratified by the arrival from England of the
Missionary brig "John Wesley." Captain Buck had
brought out seven Missionaries for New Zealand and the
Islands. They were the Revs. Messrs Malvern, Ford,
Daniels, Amos, Adams, Kirk, and Davis. During their
sojourn in Sydney, their services were in great demand;
and prominently at the opening of the Chippendale chapel.
In several places where they preached, precious souls were
led to the Saviour. Their leave-taking was at an ever-
memorable lovefeast in the York Street school-room, on
the evening of the 30th. The presence of so many devoted
servants of God and their spiritual labours gave an impetus
to the Societies in and around the city.

On the 29th of July, the twenty-ninth annual District

Meeting of New South Wales assembled, a preparatory
sermon having by appointment been preached by Mr.
Turner. The meeting was one of importance and interest.
It exhibited the development of the Church during the
General Superintendent's first year, and in this respect was
highly satisfactory. All the Connexional funds showed an
increase ; and the schedule of members, an increase of two
hundred and ninety in the District. The Sydney Circuit
was divided,—Chippendale, Newtown, and Canterbury
being the chief places of the separated portion, which took
with it one third of the members. The Rev. Frederick
Lewis was appointed to the Chippendale Circuit, and for
this Circuit scarcely a more eligible appointment could
have been found. To great wisdom and affability he
added quenchless zeal. The published notice of the
meeting says :—"An interesting conversation was held,
respecting the claims of distant parts of the colony, viz.,
Moreton Bay, New England, Clarence River, Gipps's Land,
and the squatting districts generally, upon the sympathies of
the Wesleyan Church." During the District session two
social meetings were held; the former, attended by all
the office-bearers and Sabbath school teachers of the surrounding Circuits; the latter, by the members. [I may
add, that for some years a similar annual gathering of the
office-bearers was held, at which all appeared to profit by
the free and stimulating addresses of the visiting Ministers
and others.]

Mr. Turner's ordinary Sabbath services were attended by
cheering tokens of the presence of God. On Sabbath
evenings, from time to time, the hearts of sinners were
broken by the hammer of God's truth; and the basement
school-room of York Street church was the birthplace of
many souls. The Chippendale chapel was crowded, at the
first lovefeast held in it, which Mr. Turner conducted.
The testimonies to the saving power of grace were followed

by the cries of conviction and distress ; and to a late hour
the sorrows of penitents, and praises of new-born souls,
were mingled around the altar of prayer. That night, and
next day, many found peace with God. He had a large
harvest of souls that winter.

In September, he attended the military funeral of
Quartermaster Moore, of the 50th regiment, who had
died very suddenly. The occasion drew around the grave
some thousands of persons, who were solemnly admonished
to apply their hearts unto wisdom. The Quarterly Meeting
returns showed an increase of members.

On the 31st of October, the Rev. John M'Kenny was
called home to God. Increasing infirmities, traceable to
his twenty-two years' residence in India, had compelled him
to retire from the active work, at the late District Meeting ;
and since then he had resided at Stanmore. From the
nature of his illness, he had been unable to converse,
towards the last ; but he had left satisfactory evidence of
his interest in Christ. Part of the funeral obsequies were
observed in the York Street church, and his remains were
interred in the Sydney burial ground. The funeral sermon
was preached by the Rev. T. B. Harris, after which Mr.
Turner read a brief memorial statement.

Mr. Turner's anxieties and exhaustive labours were now
telling upon his health, so much so, that a thorough change was
considered necessary. Mr. Boyce, with characteristic kindness, undertook his pulpit work for a few weeks, to admit of
his taking a sea voyage, in pursuit of health. He embarked
on board the steamer "Juno" on November 30th, somewhat depressed by the necessity for his doing so. After a
stoppage of two hours at Twofold Bay, he finished an
agreeable trip to Melbourne on Saturday night. He enjoyed
the early Sabbath morning walk of six miles to the home of
his friend, Mr. Bell. On attending a delightful service in
Collins Street, at which he had heard Mr. Sweetman preach,

he found himself surrounded by several Tasmanian friends, who were right glad to greet him. After dining, he visited Collingwood, where Mr. Lowe preached a profitable sermon. His notes say:—"The congregation was good and deeply attentive, but the chapel is a miserable affair. Here I found one of my greatly endeared spiritual children, Mr. Walter Powell, formerly of Launceston, in charge of a very interesting Sabbath school. I addressed a few words to encourage and stimulate the congregation before they parted. Several souls have lately been converted to God. At the evening services, I assisted Mr. Sweetman in the administration of the Lord's Supper.

"Monday morning brought mingled pleasure and pain. With our friends in Melbourne and its vicinity it was not as when the candle of the Lord had shone brightly. Afternoon, by steamer to Geelong. At wharf, after dark; saw light in chapel; found a large number separating from their prayer-meeting. Was again surrounded by many, who had in former years been objects of my pastoral care in Van Diemen's Land. Here I met with that good man, Mr. Joseph Lowe, to whom, as an instrument, I owe my conversion to God. Mr. Lowe was very useful in the Nantwich Circuit at that period; and, blessed be God, he has through every succeeding year been using his talents for the Divine glory; and now, in his old age, he is bearing golden fruits. We met and parted, a father and son in the kingdom and patience of Jesus.

"Tuesday.—An early stroll through Geelong streets. The site is excellent, and the town well laid out; several large vessels in the Bay loading with wool for England. In the afternoon visited the Barabool Hills; greatly pleased with the soil and scenery. Methodism has taken a firm hold in Geelong. A handsome and substantial chapel has been erected, and the congregation are saying, 'We want a gallery.' In the afternoon returned to Melbourne,—my feeble frame wearied out, but my mind refreshed.

"Wednesday.—In early afternoon left for Adelaide. By two P.M. on Thursday made Port Fairy, a bleak-looking harbour, with four wrecks visible on the beach : by eight P.M. were in Portland Bay; could not go ashore, but was glad to learn that the cause here is progressing under Mr. Witton's labours. By ten on Saturday night the steamer reached Adelaide, where I received a hearty welcome from Brother and Sister Draper.

"Sunday.—One of the most sultry days I ever experienced. Excellent sermon from Mr. Draper* in Gawler Place, and in the afternoon at Hindley Street. I ventured to conduct the evening service in Gawler Place, and assisted Mr. Draper in dispensing the Lord's Supper. Several present had been under my personal charge in Van Diemen's Land. Suffered much afterwards.

"Monday.—Though very languid, visited several families.

"Tuesday.—Profitable afternoon at North Adelaide. Preached there ;—congregation good ;—prospect cheering ; —situation superior to that of South Adelaide.

"Wednesday.—Accompanied Mr. Draper to the Glen Ormond mines, and with the captain went through the shaft many fathoms underground. I felt for the poor men shut out from the light of heaven, and breathing a most impure atmosphere. But even there, with the love of Christ in their hearts, these pious Cornishmen can be happy. In the

* The name of Daniel James Draper is honoured in the memory of Australians. After thirty years of successful toil as a Christian Minister, during trying periods of our Colonial Church history, he visited England as the representative of the Australasian Conference. The triumphs of grace in him on board the steamship " London," as she foundered in the Bay of Biscay, on January 11th, 1866, have added lustre to his life in the service of Christ.

evening heard our young Minister in Gawler Place chapel, from, ' God forbid that I should glory, save in the cross of our Lord Jesus Christ.' His manner is warm, and address pointed ; his aim evidently to do the people good. His ministry has been well received in Adelaide, and the Lord has made him a blessing among the people.

" Thursday,—After visiting an institution for the welfare of the aboriginals, spent an hour or two in company with Mr. and Mrs. Longbottom, our retired Minister and his excellent wife ; and with Messrs. Draper, Harcourt, and Thrum.

" Friday.—A dreadful day. About ten in the morning, as I was walking to visit a friend, I saw several singular-looking spiral clouds moving in the distance. Suddenly it began to blow, and I hastened homewards. By the time I reached the Mission house, the whole city was enveloped in a cloud of dust, which increased for an hour, when the atmosphere became so dense and dark that we could not discern an object many yards distant. I thought of the black Egyptian night ; that darkness which might be felt. The smell was like mud. Our Sydney ' brickfielders ' cannot half equal the Adelaide storm of dust. It was followed by heavy rain, which so flooded the streets that persons could scarcely move out of doors. Sydney rose in my estimation.

" Saturday.—Morning with the brethren, in earnest conversation on the work of God in the colony. I came to the conclusion that, supposing funds could not be raised in the colony at once for entering the many open doors, a thousand pounds would be well invested by our Committee in sending and sustaining two or three additional Ministers ; for I am sure that, in a few years, it would be repaid with great interest. South Australia has a great destiny. In the afternoon said ' farewell ' to my numerous kind friends, and went to the port to embark.

" Sunday.—The tide not answering, went ashore, and attended the Church service. At midday anchor was raised, and we put to sea. After crossing the bar, we met the ' China ' immigrant ship, inward bound. Captain Lindsay recognised me at once from the deck of the vessel. We had had pleasing interviews in New Zealand many years before. In the evening I held public service in the saloon. All listened with deep attention. Early on Thursday morning we ran up to William's Town. Had much interesting conversation with Mr. Sweetman, and was happy to find that it had been arranged for Mr. Tuckfield to visit Gipps's Land.

" Friday.—One of the hottest days I ever knew in any land.

" Saturday, Christmas Day.—Left at noon. In the evening I expounded the word of God to some of the sailors and steerage passengers.

" Sunday morning.—With the captain's kind permission I read the service on deck, and preached. We coaled at Twofold Bay. Here I visited a Presbyterian settler, and baptized his child. By Thursday noon we were safely anchored in our desired haven. I shall not attempt to describe my grateful feeling on finding my family all in health and comfort, our Church in peace and prosperity, and my health so far improved as to justify the hope that I shall be again equal to the duties of my ministerial and pastoral charge."

He hastened to devote his recruited vigour to the service of God's Church. On January 3rd, that year a public holiday, he took part in a camp meeting at Chippendale. Many hearty labourers assisted the Ministers of the city, and God gave them to rejoice over about a score of souls who found peace through believing. A similar service was held near the Flagstaff Hill on the anniversary of the colony.

On February 14th, at the York Street Chapel Anniversary, the project of erecting a gallery was submitted to the congregation. The want of more accommodation had been increasingly felt for some time. He spent the next Sabbath in Bathurst, preaching for the Foreign Missions. Major-General Stewart presided at the public meeting. The Surrey Hills and Chippendale Chapel Anniversaries had his hearty assistance. In June the Sydney Wesleyan Sabbath School Society held their yearly celebration, at which he addressed over eight hundred children in York Street church. The Report submitted at the public meeting represented fourteen schools, one hundred and twenty teachers, and one thousand two hundred and twenty-eight scholars. About the same time he had intense delight in addressing a crowd of Sabbath scholars representing various denominations. This was in the afternoon of the Sabbath on which the new galleries were opened. The various managers of Dissenting schools in the city, as well as some of the nearer Wesleyan Superintendents, brought their children to York Street church. There had never been so many Sabbath school children together before in the city.

During that month one of his earliest Sydney friends, Mr. Launcelot Iredale, departed this life. For many years he had been a respected citizen, and had been elected to civic honours. In every way in his power he had evinced strong attachment to Wesleyan Methodism. In 1840 he had presented as a free gift to the Society the original chapel in Bourke Street, which had cost £400; and, during the year before his death, he had taken deep interest in the new erection. The Missionary Society from time to time had been relieved of expense by the open-handedness with which he had shown hospitality to its agents and their families, when travelling to and from their stations.

The next District Meeting divided Mr. Turner's Circuit a second time; Surrey Hills, Paddington, and Waverley formed the new Circuit, and were placed under the charge of the Rev. Benjamin Hurst, a Minister of much energy of character; an able preacher, and eminently a man of progress.

The early services of 1849, his last year in the Circuit, were entered upon with more than usual earnestness and solemnity. His active sympathies and uniformly laborious zeal had won upon the Sydney population, and his congregations were usually of the best. It was no uncommon thing for forms to be carried from the school-room to the aisles of the crowded church, upon the Sabbath evening; or for the large double school-room to be well filled at the after prayer-meeting. On January 26th that year, the more zealous members of the Church held a camp-meeting at Macquarie Place, to counter-attract young people seeking holiday pleasures, and, if possible, to arrest the careless. In this service Mr. Turner, though he needed a holiday as much as any man in Sydney, laboured most heartily. A continuation revival service was held in the evening at York Street. It was a lovefeast. At that meeting a blessed work broke out, and the altar was crowded with penitents. The flame grew brighter and hotter on the following Sabbath, and on the Monday, at an immense public prayer-meeting, a large number entered into liberty. Among these was the writer of this memoir. He had been pierced by the arrows of conviction at the lovefeast on Friday night, and, after three days' distress under a sense of sin, was led that evening, by his father's hand, to a penitent form ; and, while the voice he knew and loved so well, —his father's voice,—was leading the large assembly with the words,—

> " My God is reconciled,
> His pardoning voice I hear,"

he was enabled by faith to join, and sing,—

> " He owns me for His child,
> I can no longer fear."

" Sing it again, friends," said the overjoyed Minister; and we sang it again and again.

On the Wednesday, while the good work was blessedly going on in Sydney, Mr. Turner visited Illawarra. The tub-steamer, by courtesy denominated " The William the Fourth," was nine hours making the voyage to Wollongong; fifty miles. He preached the same evening to a good congregation. The next day he rode to Gerringong; about thirty-five miles of the roughest travelling he had ever known. But he was more than delighted with the unrivalled scenery, from parts of the journey. He preached at Mr. Black's, " to a delightful congregation." The next evening he preached at Spring Hill, and administered the Lord's Supper. By Saturday evening he had returned as far as Dapto, to Mr. Somerville's. On Sabbath morning he preached in the little new chapel of that village, from, " There is joy in heaven among the angels of God," &c. As there was very deep feeling, he followed up the service by a lovefeast and penitent-meeting, which lasted till four o'clock. Then he began to feel hungry. After refreshment he rode eight miles into Wollongong, where he preached, and administered the Lord's Supper. During the next three days he visited and prayed with the people, and preached ; and on leaving again for the city, on Thursday, felt comforted by knowing that his visit had been " the occasion of good to many."

The District Meeting of that year appointed him to Parramatta. The three years' arduous city toil had not been for nought. Many scores of souls had been won to Christ ; several new schools had been initiated, and were now in healthy operation. The churches at Surrey Hills and at Chippendale had been built; the accommodation at York Street had been increased ; sundry new preaching stations had been taken up. The Circuit had been twice divided, and each separated part had given promise of more rapid establishment and furtherance of the work nearest his heart. In securing these results he had been heartily assisted by two excellent colleagues, the Rev. S. Wilkinson, and, as his successor, the Rev. T. B. Harris. Each of these Ministers had enjoyed, in a high degree, the affection of the people, and the smile of God upon his labours.

Those three years were the most important which up to that time Sydney Methodism had known. Mr. Boyce's presence, and his influence with the home Committee, supplied the sinews of war for the beginning of several important enterprises, and Mr. Turner's energy and aptitude enhanced their value within his Circuit. He had found a public impression in favour of Methodism, and he maintained and increased it : and the placing at that time of his zealous brethren, Lewis and Hurst, in charge of important centres of population, gave to our Church a most commanding opportunity to develop itself, if wise and faithful, through the host of willing friends of Zion, into a mighty agency of evangelism throughout the growing city and its suburbs.

CHAPTER XIX.

1849-1852.

PARRAMATTA,—to many the dearest spot on earth: for many of its lovely homes, which from the earliest years of the colony had been held by worthy families, and the vineyards and orchards, in which as children they had romped, now afforded them retirement for fond or pensive meditation. But to as many more, who knew it from necessity, it was the dullest. The changes since effected by the railway have somewhat improved its general character. The numerous available sites for rural homes, within an hour's reach from the city, have tempted many families; and the growth of colonial population has stimulated the industries of orange and vine growing and orchard culture, for which the surrounding country is famed. New folk and fancies have somewhat modified the ideas of the people, but at the date of this narrative their quietude was proverbial. It was not inappropriately that a city reporter, in chronicling a memorable hunt in the vicinity of city sportsmen, said, " Then Parramatta turned round and went to sleep again."

Of the founders of large families resident there, not a few were pious, God-fearing persons; and of this number some were Wesleyans. Several valuable public men in Methodism had begun their labours there. The dull conservatism, however, which had marked its commercial and social life, had prevailed in matters more important. And though the Wesleyan Ministers who since 1820 had successively occupied the station, had experienced much kindness, they had in general found it a depressing appointment. Mr. Turner had laboured there in early times for a few months, and had since then often visited it; so that he knew well its wants. He had many friends there; and, being received with kindness, entered upon his work with cheerfulness and energy.

There were two chapels in the town, the second being a mistake of the Centenary year; and several scattered Societies in the country, at distances of six, eight, and ten miles from home. Mr. Turner had no colleague, and the staff of effective preachers at the time was inadequate for the whole work. Under the circumstances, he laboured harder than was prudent. His ordinary public work was six or seven times preaching, besides two classes and prayer-meetings, weekly. For three months he grieved much that he saw but little ·encouragement. He spoke of his work as "like so much ploughing on a rock." Sometimes, when "the old standards" would remind him that so many of God's servants, during thirty years, had had similar discouragement, he would reply, "Ah, well! something must be wrong. I cannot be happy, unless I see the work of God prosper." What he meant by the work prospering was not simply having an interested congregation, and a hearty acceptance among the people, but the quickening power of the Holy Ghost, believers sanctified, and sinners saved.

Recreation meant change of work. In April he visited Goulburn and neighbouring towns, in the hope that an evangelistic tour of a fortnight in that salubrious region would benefit both himself and the several communities in his round. The journey gave him "the most severe shaking he ever had." On reaching Goulburn he found "its buildings far in advance" of what he had expected. The plains were "brown through the protracted drought." At Queanteyan he preached twice with freedom, and on the Monday night gave a missionary speech, which occupied an hour and a half. On Tuesday night he preached at Gunning, having travelled forty-five miles that day. Next day he preached in the forenoon, attended a tea-meeting in the afternoon, and a Missionary meeting at night. His Thursday's work was a full day's travel and four times preaching by the way. One of the places was Wheeo, since famous as the rendezvous of bushrangers. On Friday he journeyed to Crookwell, Mr. Oake's station, and preached at night. After a full Sabbath's work in Goulburn, he reached home on Wednesday, all the better for the bracing air of the table land district, and mentally and spiritually refreshed by the free engagements of his roving commission. That fortnight's tour is perhaps not an unfair specimen of the occasional " Recreations of a country " Methodist " Parson " in New South Wales, when enjoying the honour of being a deputation to an inland district.

In Parramatta were a few devoted men who felt for God's cause. Their Minister's stirring pulpit appeals, and earnest labours for souls, awoke and stimulated their reserve force of spiritual life, and they worked hard. Frequently the Sabbath evening prayer-meetings became services of revival power. Several wanderers were restored, and some few penitents found the Saviour. At these times Mr. Turner had not always the self-restraint called for. His strength for the day having been pretty nearly exhausted by fifteen or twenty miles' travelling and three services, he would just open the prayer-meeting he had called after the sermon, leave the Hymn-Book with some Local Preacher or Leader, run into his house next door, exchange his flannel vest, wringing wet with perspiration, for a dry one, and then return to do battle with the devil and unbelief. He often earnestly engaged in prayer several times in the same meeting.

As he had been forewarned, these undue labours, and the excitement connected with them, proved too much for his physical strength. An attack of bronchitis came on, which enfeebled him very much. Medical advisers and friends counselled him to rest wholly from public work for a time. In view of his family his case became serious. Several times during the previous four years he had overtaxed his strength, and been temporarily laid aside; and it now became evident that his zeal was rapidly consuming his vital force. His ardent temperament, an occasion of danger with him as a Methodist preacher anywhere, was peculiarly so where the atmosphere was unfriendly or the labour undue. As a matter of duty to his family, he reluctantly undertook a voyage to Melbourne. The neat little clipper schooner "Favourite," a model to look at, took his fancy in preference to the steamer, and there were friends among his fellow passengers. During the voyage much bad weather was experienced, and the craft had to shelter in Twofold Bay. She was twelve days reaching Melbourne, but the sea air had invigorated his lungs and appetite, and considerably recruited his strength. He found Melbourne distracted with the gold fever. In company with his son-in-law, the Rev. John Harcourt, he paid a brief visit to Mount Alexander, where twenty thousand persons were congregated. He met many Wesleyan friends, who were doing well. One party of five had cleared one hundred pounds in five days. Only one whom he knew spoke unfavourably of gold digging. Feeling benefitted by the change, and hoping for further improvement by the return voyage, he took passage for Sydney by the "Hirondelle," though in Melbourne he had been pressed by invitation to visit Van Diemen's Land. The voyage was tedious, and the latter part of it rough. Cold south-east winds, with much rainy weather, renewed his cold, and when he rejoined his family he was scarcely, if anything, better than when he had left them. The weakness in his chest was great, and he was quite unfit for work. He talked to the people a little on the first two Thursday evenings, and afterwards resumed his Sabbath labour with tolerable comfort.

Mr. Turner was now fifty-eight years of age, and being possessed of uncommon energy and a good flow of spirits, the prospect of early falling out of the ranks of an active working ministry was very painful to him. He had a large family, many of whom were still young; and except under occasional attacks, the result usually of undue exertion, he was lively and vigorous. He had the conviction that a voyage to England and back, with the thorough change and pleasure it would afford, would do him permanent good, and secure him strength for several years' added labour. The General Superintendent did not feel free to sanction his going, without the consent of the Committee. On the 30th of January he posted a letter to the Committee, requesting the required permission. A copy of the letter is before me. It modestly alluded to thirty years' faithful services, according to his ability, and suggested that he might, if spared to see England, by his presence exert so much influence in the interest of Missions as would cover the extra expenses to be incurred by his voyage. For several months he anticipated a favourable reply, but from some unaccountable cause he never received a line from the Committee upon the subject. With this he was much grieved, and he did not renew the application. His family hoped that there was some postal miscarriage.

His few letters written at this date which have come to my hand exhibit a delightful spirit of Christian confidence and submission; and his correspondence with the members of his family especially, scattered throughout the colonies, breathe a loving and faithful concern for their highest welfare.

Early in June Mr. Turner had an attack of lumbago. It was immediately followed by ophthalmia, from which he suffered acutely, and was confined to his room for more than a week. While very feeble, he attempted a Sabbath morning service, but found himself unequal to it.   He wrote : " I should be glad to be kept quiet for two months, till winter shall have passed away.   What the District Meeting will do with us I know not, but suppose I shall not be allowed to lay aside at present."   He greatly enjoyed this month a visit from his friend, Mr. Henry Hopkins, of Hobart Town.   Thirty years before they had been associated in loving Christian labours in Hobart Town, and through the whole succeeding time had enjoyed a sanctified intimate friendship.   I feel it a dutiful obligation to name Mr. Hopkins as among the foremost of the successful merchants in the churches of the southern world who have honoured God with their substance. The Christian character shone in his valuable life.   His liberal donations towards religious purposes were not by legacy, but by consecration during his life.

The gold mania was making sad work with the congregations and Societies of the Parramatta Circuit.   Inquiries by pastor or leader for absentees from church or class were met by the answer, " Off to the Diggings." Many returned wofully disappointed. To get a very little gold, they had expended much silver, besides suffering physical hardship and spiritual loss. The Church excitement and derangement from this cause continued and increased for the rest of his term in the Circuit.

The District Meeting re-appointed him, regretting, at the same time, that, from the paucity of Ministers and of funds, the way did not appear by which they could render him any effective assistance. During the whole of the December quarter he was entirely laid aside from public work. The spiritual wants of the Diggings, south and west, were attracting much attention ; and at the General Superintendent's request, Mr. Turner, while still an invalid, and in part with a view to his health, went on a ministerial visit of inquiry and observation to Braidwood. He was driven by the writer of these memorials. The first Sabbath was spent at Goulburn. Monday's journey of sixty miles to Braidwood was much enjoyed, the course lying through a magnificent valley or series of rich plains. Tuesday and Wednesday were spent at Braidwood and Major's Creek. There were the usual scenes of vice prevailing at new goldfield towns. But there were several pious Wesleyans at the latter place, who honoured God by their worship and testimony. The weather generally was fine ; and though the toil of travel was overmuch, the three hundred and fifty miles' tour was, upon the whole, an enjoyment. Upon his return journey an old forsaken road had been followed : the mistake was only found out just as night and rain had set in together. It was an awkward country for strangers, and for some time there appeared every probability of his camping out in the wet, without fire or food, which in his state of health would have been very serious. Whether his lungs were weak or strong, he made the bush ring again and again with his "cooee." But its echo was the only reply. This was before the days of buggies, and the old gig was kept jolting on at the supposed rate of a mile in half an hour, till patience was rewarded. A shepherd's dog replied to the "cooees," and in a short time a refuge was found, and the supper of damper and mutton was enjoyed. It is hoped that the kindly words and prayers of the servant of God, welcomed in that lonely bark hut, cheered on the struggling shepherd and his wife in after years, and that their bright-eyed little children have learned to sing of Jesus from the hymn-book left with them.

In March he wrote to his eldest son as follows :—" My health is much better, but it is now pretty certain that I shall not be ever equal to the regular ministry again. My chest is very, very weak, and with the slightest change to damp and cold I become oppressed like an asthmatical person ; but I am encouraged to hope I may for a while be spared to my family, and do good in a smaller way. Mr. Morris, from India, is at Adelaide, on his way to the colony, and should he come to Parramatta, I shall seek to leave it before winter sets in ; for it is more damp and cold here than in the neighbourhood of Sydney, to which locality we shall probably direct our attention for the present, if we can procure a suitable dwelling. Retiring will be a trial to me, but I will try cheerfully to submit. I have been long favoured with health and vigour, and it would be wicked in me to complain."

The foregoing appears to have been his first written anticipation of retiring wholly from the work. Circumstances favoured him so far that at the end of the quarter arrangements were completed for his removal from Parramatta. He carried with him the affection of the Church, and esteem of the community, and left not a few who had been savingly benefitted by his ministry.

CHAPTER XX.

1852–1854.

The rents of houses suitable for his family, close to Sydney, were beyond his means; but he was fortunate in securing a very comfortable residence in a salubrious and retired part of the eastern suburbs, at a distance of three miles from the centre of the city. The site commanded a lovely view of the harbour, and the premises were all that his family could reasonably desire. Thus free from ministerial care, in a short time his spirits rose, and his health improved. In May he wrote, " I feel more vigorous than I have done for eight months past, and hope to have strength to work again in my Master's vineyard." In June he began to visit about the hamlet, distributing tracts, and inducing parents to send their children to the Sabbath school, in which the members of his family took an active part. He formed a class in his house, and regularly met it when able. In July he resumed preaching, taking a morning appointment at New Town.

The District Meeting of that year, as had been anticipated, made him a Supernumerary. The following is the official record :—

" Brother Turner's health having so far failed during the past year as to render his retirement from the labours of his Circuit absolutely necessary for the preservation of his life, we unanimously recommend that he appear on the Minutes of Conference of 1853 as a Supernumerary.

" We desire to express, on this occasion, our high sense

of Brother Turner's faithful labours during the thirty-one years in which he has been actively engaged in the Mission field,—in New Zealand, Tonga, and the Australian colonies. His consistent walk with God, his truly Christian amiability of disposition, his energetic and lively preaching, have rendered him an object of sincere attachment to all who have been placed in contact with him." *

The decision of his brethren was in entire harmony with his judgment, though looking forward to it had cost him many months of deep feeling. No man had loved the active service of Christ's Church more than he had. He had not felt any part of it irksome, nor had he grudged the sacrifices it had involved. It had been his life, and it would have been strange had his " sitting down " not caused him feeling. At the meeting alluded to, all the brethren expressed the kindliest sentiments of regard and sympathy; but they were unanimous in the opinion that, for him to attempt to resume the regular work, would probably terminate his life. There was, on the other hand, the likelihood that, in the retirement of a Supernumerary's position, he might long be spared to his family and the Church, and indeed enjoy a lengthened term of peace and usefulness. The step having been taken with his full concurrence, he never in any degree regretted it, though at times he was eager for more active employment.

The Rev. Robert Young was deputed to visit the Australasian Churches and Missions on behalf of the British Conference, preliminary to their being formed into a separate Conference. Mr. Young attended the District Meeting held in Sydney in 1853. Mr. Turner attended most of its sittings, and he felt it an occasion of gratitude to God that, as he was retiring, one of his sons was recommended to the work of the ministry.

Messrs. Young and Boyce, the Deputation to Auckland,

* Minutes of Sydney District Meeting, 1852.

expressed a wish that Mr. Turner would accompany Mr. Young on his projected visit to New Zealand and the South Seas. The prospect of revisiting the scenes of his early labours afforded him much pleasure, and family considerations alone presented a difficulty. At that juncture the Rev. Peter Turner arrived from the islands, and was welcomed as a temporary resident with Mr. Turner's family, and the island trip was taken. The subjoined narrative of the tour is compiled and extracted from his note-book.

The voyage to Auckland occupied nine days, ending September 8th. Messrs. Boyce and Young suffered not a little from sea-sickness. Mr. Boyce did not proceed with the "John Wesley" to Tonga, &c.; but journeyed through New Zealand to Wellington, (Cook's Straits,) and thence returned to Sydney. They anchored in rough weather, and were landed at some risk, and found that the Missionaries from several stations had been some time waiting. He was greatly pleased with the admirable spirit of wisdom, prudence, and piety with which Mr. Young conducted the business of the District Meeting. He heard the Reports of several of the stations read, and was glad to find the brethren in general so prudently and piously prosecuting their work, notwithstanding many difficulties. The rapid decrease of the native population in every part of the land was painfully evident. Of one session of the meeting he wrote, " O, it was a season of mercy and love ! The Chairman affectingly exclaimed, ' Lo, God is here!' My soul did indeed praise the Lord for such a body of men consecrated to His cause in New Zealand. Surely better days are before it." Mr. Turner spoke at the Missionary Meeting, but felt himself " tongue-tied and barren."

He visited at the " Three Kings," the Native Training Institution, then under the effective management of the Rev. Alexander Reid, who had been selected in England for that post. The roll numbered some thirty females, and nearly one hundred men and boys. One of the native Ministers delighted to meet in Mr. Turner his first teacher when a boy. The village and surroundings of Epsom were very charming. He visited the college presided over by the Rev. J. H. Fletcher. There were forty boarders and thirty day scholars present. It was then "justly regarded as the best college in the land." There was good feeling at the public weekly prayer-meeting of the Auckland Society; fifty were present. Among old friends and acquaintances who called after him was a former servant, Mary Allen, who had accompanied his family to New Zealand in 1836. From regard for her former master, she had travelled many miles, with her twin children, but three weeks old, for him to baptize. He visited Onehunga, the pensioner settlement, a fertile, lovely place, where he noticed a good store, managed by a Maori.

Mr. Turner was induced to conduct a native service at the Three Kings Institution. His heart warmed, and his tongue was free. He was astonished at his liberty in preaching. "Though I conducted the whole service, Mr. Reid only detected one mistake." At the Maori lovefeast in Auckland the testimonies to the truth and power of grace were quite equal to anything he had ever heard among his own countrymen. He spent most of his last Sabbath in New Zealand on board the brig. At eleven A.M., and at 5 P.M., he preached to the crew, and passed the interval with a dying Tongan who was on board. Far from his home and friends, Sampson said, "I am not afraid to die, for Jesus is my Saviour."

"Monday, October 10th.—Have said 'Farewell' to the city, with its fine churches and muddy lanes. Five P.M. The brig was tacking in the Gulf of Hauraki, near the spot where, in 1840, poor Bumby was drowned. On the other side of the gulf, beautifully situated, is the residence of

Patuone,* our deliverer from apparent destruction when fleeing for our lives from Whangaroa, in 1827. I met him in Auckland Street, on the day of my landing, when his face beamed with pleasure as I saluted him as our kaiwakaora.

"Tuesday morning.—Have just passed the Great Barrier Island, on which a copper-mine is being wrought.

"Tuesday, 18th.—Last evening the vessel suddenly lurched, and threw my head violently against the boom, which knocked me down with great force on to my back. I suffered much all night. This morning for the first time was absent from the breakfast table. Am thankful no bone was injured."

On Friday, the 21st, Nukualofa was sighted; and, with the view, came a rush of memory and of feeling. He gazed with peculiar emotion on the familiar outline of the old hill, and upon the chapel which crowned it. He says, "How wonderful the dealings of Heaven with me! Twenty-two years ago I was removed from this place, a sick and, as some supposed, a dying man; yet, after so many changes in many lands, here I am in tolerable health, to visit the scenes of early labour." The arrival was sudden and unexpected. But few natives were on the shore when the ship's boat reached it. Mr. Turner's name had been a household word in the group; and, so soon as it was known that he had come, there was general joy. The greeting of Messrs. Amos and Adams was very cordial. Mr. Turner wrote :—
"The brethren appear very hearty in their work; but, alas! some of them are very sickly and feeble. Mr. Adams, a most devoted and excellent Missionary, appears very delicate, and fears a change to a more bracing atmosphere will be absolutely necessary. Mr. Millard urges a removal

---

* Patuone is now (1870) a venerable chieftain, bending under the weight of a hundred years, and is known as Etuhera Maihi. He lives alone.

at once, as the only means of saving his life. Visited the natives in their different *abcs*. Many remembered me well. Ebalahama Vakatuola, Abraham, brother to the late king, and one of the late converts, was nearly frantic with joy. I sought out and found Setalaki Mumui, formerly an interesting scholar, but now chief justice, and believed to be the most intelligent man in the land. Alas! fell disease has seized him. He received me with great delight. I took up his Tongan Book of Psalms, and read a portion for him. By his side was one of his manuscript sermons; well written. He is of the royal family, and has been a first-rate Local Preacher. I was greatly pleased with the spirit and manners of the king and queen. It is scarcely possible for any man to stand higher in the esteem of Ministers and people than he does. His piety is of the highest order, and his wisdom, prudence, and firmness call forth the praise of all under his government. The queen is deeply devoted to the interests of her husband. She is a godly woman, and is a useful Class-Leader."

There were three hundred present at the six o'clock Sunday morning prayer-meeting. Mr. Turner was impressed by the manifest power with God of those who prayed, and with the devotional and warm ascription, *Faka fa tai!* "Praise to God," so general throughout the meeting. At nine A.M. Mr. Young preached, and several, including the king, engaged in prayer. Mr. Turner conducted the afternoon service, but felt the restraint of being publicly interpreted, for the first time for many years.

At Bea, there was pointed out to him the spot on which King George had recently pardoned the rebel chiefs. The incidents connected with that event are among the finest examples of Christian heroism and honour ever recorded.

"We afterwards passed the largest tree in the island. It is called the 'orava,' and is of the banyan species. Its girth is not much less than fifty yards, and its branches are widely spread. We also went to see the much honoured Kolo, the royal city of Tonga. The Faitokas, burial places, are remarkable; they are raised mounds, some of them fifty yards square, surrounded by two or three tiers of massive stones, hewn from their native rocks, and said to have been brought from an island leeward of Tonga. But how they had been quarried or conveyed was a wonder. We measured one, and found it twenty-two and a half feet long, six feet wide, and seven feet deep. No vessel the Tongans now have, could have borne the weight of these stones."

Most of Thursday was spent in reviewing seven schools, and the visitors were much surprised and pleased with the knowledge exhibited. The king took leave of his household and people on the eve of embarking for Sydney. He had projected the visit, with the view of furthering the interests of the people; and the step was approved by the Missionaries. The demonstrations of his people, on his parting from them, were most affecting. Their adieus were given and repeated amid many tears, at the beach, in the surf, and on the ship's deck. A run of twenty-five hours carried them to Vavau. The entrance affords a picturesque view of the main land and of twenty islands. The spacious harbour, with its numerous coves and inlets, somewhat resembles Port Jackson. The brig anchored in a lovely bay which would hold the whole British fleet. The chief drawback to it is the too great depth for anchorage.

"Vavau has been our best and largest Mission in these islands. Formerly three Mission families resided here; now only one, and he, Mr. Daniels, looks poorly. The press is here, and is actively worked under his direction by an English resident, a New Zealander, and a Tongan. The chapel is a substantial native building, one hundred feet by forty-five feet. A good school-house stands close by.

I visited the graves of the brethren, Francis Wilson and David Cargill. At a lovefeast, several references were made amid much emotion to the gracious outpouring of the Holy Spirit in 1834, in connexion with the labours and prayers of the Rev. Peter Turner, when occurred, unquestionably, one of the most extensive revivals of religion since the Pentecost. I attempted to speak through an interpreter, but my feelings were too much for such restraint, and my full soul found unexpected vent in the Tongan language."

His fortnight's association with the Tonguese had so revived his remembrance of the language, that he could understand all that was said in it, and could readily make himself understood. Many of the natives seriously begged him to return, and labour for a few years among them. He was much pleased with a view from Talau, a remarkable hill two miles from the station. Of a great part of the group, he wrote, " Every spot of each isle appears clothed with luxuriant foliage. Yet only here and there is it cultivated. Under English culture these islands would sustain several hundred thousand persons, whereas the present population is but some eight or ten thousand. The difficulty would be want of water; but as there are many elevations, reservoirs could be formed in most places."

On Thursday, November the 23rd, the anniversary of Mr. Turner's arrival in Tonga twenty-six years before, he bade farewell to Tonga. Under its bright green sod was resting the dust of hundreds of Tonguese who had slept in Jesus, and with them that of holy men and women who had told them of Christ their Life. Together they would live again in the Resurrection morning. " I felt for Brother Daniel in bidding him ' good bye.' He is alone with his family at this important station, has got the language well, and appears quite happy in the work, and bent upon doing all the good in his power."

He landed with Mr. Young at Lakemba, Fiji, on Sunday,

during morning worship.   Their unexpected presence in the
chapel did not interrupt devotion ; Mr. Polglase went on
fluently preaching to a chapel full of deeply attentive
hearers.   The Missionary, with Messrs. Lyth, Binner, and
Colliss, gave them a cordial greeting, and their Sabbath
intercourse was much enjoyed.   The Christian natives of
Lakemba are considerably removed from the pure Fijian
type, having traded and intermarried with the Tonguese for
many years.   Among the preachers was Joel Bulu, a choice
man from Tonga, a Native Assistant Missionary.   Not far
distant was a town of Tonguese numbering some two
hundred persons.   Nearly all the twenty islands of Lakemba
had lotued.   At the native lovefeast, the bread used was a
compound of arrowroot and taro, sweetened by the juice of
the native fi-plant : its taste was not unpleasant.   Though
the Fiji dialect differs much from that of New Zealand and
also of Tonga, Mr. Turner observed many words that he
could understand.

" Monday afternoon.—Am greatly pleased with Mr. and
Mrs. Lyth and Mr. Polglase.   While my Mission friends
were enjoying their English correspondence, I climbed a
hill to have a view.   The valleys in general are very rich,
producing food in abundance.   The principal of them have
the advantage over Tonga, in possessing small streams.
Went through the Fiji kolo, or town, one of the most
wretched, filthy places that ever I was in.   It is surrounded
by a moat full of filthy water and mud, the home of myriads
of mosquitoes.   Tuiniau is one of the fattest, grossest
men I ever saw; a real Eglon...Saw a Fijian woman
making pottery......Visited the Tongan burial-ground, two
miles distant, where lie the remains of some of my old
friends.   Their graves give proof of affectionate remembrance.   At some distance is the grave of Tubou Totai and
Lajiki, two Tongan brothers, chiefs of the first rank, and to
whom, in 1826, I felt warmly attached.   They had become

restless and unsteady, and had finished their course in Fiji, with but little hope in their death. The examination of some of Mr. Colliss's four hundred scholars gave evidence of successful teaching, under a modification of the Glasgow system."

The notes of an English wedding are given. Many Tonguese were present on the happy occasion of the marriage of Miss Fletcher and the Rev. John Polglase. It was arranged for King George to take part in the solemnities. He read the Marriage Service in the Tongan language.

Much has been written of King George as a Christian and as a sovereign. He excels as a preacher, and I append notes of a sermon Mr. Turner heard him preach during his visit to Fiji. The king of Lakemba and his wife were among the hearers.

Text, Hosea iv. 6: "My people are destroyed for lack of knowledge." After a few introductory remarks, he pointed out,—

I. *The great evil of ignorance*, and

II. *What the people suffering from it should seek for.*

I. (*a.*) *Man the noblest creature of God.*

Made in His image. To know Him. To love Him. To serve Him for ever. In proof of man's greatness: (1.) Appointed the ruler of this lower world. (2.) Redeemed by the sufferings and death of Christ.

(*b.*) *Man now fallen from God.*

Suffers under his great ignorance of Him. God's image, excellence, or dignity is gone from him. Is now a weak, degraded mortal; exposed to everlasting damnation.

Addressing the people of the Friendly and Fiji Islands, and designating the chiefs, *matabulus*, and common people, he asked whether his statements were not true.

II. *What the people who are ignorant should seek,—instruction.*

(*a.*) *By learning to read.*

Chiefs and parents should send their children to school. Can anything good or noble or wise be performed without knowledge? The prevailing error in Fiji is, that accepting the *lotu* is sufficient. "Ignorant *lotu* is worthless."

(*b.*) *Specially by obtaining the knowledge of the Bible.* This is "the great property, or riches."

(*c.*) *But this knowledge must be sought by and from the Holy Ghost.*

The cannibalism of Fiji is, perhaps, the most revolting in the world. Mr. Turner heard the following instances credibly related. A Fijian clubbed his wife, and, while the little one was crying for its mother, he cut off one of her hands, and threw it to the child to comfort it...Occasionally, when about to eat a man, they fasten him to a tree alive. They then cut off his hands or other portions of the body, and bake them before him, and offer him a part of himself to eat.

Joel Bulu, who delighted to acknowledge himself as one of Mr. Turner's children, was asked what he thought of the subjugation of the whole of Fiji to Christianity. He replied, "The thing is certain, but I think the progress will be slow." Mr. Turner had an interview with two resident French priests. They were of agreeable manners, and spoke the Tongan language fluently. They had but a miserable existence at Lakemba, and were not making any converts. Frequently they were unable to get any one to cook a few yams for them.

On the 14th they reached Ovalau, the scenery of which, and of the great island generally, was very bold. During their stay they had much pleasing intercourse with Messrs. Calvert, Joseph Waterhouse, and Hazlewood, all devoted Missionaries. He visited the tomb of the sainted John Hunt. [Two years before, while he had been preaching his memorial sermon in the York Street church, a young convert, Mr. John Crawford, had been filled with an intense desire to go to Fiji as a Missionary. He afterwards went and died there.] Mr. Turner wrote to brother Moore of Bua, whom he regretted he could not get to see, but of whom "all the brethren gave an excellent account, as a · devoted and useful Missionary."

He saw Bau, the veriest hell upon earth, also Thakombau, and his great house appropriated to strangers, where the most violent cannibal tragedies have been enacted. "Mr· Joseph Waterhouse is about to reside in Bau. Poor young man ! he will need all the nerve, prudence, and zeal he can obtain. To take a delicate wife to such a place must be more than commonly trying; but he does not seem appalled. If Bau once submits to Jesus, all Fiji will soon follow."

From what he saw of the Fiji Mission field, Mr. Turner was led to coincide with Joel Bulu's opinion. Wondrous success had been achieved. But the ignorance and fearfully depraved character of the masses of the islanders called for continual intercession with God, and persevering, zealous effort.

On Friday, November 18th, as the "Wesley" passed the outer reef, homeward bound, he said, "Farewell, Fiji ! dark, cannibal Fiji, farewell ! The Sun of Righteousness has arisen upon thy children." Twelve days afterwards he was recounting his adventures and mercies to his own children at home.

The last month of the year was happily spent in the bosom of his family, and in receiving visits from ministerial and other friends. On New Year's Eve, after a very hot day, he was attacked by cholera. For many hours it threatened his life. Through great mercy he recovered in a few days. A few weeks before he had left for the islands Mr. Thomas Turner, his eldest son, resident at Launceston, had been at the point of death; and for a time his father had thought of visiting him instead of taking the voyage by the "Wesley." While Mr. Turner, senior, was away, a trip to Sydney and several weeks' rest from office work had considerably restored his son's strength. Upon his return from the islands, his father became very anxious to see him, and made early arrangements to do so, going *via* Melbourne.   On reaching that city he met a young friend who had just come over from Launceston, who gave him sorrowful tidings. Mr. T. J. Crouch had but two or three days before left his son on board the "Lizzie Webber," in the Launceston harbour, mortally ill; and he was then on his way to Sydney, hoping that he might be spared to see his father once more before he should die.   With an anxious, troubled heart, the good old man voyaged homeward the next day, and for three days at sea was in great suspense. The Launceston brig had not reached Sydney when he arrived there.   For three days more his suspense was continued, and then the captain reported that his eldest son had died four days previously.

"Even so, Father, for so it seemed good in Thy sight." Though the dear old man was able to say this, it was from a crushed heart. Though it is his brother who writes, he feels free to say that few young men have more deserved the sorrow which his untimely removal caused.   From his boyhood his spirit and life had won the admiration and love of many friends.   His manner had been somewhat reserved, but he had evinced a nobly unselfish nature. As a son and brother he had been dutiful, loving, and prudent in a high degree.   He had cheerfully rendered conscientious labour to the Church of Christ as a Sabbath school teacher, church trustee, and otherwise.   His medical advisers had sought to dissuade him from taking the voyage, believing he would not survive it; but he was so anxious again to see his father, that he was willing, in that hope, to risk an ocean grave.   His sufferings on board were great; but he evinced the utmost Christian resignation.   The only impatience he showed was to see his father.   To one on board he said, " O, my father is such a good man I would give all I have to see him again ! " His latest words were, " I am happy now ! I am happy ! "

" The sea shall give up her dead."

The bereaved family bowed in submission to the Hand which had smitten. The providence was all mysterious. The steamer by which Mr. Turner was returning to Sydney ordinarily called in at Twofold Bay ; but on that trip she did not : had she done so, his father would have found his son on board the brig, lying there windbound, upon the last day but one of his earthly life.

" Thou art my hiding place," was his comfort in affliction, and the work of God was his solace. A supply was needed at Chippendale the next Sabbath morning, and he undertook the service. Calmly and in tones of heavenly resignation he announced the text: " The Lord gave, and the Lord hath taken away ; blessed be the Name of the Lord."

A few weeks after this he visited Brisbane, Moreton Bay, where his now eldest son and two of his daughters were residing. The trip was taken partly with the view of forming an opinion of Brisbane, as suitable or otherwise for his place of residence for the remainder of his days. The climate was reported dry and agreeable, and two of his family were settled there. The opinion he formed was more favourable than he anticipated it would be. Brisbane was then a quiet town of about two thousand inhabitants, its population comprising many agreeable families. The expense of living there would be much less than in Sydney, where his cottage rent, two miles from town, was about to be increased from £78 to £225 per annum. After serious consideration, he decided to make Brisbane his future home, believing the arrangement would prolong his life, and afford him a quiet sphere of usefulness with his family, and in the church of that young community.

1855–1864.

His decision to found a family home, amidst a young and comparatively small population, five hundred miles distant, did not commend itself to all his Sydney friends: however, he thought he saw the Pillar of Cloud. For some time he sojourned with his son resident in Brisbane. He purchased an acre of land in the outskirts of the town, an eligible building site, with a fine view, and on it he erected a roomy cottage, the first home he ever owned, and, as the event proved, the last. From his boyhood he had loved gardening, and during his missionary career he had excelled in the recreative art. Many a wilderness of Mission premises had been redeemed and made fruitful by his industry and skill. His own table had been kept well supplied with vegetables, and perchance that of his successors with fruit. And now with the idea—a peculiar sensation to a Methodist Minister—of its being his last home on earth, the laying out, stocking, and cultivating his garden afforded him ample scope for his favourite pastime.

The townspeople, who were of a quiet turn, comprised many agreeable families, and soon supplied a pleasant circle of friends. Methodism had a living representation in a small society, and had recently shown signs of vigour. It had been established by the labours of the Rev. William Moore and the Rev. John Watsford. The Rev. S. G. Millard, the then resident Minister, hailed the arrival of

Mr. Turner's family, as so much additional power to the cause of God. The parents early began to visit the sick and poor, and their children found work in the Sabbath school. The family correspondence of that winter shows that the removal to Moreton Bay had given them general pleasure. The climate, the new friendships, the work and prospective work in the Church, were alluded to with satisfaction. But summer came, and with it another story as to Brisbane climate.

Mr. Turner looked forward with great interest to the first Australasian Conference, and readily yielded to numerous invitations to attend it. He had been the cotemporary and immediate successor of Samuel Leigh, the first Methodist Missionary in the Southern World; had watched the struggles and shared the triumphs of Methodism for more than thirty years : he had seen the tyranny of heathenism and the not less hateful tyranny of convictism overcome; had been present at the planting of churches, cities, and colonies, and had watched them flourish in their youth. His heart was still young. He loved Methodism and its preachers, and thought but little of a thousand miles' voyaging, to be at its first Conference in this hemisphere.

He reached Sydney on the 7th of January, 1855, in time to attend the covenant service, and pleasantly spent the next week among friends in the city, and at Parramatta; but he did not feel equal to preaching.

The labours of forty years had planted the form of religion known as Wesleyan Methodism in Van Diemen's Land, New Zealand, Tonga, Samoa, and Fiji, as well as upon the vast Australian continent, where its chain of stations stretched for three thousand miles. The future of this vast religious organization was important, and it was felt that the field could not longer be well worked from London as the official centre. Its exigencies had more than once baffled the wisdom of the Committee. And though the utmost loyalty to the parent Church had prevailed throughout, self-government had become a necessity. The Methodism of Australasia, including the Mission stations, comprised 78 Ministers and 7 Supernumeraries, 31 Ministers on trial, 19,897 Church members, and 83,000 hearers. Sundry preliminaries had been settled, and a constitution agreed upon. The Australasian Conference had been authorized, and its first sessions had been anticipated with much Christian interest on both sides of the world.

The Ministers to the number of forty met in the York Street church, on the morning of Thursday, January 18th, 1855. The Rev. W. B. Boyce, whose important services as General Superintendent for nine years had won for him the highest esteem of his brethren, was the President, by appointment of the British Conference. The occasion was one of solemn interest to all. There were the founders of a mighty work of God which, during their day, had outgrown their most ardent anticipations; and there were young Ministers, whose earliest religious instruction had been received at their feet. Before them were momentous questions, and upon their decisions seemed to rest in great degree the advancement of the Church of Christ. Never was Christian zeal more sacredly tempered with humility, than when they rose to sing, as their opening hymn,

> " Except the Lord conduct the plan,
> The best concerted schemes are vain,
> And never can succeed."

The first prayer was offered by Mr. Turner, the sole representative of the first decade. During his prayer, and those which followed, by Messrs. Hull, Schofield, Eggleston, and Hurst, a most gracious influence prevailed. The Rev. John Allen Manton was chosen Secretary, and the Rev. Stephen Rabone and H. H. Gaud, sub-Secretaries. As the English mail with official despatches for the Conference

arrived that morning, the afternoon session for the day
lapsed. The Conference prayer-meeting held in the evening
was largely attended, and was " a blessed season." At five
A.M. on the next and succeeding days, the President and
some of the fathers in the ministry met a number of the
young brethren to hearten and counsel them in reference to
their work. The Conference sermon was based on the
address to the Church at Ephesus. It was preached by the
Rev. Thomas T. N. Hull, and was regarded as one of the
most eloquent and powerful discourses delivered in
Sydney. The Ministers present will not soon forget their
emotion and vows under the word that night. Among the
arrangements of that first Conference was the founding of
Horton College, in Tasmania. The Rev. J. A. Manton
was appointed Principal.

Mr. Turner felt a great interest in the numerous
aborigines of the Moreton Bay district. With others he
had sought to establish a Mission among them ; and he
deeply regretted that he could not induce the Conference to
make some special provision for their instruction.

As the Brisbane Circuit Minister was about to remove,
he was properly concerned as to his successor. He wrote,
".Were I in charge of the Circuit, or my subsistence de-
pending upon it, I could scarcely feel more." The appointment of the Rev. W. J. K. Piddington, a young Minister of
fine spirit and enterprise, was soon followed by the erection
of a new town chapel. In this enterprise Mr. Turner and
his family took much interest from the beginning. A vast
Gothic sanctuary, forty feet by eighty in the clear, was a
long way in advance of the Methodist part of Brisbane ;
but after its successful opening by the Rev. John Eggleston
in January, 1856, its sittings were in demand.

Of this term I have nothing by which to link my narrative. In ordinary fine weather, Mr. Turner was wont to
enjoy gardening for an hour or two before breakfast, and

also in the early forenoon. He would spend the middle of the day in reading or in correspondence, and fill up his afternoons by services of love or mercy in the neighbourhood. The various public charities found him an active worker upon Committees. His class increased in numbers, and engaged much of his time. He never knew what it was to be dull, and was accustomed to say, " The lines have fallen to me in pleasant places; I have a goodly heritage." Christian visitors to his cottage, nestling in roses and jessamine, and to his lively group of children within, thought so too.

In May, 1857, he again visited Sydney, the occasion being the marriage, on the same day, of two of his family. Of the celebration, which took place in the Surrey Hills church, he wrote home, " I never performed a service for any member of my family with more perfect satisfaction." He spent the Sabbath and a day or two at Parramatta, enjoying the kind hospitality of his friends the Howisons. Mr. Rabone accompanied him to Windsor, where they assisted Messrs. Watkin and Peter Turner at a Missionary Meeting.

He spent two Sabbaths at Maitland, where the writer of this memoir was stationed as Mr. Chapman's colleague. He was accompanied by one of his daughters, and wrote, " We were cordially entertained by Mr. and Mrs. Owen, and never was I more kindly treated." Simultaneously the Rev. J. Eggleston visited the Hunter as a Missionary Deputation. Torrents of rain and miles of mud caused several postponements. Methodism, however, can find enterprises for all weathers. While enjoying a social hour with Mr. Joseph Ede Pearce, one of the best specimens of a Cornish Methodist, I suggested that a more profitable nvestment of time and labour might be made by the visiting Ministers than in travelling the country roads up to their horses' girths in mud, to spend their eloquence upon empty seats. Could they not give an evening to a representative meeting of the town congregation, and assist in initiating a new church-building scheme ? West Maitland had for years been a flourishing commercial town, and an important Methodist centre ; but the town interest had been hampered by the want of a larger and better church. The suggestion was accepted by the Superintendent. The heads of families, to the number of about fifty, were invited. Some thirty attended, and enjoyed their tea and the graceful attentions of two or three ladies only. The proposal to build was talked over, and, in a few minutes, the sum of *nine hundred pounds* was promised. The subscription list was considerably increased the next day. The result was the erection of a fine church, ninety feet by fifty-three feet, at an expense of *six thousand pounds*.

" The rains descended and the floods came." Mr. Turner was one of the last persons who re-crossed to the Maitland side of the Hunter, before its first flood of that year ; and he but barely saved himself a week's imprisonment by the flood. That June flood, 1857, was the first of any importance which had occurred on the Hunter during many, perhaps twenty, years. It was, however, followed in July and in August by others much more disastrous. On Sunday, August 8th, the rich alluvial flats, for miles studded by the homes of industrious tenant farmers, were flooded to a depth of from two to twelve feet ; and the various villages and small towns were crowded with refugees, many of whom had narrowly escaped drowning. About two-thirds of West Maitland were flooded. Four hundred refugees were accommodated in public buildings or by private friends on the higher parts of the town. Among several disasters to buildings was one to the Wesleyan Mission house. A corner of its foundation was underrun by the flood current, and a large part of the two-story building fell to the ground. The families of the Rev.

B. Chapman and his brother-in-law, the Rev. Theophilus Taylor, and the household servants and myself, had a very narrow escape. We had been barely rescued by brave volunteers when the falling in occurred. The repairs cost some hundreds of pounds.

Mr. Turner regained his home in good health and spirits after a happy six weeks' tour. At the close of the winter he wrote, "I am now much more healthy and vigorous than for some years past ; and I have plenty of work in assisting our young Minister in the Circuit." The September mail brought tidings of the happy death of Mrs. Turner's mother, aged eighty-three. She had lived in union with the Church for thirty-five years.

He was much gratified by affectionate remembrances of him by friends at a distance ;—by one instance in particular. A kind friend in Hobart Town made him an overture to leave Brisbane, and remove to that city, to live among his former friends there. He would be at liberty to do just what public work he might feel equal to. The removal expenses of his family would be paid, and a liberal main-tenance would be provided for them. Though he was much attached to Hobart Town, and to many there, he could not see his way clear to accept the generous offer. He was now advanced in years, and the Tasmanian climate would be too severe for him. Further, the arrange-ment so kindly proposed did not suit his independent spirit. On the question of the maintenance of Supernu-merary Ministers, Mr. Turner always held the common-sense opinion that no Minister should be subjected to the temptation to labour, for the sake of family maintenance, longer than he could work efficiently, and also, from that time, a moderate but sufficient allowance should be secured to him, not by friendship or other private source, but by the funds of the Church he had served during his years of vigour.

Mr. Turner loved the Superintendent, Mr. Piddington, as

well for his ministerial as his personal qualities; and in
Circuit affairs and work gave him most cordially his utmost
assistance. On the first of January, 1858, the Eagle Farm
chapel was re-opened, and on that day week he re-opened
one at Fortitude Valley, after enlargement. In this suburb
of Brisbane he seemed to take a special interest. When
there had been but a scattered community, he had preached
out of doors. An innkeeper named Lowden, who somehow
seemed to take a great liking to him, not wishing to see him
exerting himself under the hot sun, offered him the use of
his large room, which was well furnished with seats. The
services were continued in that room for some time. Then
another publican offered land for a church, and a good
donation towards the erection. Including the Abbot Street
church, there had been, during his first four years in Brisbane, four erections of churches, much of the credit of which
was due to Mr. Piddington's enterprise. A Wesleyan
church was at this date being built at Ipswich.

During the winter of 1858 Mr. Turner was laid aside by sickness, and for a time serious results were feared. I visited him
from Sydney during his recovery, and found him cheerful,
though much reduced and enfeebled. I sought very
earnestly to induce him to write an autobiography, for the
gratification of his family and numerous friends. He manifested the greatest reluctance for many days,—his objections
always being given in the spirit of Christian humility. I
pleaded that probably such a manual would do good in
encouraging young Ministers, and possibly in reviving the
missionary spirit. By these considerations alone, I succeeded in getting him to prepare the personal narrative
from which much of this biography has been written. He
wrote from memory, and from reference to Missionary
Notices, and manuscript scraps which he had preserved.
He began at once, and for many weeks devoted occasional
hours of each day to the work.

The Conference of 1859 being held in Sydney, afforded him another pleasant change. His letters home are miscellanea of Methodist intelligence, but give prominence to Moreton Bay affairs. " I have had to contend for Moreton Bay, as for my life." Infirmity and affliction somewhat marred the enjoyment of the visit, but his diary is that of an active, spiritually-minded traveller. Some weeks after his return he gave to a member of his family the following account of his illness. " The second day I was in Sydney, I had a sore attack of inflammation in the eyes, which blinded me for some time. Recovering from that, I took a severe cold, which brought on inflammation in the chest, accompanied by a most racking cough. Last, but not least, a very bad carbuncle was all the while forming on the back part of the left thigh, deep among the sinews. I suffered not a little during my return voyage, and my agony in walking home from the steamer, at twelve o'clock on Sunday night, I will not attempt to describe. I have been in Dr. Bell's hands ever since, and kept in bed for a fortnight. Two days ago I got up, and upon crutches (the first I have ever had cause to use) took a journey into the back garden, from which I returned to bed, really exhausted. My sensitive nature shrinks from pain, yet I feel assured it is all well, and try to pray,

> ' With me in the fire remain,
>   Till like burnish'd gold I shine,
>   Meet through consecrated pain,
>   To see the Face Divine.' "

In the spring he paid a visit to one of his daughters resident at the Darling Downs. He was " charmed with his grandchildren and their home at Rosalie." He quite enjoyed their family prayers, and his special public services with them. During his return journey, he preached in the large room of the Sovereign Hotel at Tonomba, and did a full Sabbath's work at Ipswich.

Early in December he experienced a severe trial in the removal to Geelong of his son. He had been a resident of Brisbane, and for five years had been Mr. Turner's daily companion.

The next two years were a transition period. The whole community arose from something like bucolic quietude into the excitement of finding themselves political pioneers in a new and independent colony. Moreton Bay had been discovered by Captain Cook in 1770. Its settlement, however, had dated as recently as 1823, when, upon the discovery of the Brisbane River, the New South Wales Government established a penal station on its banks. In 1841, when transportation to that colony ceased, the northern part of it was thrown open to free settlement, and from that date it had been occupied chiefly for pastoral purposes, remaining part of New South Wales, and sending representatives to its Parliament. Its increased importance and ascertained resources, however, led to its being formed, at the date of our narrative, 1859, into an independent colony, under the name of Queensland, with representative government,—its first Governor being Sir George Ferguson Bowen, Bart. Queensland is the largest of the Australian colonies, embracing the whole of the North Eastern portion of the vast continent. Its eastern coast-line boundary extends for thirteen hundred miles, from Point Danger, in lat. 28° 8′ S., to Cape York, in lat. 10° 40′ S.

In January, 1861, Mr. Turner again visited Sydney, partly to enjoy the Conference, at which Dr. Jobson would be present, and partly to accompany his daughter, Mrs. Jordan, so far on her way to England. In his place in the Queensland Parliament, Mr. Jordan had initiated a liberal land and immigration scheme, which quickly found general favour, and passed into law. To carry out some of its provisions, the government arranged for his services in England, and sent him home as Immigration Agent for the colony.

Mr. Turner had a free and joyous Sabbath, hearing Dr. Jobson and Mr. Dare. He wrote home, " It is many years since the depths of my soul were so stirred, as on Sunday morning, when the Doctor preached from, ' God is love.' O ! what melting power attended the word ! Dare is a fine fellow, and when he gets the Doctor's maturity in the work, will be a first-rate man. He looks you into love. We had a splendid meeting last night at York Street, to give Dr. Jobson a hearty greeting. His reply to the address presented was most effective. There was the grandeur of simplicity, holy zeal in its greatest fervour.......Pray for me that I may return home, a holier and better man."

When the " La Hogue " had got to sea, Mr. Turner spent a few days with the Mantons and other friends. Of the Conference, he wrote, " It opened well, and has progressed in a good spirit. Poor Hessel is going home, and I fear, there to die. Poor Adams, too, is obliged to take his children home. Heard Rabone preach his official sermon as President,—a good sermon to a good congregation."

He took little part in the discussions of Conference, except such as related to Queensland appointments. For three years he had assisted to his utmost the Rev. Samuel Wilkinson in Brisbane ; but he now felt that the future of Methodism in that city and colony was a matter of moment, and depended, in a good degree, upon the earliest appointments to be made. Brisbane was now the seat of government, and a large influx of population might be looked for during the next Minister's term.

Conference over, he visited Newcastle and Maitland on his way home. He was very weary when he reached the steamer late at night. The saloon was crowded with passengers, some of them rather too lively. It was race week, and all the berths were " taken ; " so he had free selection between a berth under the table, and one on top of it, with the prospect of a roll off. While he was studying his situation, two gents of the turf stood near a very comfortable berth, loudly disputing the ownership. Mr. Turner looked on and mentally judged that it belonged to neither ; so just when they were about getting to blows, he quietly settled himself down in the berth for sleep. The disputants looked at the old Minister and at each other ; and then settled the difficulty by leaving him to enjoy a good night's rest.

Mr. Turner's family had now all grown up, and in the providence of God were settled in different parts of the colonies. Though several were in Queensland, he much inclined to move towards Sydney, where Mrs. Turner and he might more reasonably hope to see them all in turn. He seriously projected arrangements with this view, when the removal of one of his sons to New Zealand altered his mind.

He had lived an exceedingly active life, and when well had taken, under the constraint of his generous nature, an ardent interest in all matters of public local concern, as well as in those of the State and the Church. Since he had been freed from the cares and responsibilities of a Circuit Minister, his public-spiritedness had developed itself into a marked feature of character. The interest which different members of his family had in Queensland fairly took hold of his own sympathies, and he became warmly and zealously concerned for all that affected her welfare, educational, social, religious, and political. Queensland and he were one. His letters are full of references to public institutions and questions, clauses in land acts, the founding of new settlements, corporation works, and kindred topics. From the wisdom and force of character for which he had been long known in the district, prior to its being erected into a separate colony, he received respectful notice by public men ; and his letters reproduce with much care sundry conversations with the representatives of political progress. He liked to listen from the

Speaker's gallery to a good speech, and to hail the victory of those he considered the friends of the colony. He early visited some experimental cotton plantations a few miles from town, and with much delight noted the progress of the industry. His letters comment with the zest and ardour of a young colonist upon the stock travelling to new runs in the north, and on the arrival from the other colonies of intending settlers.

The anticipations of the rapid progress of the colony which Mr. Turner shared with the early friends of Queensland have been fully realized. The following statistical statements, which will be of interest to English readers, are taken from the last monthly summary of the "Brisbane Courier," December, 1870.

"The population has increased about fourfold. In 1860 there were forty-one public schools, attended by one thousand eight hundred and ninety pupils. At the end of last year there were one hundred and ninety-two schools, and thirteen thousand four hundred and seventy-two scholars. During the present year, when the system of free education came into operation, the number of children attending the public schools has increased by one-third. At the time of separation there were six charitable institutions, giving relief to three hundred and ninety-seven persons; now there are sixteen such institutions, and between two and three thousand people derive benefit from them.

"Coming now to the figures which show the increase in the production of the colony, we find that from 1860 to the present year more than seven hundred and fifty thousand acres of land have been sold, and the number of pastoral leaseholds has increased from thirteen hundred to three thousand five hundred. There were forty-one millions of acres under lease in 1860, and nearly one hundred and seventy-two millions in 1869. The area of land under cultivation has increased from three thousand three hundred

and fifty-three acres to forty-seven thousand six hundred
and thirty-four acres. Since separation two entirely new
branches of agricultural industry have come into existence.
In 1860 there were fourteen acres of land under cotton culture ; in 1869 there were fourteen thousand four hundred and
twenty-six acres. The cultivation of cotton has no doubt
been stimulated by the protective policy of successive
governments with regard to this product. Cotton growing
is almost entirely confined to the Ipswich district. But
there is every reason to believe that cotton cultivation will
soon extend and flourish in every part of the colony where
cheap labour is available during the picking season. The
other branch of agricultural industry to which we refer, sugar
planting, has practically received no direct encouragement.
It has succeeded, simply because it is suited to the soil and
climate of the coast lands of Queensland. The progress of
that industry has been really surprising. Its commencement dates only six years back. In 1865, ninety-three acres
were under cultivation with sugar-cane; in 1869 there
were five thousand one hundred and sixty-five acres
planted. During the present year the additional quantity
of land taken up for the purpose has been very great,
although no figures have yet been published, giving the
exact amount. It is well known to be a fact that in a year
or two hence the production of sugar will be greater than
will provide for the consumption of this colony, and will
then take a place amongst our more important exports.
Under the head of production there must also be included
the increase in live stock. Since separation, the number
of horses has increased from twenty-three thousand to
seventy-one thousand ; of cattle, from four hundred and
thirty-two thousand to eight hundred and ninety thousand ;
of sheep, from three millions to eight and a half millions.
There were thirteen manufacturing establishments, including mills, in 1860; now there are two hundred and fifty.

" Another proof of progress is afforded by the figures under the head of what the Registrar-General terms 'Intercharge.' Some of them can most conveniently be given in a tabular form, in which the first year after separation and last year (1869) are compared.

	1860.	1869.
Letters posted	199,168	1,704,370
Newspapers posted	149,236	1,087,345
Shipping, inwards, tons	45,796	145,213
Ditto, outwards, tons	39,503	142,802
Total imports	£742,023	£1,804,578
Total exports	£523,477	£2,166,806
Export of wool	£444,168	£1,098,149
Export of tallow	£25,628	£166,609
Export of gold	£14,576	£523,045
Export of copper	£50	£87,268
Export of cotton	*nil.*	£51,217

It comes under the same heading of ' Intercharge ' to note that since separation two hundred and eight miles of railway have been opened for traffic, and an electric telegraph system has been established, which includes two thousand one hundred and eighty-two miles of wire.

" Perhaps the best proof of the progress of the colony is afforded by the fact that the number of the depositors in the Government Savings Bank steadily increased from one hundred and sixty-three in 1860 to five thousand three hundred and twenty-seven in 1869, and the business to credit of the bank from £7,545 to £300,522. The advances made by the different Joint Stock Banks amounted to £490,861 in 1860. In 1865 the amount exceeded two millions; but, notwithstanding the commercial crisis of 1866, the effects of which are still felt, the banks made advances last year to the extent of £1,576,747."

To his daughter in England, Mr. Turner wrote :—" You will be glad to hear that we continue to be blest with every family comfort, and the smile of our Heavenly Father. I never delighted in my garden more than now. Everything is looking charming. The loquat trees are loaded with ripening bunches,—the mulberry tree bends almost to the ground beneath its weight of finest fruit. The early peaches will be abundant and are coming forward rapidly. Three orange trees are in full bloom. The pine-apples are doing pretty well, but there has been too much wet for them.... Our beloved Methodism is making sure progress; we continue to enjoy the ministry of Mr. Fletcher....Brisbane is becoming greatly enlarged and improved. Although more than twelve hundred persons have arrived within the last few months, the want of labour is as great as ever."

Mrs. Jordan had visited her aged relatives in England, and her husband had preached in one of their homes. In Mr. Turner's reply to her notice of this visit, he says, " I feel humbled and grateful on learning that I am remembered so affectionately in the places in which I spent my early days.

      ' O, to grace how great a debtor ! '

May I be faithful unto death ! " In November, he wrote :— " A fortnight ago I was at Ipswich, assisting them at their third chapel anniversary; they have done a noble thing in clearing off their debt of more than £400."

For two or three years he had been the subject of a painful affliction, which at times had been almost insufferable. By much care, however, he had been enabled to enjoy life in comfort ; but the disease now gained upon his constitution, and he was for several weeks wholly laid aside as " the Lord's prisoner." He wrote, " With the blessing of God on the careful use of well-directed means, I hope to recover my health ; if not, the will of the Lord be done. My poor old frame has not had so serious a shake for a long time. I hope it has been sanctified to my best interest, and that I shall be more careful to be found of my God in peace, when He shall call me." His correspondence of this date breathes gratitude for family mercies, and deep concern for the spiritual welfare of his children.

The first immigrant vessel to Queensland, the "Wansfell," arrived on November 14th. The next day he visited some of the immigrants; and his words of kindly counsel did not seem the less welcome as coming from an old man.

The Christmas was spent with his daughter, Mrs. Kent, and her family, at Rosalie. He was much pleased with the improvements on the station in two years. An unusually heavy fall of rain prevented his being driven; so he ventured to ride on horseback most of the way, and was pleased with his exploit; sixty-three miles in two days. "I was only troubled with too many good things......Besides daily family prayer I preached for them three times, and gave two missionary lectures on New Zealand and the Friendly Islands. I spent one of the three Sabbaths at Iondaryan, a very large squatting station, fifteen miles from Rosalie, and preached in their beautiful little church morning and evening."

I extract a few notes from his early letters of next year. "Lizzie writes of my eldest sister, Mary, having been suddenly called to heaven, aged seventy-four, and of my sister Martha, also pious, supposed to be dying. I do not really sorrow for them. They are safe and happy... The weather for some weeks past has been dry, hot, and at times extremely sultry. My chest has been very weak and sore, but I am better again. Preached with great freedom and strength yesterday morning in Albert Street chapel. Got quite as warm as in by-gone days."

Writing in the autumn, he says, "My late indisposition has left my chest in so weakly a state that I fear my preaching days are ended. My class, I fear, will have to be led by another; for, besides my chest affection, my deafness has much increased. But, thank God, I do not grieve or repine at increasing infirmities, for the Lord has indeed dealt well with His unworthy servant for many years. I rejoice and praise God for having enabled me to work so long, and happily too. I am seeking a full meetness for the inheritance above......The Rev. Mr. Slatyer of Sydney is here on a visit for his health. Yesterday I heard him twice, and two better sermons I never wish to hear..... My class now numbers twenty, and we have had some blessed meetings of late. But we greatly need a breaking down among the sinners and formalists in our congregation...... Tenders for our new parsonage on the hill are to be opened this week."

Mr. Turner's July letter to England says, "I must not complain of a little temporary indisposition in the middle of my seventieth year.......I am still pretty well able to attend to my pet gardens as in days when we used to walk together and talk there......At all the public meetings of the Churches in Brisbane I am still called to take a part. Such honour have not all God's aged saints. O, may I triumph at last!"

He much enjoyed the intimate friendship of many excellent Ministers of other Churches. The Bishop of Brisbane familiarly visited him, and as a Christian friend talked over the spiritual needs of the colony, and of the best way of supplying them. After one of his extended pastoral tours through the length and breadth of the land, Dr. Tuffnell gave him an interesting account of the settlement and labours of sixteen Clergymen, mostly in squatting districts, somewhat after the Methodist plan. He valued frequent cordial intercourse with the Rev. Edward Griffith of the Congregational Church, whom he found a truly Christian friend.

The future of Methodism in Queensland became an anxiety, if not a temptation to him. At no previous time in his life had the cause of Christ more engaged his sympathies. He saw in the thousands of settlers all over the colony the fathers of a great people, and mourned deeply that, so far, Methodism was making no adequate provision to supply the word of life ; for the claims of the city demanded all the time and energy of its one Minister. There were no public funds by which others could be obtained or in part sustained for a time. Though the settled districts were of vast area, and were but thinly populated, if he had had but half the vigour of his earlier manhood, he "would have gone through the land, and soon," he believed, "have procured abundant means to support a few young men." But he felt himself a worn-out old man, unfit for such a tour ; and it grieved him sorely that there seemed no likelihood of timely securing a supply of Ministers of the Wesleyan Church.

Brisbane was then a station of the Sydney District, and the Rev. J. H. Fletcher attended the District Meeting in November. A few weeks previously, in a Church Extension Fund Committee Meeting in Sydney, I requested that a movement might be set afoot for securing additional Ministers from England for New South Wales and Queensland. The project, which was declined at that meeting, was taken up and forwarded by some spirited laymen. The result was the arrival, within a few months, of five or six Ministers for New South Wales, the cost of whose passages was paid for by the Methodists of that colony. At the same time three arrived for Queensland, whose expenses were borne by the people there. This addition of working power, and the erection of Queensland into a separate District, gave Mr. Turner the greatest satisfaction.

During the eight years which have followed, young Methodism in Queensland has had to cope with great difficulties, such as, in my opinion, ought to have been relieved or much reduced by the foresight and liberality of the parent Church in England. With a much more extensive area than that covered by any similar Methodist population in the world, with its friends all young colonists having everything to do, and most of them having nothing but their muscles to do it with, it has had but very few Ministers. Most of these have been young and inexperienced men, and their stations in some instances are two and three hundred miles apart. Methodism has, it is true, struggled into a hopeful position. If, however, it had received timely assistance in the shape of say, *a thousand pounds* a year for five years, for the wise establishment and extension of the work, it would by this time have created for itself so much favour and power in the colony as to cause a mighty influence to be felt upon the rising nation there in all the future. I feel it right to add, that Queensland owes very little to the practical sympathy of the Australasian Methodists generally.

The Government of Queensland had adopted the national system of education, with which the public generally were satisfied. The Roman and Anglican Bishops, however, were unfriendly to the system, and did their best to have it superseded. Mr. Turner did not scruple to lend his influence on the side of the existing system, judging it much more likely to serve the interests of the country than the denominational.

In March Mr. Turner had a severe illness. He wrote, " In Brisbane we have been suffering from heat and moisture. We have had a good share of disease. Bilious, or gastric, fever has been fatal to many, especially children. For the last ten days I have been its victim. Our kind medical friend, Dr. Hobbs, has me under his charge, and has limited my diet to gruel and rice-water. I must not even taste broth. and my journeys are only to be between the bed and the sofa. I am trying to submit to my Heavenly Father's will, fully assured that I am in the best of hands, both for body and soul. I am not in severe suffering, but am weak and depressed at times, with much maziness in the head."

When the winter had passed, he wrote to one of his children, "While I have been mercifully saved from serious sickness, I have had through this winter a good share of those lesser ailments which make 'the grasshopper a burden.'......Don't regard me, my dear child, as uttering the language of complaint. O, no! 'Thou hast dealt well with Thy servant, O Lord.' Mine has been, and continues to be, a life of mercy. While my physical strength is weakened upon the way to the tomb, I desire, and to some extent labour to secure,—

> 'That strength which pain and death defies,
> Most vigorous when the body dies.'"

In August I again visited our Brisbane home. The changes of five years had told somewhat upon my father's strength and appearance. But he retained his characteristic cheerfulness, and was evidently ripening for heaven. His garden, which was full of bloom and beauty, still had daily care; and, as far as strength would allow, he pursued his favourite work of love, visiting among the sick and poor. We had a drive to Ipswich and back, in the hottest weather I ever experienced. The journey was too much for him. While on the road he became very ill, and he was for several days a great sufferer. His intercourse with me, which was almost hourly for many days, was chiefly upon Divine things. A month later he resumed preaching, and hoped "the Lord would yet enable him to do a little good in His Name,—bearing fruit in old age."

A revival had broken out in Melbourne, in connexion with the labours of the Rev. William Taylor, of the California Conference. Writing to his daughter, Mrs. Harcourt, he says, "Your last did me good, raising my drooping spirits. It led me back to days gone by, when my soul lived in revival scenes like these, though on a smaller scale. In Hobart Town, Launceston, and Sydney, we were privileged to see the Lord's hand made bare in the conversion of many souls, for which I still bless His name. But, alas! I mourn that these are almost exclusively things of the past with me. It has been a rare thing here to rejoice over the return of a single prodigal. Still I hope a brighter day is dawning upon us. The gladdening news which I have published is not without its effect. At our lovefeast on Wednesday evening, two young men bore satisfactory testimony to their having within the last fortnight obtained a clear sense of their acceptance with God. I preached for the Baptist friends on Sunday morning, when I did not forget to tell them of the Almighty Spirit's glorious work in Melbourne."

The letter to which Mr. Turner was replying had urged upon him the desirableness of supplying the material from which in the future his memoir might be written. He answered as follows :—" I must now try to set your mind at rest as to a history of my poor life and labours, written by myself. Some five or six years ago I commenced, not to make a book but, to write for my children a narrative of events in my life, in their chronological order of occurrence. I brought it down to the date of our arrival in Sydney, when my journal entries ended. Then I grew discouraged, and gave up. When George visited us a few weeks ago, I allowed him to take what I had written. I laid no embargo upon him in the matter. It contains a good deal that may become interesting relative to the early history of our New Zealand and Tonga Missions. If any history were to be written without data, it would be an incongruous jumble of events, not quite true in themselves, and painfully misleading to others. Not a few such did I meet with, to my great grief, in the Life of Samuel Leigh, by Strachan,—things recorded as said and done by Mr. Leigh in New Zealand, which could only apply to myself and brethren, and which did not transpire till long after Mr. Leigh had left New Zealand. That blessed man, John Hunt, fell into the same error, to some extent, in writing the Life of the Rev. William Cross."

Early in December Mr. Turner visited Maryborough, about two hundred miles north of Brisbane. A letter to one of his children contains the following account of his tour:—"My visit there was to prepare the way for the reception of one of the three young Ministers now expected; and I am happy to say my mission was prosperous beyond expectation. I found many who had been worshippers with us in other lands, and who were quite prepared to give the expected one a warm reception, and do all in their power towards his support. During the week I was there I preached three times to good congregations, visited many families, bought for church purposes two good allotments of ground in a central situation for one hundred pounds, half cash down, which I personally begged in the town. For the balance, which friends promised to collect, I gave a six months' promissory note with good names. I had the transfer made, and deeds handed over. I have not for many years spent a more laborious or profitable week; but I afterwards suffered a good deal from the over exertion. Mr. Fletcher, accompanied by Mr. Sutherland, visited Rockhampton at the same time, for the same purpose. He met with some encouragement, but land there is high. Unhappily we have allowed others to take the lead in that go-a-head place, and we shall suffer for our neglect. We are glad the young men are coming, and now wish there were four instead of three. But we hope to get another appointed by the Melbourne Conference, and then shall occupy Warwick, Towomba, Maryborough, and Rockhampton, as well as Ipswich, and have two men in Brisbane."

On the ninth of January he solemnized the marriage of

his youngest daughter, and his correspondence notices the event with a fond father's delight.

The Rev. Messrs. Dixson, Woodhouse, and Olden arrived at the end of that month. Of their introductory labours Mr. Turner wrote, " They have commenced their ministry like men who intend to succeed in winning souls to Christ. They have been well received and spoken of by all who have heard them."* Like their brethren who arrived about the same time in New South Wales, these young Ministers had had all the advantages of the Richmond Institution.

During the first week in April he was seized with a serious attack of inflammation of the bowels, similar to those by which on two or three former occasions his life had been imperilled. Through Divine mercy, however, the skill of medical friends relieved him, and in a few days he was himself again. One of the earliest public meetings he was able to attend was the valedictory service to the Rev. J. H. Fletcher, recently appointed President of the Newington College. They had spent three years together in intimate Christian communion and ministerial co-operation. Throughout the term Mr. Turner had personally profited in a high degree by Mr. Fletcher's ministry.

In May he had the unexpected pleasure of welcoming his daughter from England. Mr. Jordan had conceived it his duty to pay a hurried visit to Queensland, in the interest of immigration.

The latest reference I know of made by Mr. Turner to

* The Rev. Benjamin Dixson from Leeds was a young Minister whose ability and zeal were owned of God, and gave great promise to the Church in Australia. After successful labour at Rockhampton, where he laid the foundation of Methodism, he was appointed to the important district of Port Denison. A few days after his arrival, he was seized with gastric fever at Bowen, and died on May 5th, 1866.

his own public labours is dated July 7th :—" I have once again tried to preach, and to meet my class."

As the winter wore on, his friends thought they saw a decay of power. Of this, however, he did not appear to be conscious. The ardour of his temperament suffered little abatement, and he continued to evince his interest in the church and colony. Every sign of progress and opening for usefulness engaged his attention and animated conversation. He was wont to say almost in the tone of impatient zeal, " If I had but the physical strength of gone-by days, I would like to visit every town and station in Queensland and preach the Gospel." Infirmity often kept him from his class, but at such times he would most devoutly pray that the Lord would " bless each member." His late visit to Maryborough had been made a blessing to his soul, and he hoped to go again, when the new chapel should be opened.

Early in November he had the gratification of being often in the company of the Rev. W. Taylor, who was then engaged in special services in Queensland. He had much sympathy with that Minister and his work. He said to him one day very solemnly, " Brother Taylor, God has raised you up at a most interesting period of the world to do a very important work. I prayed that I might live to see and hear you, and God has answered my prayer. My work is done, but it is a great joy to me to see that God is raising up such workers : God bless you, my brother."

Reference has been made to a disease from which he suffered much pain. None, save a few members of his family, knew what extreme torture he endured. On the 18th of October his medical attendants apprised him that it was necessary for him to undergo a critical surgical operation, which they desired to perform, and which, they stated their conviction, they could safely carry him through. He remained perfectly calm, and readily and cheerfully consented. He trusted his doctors, and stated his confidence that God would give him strength to bear the trial, would bring him through it, and perhaps add years to his life. Counsel having been taken with several of the most skilful medical men of the city, an appointment was made, as advised.

On the following day he wrote to his son-in-law, as he had been accustomed to do monthly, during his former residence in England. I copy the letter, as it is the last he is known to have written.

" BRISBANE, *October* 19*th*, 1864.

" MY DEAR SON,

" By the mercy of God, I still live in this dying world, but in all human probability my days below will not be many. I was apparently in an improved state when you left, but the return of those dreadful spasms has thrown me back again, and occasioned me much suffering. Dear Emma is paying us a short visit, (Annie's state would not allow of her coming also,) and she proposed a homœopathic lotion for me, which, for several days, had most beneficial effect; but on Sunday last the worst symptoms returned with great violence, and continued through the night. Monday morning we called in Drs. Hobbs and Bell again. They came and diligently sought for what they expected to find, a ' stone in the bladder.' That such is the case they are fully satisfied, and that this has been the cause of my long and severe suffering. Also, they assure me, that unless this be removed, my sufferings must continue to increase. They advise me (my personal friends and medical advisers) to submit to this operation without delay. They do not fear any evil consequences from the use of chloroform, but by the blessing of God they may not only give present, but permanent relief, and in all probability add years to my life. Since this painful discovery, we have had many sighs and tears, accompanied by earnest entreaties to Heaven for Divine guidance and support. Prayer has been already heard and answered in the renewed strength and peace of my own soul. I have been greatly blessed in my soul this morning, more than in many months past. Looking at the case in all its bearings, I calmly conclude the doctors are right in their views of the matter, and therefore I think it right to submit to this, as my Heavenly Father's will.

"My nature shrinks from suffering; but to continue on earth with an increase to present suffering is what I could not choose at my Father's hand, *unless coupled with strong assurance that I should thereby advance His praise.* On the other hand, should I die under the operation, I should calmly pass away from the sorrows of earth to the joys of heaven, and my much-loved children will know I am gone to my Father's house above. Unless stronger reasons be advanced against it by my dearest ones and best friends, I shall, I believe, submit to this thing as the will of my Heavenly Father. O, may we in this be guided aright!

"Mamma has prepared a letter for dear Lizzie, in which will be found all family news. The prints will supply all you can desire in reference to politics, progress of the colony, &c. Church affairs much as when you left. I shall conclude with a suffering, perhaps a dying, father's love and blessing to his dear children, and their very, very dear children. O, may the goodwill of our Heavenly Father rest upon you, and His best blessing upon your labours! Amen! Amen! Amen!

"(Signed,) NATHANIEL TURNER.

"H. JORDAN, ESQ.,
    17, *Gracechurch Street,*
        London."

On Tuesday morning, November the 7th, he prepared for what he well knew might prove a mortal suffering; and nothing could exceed the tranquil confidence with which he did so. Though very feeble, he arose earlier than usual, and shaved and dressed as for a Sabbath service. He breakfasted, and had prayer with his family, including Mr. and Mrs. Crouch of Melbourne. The tones and words of that family worship were so loving and solemn that all were bathed in tears. When the surgeons were all in readiness, he affectionately embraced his wife, and said, "You must help me to be brave." His illness had occasioned much sympathy in the community, and especially in the Church; and while the operation was being performed, a special prayer-meeting was held in the Abbot Street chapel, for its success.

Though their patient was over threescore years and ten, and though the disease had made considerable progress, the operation was successful. Mr. Turner was full of praise and hope. For about a fortnight he appeared to be rapidly recovering; his medical friends said, "Nothing could be better." Indeed, he more than hoped for a perfect recovery; and in the manuscript draft of the preaching appointments for the ensuing Sydney Conference, his name stood, with his consent, in its customary place, under that of the President. Towards the end of the month, however, an attack of diarrhœa set in, which, in his very reduced state, baffled the utmost skill and the kindest attention of his medical and other friends.

The visits of Christian Ministers and other pious friends were greatly blessed to him. The Rev. Dr. Tuffnell with much tenderness and affection visited him repeatedly, and prayed with him. He profited much by the hours he spent with Mr. Fletcher, who twice went down from Ipswich to see him. For many weeks his Bible was his constant companion, and his family were pleased with the accuracy with which he would direct them to any passage he desired read to him. He found special comfort in the presence of his daughter, Mrs. Kent, who, far from her home, arranged to spend much time with him, reading to him the Word of God, and the comforting and animating hymns he had so long used and admired.

While lying on his mortal couch, prayer and praise were his constant employment. His mind was not once for a moment disturbed by worldly care, nor did he express a wish as to his temporal affairs. His only anxiety was, lest, under the influence of pain, he should in any degree dishonour God, whose gentleness and love he hourly acknowledged. He said, "I do not murmur, but I cannot help moaning. Lord, help me! O, do not suffer me to grieve Thee! Pity Thy poor worm: help me patiently to bear all I may have to pass through! The cross was the light of his mind, and the home of his heart: he often said, while the raising of his emaciated hand expressed his confidence,—

> "Other refuge have I none,
> Hangs my helpless soul on Thee."

The utter unavailing of human merit which he had so prominently and so long set forth to others he "steadfastly in death declared;" and his friends understood the emphasis of his triumphant words,—

> "Kept by the power of *Grace Divine*,
> I have the faith maintained."

Calmness was in his manner, and gratitude and humility were in his tones, as he uttered the following remarkable sentence: "For more than fifty years I have loved and served God; I have made many mistakes, but I am not conscious of having once wickedly departed from Him."

Once only, as far as is known, was he permitted during his last illness to be harassed by Satan. On the Friday before his death, he said to Mr. Jarrot, a good old leader: "I have had a most distressing struggle with the enemy of my soul; but, O, I obtained such a glorious victory, that I feel as if God were about to raise me up again, and add years of usefulness to my life."

He expressed a desire to partake once more of the memorials of his Saviour's love, and it was arranged that he should do so the next morning. During the night he rested very little, and in the morning, feeling drowsy, he became very anxious lest he should in any way during the sacramental service dishonour his Saviour. To his son he said, "Don't let me be agitated;" to Mrs. Turner, "I do most sincerely cast my soul on Christ. There I rest. 'Other refuge have I none.' The precious blood of Jesus Christ cleanseth us from all sin." The service was conducted by the Rev. William Taylor, who wrote of it to me as follows : "It was Saturday, December 3rd: there lay the veteran soldier of Jesus, and next to his bed-side the noble wife of his youth, who had shared the toils and trials of his whole missionary career; next were their dear daughter, Jeanie, and Mr. John S. Turner, their eldest son, and his wife, and with them an old nurse. Beside these, there were the two Ministers of the Brisbane Circuit. I administered to this little congregation the emblems of the sacrificial death of Jesus. We all felt, 'It is the last time.' We did not sorrow as those who have no hope, but we all wept."

When reminded that he would meet many in heaven whom he had been honoured in leading to God, he replied, "O yes! But I shall see my blessed Saviour there!" There is one to whom especially the looks, words, and incidents of those days of suffering and of triumph are all memorable. As he fondly stroked her hand, he looked upon the wedding-ring, and smiling, said, "'Till death us do part.' You cannot go with me over Jordan, but you can come to the brink; and when you leave me, Jesus will take me up. You must be brave! 'Thy Maker is thine Husband;' you will soon follow me."

Throughout his last Sabbath he was very peaceful and happy. After the morning public service, many friends called to have a moment with him, and to shake his hand once more. To each he said most touchingly, " God bless you, my brother," " Live to God," or some such few words. His expressions of triumph suggested to the Rev. W. Taylor the dying sentiments of Bishop M'Kendree, and in his softest notes he sang to him the stanzas in which they have been preserved. During the time of singing, Mr. Turner's countenance beamed with more than earthly delight, and he waved his hand in token of his own triumph. He continued for some time in an ecstasy, saying distinctly, though very feebly, " Praise God ! Praise God ! Praise God !" Presently, when he had quieted down, Mr. Taylor told him of an incident in the last triumph of an eminent Christian physician of Washington. When he was dying, Dr. Sewell shouted aloud the praises of God. His attendant physicians admonished him against exhausting his strength, and said, " Don't exert yourself, Dr. Sewell : whisper, Doctor, whisper." The dying saint exclaimed, " Let angels whisper ; but a soul redeemed and cleansed by the blood of Jesus ! O ! if I had a voice, I would shout that all the world might hear, and proclaim the saving power of Jesus. Victory ! Victory ! through the blood of the Lamb." The incident but expressed Mr. Turner's feelings. In the afternoon more kind friends called than could be admitted to see him. He said, " Tell them all I am truly grateful for their kindness, I love them all, and would most gladly see them all, but poor human nature is almost gone, I shall soon be in heaven." Many went into the verandah, and from the window saw his face for the last time.

His physician, Dr. Hobbs, called to see him. Mr. Turner took him by the hand, and said affectionately, " Doctor, you have done your best ; I want to thank God for all your kindness to me and mine." There was such a touching tenderness in his manner and tone that all present were moved to tears. Still holding him by the hand, he added, "The precious blood of Jesus that cleanseth me from all sin is efficacious for you, Doctor. God bless you." "Give my best love to all my friends, and tell them I am thankful for their sympathy." To Mrs. Turner he said, "Let me go, do let me go." She answered, "We will, dear, we will." He replied, "Yes; but not cheerfully;" and when she had answered, "Yes, we will, dear," he said with much content, "That's right."

He passed Sunday night without much suffering, Mrs. Turner and their son being with him. During nearly the whole of Monday his daughter Martha was at his side. She left him at six o'clock, not thinking the end was near. In about an hour a change was observed. Mrs. Turner and her daughter Jeanie, and Mr. and Mrs. John Turner, with Mr. Brooks and the nurse, watched in the chamber of death. He did not appear to suffer much, but had some difficulty in breathing. He once said, "Raise me up." When this had been done, he said, "I am going home; but all is well. Praise my God! All is well." He kissed his frail daughter Jeanie, a loving child of God, and said to her, "The blood of Jesus Christ, God's Son, cleanseth me from all sin." After a short sickness, he said again, "I am going home. All is well."

About eleven o'clock, while the pallor of death lay upon his brow, he said, "You will please all retire to bed, and I will take a quiet sleep, and I shall be able to talk with you in the morning." Mrs. Turner asked whether Mr. Taylor, who had come in, should not once more pray with him. He assented, and then clearly and calmly whispered a distinct response to each petition of the last prayer he heard on earth. For nearly an hour his family stood near, watching the peace and light of that midnight hour. They

caught a few words faintly spoken......It was nearly twelve
o'clock......So peacefully had he passed away, that they
did not know the exact moment. The last words he spoke
on earth were, " Farewell. All is well."

In the Brisbane Cemetery, in a spot he had himself
chosen, he rests from his labours. He is indeed "taking
a quiet sleep, and will be able to talk with us again in the
morning."

"FOR THEM ALSO WHICH SLEEP IN JESUS WILL GOD
BRING WITH HIM."

CHAPTER XXII.

A FIRST interview with a stranger would reveal Mr. Turner's true nature, and it was but little modified by circumstances at any period of his life. Of a vigorous and wiry constitution, an ardent temperament, and a tender and affectionate spirit, his look, voice, and manner would at once show the man. General good-will came to him by the right of nature ; yet, through life, he was helped by decision of character and high-spiritedness.

His mental endowments, if not of the highest order, were considerable, and, as the result of their faithful employment showed, were eminently suited to the sphere and service of his life. Having clearly perceived and vigorously grasped truth, he held it firmly. He avoided mere speculations on religious subjects, but had fixed and comprehensive views of Christian experience and duty. Though he entered upon his public work without that degree of mental culture he could have desired, his diligence in study early secured him honourable and gratifying recognition in the pulpit, on the platform, and in the social circle.

The grace of God exhibited its beauty and power in his life of love and blessing. His personal conversion was a demonstrated fact. Comparative loneliness in his early religious life had led him to strive with God in prayer, and his Church anxieties and exercises had served to mature his piety. He made the cross of Christ his home. There his affections were kindled and his powers exalted. He

cherished the love of the Spirit, and daily walked in Hi
light.

Mr. Turner firmly trusted in the Providence of God, for he
had been its child: and he never forgot that in the early
struggles by which he had acquired a power for usefulness
he had been Divinely aided. Experience suggested faith
as well as thought; and when public responsibilities or
family cares pressed, he found both the will and power to
" commit his way unto the Lord." In personal peril or
affliction, or when the life or interest of a child was
threatened, or in any other exigency, he was accustomed to
say, " The Lord will provide." In this respect, his counsel
as a friend, or his correspondence as a father, was but the
voice of his own life.

His trust in God was more than habit. It was an ever-
repeated act in prayer, and, like all life with him, was
real though unobtrusive. In his house no apology was
offered or needed for religious exercises. None of his
family, and but few, if any, of their occasional visitors, can
forget the tones of intercession they overheard from his
retired room, his garden path, or his way-side walk. He
knew the way to God, and in the tranquil light and beauty
of his course, day by day, illustrated the duty and its corresponding promise : " Be careful for nothing, but in everything by prayer and supplication, with thanksgiving, let
your requests be made known unto God. And the peace
of God, which passeth understanding, shall keep your
hearts and minds by Christ Jesus." Though he felt that
Providence was both rich and gracious, he had a keen sense
of moral responsibility, and enjoyed in peace the fruit of
righteousness. He sought to adjust all claims upon him
by the prayer he daily offered.

> " When I have lived to Thee alone,
>   Pronounce the welcome word, ' Well done ! '
>   And let me take my place above."

Mr. Turner's was a young life. No man was more cheerful, and it was an unusual thing for him to be depressed. His habits of early rising, and of out-door activity, in his garden, or pastoral visitation, or when travelling, served to develop this genial quality; which, especially during his later years, was a comfort to his family, and a joy among his friends.

The harmony of his character shone in his family and social relations. In all matters of parental duty he was anxiously careful, and in no other respects did the intensely realizing quality of his nature show itself more. To influence aright the hearts and habits of his children was made his daily care. His circumstances were limited; and often when surrounding influences were unfriendly to family training and advantage, his spirits were weighted with fear. Sacrifices were made again and again to afford his children the best education he could secure them; and he had few pleasures greater than in watching the result. A fond but faithful father, he was the head of his family, and maintained authority and administered discipline in a serious spirit. He interested himself personally in the mental progress and religious welfare of every child, influencing in the study of Holy Scripture, in the selection of companions, and, with especial care, in the observance of the Sabbath. And though the best sermon he ever preached to his children was his own example at home, they can never forget with what tearful earnestness he wrestled and watched, worked and waited, for their conversion.

Mr. Turner was a good type of "the old school" of Methodist preachers. Reconciliation with God, and the holiness and privileges of believers, were his favourite themes. When he had selected a subject, he well thought it out, and prepared an ample outline. It was his custom to study, walking; and, when convenient, to think aloud. Some Ministers practise preaching before the empty pews of their churches. He preferred his garden, and a congregation of plants and flowers. His pulpit delivery of the truth was loving, but bold; direct, but careful. If any one quality of his nature dominated there, it was his tenderness. His voice, which could thunder on occasions, was the expressive medium of sympathy or of assurance. A believer in " present salvation," he preached for results, and had them. Why? Primarily, because the Holy Spirit accompanied the word. But also from another cause, very important, though secondary :—his loving pastoral toil, in season and out of season, and the weight of his personal and ministerial character, had affected the moral conscience of the community. It was this which secured him large congregations in the towns in which he regularly ministered. His animated preaching had a telling effect upon all classes of hearers, for he found his oratory in their hearts.

He is affectionately remembered as a Christian pastor. He understood that the value of a sermon was in its adaptation to the case of the hearers, and in the welcome with which it would be received. He therefore visited from house to house as systematically and frequently as other duties would permit; and thus was able to influence by the truth the inner life of every member. Where there were the sick and sinful for whom no one else seemed to care, he found time to talk and pray with them. His special addresses to the " members of Society " were frequent, and of the most faithful and profiting character. Few Ministers excelled him in leading prayer-meetings. Under an ordinarily prosperous state of the Church, these were lively seasons; for his spirit and faith, during the exercises, had a holy infection.

The children and youth of his congregation loved him as a father or friend. It was his custom, when circumstances would allow, to have an hour weekly, generally on a Saturday afternoon, with such of the elder children as could be got together, that he might talk and pray with them. His

Bible classes in Tasmania and in Sydney were fruitful in developing the powers of young men for public usefulness. His systematic and kind attention to the young converts in different Circuits supplied several valuable workers. He did not believe in doing ministerial work by proxy, and in no relation to any part of the Church, if he could help it, would he commit to others the labour or responsibility properly his own. He was a true lover of progress, and sought to extend the work of God. Where doors of usefulness were not open, he would either find a key, or break them open.

The *régime* under which he laboured as a Missionary afforded small scope for administration of Circuit affairs, as now known. The relations of the missionary brethren to each other, to their stations, and to the Home Committee, differed widely from those of their successors as Circuit Superintendents in Australia. In his Circuits, however, Mr. Turner maintained discipline in love.

He was not of that class who are sought and respected for what can be got out of them. His good name and friendship remained when in the feebleness of years he sought retirement. The Rev. William Curnow, the esteemed Minister of the Ipswich Circuit, near Brisbane, wrote of him : " Though a Supernumerary, his intense interest in the work of God struck me much. When his powers were enfeebled, he lost none of his zeal and fire. Instead of standing aside as a censor of the more active Ministers, he drew near as a sympathizer and fellow toiler, to the full measure of his strength. The thing that impressed me most in him was his unaffected interest in young men. He had no jealousy and no reserve with those who were greatly his juniors. He would counsel, or criticize, or encourage, with unfailing good nature and success. No one could say that he grew hard or crusty when he grew old. His childlike spirit, his gleeful face, and his singularly transparent manners, were a benediction to many."

Mr. Turner's religious sympathies were truly catholic. Forms of Church government or shades of Christian doctrine did not veil from his view the manifold beauties of Christianity. A loyal Wesleyan Methodist, he was known and honoured as a lover of all godly men, and a helper of every good cause.

He was a good citizen. Suffering and want found relief at his hand to his utmost ability. He read the newspaper, and watched with patriotic interest every sign of civic progress or of social danger in the community. He was a true Briton, but cherished the high hopes of an intelligent Australian colonist.

Those who knew him had a true friend. Rich in charity which thinketh no evil, he hated suspicion and narrowness. Children are judges of men, and he was always a favourite with children. The little ones climbed his knees, and the older boys and girls delighted in his stories. In company he was cheerful, inquiring, and communicative; and in correspondence, free, spiritual, and affectionate.

Rewarded openly, his success was received with humility and gratitude. Whether in the morning of life breaking up new ground, or in its noonday strength establishing the churches, or in the hush of eventide awaiting the Master's voice, he ever sang, "Now thanks be unto God, which always causeth us to triumph in Christ, in every place."

It remains to be said that if God gave him honour everywhere, there was a secret in it. That secret was simply this,—he lived with God, and maintained his Christian simplicity to the last. His course was

"Like the aloe, green and well liking till the last best summer of its age,
When it putteth forth its golden bells, and mingleth glory with
corruption."

An interesting incident, (which escaped insertion in its proper place in this volume,) the result of the Rev. N. Turner's ministry in New Zealand, was narrated by the Rev. George Scott, who was for many years our valued Missionary in Sweden, at the Annual Meeting of the Society at Exeter Hall, in 1865, to the effect that a Swedish sailor was brought to God under a sermon preached by Mr. Turner on board his ship, when anchored off the coast of New Zealand. This worthy seaman was afterwards employed as a sailor colporteur in Sweden, and we doubt not did good service in the cause of his Redeemer. The bread thus cast upon the waters was found after many days.

.*. On page 24, the Princes Street church property is described as the oldest in the Southern World held by the Wesleyan Connexion. The correct reading is, that this property is the oldest but one.

THE END.

LONDON:

PRINTED BY WILLIAM NICHOLS,

46, HOXTON SQUARE.

www.ingramcontent.com/pod-product-compliance
Lightning Source LLC
Chambersburg PA
CBHW021806110726
47902CB00006B/1669